ALSO BY SHARMA SHIELDS

Favorite Monster

THE
SASQUATCH
HUNTER'S
ALMANAC

THE
SASQUATCH
HUNTER'S
ALMANAC

A NOVEL

SHARMA SHIELDS

HENRY HOLT AND COMPANY
NEW YORK

HOLT PAPERBACKS
HENRY HOLT AND COMPANY, LLC
PUBLISHERS SINCE 1866
175 FIFTH AVENUE
NEW YORK, NEW YORK 10010
WWW.HENRYHOLT.COM

A HOLT PAPERBACK® AND ® ARE REGISTERED
TRADEMARKS OF HENRY HOLT AND COMPANY, LLC.

ANNA SWIR, "SHE DOES NOT REMEMBER," FROM *TALKING TO
MY BODY*, TRANSLATED BY CZESLAW MILOSZ AND LEONARD
NATHAN. COPYRIGHT © 1996 BY CZESLAW MILOSZ AND
LEONARD NATHAN. REPRINTED WITH THE PERMISSION OF
THE PERMISSIONS COMPANY, INC., ON BEHALF OF COPPER
CANYON PRESS, WWW.COPPERCANYONPRESS.ORG.

LIBRARY OF CONGRESS CATALOGING-IN-PUBLICATION DATA

SHIELDS, SHARMA.
  THE SASQUATCH HUNTER'S ALMANAC : A NOVEL / SHARMA SHIELDS.—
FIRST EDITION.
    PAGES ; CM
    ISBN 978-1-62779-199-1 (SOFTCOVER)—ISBN 978-1-62779-200-4 (EBOOK)
1. CONFLICT OF GENERATIONS—FICTION.   2. SASQUATCH—FICTION.
3. ANIMALS, MYTHICAL—FICTION.   4. DOMESTIC FICTION.   I. TITLE.
  PS3619.H5429S27 2015
  813'.6—DC23   2014020085

HENRY HOLT BOOKS ARE AVAILABLE FOR SPECIAL
PROMOTIONS AND PREMIUMS. FOR DETAILS CONTACT:
DIRECTOR, SPECIAL MARKETS.

FIRST EDITION 2015

DESIGNED BY MERYL SUSSMAN LEVAVI

PRINTED IN THE UNITED STATES OF AMERICA

1   3   5   7   9   10   8   6   4   2

For my parents

For my sisters and brother

For Henry and Louise

For Sam

She was an evil stepmother.
In her old age she is slowly dying
in an empty hovel.

She shudders
like a wad of burning paper.
She does not remember that she was evil.
But she knows
that she feels cold.

—ANNA SWIR
"She Does Not Remember"

Because we are human
We assign human emotions to Sasquatch.

—SHERMAN ALEXIE
"The Sasquatch Poems"

CONTENTS

THE
SASQUATCH
HUNTER'S
ALMANAC

1943

THE HANDSOME GUEST

ELI ROEBUCK LIVED WITH HIS PARENTS, GREG AND AGNES, IN A tiny cabin near Stateline. Greg arranged a little rock border right where the line ran so that Eli could stand with one foot in Idaho and one foot in Washington and sense through the soles of his boots the difference between the two.

Washington sap smelled sweeter. The soil was softer and less rocky. Idaho earth baked and hardened and stank like eggs. Or so Eli imagined. In reality, the environment was seamless, dry white-pine forest littered with decomposing needles and loose rock, and, above, a hawk wheeling in the beryl blue sky. In the winter, snow fell and transformed the uneven terrain into a smooth white plain. Then it melted and the world returned to him as it had always been: faded brown and faded green, jagged and inviting.

Other children hated living here. They wanted to be in Lilac City or Seattle or even Boise, where there were large toy stores and more cars than animals in the streets. Eli liked it here. He liked his house, he liked the forest, and he liked his parents. He was a happy kid.

Eli's mother was not so happy. She was a slight young woman with a delicate brow and a low, serious voice. She rarely smiled. Eli had once heard his father say to her, "I don't know what makes you happy, Agnes. I wish I knew. I wish you'd tell me." Eli wished she'd tell him, too, but she ignored most of what Eli's dad said.

Like Eli, she was happiest when outdoors. She disappeared for long walks in the forest, following the finespun deer paths to areas where Eli was forbidden. If Eli ran after her and took up her hand, hoping to accompany her, she shook him gently away. She wanted to be alone, she said, to collect her thoughts. Eli pictured her kneeling on the forest floor, gathering her thoughts—glowing amber orbs—to her breast. Too in love with her to argue, he gave her anything she wanted, even her freedom. Sometimes she left Eli alone for hours, not coming home until just before dinner.

Eli would pace the front yard, scared, near tears; he would watch the forest until she limped into view. She always returned, tired but radiant, apologetic and affectionate. She would take up Eli's hand and hurry inside to make supper. They would work side by side, Eli giddy with relief, singing songs and chatting amiably, until Eli's dad called to them from the foyer. Then her mood would darken, a shift as unsurprising as the sunset.

Eli wondered: What did she do in the forest? What was it there that made her so happy?

He awoke one morning and his mother washed his face and ears and combed his hair and put him in his Sunday best. She forbade him to go outside, because, she explained, she wanted him to meet someone very dear to her. Eli's father had left for work hours ago, when it was still cool and dark. Already the day's heat was pushing into the house.

"Who is it?" Eli said. "Is it a friend of Dad's?"

Agnes leaned over her hand mirror, pinching her cheekbones. "It's a stranger, darling. You'll see. He's very interesting. The most interesting man I've ever met. You'll like him."

Eli helped Agnes with the broom and the dustpan, careful not to dirty his clothes. Something savory baked in the oven. The house grew hotter yet and groaned.

Finally the visitor arrived. Hearing the knock, Agnes raced to the door and swept it open.

There stood her guest, "the most interesting man."

Eli tried not to stare. He did not see a man at all. What he saw was an enormous ape crushed into a filthy pin-striped suit. He remembered a book from school about exotic beasts, the giant apes who lived in *the savage countries of the world,* and the guest resembled those creatures: deep hooded brow, small blank eyes, thin-lipped mouth like a long pink gash. And the hair! The guest was so hairy that Eli was unsure of the color of his skin: Beneath the thick brown fur, his flesh—tough and charred, like strips of dried deer meat—appeared red in some places, purple in others. The guest even smelled of hair, badly, like a musty bearskin rug singed with a lit match.

Eli was horrified and delighted.

Remembering his manners, he stepped to the side and said politely, "Please, sir, come in."

The guest's small, round eyes raked over Eli. He cleared his throat and lumbered into the room, swinging his powerful arms. *Well,* Eli thought, *he* walks *like a man, even if he doesn't exactly* look *like one.* But then Eli noticed the guest's wide, shoeless feet, two hairy sleds that moved noiselessly over the wooden floorboards as though through a soft snow.

"Do you want some tea?" his mother asked. "It's scalding hot, just the way you like it."

The guest spoke. The noise startled Eli, a short sentence of senseless bleats and hoots. Agnes responded as if she understood. She handed over the teacup, and the guest handled it clumsily before dropping it, with a roar of annoyance, onto the floor. Eli hurried to clean up the mess himself. He didn't even wince when a piece of china stuck him in the index finger. His mom offered her guest the teapot instead, and he drank greedily from its spout. Eli watched in sick fascination.

"What's your name?" Eli asked, gazing up at the hairy beast as he gulped and slobbered.

"Eli," his mother said. "It's rude to stare. This is Mr. Krantz. He's a dear friend. What do you think of the house, Mr. Krantz?"

Mr. Krantz was about to toss the empty teapot on the floor, but Eli—always a quick boy—reached up on tiptoe to take it from him.

"Here, Mr. Krantz," he said kindly. "Let me help you."

Mr. Krantz released the pot. He briefly patted Eli's head, and the impact made Eli's teeth clatter.

"I'm happy you've met my son," Eli's mom said to Mr. Krantz. "I can tell Eli likes you. He admires strong men."

Eli had never stated this aloud, but he supposed his mother was right; there was much to admire about Mr. Krantz. For one: his immensity. He was easily the largest person Eli had ever seen, over seven feet tall, and three or four times heavier than Eli's own dad. Second: his hairiness. He was as furry and sleek as a grizzly bear. Last: his unpredictability. Eli found unpredictability the most alluring trait of all. Now, for instance, Mr. Krantz was fondling a houseplant. If Eli so much as sneezed in a houseplant's direction, his mother scowled, but she watched Mr. Krantz patiently as he broke a leaf and then held it up to his nose, sniffing it.

Mr. Krantz held the ruined leaf out toward Eli, like it was a gift.

"Hydrangea," Eli said, touching its edge.

Mr. Krantz put the leaf in his mouth.

"Poor thing!" Eli's mom said. "You're famished. I made biscuits. The ones I've brought you before, Mr. Krantz. *Drenched* in butter."

She hurried to the kitchen, humming. Eli smiled. Here was another reason to like Mr. Krantz. He clearly made his mother very happy.

Mr. Krantz abandoned the plant and moved to the piano, where he rested one of his long bowed hands on the keys and then leapt in surprise at the tinny noise they imparted. Astonished, then curious, he leaned over the keyboard and poked at it softly with one rough yellow talon. *Plonk. Plonk. Plonk.* He bared his teeth in delight and hopped up and down for a moment, looking over at Eli for encouragement (which the boy gave by means of a friendly nod), and then he began to bang away at the keyboard enthusiastically, hooting in time with the music. Eli jumped up and down, too, clapping his hands. What a funny sort of man was Mr. Krantz! So funny, in fact, that as he waggled and spun to the music, the button of his ill-fitting pants burst open. Underneath, he wore nothing at all. No underdrawers! For one awkward moment, Eli glimpsed the lopsided bulging serpent of Mr. Krantz's penis. That, too, was impressive. It dwarfed even his father's, which Eli had always before assumed, with a sort of horrified reverence, was *the Longest Penis in the World*. Well, apparently not. Mr. Krantz put Eli's dad to shame in that category, too, and in the category of *Having Fun*.

This was something he had heard his mother say—a funny thing coming from her, as she herself was always so stern and serious. "Oh, your father," she'd said to Eli. "He doesn't know how to *have fun*."

Eli had gone along with her. *A stick in the mud. Right you are. Sure.*

Privately, Eli disagreed. It was true: His father was a hardworking man, juggling three jobs at a time. He worked on the weekends for the telephone companies, stringing up telephone wires. He worked as a ranch hand, too, down at old Haywood Anderson's farm. And after long days of hammering barbed wire and repairing irrigation ditches, he walked to town most nights to bartend at a flea trap called the Tin Hut. His plan was to own the bar outright one day, and so he worked and scrimped and saved.

"One day it will be a fancy place," he told his son. "Exclusive. You'll have to wear silk pants to get in there."

But when his dad wasn't working, he was home. And those times, to Eli, were the best times. Despite his mom's accusations, Eli loved his dad. They played cards together, rummy and blackjack and King's Corner (which remained Eli's favorite, despite his dad's insistence that it was a child's game), and they went on walks, his dad pointing out wildlife and good trees for climbing. Sometimes he came home with a tractor from the ranch or a lawn mower, and he would let Eli drive or push them. If he came home with a horse, he would let Eli ride until he could hardly walk. When they went hunting together, he let Eli hold his new rifle, let him aim and fire (he had yet to kill anything, though his dad's shot was always dead-on). When Dad was home, Mom was absent. She was on one of her epic strolls, or she remained in the kitchen, baking or cooking soups. "Come play," Eli would beg, but she would always refuse.

One day his father brought home a new phonograph, and Eli watched in amused disbelief as his parents threaded their limbs together and waltzed haphazardly across the living room floor, bumping into the table and chairs and sofa, laughing and singing. But that was a long time ago, a year or more. There had been little contact between his parents since, aside from the sad comments they made about each other to Eli. Things like, *He's no fun* and *She wants fancy things.*

You're wrong, Eli wanted to say but didn't. *He's fun! She doesn't care for fancy things at all!* Eli wished they would say nice things about each other. He wished, right now, that they would speak to each other with the same easy tone his mother used with Mr. Krantz.

Mr. Krantz had noticed his burst fly and fumbled with the button hopelessly. He gave Eli an embarrassed shrug. Eli put up one finger and then went racing into his parents' bedroom. He plucked from the bureau the longest belt he could find and returned to Mr. Krantz, presenting it with a triumphant flourish.

Mr. Krantz smiled at Eli with his broad ape mouth. He held the belt to his chest for a moment and then wrapped it tautly about his waist. He had to force a new hole through the leather to fasten it, but it worked well enough, and Eli felt proud of himself. He was an excellent host. Mr. Krantz spun in a circle for Eli and grinned. Eli applauded.

It was funny to see his dad's slick, oiled belt encircling the filthy fabric of Mr. Krantz's suit. It looked as though Mr. Krantz had rolled in the mud on his way to their house. Where, Eli wondered, did Mr. Krantz buy his clothes? He looked silly in clothes. He kept pulling at the sleeves and elbows and legs, obviously uncomfortable. And those wide flat feet! Eli's gaze kept falling to them. He wished he could touch them. They would be hot against his fingers, furry and powerful and new.

Eli's mom returned to the living room, holding the good silver tray perpendicular to her chest. It bore a pile of lovely golden biscuits. Eli's mouth watered. In their hurry to prepare for Mr. Krantz, they had forgotten about Eli's breakfast. He went to grab a biscuit, but his mother shifted the tray away from him.

"These are for Mr. Krantz," she said sharply.

"I only want *one*," Eli insisted, and then flushed, embarrassed by his own rudeness.

Mr. Krantz stopped his piano-playing and his funny little dance and approached the tray. He drooled onto his dirty lapel.

"These are for Mr. *Krantz*," she said again. She placed the tray down on the coffee table with an inviting smile at her guest and took an athletic step backward, perhaps anticipating what Mr. Krantz would do next.

He lunged, batting the tray's steaming baked goods with those monstrous yellow and purple hands of his, scattering many of the biscuits onto the floor but managing to shovel several of them into his mouth at once. How he ate! They must have been very hot, Eli guessed, listening to Mr. Krantz's loud, staccato whimpering, but how tasty they must have been, too, for he moaned happily, licking his lips with a long, menacing tongue. Eli watched sadly as Mr. Krantz devoured every morsel; he even crouched doglike on the floor and lapped up the fallen soldiers. Eli looked up at Agnes, sure that she would disapprove of Mr. Krantz's barbaric behavior, but she only gazed at her guest affectionately, as one might gaze at a favorite pet or, Eli realized, with a sudden maturity that had so far always eluded him, an adored sweetheart. This was not the look of a woman disgusted. She was transported, elevated. She was maniacally content.

"I have a piano lesson in an hour," Eli said loudly.

Agnes waved him aside. By then his dad would be home, she said, and he could walk Eli to his lesson.

Eli frowned. "But you *always* take me."

His voice was so whiny. The voice of a much smaller boy. He hated himself for it, and then he hated his mom for it, and then, very briefly, he hated Mr. Krantz.

But Mr. Krantz was back on his feet now, swiping at his chest and arms, releasing small crumbs so that they drifted snowlike onto the Oriental carpet. Eli waited for him to drop back down into a crouch and lick up every last tiny remnant, but Mr. Krantz withheld himself, staring longingly at the crumbs but seeming to remember that he was a guest, or maybe simply feeling that his immense hunger had, however temporarily, been satisfied. He looked up at Eli's face, his expression apologetic now. He gestured at the empty tray.

"It's okay, Mr. Krantz," Eli lied. "I'm not hungry, anyway."

Mr. Krantz ruffled Eli's hair and then lifted his gaze to the face of the woman watching him. Eli's mom had grown very still, standing before Mr. Krantz like a blossomed flower, her face open and shining. Seeing her, Mr. Krantz's eyes gleamed with a new hunger. Crazily so. Eli, uncomfortable, reached for his mother's skirt and tugged.

She dropped to his side. She wrapped her arms around him and kissed his face.

"Oh, my baby," she said to him. "How I'll miss you."

"Miss me? My piano lesson is only an hour. I'll be home for stew."

His mother blinked at him heavily, as if she were fighting sleep, and then she drew him fast to her breast. She smelled of Palmolive and cake batter. Eli would never forget the warmth of her smell.

"I do love you," she said. "Never doubt it, sweetheart."

Eli wavered, confused. She went to the closet and retrieved a packed suitcase. She groaned lifting it, and Mr. Krantz came forward to take it from her.

"Mr. Krantz," she said bravely, straightening and extending her hand. "I'm ready."

Mr. Krantz swallowed up her hand with his free one. They went out the door together, the woman lean and pale and barely breathing, the other hairy and dark and panting like a dog in heat. Like Mr. Krantz, Agnes was barefoot. Their feet pressed into the mud of the yard, winding toward the forest. Large prints, small prints; monstrous feet, dainty feet; heaviness, freedom.

His mother did not turn toward him again, but Mr. Krantz turned as he reached the small line of stones parting Washington State from Idaho. The guest sorrowed for him, Eli could see. It was Mr. Krantz's attempt at an apology.

Eli panicked.

"Come back," Eli called after them. "You can't leave!"

Mr. Krantz put an enormous hand on the small of Agnes's back. She lowered her head. They hastened into the woods together, extinguished by the trees.

Eli hated Mr. Krantz then. He was not a man at all but an animal. Like an animal, he took what he wanted, regardless of who suffered for it. He was just the same as a bear or a cougar or any other woodland predator.

But, then, what did that make Eli's mother? Who was she?

Woman. Mom. Animal. Wife.

Maybe just nothing, Eli thought. *Maybe she wants to be nothing.* And he wished he could make her nothing, too.

He considered following them. The sun slanted down and baked the footprints into place. He thought of his dad. He returned to the house, the door smacking shut behind him. The room smelled of biscuits, of simmering stew. Eli sat on the sofa and folded his hands in his lap. He furrowed his tiny brow.

He would wait for his dad. He would go to his piano lesson.

Most important, he would think up a better story than the one he had just witnessed.

His dad was a practical man.

He would not believe a word of it.

1945

THE BOTTOMLESS PIT

ELI WAS ONLY TEN YEARS OLD WHEN GREG ROEBUCK, THE BOY'S hardworking father, found the family dog struck dead by a car.

The dog's name was Hermit. He had been the perfect companion for Greg's lonely son. Frost stitched the body to the side of the road. Greg pried it free, the wind stinging his eyes. He carried the body back to the house.

He went to wash his hands in the sink, thinking only of his son. He dreaded Eli's reaction. The boy had already lost his mother. And now this. What sort of unmoored life would Eli live if his childhood proved only a steady parade of loss?

When Eli arrived from school, Greg met him on the dirt road that led to the house. The fields were heavy and frozen and stank of manure. Greg, tongue-tied, motioned grimly: *Follow me*. The boy tensed. It began to snow. They entered the house together. Eli did not drop his rucksack to the ground or remove his coat.

In the kitchen, Greg mumbled an apology. He had covered Hermit's body with an old blue quilt, and he whipped it aside now as though unveiling a prize. *You asshole*, Greg chided himself. *Slowly, now. Slowly!*

He had rested the dog on the table, and he chided himself for that, too, given his son's already timid appetite.

Greg could not bring himself to look Eli in the face; he heard only the great intake of breath, the fumbling of his boy's fingers over Hermit's body, and then a series of brief, staccato questions delivered almost professionally: *When? Where? Who did this? How long was he there? Did it hurt him? Is he gone forever? Can we save him? Why is there so little blood? This doesn't even really look like Hermit, does it?*

The questions droned on, weird and touching, and Greg offered few answers. He reached out like a blind man and randomly patted his son's shoulders, wondering if this offered any comfort at all or if it only registered faintly to the boy, like raindrops, maybe, or like tears.

Greg had felt similarly useless when Agnes left. Like Hermit, she was gone, both disappearances untimely and permanent.

The boy was crying now, his questions finished for the time being, his little heart accepting in throbbing registers the fullness of its wreckage.

"Whatever you want for dinner tonight," Greg said. "Muffins. Candies. Root beer."

Eli could not respond, could only turn and run from the room, to his bedroom, to his bed. Greg heard the small mattress receive him with a groan. Uncertain of what to say or how to proceed, Greg went to the door and listened to Eli's earnest, desperate prayers.

"God," the boy pleaded, "I'll do anything. Please bring Hermit back. This is a dream. Say it's a bad dream. Wake me up, God. Wake me up. Wake me up! Please, God, wake me up."

Greg stood quietly in the hallway, rooted to the floor by the deep strands of his son's woe; he was strengthened somehow by the purity of these strands, their unfathomable depth and beauty. How pierced the earth was, too, how altered. Around their tiny woodland home, the air seemed to shimmer and thicken. The new world, Greg saw, was a place of great love and great loss.

Eli whispered himself into a fitful sleep and later, much later, emerged. Greg had removed the dog's carcass to the woodpile outside. He sat now with the newspaper on his lap, the newly washed surface of the kitchen table gleaming like the belly of a fish.

"I want to bury him," Eli said.

"It's done," Greg lied, wanting to save the boy the pain of the activity, the horrible labor involved. "He's already buried."

Eli began to cry. "Then we'll dig him up. I want to see him again. I want to clip some of his fur. I want to bury him. Me."

He sobbed, utterly broken.

It was not uncommon for Greg to scold himself for being a poor father, but now, too, he was a liar.

"Eli. Don't fret. He's there. He's right there. I just thought—well, it doesn't matter what I thought. Anyway. If you want to bury him, then that's what we'll do."

Relief crossed the boy's face, a look that was so close to joy that Greg felt unburdened. *Yes,* he thought. *This is a good activity for a boy and a dad to do together. Bury the family dog. And tomorrow—a* Saturday, the only day this week that Greg didn't work—*we'll go to town together to choose a new dog.*

And they did.

THE NEW DOG had no name for nearly a full week, but then, out of the blue, Eli began calling her Mother.

Greg disliked the dog. He had disliked Hermit, too, in the beginning. He didn't like dogs, generally speaking. He liked animals with a purpose: horses, cows, pigs; animals to pull, milk, eat. He had brought Hermit home not long after Agnes's departure, at the suggestion of a friend, to make their motherless, wifeless household appear less lonely. It was a strategy that had, to Greg's relief, worked. Eli became happier, dedicating himself again to his schoolwork, so long as the dog remained by his side, Hermit's tail slapping out a friendly beat on the battered wood floor. Eli's grades improved, his friendships improved, his relationship with his father improved. And, either out of a feeling of gratefulness or just because Hermit was such a good-hearted dog, Greg, too, began to love the animal. Not the way he loved Eli. But just enough. The three of them made a respectable family.

But the new dog was strange. She was a mutt, part Welsh terrier, part some-other-breed-he-couldn't-remember, a breed that, the breeder told him, had delicate bones. She was shaggy like a terrier, with a terrier's round wet nose, a nose that shocked Greg when she pressed it like a soggy sponge into his hand or bare leg, a thankfully infrequent behavior. But he definitely did think of the word *delicate* when he saw her—she *was* delicate, not doglike at all but graceful, careful, like a long-limbed bird. Hermit had been overeager, sliding across the floorboards when Eli came home, racing frantically and clumsily around corners, but the new dog literally stepped, that cold black nose in the air, like some well-trained Spanish show horse, from one corner of the house to another, lifting each foot off the floor with a gait suitable for dressage, as though disgusted by Greg's housekeeping. When she wasn't traipsing about the house like an elegant snob, she sat dolefully in the corner, staring out the window, or she turned those black shining eyes on Greg. Regarding him, she seemed unimpressed.

Mother enjoyed Eli and she abbreviated the boy's grief, but, compared with Hermit, she was measured and fussy. She would sit with Eli at the couch, for example, but she would not approach the boy if he sat in his father's recliner. Or she would greet Eli at the back door when he returned from school, the door facing the woods, but never the front door, facing the road. The boy changed his habits to suit her, but Greg was annoyed. He wanted to return the dog and find a more affectionate one, although he could never bring himself to suggest this to his son. Eli already loved her, and

Greg begrudgingly tried to accept this love. But she reminded him of something, or someone, although he couldn't quite think of what or who it was, not until Eli called her Mother.

It was true. Eli's mother. The damn dog reminded him of Agnes.

Despite the wild red rage that flamed in him when he connected dog with woman, Greg could not bring himself, despite the years of rejection and regret, to hate the dog fully. Not yet. Eli loved her. Eli was quick to forgive her quirks, and the dog, in turn, became almost, if not quite, affectionate with him. It was not unlike the odd mother-and-son relationship that Greg had witnessed when Eli was little. It had been a relationship that comforted him as well as frightened him, with its easy floating intimacy, its foreign, accepting quiet. Greg's own mother had been effusive, tender to the point of discomfort. Not so with Agnes. She had been attentive but distant, kind but aloof. In some moments he found her to be the best sort of mother possible, a mother who never raised her voice in anger or sighed in annoyance, but in other moments he found it bizarre—disturbing, even—that she sometimes did not notice Eli at all. There was, for example, the incident with the wood chipper, when Eli had shoved his little fist into its maw, curious. It was off, thank God, but Greg, pulling weeds from the flower bed, had launched to his feet with an angry shout, warning the toddler never to approach the machine again, all while Agnes stared vacantly into the trees, her face as black and unreadable as a crow's. Later, Greg had asked her how she had not noticed. She had been standing with Eli, practically on top of him. How had she not seen what he was about to do, what he did? What if the wood chipper had been on? What if Eli had managed, being a smart boy, to turn it on right at that very instant?

Agnes had turned toward him, her face still empty. "There are people who worry. There are people who don't."

A little worry, Greg argued, was a good thing where a child was concerned. A boy as smart as Eli, as smart and as fragile, well, to go through parenthood with blinders on was unacceptable. Absolutely unacceptable.

Agnes had smiled at him, and the smile reduced him, as always it did, to an insignificant, paltry thing: a man, a husband, a father— the ridiculous sex. As he spoke, his anger and worry waned.

What right did he have to tell a woman how to be? Wasn't Eli growing up to be a marvelous boy, a truly kind and rational and generous child, a child rumored by other parents and the schoolhouse to be, in fact, brilliant? Men had no rights in these matters, and Greg was ashamed. After all, he was not in the house daylong, as she was. She knew Eli best. And he supposed, as many men supposed, that she loved her child more than he did. He backed off. His wife expressed no gratitude and no annoyance with him either way. If anything, she seemed simply bored with the whole affair.

And that was how Mother behaved, too. Bored. Not angry or tense, not furtive or sad. Just bored. At night, Greg passed by his son's room, saying hello and good night on his way to work; he held down the night shift at a filthy pub, a job that was easy and decent despite the long, late hours. Usually Eli would already be asleep, one hand clutching the fur on Mother's back. Mother, however, never slept. She lay very still, statuesque, but Greg had not once seen the dog's eyes close. She didn't even bother to raise her head to study Greg—she merely combed him over with her eyes, judgeless but uninviting. God, the boredom!

And, like Agnes, the dog simply lay there, visibly but joylessly caring for his son. Greg wondered if she would suddenly up and disappear, just mysteriously vanish. He considered purchasing another dog straightaway, to soften the blow of such a departure. Or he could put the dog down now and save them all from an even bigger misery down the road.

Most days, Greg found additional work mending fences or loading hay or repairing downed power lines, and he would sleep only two or three hours before rising and heading out to work again, his brain sloshing in his skull like a bowl of cold soup. It was dangerous to work in such a twilight state, especially driving testy machinery or climbing the bald telephone poles, but others did the work drunk or just plain boggled with stupidity. Greg was surefooted, small but coordinated, his hands as deft as a raccoon's, and he performed as well on no sleep as other workers did on a full night's rest. He took whatever job was offered to him: He was saving for his son's schooling. Eli deserved all he could provide. Greg had little else to give the boy if he died, other than the furniture and his good rifle, so he worked and saved.

When he left in the morning, he would knock on the door to his son's room and say, "Leaving now. Go to school. Feed the dog."

The boy never needed to be told these things, but Greg liked to have a reason to look in on him, his yellow tufts of hair poking up from the blankets, the room awash with the sweet smells of his boyhood, smells of salty earth and maple syrup and warm, fetid sleep. Rarely, the boy stirred, but sometimes he lifted his head from the blankets just long enough to say, without opening his eyes, "Goodbye, Daddy," and Greg's heart filled and spilled over. He loved his son. He was not, he knew, the world's best father. But, *goddamn it,* he did love his son.

One morning, on the way to scale poles just outside Wallace, Idaho, Greg poked his head into his son's room and saw that he slept alone. He said goodbye and gave the boy a kiss on the forehead. Eli grumbled something and turned over, taking with him most of the blankets and a corner of the fitted sheet. Greg stood and gazed for a moment, embraced by the old, sleepy sensation of love. Then he went into the kitchen to retrieve his thermos of coffee and his lunch: some salami, a hard knob of cheese, and a round rock of a plum, dried to a small black husk. The same food sat in another satchel in the fridge, ready for Eli to ferry to school. Greg went to the front door and pulled on his work boots and began to tie the laces. He was energized and hopeful despite his short night

of sleep. As he finished tying his right boot, Greg heard a soft snuf-
fling noise. He raised his eyes to find Mother staring at him, her
nose wet from the water dish, or maybe from drinking out of the
toilet, something Hermit had loved to do, although Mother likely
believed herself too good for such a lowbrow habit.

Greg smiled at the dog and patted his leg. "Here, girl. Here,
Mother."

Mother did not so much glare at him as raise her eyebrows with
incredulity.

"Come here," he said softly. "Come here, Agnes."

The dog moved forward hesitantly.

Greg opened the palm of his hand.

"Agnes," he said. "I thought so."

Mother peered at the palm of his hand with a regal expression,
as though staring down into a pit of snakes. She did not move
closer.

Greg wanted to cradle the dog for a moment. Not in any weird,
sexual way, he told himself. Just to feel her warmth, anything's
warmth, curled against him. Mother yipped in protest as he grabbed
her collar and pulled her to his chest.

"Stay," he said. "Stay. Mother. Agnes. Stay put."

She squirmed against him and he held her there harder. Her
breath came in a labored wheeze. *Stop,* he told himself. *Stop it, or
you'll choke her to death.* He couldn't stop. He crushed her to him
with more force, his own breath coming in urgent, clumsy gulps.

A horn sounded. The truck bound for Wallace. Greg released
the dog and stood. Mother scampered, whimpering, away from
him, and Greg thought, *Good.* He felt enormous, powerful, post-
coital. And also: delusional, concerned, filled with an ominous
regret. Had he hurt her? He saw her curl into a ball near her food
dish, her indifferent face clearly expressing, *You cannot reach me.
Ever. You'll never reach me.* The expression meant she was okay,
okay enough for him to be annoyed again, to want to give her a

solid crippling kick, but he hurried from the house instead, shutting the door firmly behind him.

When Greg returned later, drained and irritated, he found Eli on the couch with the dog, looking over his arithmetic lesson.

A bright boy, brighter than Greg had ever been. Very much like Agnes. He could be an engineer, even a doctor. The dog, he noticed, leaned over the book, too, as though reading along.

"She's smart," Eli laughed. "Look how smart she is."

"Oh, I have no doubt," Greg said. He sat down to unlace his boots and noticed the dog peek at him warily—just for a moment— and was pleased when she quickly looked away. So. He had affected her. He felt satisfied. He rubbed at one of his sore shoulders and sat there on the old bench, leaning against the wall, listening to the heavy panting of the heating register.

"You know, son," he said. "I've been meaning to ask you."

"Hmm?" Eli said, half listening.

"I've been meaning to ask you about this dog here."

"Mother," Eli said. He didn't look up from his work, only turned his pencil over and erased what must have been a wrong answer.

"This dog here of yours. Meaning to ask how you came up with the name you did. It's a queer name for a dog. Especially for a dog that's not, you know, a mother."

Eli stared into his book. A moment's silence passed.

"It's just," Greg continued, tugging at a callus on his palm, "I'm curious. Why Mother? Why not Angela or Katie or Mutt or Aloysius? Good gravy, why not Spot or Fuzzy or any other normal dog name? Why Mother?"

"You don't like the name," Eli said, and looked up at him, his eyes filling with tears.

"Well," Greg said, "I didn't say that. Don't go crying on me, son, you're nearly full-grown. Let's not have tears here, now. You know I hate that. Tears are the tools of manipulation. I've always said it."

"You hate the name," Eli repeated.

"Tell me how come."

"Because—" he began. Then stopped, shook his head as though freeing water from his ears, and began again. "Because the man— her first owner—called her a first-rate bitch. He pointed at her and said, 'She's a first-rate bitch.' And you said, 'We'll take her, then,' even though I wanted a different one. I wanted the one who wouldn't drink his mom's milk, who had to be fed from the bottle. But you didn't want him. And also," and he looked up at Greg's face again, brave the way only children can be, and said accusatorily, "and you called Mother a damn bitch once. I heard you."

"I did not. I never said such a thing to your mother. Not once. Not ever."

"Not *to* her. You said it *about* her. After she left. You said, 'If I could get my hands around that damn bitch's neck, I'd kill her.' That's what you said to Uncle Frome. And Uncle Frome said, 'Now, now, that's no way to speak.' And you said, 'That damn bitch. I'll kill her! I'll kill her for what she did!'"

The boy finished his exclamation and then buried his face into his dog's body, the bravery stripped from his face, his deepest secrets dredged and discovered.

Greg, too, felt ruined. He wanted to put his arms around his son, console him and explain why, *why,* he'd said such horrible things, but the dog had risen and stood between them, and Greg worried that if he came too close to her, he would take her up in his arms and swing her sideways against the wall and smash her head open, spatter her brains against the wainscoting.

So instead he said, "I was angry. Very angry with her. For what she did. For leaving us. For leaving you. I was angry because it wasn't fair to you, Eli, what she did."

"She loved me," Eli said, crying freely now. The dog went closer to him and nosed the boy in the arm, as though to say, *Yes,* as though to say, *Hate your father, as I do.* "She loved me; I know it."

That may be so, Greg thought, *she loved you, but she didn't love you* enough. That was the thing. Anyone could love. Anyone could say they loved their husband or child or wife or dog. They could be out in public and behave with perfect respectability, so that people would say, as was often said of his wife, *What a wonderful person. What a wonderful mother. What a wonderful, calm, loving woman.* Anyone could perform such an act. But to actually love, to love enough to commit to unhappiness, *that* was real love. When his wife would say to him, *I wish we could travel, Greg; I wish we could go dancing; I wish we could drink beer until we black out and then do nothing tomorrow but vomit and fuck and then drink some more,* Greg would frown. Yes, he wanted those things. They sounded like good fun. But they had a child now, he would say, a responsibility, and they owed it to Eli to be constant, reliable parents. Agnes would listen raptly with what Greg assumed was the pure, quiet understanding of love but with what he realized now was sheer bafflement at the depth of his own affection.

"It's so easy for you," she'd told him once, "to love and not grow bitter. It's hard for me, Greg. I'm just not good at it. The more I love, the more bitter I become."

"But you do love Eli?" Greg had pressed, worried.

"Oh, yes. I love him. Of course I do."

And Greg's worry had immediately deflated; he had decided that she was simply tired.

So many mothers were. So very tired. So very fed up with the young children they watched day in and day out. He understood it all in a way that most husbands did not. She would say that to him, even—*You're very understanding, Greg*—but she would say it with a sorrowful tone, as though she wished he would beat her, or tongue-lash her, or choke her during sex, as she had once read about in a dirty book she'd found at a friend's house. When she'd told him of the latter discovery, Greg had ignored it. He had not taken her seriously when she'd mentioned the choking, had not accepted the tacit invitation suggested there, but maybe he should have taken it very seriously indeed. Maybe a little roughhousing would have gone a long way.

Did it matter, though? No. Probably not. In the end, she didn't love them enough. She didn't love Greg and she didn't love Eli. Not enough. That was what had really shocked him. That her love for Greg had an ending point was not surprising. Such was the way with wives and husbands. But the love for her own son? A mother's love was supposed to be unfathomable, like an ocean without a floor—reaching, spiraling into nowhere, into infinity—but her love had stopped before it even began.

What if she had seen Eli in the aftermath, when he had screamed and sobbed for her return, when he had been unable to sleep at night because he ached to hear her voice, ached to embrace her soft body in its worn nightgown and darned socks? When he had asked his father, over and over: *Will she return? When? Where is she? Did she send a letter? Did she phone yet?* If she had seen these things, heard these things, Greg wondered, would she have returned? Or would it have only made her more cocksure that her abandonment had been the right idea all along?

The right idea, Greg surmised. Yes, doubtlessly. She was always cocksure. She would not return. The more they wanted her to return, the less likely the possibility.

"So why," Greg said to the dog now, who sat nosing his son's weeping, supine form on the rotting couch, "why are you here now?"

The dog ignored him, as did the boy. Greg rose and took his son up into his arms and carried him to bed. The boy hadn't eaten dinner, but he was clearly spent from his refreshed woe. Greg was almost grateful when Mother entered. She moved into the room's farthest corner and sat on her haunches, raising her long chin high. She waited patiently for Greg to leave. When he did, he heard her trot across the floor and climb onto the bed, too. No doubt she felt safest with the boy. That made sense. Greg wanted to take a club to her head.

Greg went to the kitchen to eat leftover bread and gravy, which he reheated on the stove. He sat at the little table in the kitchen—more of a stool than a table, really—and noisily sopped up the food with a spoon. Then he sat there for a good several minutes, thinking of little and enjoying the silence. He considered rising and taking up the papers in the living room, but the idea of moving even one inch exhausted him, and so he merely tucked his chin down and fell asleep there, sitting up, as he did sometimes, his plate so clean before him that his last thought was that he could go swimming in it and how refreshing it would be to swim into the milk-white ceramic, like pushing through the supple, supportive fabric of the moon.

And then, with a sharp cry, he awoke. The room had darkened, the single bulb had burned out over his head, but the moonlight pushed through the window, illuminating the kitchen in a deathly bluish gray. Perhaps because of his earlier reverie, Greg worried for a moment that the world had flooded, that they were underwater. But as quickly as this notion appeared, it dissolved. Greg then noticed the black form of an animal in the doorway, an animal that gazed at him with wet, affectionate eyes. Mother.

"Why are you looking at me like that?" he asked her.

She floated to him, stood at his feet.

"Don't look at me like that," Greg warned her.

Her eyes never left his.

He stood, his knees wobbling, remembering how Agnes would come to him every now and again, with this same wet, desperate look, this same longing for love. How grateful he would be in those moments, how immediately forgiving of all of her prior coldness and cruelty, and he would lift her and take her with him into the bedroom and strip her down and be with her, inside her, around her, and she on top of him and beneath him, and then in front of him, like a dog.

That was the worst thought, when it came to him, *like a dog.* The animal gazed up at him with that same question in its eyes. It mocked his loneliness.

"Leave me be."

He scooted the dog out of the way with his foot.

He made sure to lock the bedroom door behind him.

That was the thing he remembered later: that he had locked the door, that he had checked the lock, made sure it was fast. So how was it that he awoke, hours later, the dog sitting right beside him on the bed, staring down into his face with a terrible silent urgency, an expression that immediately panicked and excited him?

He trembled as he rose and pulled on his robe. He lifted the animal into his arms and felt her go gratefully slack. What he wanted to do, what he wished more than anything to do, was lie down with her, wrap his arms around her, burrow his head into her stinking dog flesh, and weep. Instead, he went outdoors, marching for the woods, stopping once before the rusted spade, awkwardly packaging Mother beneath one arm so that he could take up the spade in his free hand. He continued this way, through the sparse snow, for several minutes. It was as if she knew what he would do. She remained where he set her down, waiting. The earth was cold, difficult to puncture, but he strained and heaved, more convinced with each thrust. It was better this way. Better for them all. She would be gone, and he would sleep, and, later, he and Eli would drive to town for a new dog. There would be some sort of necessary lie about the dog's disappearance (carried off by raccoons or coyotes, he thought, stolen by some stranger driving a beige truck, merely gone, just gone, something the boy already knew all about).

This last thought occurred to him as he began to shovel dirt over the dog's head. Mother shook the dirt off and looked up at him from the recesses of the deep hole. He shoveled more dirt down onto her. He was crying now, telling himself, *No, no, don't do this. Even if she is the ghost, even if she is.* He stopped digging, thinking of Eli. He could not bury Mother alive, after all.

How Greg sobbed then. How lost he was! All of his life had tunneled toward this one dark hole in the woods. If he buried this dog, he would never rise from it. It would be the final descent of his soul. The dog gazed up at him calmly.

"You damn-it-all heartless bitch," Greg said, and wormed onto his belly, reaching for the animal.

How far down had he dug this hole? He was amazed at its depth. It seemed implausible that he could have dug down this far in such a short amount of time, straight through the frozen earth. He could not reach the dog. His fingers scrabbled at her ears. "Up on your hind legs, damn you," he said, but the dog lay down on the dirt with her head on her paws.

"Tomorrow, then," he said. He was bone-weary. He had never felt so tired. He rose, groaning, and made for the house.

Tomorrow, Greg decided numbly as he walked, he would form a phony search party with his son, and they would come across the hole together, and he would make a big show of returning to the house for a ladder, and Eli would regard him as a hero, and all would be well.

And, he resolved: Mother would live with them again, unmolested this time. Greg slouched back toward the house, dragging the spade behind him. His shoulders and spine throbbed. He would treat her right, better than ever, and maybe the ghost would recede and the animal would come forth, or some such bullshit. Greg didn't know. But he wouldn't harm another hair on her head, not when Eli's feelings were at stake. He went to bed feeling a bit of hope, and also a bit of gratitude that Mother was nowhere near the house. For the first time since her arrival, he slept dreamlessly.

The next morning began as Greg had expected: Eli rising, Eli calling for Mother, Eli arriving at his bedside, tearstained, to beg for his help in finding her.

"Sure, buddy," Greg said, and nearly screamed as he sat up, the soreness in his back splitting open like the maw of a volcano. "Sure. Let's go a-lookin'."

They pulled on their coats and boots and went outside. Greg noticed the tracks in the earth from where he had plodded, to and fro, the night before, and he watched his son's face for any sign of recognition, but Eli looked only side to side, every now and again throwing back his head and baying, "Mother! Moooooother!" It was a heartbreaking caterwaul, and Greg knew Mother was not the sort of dog to bark in response. She would remain silent in that deep hole, waiting for them. Always, it seemed, she was waiting.

Eli reached the hole first and stood at its lip for a moment, looking back at his father in delight and then saying very loudly, "Wow!"

So he's found her, Greg thought, and heaved a sigh of acceptance.

Then, to Greg's shock and alarm, Eli picked up a giant rock and hurled it as hard as he could into the darkness. Greg cried out, "Don't," baffled that his son would attack his dog in such violent fashion, but when he arrived at the mouth of the hole he saw that there was no dog visible. There was nothing visible at all. No dirt floor, even. Nothing but an endless blackness. The hole receded into the earth and kept receding, down and down, like a well that had been opened and abandoned.

"This can't be right," he mumbled.

Eli hoisted a fallen tree branch and flung it like a javelin into the hole. They listened to the dull thud of its impact on the dirt walls, waiting for some sound of a watery or rocky bottom, but there was nothing, just eventual silence. Greg backed away from the hole and urged his son to do the same.

"But," Eli said, rising hesitantly from an uprooted tree stump that he was attempting to roll toward the opening, "this will be so great."

Greg looked around him: Perhaps he was at the wrong hole—but how could that be? He knew these woods so well. He had followed his well-worn pathway here; he could still make out his fresher tracks from the night before; everything—everything—suggested that he had been here only a few hours prior, that he had dug this bottomless pit himself.

"Eli," he said. "Move away. Move back now. Come here."

The boy sobered, his grin fading. A sound issued from the hole—a long, womanly wail.

Part animal, surely, but also human.

What pain it bellowed! What heartache!

"Mother," Eli cried. He fell to his knees, crawling to the opening, peering into the face of its irretrievable, unfathomable blackness. "Mommy!"

Greg lunged. There was nothing left in him but love for his son, nothing but horror at the potential loss of him.

He grabbed the boy's collar.

He pulled.

1955

S'CWENE'Y'TI

Eli Roebuck, twenty years old, sat in a crowded bar in downtown Seattle, nursing his drink and wondering if he was the only person at his table who was a virgin.

He had agreed to this blind date only because he was deeply taken with the date's organizer, a long-throated nursing student named Bethesda Green.

Beth raised her eyebrows at him. *Whaddaya think?*

Eli nodded politely. The blind date, Gladys Johnson, was one of Beth's two roommates. She was admittedly good-looking. She had lustrous dark hair, good clothes, perfect posture, and a thin, painted mouth. She sat calmly next to Eli, smoking cigarette after cigarette with her elegant chin lifted high over a plate of raw oysters, which she never touched.

"I like your bracelet," Eli told her.

She lowered her cigarette and squared her handsome chest at him. "My bangle, you mean? How dear of you to notice it. Thank you." The bangle on her wrist flashed as she smoked. "A gift from an old beau. James was his name. Cardinal James. Named for a bird. Poor Cardinal. A silly boy I hardly cared for at all. Goodness, he loved me. Died in a car wreck. The poor thing. Tragic."

She returned to her cigarette, and Eli, flummoxed, fumbled for a response. Beth rushed in to save him with her clear, confident laugh.

"Gloomy Gladys we call her," Beth said. "You can always trust Gladys to bring our heads out of the clouds. Isn't that so, Gladys?"

"He's not my first beau to have died," Gladys said.

Beth's date, Glen, cleared his throat. *Here it comes,* thought Eli irritably. Glen had an obnoxious habit of clearing his throat before he spoke.

"We're all mortal, after all," Glen said. He waved down a passing waiter and ordered another round of champagne cocktails.

"I couldn't possibly have another," Beth said when the waiter reappeared, but she accepted the cocktail handed to her and then drew her chair closer to Glen.

Glen opened one long, hulking arm, and Beth settled into it with a happy little smile.

Lucky bastard, Eli thought. Glen was a good enough guy, a fellow medical student en route to becoming a successful surgeon, but Eli wouldn't mind punching him in his gargoyle-shaped Adam's apple. How had this big-armed boob landed a knockout girl like Beth? The throat-clearing was bad enough, but then there was also the unmistakable smell of formaldehyde, from Glen's extracurricular work assisting the city undertaker. They weren't sound reasons to hate him, Eli knew, but didn't they at least render him unattractive? Maddeningly, Beth adored Glen. It was as though the sound of bubbling phlegm rang like silver tongues in her ears. It was as though the smell of formaldehyde reminded her of sex and not of death.

Women were a mystery to Eli. He had his mother to blame for that. His mother, who had chosen that hairy *beast* over his good-hearted father; how could he not regard women with distrust and wonder? He hardly remembered her now, anyway. Her memory surfaced only as an emotional scapegoat. Up she would rise, faceless, limbless, a specter with side-parted auburn hair and a strong flowery perfume. She wavered guiltily before him and he told her, *Your fault, Mother. But you loved me. I know you loved me*, and then she would dip up and down like a candle flame. Once, in a dream, he'd had sex with her, penetrating her flesh as if it were a fine gauze, and he'd woken up wet and sweating and ashamed.

So far, women had done nothing but humiliate him. Eli wanted to humiliate one of them in return, in the dark, in the nude, but in a kind, equitable way, batting the humiliation back and forth like a pink-nosed shuttlecock.

He squirmed in his chair, struggling for something to say. "Just say anything at all," Beth had advised him earlier, teasing him for his quiet nature. "Say whatever silly thing comes into your head. Women don't care what you say, so long as you say it with confidence."

He forced himself to speak now, however woodenly.

"I wouldn't mind," he said, "getting a good drunk on tonight."

Beth sat up and regarded him, bright-eyed, interested.

So, Eli mused sourly, *it's true.*

"I wouldn't mind," he continued, with more confidence, "getting so drunk that I swim in the Sound."

"There we go!" said Beth proudly.

Glen cleared his throat. "I think I'll join you, my good man."

"Funny," Gladys said, "that's precisely what Jim said before he died."

AFTER DINNER AND drinks, the four of them ambled downhill to the Pike Place Market. Somehow both women clung to Glen's arms as they walked. Eli walked slowly behind them, hands in his jacket pockets, hat low over his brow, pretending to be at ease. The perfume of the girls floated back to him, laced with the smell of formaldehyde. From the back, he noticed Gladys's good legs, plump and strong in their sheer black stockings. Her dress, too, was of a finer quality than Beth's. It was a stiff, flattering lavender, while Beth wore a floppy, homely plaid. Both women wore similar coats and hats, which Beth had told him they'd purchased together during a recent shopping trip.

"She has the most luscious taste," Beth had told him a few days before. "I ask her advice on everything fashion-wise. You two are just going to eat each other up!"

They had not fallen passionately in love, but dining with her wasn't half bad. In fact, midway through the meal, when Beth disappeared, taking her summery smile and lovely arms with her to the bathroom, Eli had realized that Gladys was very attractive. She was like a plainer, quieter moon, being drowned out by the noise and fire of the sun. When the sun set—when it left for the bathroom, say, to powder its nose—then the moon glowed quite beautifully. Maybe even more beautifully?

"Look at that man over there," Gladys had said conspiratorially, setting down her forkful of shrimp and touching Eli lightly on the wrist. "Look at how wide his shoulders are. I'll bet he plays football."

Eli had leaned into her, not really caring about the man's shoulders but thrumming slightly from the fingers that had grazed his skin. He suddenly imagined himself in bed with her, beneath her, his face covered with her glossy black hair.

"What do you think?" Gladys asked him.

"What?"

"About his shoulders? Aren't they very large? Very masculine?"

It occurred to him that she was trying to make him jealous. He lifted up his napkin and smiled into it. He was flattered.

"Oh, yes," he said, returning the napkin to his lap. "Quite masculine."

Glen, listening to them from his side of the table, cleared his throat. "I know that man. His name is Scott. I've seen him swimming at Alki Beach. You wouldn't believe this, Gladys, but shirtless he's very fat."

"No!" Gladys exclaimed. "You lie!"

"Those shoulders," Glen said, "are pink and mottled, like two raw ham hocks. He's a fatty, Gladys. Don't trust a man's beauty until you see him in the nude."

Eli considered his own small frame, his nearly hairless pallor. Glen laughed.

"I'm kidding, sweetheart," he said to Gladys, and leaned forward, snapping up her empty glass and shaking it in the air. A waiter rushed forward to retrieve it. "Really, Scott's an absolute god naked. I've nearly wept from his beauty. Truly."

Gladys turned to Eli. "I don't like big shoulders, fat or no," she said. "I mean, a man can have them, surely, but I don't think they mean he's got any real intelligence in his head."

"You know what they say about big shoulders," Glen joked, more to himself than to them.

"Now," Gladys said, "glasses are something else. Glasses indicate a *reader*, a man who is *learned*. Glasses tell a girl, *Here is a man who enjoys a good, thick book*. No, it's certain. I much prefer glasses to shoulders. Wouldn't you agree, Mr. Roebuck?"

She still insisted on calling him Mr. Roebuck, despite his protests. She was a formal girl. Eli couldn't help but admire her attempt at elegance.

Elegant or not, she was flirting with him. Eli adjusted his own spectacles on his nose and gave her a wink. Not in character for him at all, but she received the wink with a slow flutter of her own lashes, and he thought, *My God, she's the one, isn't she?* He was going to sleep with her. He could feel it in his bones. Surely a girl like this would divulge some good secrets in bed. He would be sure to keep his glasses on for the performance.

But right at that moment Beth returned, beaming.

"What'd I miss? What are you grinning about over there? You look like two jack-o'-lanterns. Plotting against me, I see."

Just like that, the sun rose, washing out the moon. A bit breathlessly, Eli watched Beth move. Glen was equally captivated, leaping to his feet and pulling out Beth's chair. Glen planted a lingering kiss on her flushed cheek. Beth pulled away with a flirty swat. She was lightly disheveled, winsome, and athletic. Eli's throat tightened. His confidence with Gladys shifted. He would never be the sort of man to attract a girl like Beth. And when there was a Beth in the world, why would anyone wish to be with a Gladys?

Next to him, Gladys re-crossed her ankles. If she noticed his love for her friend, she was unmoved. Her expression remained the same: sharp, observant, her mouth a wry red slash, her face as smooth as limestone, her hair perfect, not a black strand out of place, her posture remarkable. She reminded him of a fine white Roman statue.

And why, Eli had asked himself, would you love a statue, when you could love a living, breathing, vivid woman like Beth?

But now, walking behind the two young women, he did not take such a bleak view. In the broad grim light, bright if clouded over, it was clear that Gladys was the looker of the two. Gladys was the sort of woman destined for great things. He could see her running her own art gallery or posing, unsmiling, for the cover of a famous magazine. Beth, on the other hand, was destined only to nurture. She would be a beloved housewife, a doting mother. She had once confided to Eli that she had only entered nursing school to meet a wealthy, handsome husband. Nothing wrong with that, Eli had said. Gladys, however, had moved to Seattle from rural Washington with a more ambitious agenda: to escape her potato-farming parents and her dull sisters. She wanted excitement and recognition for her great beauty and intelligence. Beth drew up now, removing her arm from Glen's, to come and walk with Eli.

"Isn't she lovely?" she whispered.

He relished the arm she slipped through his own. He pressed it to his ribs.

"Yes," he said. "She's a looker."

"She was a beauty queen at a rodeo, you know," Beth continued eagerly. "Several times over, I think. You should ask her about it. It's a riot. She describes it as standing in manure with a tin tiara on her head." Beth laughed, shaking her pretty curls. "Gladys knee-deep in cow manure! Unholy image! I can't picture it at all!"

Eli, however, pictured it perfectly. It explained her feigned regality. She loathed her homeland. She gleamed like a polished onyx knife among those dull gray denizens. She thought every day about how to get out and how to never return; it was similar to how he believed sex would deliver him from the memory of his mother. Sinking into another woman, releasing the old ghost.

The market came into view with its cluttered awnings, its coursing crowds. A picket line of machinists stood somberly in the human traffic, holding signs about the aircraft plant. Seagulls pitched and plummeted overhead, driven crazy by the smells of fish and fried bread.

"Get back to work, you lazy bums," Glen shouted at the machinists, and they glared back at him mutely. "Union goons, the lot of you."

"Oh, leave 'em be," Beth chided. "They're true blue." To Eli she said, "My brother's a machinist, you know. Boeing is a bear. All these men want is seniority protection and a ten-cent raise."

"Fucking unions," Glen said loudly, turning back to them, "ruining this country."

"Saving it is more like it," Beth muttered, more to herself than to anyone else, but Eli heard her.

Glen put his arm around her waist and drew her away from Eli's side. "What's that, doll?"

Beth's face unclouded and she tossed her shoulders. "Nothing.

Nothing at all. Isn't it a wonderful evening? Aren't we having a splendid time?"

Beth's destiny, Eli saw sadly, was to succumb to a man in just this way. It struck him as weak and unfair.

Gladys walked next to him now. They pushed past the machinists. Eli took her elbow and guided her forward. He met the eye of one machinist and, thinking of Beth, smiled. The man noticed and nodded in return.

"Poor things," Gladys said to him. "They'll lose their jobs. It won't be worth it in the end."

"Even so," Eli said, "it's good to stand for something."

"My father stood for many things," Gladys said. "He became a drunk."

Eli thought of his own father, ill now, nearing death. He received a letter every few weeks, asking him to come home. There was not much time left to him, Eli knew, but it didn't matter. Eli did not want to return. He did not want to see his father in that bed, curling the sheet between his skeletal fingers. He did not want to see the woods, where his favorite dogs were buried, and maybe where his mother was dead, too.

"It's not a bad thing, to have opinions," Eli said.

"Every man has an opinion," Gladys countered calmly, "but a true man *acts* rather than speaks."

Eli rolled his eyes. *A true man.* How quaint. Gladys was a bit of a bore, wasn't she? Beth would never make such silly generalizations; Gladys was a phony. Eli suddenly felt that he hated Gladys and her carefully arranged perfection. She was too much like him.

And then, as if to prove him wrong, Gladys stumbled. Not just stumbled but fell, sprawling, to the cement. Eli momentarily glimpsed her complicated black underpinnings in the spectacular explosion of fabric, and his heart lurched. He rushed to help her to her feet, and she rose, sputtering, near tears, as shocked with her gracelessness as he was.

"The sidewalks here," she complained, shaking. "The gulls."

There had been no gulls near them, but Eli wrapped an arm around her waist, leading her onward, feeling protective of her and irrationally mighty.

"You are very beautiful," he said to her, thinking not of her girdle or her stockings but of her face.

She grew shy, or feigned shyness well. The shaking almost immediately stopped.

"You are a gentleman, sir," she said, but she gave his hand a squeeze that was as far from formal as the cow pastures in which she had been raised.

She wanted to be a good person, Eli thought, but she was not. No woman was. No man was, for that matter.

They walked under the awnings of the market, listening to the caterwauling of the fishmongers, smelling the fatty, metallic scent of sea life. Beth looked over her shoulder at them and smiled approvingly, noting their new closeness. She would gloat about her matchmaking abilities for years. Eli's crush on Beth would never diminish, not even when she died in her late forties—quite suddenly—of meningitis, leaving her many children motherless but aware of how lucky they'd been to have her in the first place.

For now, all four of the party—Eli, Gladys, Beth, and Glen— were healthy and well. They were capable of anything: love and sex, hatred and ruin. They had oceanic lives ahead of them, or so they believed.

A table off to the side of a florist's booth caught Eli's attention. He was still holding his date's waist as he pushed closer to it.

A man sat in a chair beside the table, his deft hands whittling a small piece of wood. On the table were a dozen or so wooden figurines. The handwritten sign before him read: DALE BIRD, FAMOUS WHITTLER OF THE SPOKAN TRIBE.

Eli stared down at the figurines, incredulous. He released Gladys almost roughly.

"May I?" he asked the man, his hands hovering over the largest of the figurines, and the man shrugged.

Eli picked up the figure. It was heavier and denser than it looked, almost as if it were petrified.

"What is it?" Gladys asked, sounding amused. "A monster?"

The man shook his head impatiently. "S'cwene'y'ti," he said. "Tall Man of Burnt Hair."

"Sounds like a monster to me," Gladys said.

Eli hardly heard her. He ran his fingers over the hulking shoulders of the figurine. He caressed the face, jagged with the impression of hair.

It was Mr. Krantz.

Mr. Krantz, with his matted fur, his small eyes, his colossal figure.

Eli remembered the smell of burnt hair. With it, his mother's floral perfume. He stroked the figure's wide flat feet.

"How much is this?" he demanded.

The man stopped whittling and considered him. "Ah. You've seen him. S'cwene'y'ti."

"How much for this?" Eli repeated, and the man, amused, shrugged again.

"Ten dollars," he said.

Eli fumbled in his pocket for a bill.

"Oh, come now," Gladys protested. "You're being rooked."

Eli brought out a five-dollar bill. He showed it to the man, and the man shook his head.

Eli began to argue with him.

"Ten dollars," the man said firmly. "Ten."

Eli looked at Gladys desperately. With her drawn white face and black hair, she seemed out of place in the colorful market. She belonged in a fairy tale, Eli felt. The one his father had read to him as a boy, the one about the huntsman who ripped out the heart of a deer. *Yes*, he thought. *Snow White.*

"You really need this ugly statue?" Gladys said to him.

"I need it," he said firmly.

She gave in, reaching into the pocket of her fine lavender dress. "Here," she told the man, careful to hold the bill so that there was no chance of grazing the man's fingers. "There's your other five, redskin."

Eli was grateful. The man took the figure from Eli to wrap it in brown paper. He handed the package back to Eli.

"They are not monsters," he said. "They are men."

Eli said that, yes, he knew this.

"They are sentenced by God to wander in doom," the man continued. "He is to be heard but never seen. A vagabond. Only the very gifted can see."

Eli wanted to hear more. Gladys tugged at his hand. "What else can you tell me?" Eli said.

"S'cwene'y'ti raped my neighbor's favorite horse."

"Please," Eli said to the man, and with his hand acknowledged Gladys, who had gasped in disgust and now looked as though she might be sick.

The man grinned at Eli; he had meant to offend her with the lewd joke.

Eli thanked the man stiffly and returned his arm to Gladys's curvy waist.

"I could just faint," Gladys said. Her head rolled onto his shoulder and he pointed his nose over her hairline, inhaling the scent of jasmine and rose. He remembered his mother's smell. *You women,* he thought, his eyes closing. *Why must you always kill me with your smell?*

"Are you okay?" Eli murmured into her hair. "I'm sorry if he shocked you."

"That old redskin was ripped. They're always ripped. We had loads of them in Omak, you know. Loads and loads. I know all about those people."

"He's a talented whittler."

Gladys scoffed. "Wasting his talent on those little monsters. Why, you should have bought one of the sparrows. They were sweet." Then, more weakly, "Can we stop for a moment?"

They stopped and Gladys lolled against him, her whole body. He pushed his hand into the small of her back for support and felt her torso jump in response. She met him, her legs surrounding one of his legs. She lifted her face to him. They kissed. It was lusty and deep.

Eli forgot about the figurine in his hand. He forgot about Mr. Krantz, about his mother. He muttered into Gladys's lips, words he hardly understood himself, and she muttered back, chewing on him, creating a new language.

"Take me home," she finally said. "Take me home with you."

She had set her sights on him, Eli realized, and she would have him. There had never been any doubt in her mind about it. She was a woman who always got exactly what she wanted.

He took up her hand and they threaded their way to the street. Beth and Glen stood together at the stairwell to the pier, watching them. Beth raised a hand, beckoning to them, but Eli didn't feel like acknowledging her. She wasn't nearly so attractive now, hair and clothes ruffled by the wind. He told himself that he'd won the better prize.

"Your place," Gladys said again. "You, me, and your little monster."

"You and me," Eli corrected, and he tucked the package deep within his coat pocket and forgot about it until the next morning.

1959

THE FUNNEL,
THE HOURGLASS,
THE WINDOW

GLADYS, FLUSH-CHEEKED, PREGNANT-BELLIED, HER HAIR FRESHLY
washed, tiptoed through the garden to where her husband stood
watching the trees.

"The starlings," Eli said. "They're flocking."

Gladys looked up, angling a pale, bejeweled wrist to shield her
eyes. She wore costly jewelry, rings and bracelets and necklaces
that clattered musically when she moved. It was her one demand of
her husband, to provide her with the very best. His own taste being
fastidious, he was proud to accommodate her. They cultivated an
appearance of greatness. When they went out to dinner together at
the club or met for lunch at the plaza, people admired them. *The
good doctor. The good doctor's wife.*

For the most part, Gladys was satisfied with their life. Eli's chosen field, podiatry, was very successful. She would have preferred
that he become a cardiologist or neurologist or surgeon, but Eli had
always been fascinated by feet and by footprints, and so she had
allowed him to choose his specialty with only mild complaint. And
good thing! His practice was booming. Their banker fell over himself when Gladys entered his branch, rushing forward to take up
her hand. The Roebucks owned a fashionable home filled with

furniture that inspired the envy of their handsome friends. Every week, Eli visited a buyer at the department store, a storklike woman who advised him on all women's finery. The stork was impeccable if unnecessary, but he seemed to like the formality of it and always sought her out for advice.

Gladys looked forward to Fridays, when her husband arrived with a box or two under his arm. He never forgot, never came home empty-handed. Gladys unwrapped the packages slowly, deliberately. Her face betrayed no excitement. The quickest way to lose a man, Gladys believed, was to show him too much gratitude. So she expertly raised her face to him and received his kiss and said tonelessly, "Thank you, dear," whether or not the purchase had pleased her.

The only thing missing from this charmed life, Gladys felt, was a child. She had already lost two—one in the first trimester and one born dead. She had named the stillborn Jonathan after her loving if ignorant father. Jonathan's birth and death had nearly killed Gladys, first from the grueling labor and then from the grief.

Instead of dying, she briefly lost her mind. Organ music played in her ears, a relentless, cheerful waltz that made her want to rise and dance until she dropped dead. Voices chattered at her. She fielded their remarks with a measured patience.

What an intelligent, refined person you are, Mrs. Dr. Roebuck.

"Oh, my darlings," she would reply. "How very kind of you to say so."

Teach us, please, how to be as elegant as you are.

"You are too kind. My poor darlings. How marvelous of you to notice."

Eli, sitting stiffly at her bedside, had once heard this and asked her, "Gladys, what are you saying? Who are you talking to?"

His voice had shattered the waltz, the voices shrieking in alarm and then gone. Gladys had seen her bedridden, disheveled image in Eli's broad red spectacles. It all came crashing down on her again.

"Leave me alone," she had moaned.

She had remained inconsolable until they mercifully drugged her to sleep.

Finally, inevitably, as the hormones and the drugs sloughed off, Gladys stabilized. Her mental health—always fragile, always a little shaky—was mostly restored.

The doctor declared her barren, and Gladys begrudgingly accepted this as the truth. She told herself she didn't want children, anyway, dirty, disgusting creatures that they were, and she refused to go to a friend's house unless their children were safely away at school or with a nanny. She lived in this frozen state for nearly two years following Jonathan's death, congratulating herself for being a modern woman, but the sight of a stroller on Main Street unsettled her and she averted her eyes from the baby even if it was a friend's child.

Rarely, only when Eli begged, she undressed for her marital duty and opened her legs to him, staring up at the ceiling while he grunted and stabbed. *Silly, perverted men,* she thought. Men would enjoy anything, as long as it was soft and wet and willing. At least her husband wasn't as bad as some.

He did annoy her sometimes, with his foot fetishes and his monster-tracking. His obsession with the outdoors, with hiking and camping and watching the trees and the sky, was incomprehensible to her. She enjoyed the smell of a rose or the vision of a pink sunset, just like any woman. But she far preferred the city and its tidy, cheerful shops to the dirt and shadow of the woods.

Still, he provided for her and loved her, and she was grateful. And now she had so much more to be grateful for: To everyone's surprise, she was pregnant. Even better, she was far along in the pregnancy, past the point of even Jonathan's stillbirth. She feared for the baby's life, but the doctors told her: All is well. Relax, think positively, drink orange juice. If possible, avoid cigarettes and alcohol and especially coffee. The baby would be "just nifty."

When the doctor had said the word *nifty,* Gladys had stiffened, but Eli had reached over and put a hand protectively on her back, and she knew that this gesture meant, *No matter, I'm here for you; I will always be here for you, and all will be well.*

So when her husband called to her to come outside and join him, Gladys went willingly. It was ten-thirty in the morning. She had been polishing the silver at the dining room table, watching him with a droll expression, wondering what had captured his interest.

Birds, apparently.

Tedious, Gladys thought, but she looked up, anyway.

And, admittedly, it was spectacular. Starlings were filthy little birds individually, Gladys thought, but as a collective unit they were magical.

Hundreds—thousands?—of starlings thickened the sky, forming a dark funnel one moment, twisting into an hourglass the next. They swelled and fell like a black wave or like an impending pestilence. Watching them was spellbinding. It was as though they had tethered her painlessly through the chest and would soon tug her airborne.

Gladys murmured her appreciation. She rested a palm on her belly and felt the baby surge, as though it, too, were bound to the flock. Eli stepped closer to her, never taking his eyes from the sky. He kissed her distractedly on the side of the head. Then he removed his glasses with their heavy lenses and began to polish them on his shirt.

The starlings rose and fell, rose and fell. They reassembled themselves into a new shape. Gladys's brow furrowed. It was as though they were spelling a word. She squinted. Yes, she thought. Yes, they were spelling a word.

She read the black letters in the sky.

DOOM.

The starlings fell apart, the word dissolving. *How silly of me*, Gladys thought. The flock sharply returned to itself, hanging in the blue as though nailed to it:

DOOM.

Gladys shoved her knuckles into her eye sockets. There, too, on the backs of her eyelids, were the starlings, white this time in a black sky.

DOOM.

Gladys cried out. She began to shake.

"What's the matter?" Eli asked her.

"The baby," she sobbed. "The baby is going to die. Not again, Eli. Oh, no, not again!"

He put a hand on her belly. It roiled under his palm. His eyebrows shot up.

"Gladys," he told her. "You're in labor."

"Doom," she bawled. "We're doomed. The baby. Us. We're all doomed."

Eli struggled with her into the house and then to the carport. Her bag was packed, ready, sitting in the foyer closet alongside their boots and shoes, and she managed in her terrible state to remind him to fetch it. He obeyed with a professional calm that irritated her. They drove to the hospital. Gladys bore her contractions silently now, but the tears fell in droves.

The baby, Gladys was sure, was dead inside her. Lost. *You dumb doomed baby.* She could feel its death plowing through her, soaring toward her heart in one dark twisting line. The starlings were inside her now.

In the sterile little room, the nurse gave her an enema. Gladys wept from the humiliation. They drugged her. She fell into a dreamless sleep.

When she awoke, the baby was placed in her arms, not only alive but lovely, a perfectly defiant little being. Its eyes were lucid, skeptical, even, and it stared at her haughtily, as though it already saw her weakness.

"But how can this be?" she asked.

The nurse brought her a mug of ice chips. "As strong as a bear cub, this little girl. Born last night near midnight."

Gladys, speechless, cupped the baby's soft pink head with one palm. The baby mewled and then shut her scowling eyes as though to sleep.

"She wanted out, I tell you," the nurse said cheerfully. "Would you like some broth?"

Gladys thought again of the starlings.

"Where is my husband?"

"At home, maybe? Sleeping one off? I'm sure he had a drink or two after the good news."

Gladys had her baby now. She was exhausted, relieved, too tired for elation. She leaned back against the pillows and shut her eyes.

"I'll take her back to the nursery so you can rest," the nurse said.

In Gladys's mind's eye, the starlings unfurled. They were regrouping.

"No," Gladys said. "Leave her here. Just for a bit. Just for a moment."

But then the baby's bright bruised eyes reopened. She began to cry. It was a small cry, but it bothered Gladys. It occurred to her that she had no idea how to take care of a baby. She had babysat children, her little sisters, but that was years ago, and she had always hated it. She didn't remember how to feed a baby or bathe her or change her diaper. She wasn't even sure how to kiss her or how to comfortably hold her. Even now, reclining with the baby on her chest, she felt as useless and rigid as a slab of petrified wood.

Was this all that motherhood was? Perpetual, mutating fear? A fear that blackened first this perspective and then shifted and obscured another?

"I've changed my mind," Gladys said as the nurse turned to leave. "I'm tired, after all. Take her. Take her now, please."

The nurse obediently retrieved the baby, scooping her up and kissing her almost roughly on the cheek. The baby's cries softened as the nurse bore her into the hallway.

Gladys listened to the cries fade. She'd feel better after some sleep, she told herself, but her heart, made of a thousand black wings, was flinging about in her chest, and she feared what she would see in her dreams.

She fought to stay awake. She was fingering the pages of a ladies' magazine when her husband ambled into the room. She could see that he was happy.

"Camille's a doll," Eli said. "Well done, Gladys."

For a moment, Gladys was confused. Then she remembered: Camille. Her grandmother's name. Also the name of her horse when she was a girl, that broad-rumped brown mare with the white star on her chest. The animal had been slow and patient, allowing Gladys to drape her in old tablecloths and braid her mane and tail. Gladys had always wanted a daughter named Camille, she'd told Eli, but the name sounded wrong now, fit for a different age and place. Camille was the name of a dead woman and a dead horse. How could she name her daughter after such things?

Better the name of a missing person, someone lost but maybe, one day, found.

"Amelia," she said.

Eli hesitated for a moment. "Okay, then."

She could tell he wasn't crazy about the name. Gladys didn't care.

"Amelia Grace," she continued.

Eli perched on the edge of her bed and patted her knee with a touch more friendly than intimate. He wore a dapper suit and a crisp bow tie. He was dressed to see patients.

"You're not going in today, are you?" Gladys pressed.

"No. Maybe. What would you like me to do?"

Gladys turned and looked out the window, her tone flat. "Do what you must."

Outside, the white pines shook lightly in a fine summer breeze. The day was so clear it felt ominous. There was nothing for that bright sky to do but blacken and wound.

The bed creaked. Eli was leaving. He kissed her head and bade her goodbye. "I'll come by tonight," he said at the door. "Rest well."

Theirs was a good marriage, Gladys reminded herself. But she suddenly wished she had a view of the parking lot. She wanted to see him get into his car. She wanted to see which way he turned, if he chose the scenic route by the river or the more direct route through town. To the left or to the right. She guessed to the left. She would like to be sure, if only to regain a little confidence.

She rested her head against the pillows and put aside her magazine. Sleep still frightened her. Regardless, it came.

Hours later, the room dark and cool, Gladys awoke. She did not feel well, only light-headed and weak. At the window were tiny strips of bright, glimmering light through the darkness, like holes punched into a sheet. For a moment she thought the drapes had been pulled. They were ravaged, moth-eaten. Gladys wrinkled her nose, disgusted. How could a hospital hang such shabby fabric?

But then the window moved. It moved like a living being. Light flickered, darkness fell away. There were no drapes, no torn fabric. The window had been covered not with curtains but with living things.

Birds.

Light split into the room and Gladys heard the starlings chattering evilly as they soared past, some of them in their excitement striking the window, drilling into it as if they meant to come inside and race down her throat.

Gladys screamed. The nurses came and clutched at her, securing her arms.

"Calm yourself," the prettier nurse hissed. "Calm yourself, Mrs. Dr. Roebuck."

Gladys shrieked and kicked. She wanted to see the baby. She wanted to walk. Her bladder was full of piss and blood, and she released it; the bed grew warm and sticky. They had wrapped her breasts, but they, too, flowed with milk. The room smelled wet and fecund, like a diseased swamp.

"You *people*," Gladys said hatefully to the nurses, her fear flowing to liquid anger. "You *peons*. Let go. Where is my daughter? Let go of me! What's happened to my Amelia?"

The nurses eyeballed each other like frightened horses. Gladys stopped thrashing and took a deep breath. The prettier nurse, noting Gladys's cooperation, nodded at her colleague, and the other released an arm and walked quickly out of the room. The prettier nurse released her grip, too, and stroked Gladys's shoulder soothingly, but Gladys could hear in her voice a thick dislike.

The other nurse returned with Amelia. She tried to hand her to Gladys, but Gladys demurred.

"No," she said. "I don't want to hold her. Just to see her. To make sure she's all right."

The baby was well, satisfied from a recent bottle and sleepy from the trials of being born. She kept her little eyes fastened tightly shut, as though refusing to look at her mother. Gladys pestered the nurses with questions about every wrinkle and discoloration and coo, but the nurses were steadfast: The baby was well; there was nothing wrong with her; she was perfect. Redness, bruising, gurgling—all of that was to be expected. Gladys half-listened, eyes and fingers roving wildly over the baby, seeking imperfections. The nurse holding the baby grew tired of supporting the child at such an awkward angle and asked Gladys again if she wanted to hold the baby herself.

"No," Gladys said. "No, I'm fine. Please. Just. Take care of her. My Amelia. Take care of her, please."

The ugly nurse straightened, bringing the baby against her shoulder, and clucked reassuringly. She was the kinder of the nurses, filled with pity. She was dowdy, fat, and a little too pale, but at least she was kind.

The other nurse—slim, pretty, skeptical—said she would ring for a doctor. She glared at Gladys with little concern, only rancor.

Gladys supplicated the kinder nurse. "The birds, you see. They're scaring me. The way they gathered at the window. Like an army. An evil army. You see?"

"You need to sleep," the pretty nurse said. "Sleep will help with the mania, with the hormones . . ."

Gladys knit her brow. Why wouldn't this woman go away?

". . . and," the pretty nurse continued, "a tranquilizer. You'll need another tranquilizer. I'll ring the doctor straightaway."

"Young lady," Gladys said, "I would like to see the head nurse, please. This is an outrage."

The pretty woman raised her chin. "I'm the head nurse, Mrs. Dr. Roebuck."

"Then you should be fired. I'll see to it that you are."

The kind nurse looked as if she was about to cry.

"Take the baby back to the nursery," the pretty nurse said, and the kind nurse obeyed quickly.

"Childbirth," the nurse said pedantically to Gladys, "can be very trying. A woman under duress may see things or hear things, but they aren't really there. A woman under duress—"

"I will see to it that you're demoted immediately," Gladys interrupted. "I'm a powerful woman. A doctor's wife."

"A podiatrist's wife," the nurse corrected.

Gladys hated her weak limbs then. In a better state, she would have leapt from the bed and smacked this pretty little brunette chicken senseless.

"Get me the doctor," Gladys ordered. "Right now."

The woman bowed her head with fake reverence, turned sharply, and hurried out of the room, her white shoes squeaking miserably against the floor.

I'll teach this rude young woman a lesson, Gladys thought. Having such a task at hand made her feel better. It gave her control.

And sure enough, as promised, Gladys worked on the woman's demotion throughout her week's stay in the hospital. She was kept on as a nurse but was forced into the night shift. Gladys took pleasure in bettering things and saw to it that the kind fat nurse took up the vacated position, despite the hospital's reluctance regarding her leadership skills.

The key to being powerful, Gladys knew, was telling people you were powerful. Eli stood at her side, lips pressed, as she ranted and raved to anyone who would listen. She leaned on them all, wronged, tearful, until they had no choice but to give in to her.

When it was time to return home, Gladys was glad for it. She left with a feeling of triumph. She had her daughter now. The pretty nurse had received her just deserts. The black starlings had dispersed. Perhaps she had imagined them after all? She could hold Amelia now, almost confidently. The baby regarded her with a hesitant trust, snuggling into her but starting at the smallest movement or sound.

I love you, Gladys thought but did not say. She didn't want to jinx things. She didn't want to spoil the girl too much. *I love you and we will be all right.*

On the day Eli drove Gladys home from the hospital, the starlings had gathered in the front yard. They blanketed the grass like a shifting black sea. Gladys clutched the baby close to her, shrinking back against the passenger seat, holding her breath.

"These damn birds," Eli said. "I've never seen anything like it."

I have, Gladys thought.

The baby jumped against her. The birds, too, jumped, rising into the sky as the wheels bore down on them, flocking with a panic that alerted Gladys to a changing of the tides. She was in charge now. Doom was hers alone to gift. Only one starling remained, frantically beating its wounded wing against the edge of the lawn in a futile attempt to follow its sisters heavenward.

With one arm supporting the baby, Gladys reached across Eli to the steering wheel.

Her husband released his own tight grip and allowed Gladys to draw them toward what briefness remained of that dark fluttering life.

1970

THE PATCHWORK CAP

It was a dreary Wednesday in early October when Eli informed Gladys that he planned to give up his flourishing podiatry practice and pursue, full-time, the region's elusive Sasquatch.

The good doctor was down on one knee as he spoke. He held her hand with both of his, as though proposing to her, and she stared obliquely into his face from where she sat in her ebony Windsor chair.

"Sasquatch," Gladys parroted. "I see."

She was taken aback by his passion. Eli was an exact man, precise to the point of agony, never a movement or word wasted; he was the sort of man who wore his glasses during sex. Now, to Gladys's astonishment, his eyes watered with emotion. He clasped her hand and then her legs, his palms hot and dry. He reminded her of their dogs, sitting by the tableside, begging for scraps. His tone was both a plea and a firm declaration.

Oh, if she were not such a down-to-earth woman, Gladys thought, she would toss herself at his feet and pound the floor with her fists!

The doctor kept his hands on her, as though worried about this possibility.

Gladys struggled to summon the correct tone. Her surprise had melted away, and in its place sat a stout and ugly rumination.

How could you do this to me? she wondered, but she couldn't say it aloud. It was too self-pitying.

It's my own fault, she thought instead. *I've let your fancies go too far. It's time to put my foot down.*

For as long as Gladys had known Eli, he had obsessed over the local legends of what she referred to as "his monsters" (a term that Eli disapproved of; "*Hominids,* Gladys," he corrected hotly. "They are great apes, more man than beast"). It did not escape Gladys's notice that he became a podiatrist due to his keen interest in arboreal footprints. On the only forest walk she'd ever taken with him, during their short engagement, he had brought her to a small clearing and showed her one of his "findings," as he called them. "The finding" was a long, oval impression in the dried mud. It certainly looked like a foot, if you squinted at it correctly, but Gladys was embarrassed by his certainty.

"Well," she'd said. "Very interesting."

He had beamed. He had driven her all the way from Lilac City to this dry, sparse forest outside Rathdrum, to tell her about his childhood. She had listened to him dully. She questioned her rationality in marrying someone with such a wild imagination. But he'd already set up his podiatry practice in Lilac City, and they'd purchased a handsome house, and he'd given her an enormous diamond ring that she enjoyed showing around. He seemed perched on the edge of success, and it was the sort of success that Gladys wanted. Besides, she'd reasoned to herself, aren't all men strange? Don't all men have disagreeable hobbies? Some men frequented seedy bars and flirted with loose women. Some men drank too much and beat their wives. At least, for all of his strangeness, Eli was a loyal husband and prodigious provider.

And so it was a conscious—and erroneous, she saw now— decision to accept and even encourage his interests. It was a boyhood hobby, nothing more. She pretended to find it endearing when he returned from the library late in the evenings with a few Xeroxed articles from the *Seattle P-I*, from *The Wenatchee World* or *The Lilac City Monitor*, mentioning in some small way a random (purported) sighting. Twice a year he left town to camp in the Selkirks, to spend a week combing the densely treed hillsides for evidence. He even made molds from these footprints, a few of which sat hidden away in his den (she would not permit them in the dining or living room), chunky monoliths that Gladys dusted once a week with a resolute wifely cheerfulness. It was nonsense, but she allowed it, mainly because he kept it to himself and for the most part didn't bring it up at dinner parties or bridge games.

When he did bring it up, it was keenly embarrassing. For a time he became obsessed with the Patterson-Gimlin film, which he called *Patt-Gim*. They had watched the interview on late-night television. Eli had grown so agitated during the interview that he spilled his Tom Collins all over the new tan club chair. Gladys had gotten down on all fours to scrub the fabric clear of lemon and sugar, but Eli remained on his feet, staring at the television with a look of complete madness. The next night, at a dinner party with one of his partners, he brought up *Patt-Gim* and spoke passionately about it for a few minutes, all while his colleagues and their wives smiled into their drinks. One of the wives caught Gladys's eye and grimaced pityingly. Gladys was beside herself with anger and frustration. Rattled, concerned, she berated Eli on the way home for his puerile behavior.

"People don't believe in your monsters," she said as he drove. "It's humiliating."

"Hominids," he corrected. "Or hominins, maybe. But not monsters, Gladys."

She had never been so annoyed with him. They went inside, paid the babysitter, and readied for bed. Gladys had given him the cold shoulder for the rest of the short evening, although, as usual, he failed to notice.

But now Gladys wished she had fought him harder, had killed the conversation then, before it all went too far. She looked at him and saw a dreaming little boy. She was exhausted by his silliness. She wanted to slap him.

"We're on the cusp of greatness," Eli pressed. "He's out there, waiting to be discovered. Clever fellow, evasive but waiting for us, whether he knows it or not."

Gladys put her palms over her ears. "Stop talking, please. I have a terrible headache."

"There's nothing to be ashamed of, Gladys," he said. "This is science. It's about discovery. Self-discovery, even. The more we know about Sasquatch, the more we'll know of one another. I wish I was out there, filming my own footage. I wish I could get my hands on that footage, to watch it again. It just replays endlessly in my mind. An endless loop."

What could she do? Other than chide and beg, which only added to the humiliation, there was no sure way to shut him up. She was the wife. It was her job to support him, to get out of his way, or, at the very least, to give the impression of supporting him, et cetera. Their future was in her hands. She would have to say something strategic to snap him out of his dreamland.

She began with a neutral phrase—*an amazing idea*—meaning to add, however, that she disapproved, and also to say, with some derision, that the whole business was batty.

It was too late. He had already lunged from his knees to embrace her. Gladys cried out as though expecting to be slugged, and then she felt herself wrapped in his familiar, spindly arms. She stopped breathing for a moment, baffled and overwhelmed. When he pulled away, there were tears rolling down his cheeks—actual tears! She had never seen him cry, except when his father had died, but even then there had been only an ugly open quaking of the mouth, a facial bleariness. But now he cried from relief, as freely as a child.

"I worried so much," he said, "about what you would say. I thought you would fight me tooth and nail. What a shock this must be to you, Gladys. But I feel—" He stopped here, releasing her and bringing clasped fingers to his heart. "I feel that if I don't do this, I will die. I will die a sudden horrible death. Have you ever felt that way about something? That you must either commit fully to the task at hand or die an agonizing death?"

He was not really asking the question of her, only marveling over his own appetites, and so Gladys said nothing, although what she thought was, *Yes. I felt that way about marrying you. All of those long years ago.* Perhaps not so much because of an extraordinary love for him but because it meant that she would be released from the tedium of her girlhood, a life that had been comfortable enough but as shineless and unsupportive as an old, beat-up pair of shoes. She had wanted stability, status, success. And Eli, to his credit, had so far brought her those things.

And now what? Would she lose everything?

"I do support you," Gladys said, through gritted teeth. "But what of Amelia?" she asked. "What of her future?"

Eli rose to his feet. "I don't want you worrying about money, Gladys. I won't leave you in the poorhouse. I still have my license, after all. I'll keep a few patients from the practice. The patients will come here, to the house, for treatment. Just a handful of them, enough to keep us comfortable. You won't want for anything."

"But just enough? What does that mean?"

"You know, dear, it wouldn't hurt us to live in a smaller house, in a more modest neighborhood, with more modest things."

Gladys blanched. "You can't mean you'd sell the house?"

"Fact is," he continued, fidgeting, "this could be a gold mine. If I can prove his existence, just think of it. The money. The fame! Imagine if I produced a verifiable corpse! There's nothing we'll want for. And I believe I know how to find him. I believe I have an advantage. I practically know him personally."

Gladys hesitated. Her husband was mad, she feared, but she was comforted by his promises of money and fame. She was not ashamed of her desire for wealth. She was a grown woman, after all, and deserving. And she wanted the best for her daughter. She wanted the best clothes for her, the best education. God forbid the child should attend public school or community college.

Gladys felt herself giving in; she had no choice but to accept his empty promises. His Northwest ape! His Sasquatch! It was ridiculous, Gladys knew. But watching him as he paced excitedly back and forth, she was temporarily appeased by his ardor.

"Okay, then," she said. "You have my blessing, Eli. Godspeed."

To her own ear, she sounded Shakespearian. She was pleased with herself. Eli, even more pleased, kissed her flush on the mouth, and the kiss becalmed her. She was the perfect wife, and he was the adventuresome husband who would win them glory.

Why not? The world was filled with strange things. Maybe he would find one of them.

The conversation over, Eli went to pack for his next expedition and Gladys rose and began to tidy the house. She went about her tasks cheerfully enough, but as she returned some wayward shoes to the foyer closet, a hard knot formed in her gut.

What, exactly, had she agreed to?

The knot tightened as Eli put his bags in his car.

She was agreeing, she sensed, to their doom. She thought of the black birds all those year ago, which she had written off as no more than birthing hormones. She'd experienced other "episodes," as Eli called them, but none of them had been so intense.

But now the starlings flooded her vision again. The world darkened.

She was agreeing to change. Change was a bad thing. It only brought about more change. She wanted nothing to change, nothing at all.

She raced into the driveway to flag down Eli's car and demand that he stay. He mistook her waving arms as a fond farewell, and he waved back at her through the car window. She could see his grin clearly as he backed out. Could he not see her downturned mouth?

Eli. Get back here. Right this instant.

She stomped her foot, shook a fist.

He sped away with a last wave.

Reentering the house, Gladys was very aware of her vulnerability. She was a woman, alone. What if a thief came? A rapist?

What if Eli was killed in the wilderness by a mountain lion or by a falling tree? These things happened. How would they even locate him? What would become of Amelia? What would become of Gladys herself?

What if he met another woman? A female cryptozoologist? Someone more to his liking?

Gladys had been lovelier as a young woman but she was older now, thick in the waist and throat, too dedicated to one man. She was all used up. Who would have her?

Stop it. You're being silly.

She shoveled the shoes into the closet without her usual orderliness. She went to the kitchen and wrote down the list for the maid.

TO DO:
Dust all rooms on first floor.
Dishes.
Do ALL laundry (don't forget the towels this time).

She stopped there. The letter *D* rose before her with its fat, pregnant belly. *DOOM,* she saw. She wrote quickly, *Whatever else you can fit in,* and underlined it, and put several exclamation points following. Then she started on the menu for the cook.

Dinner, she began, then, seeing again the oppressive letter, crumpled up the paper and, with weak fingers, started again. *Supper,* she wrote, and felt that it was a more noble term for the evening meal, but her fingers shook so strongly that she could not write another word.

The maid arrived, and then the cook, and by then Gladys had regained her excellent posture, if not her usual confidence. Amelia returned from school and droned on about her classmates. Gladys sat across from her at the dinner table and mechanically ate. Left to her own devices, the cook had served them peasant food: beans, meat, over-steamed greens. It tasted wretched, but Gladys choked it down. Uncertain of what to do then, Gladys excused herself for bed.

"Mom, no," Amelia cried. "You'll miss *Hee Haw!*"

"Trash," Gladys said. "Nothing but hicks and whores."

"It's my favorite show. It's *comedy.*"

"Hicks and whores."

Amelia sulked. Gladys left her at the table and climbed the stairs to her room.

She slept fitfully and awoke in the morning with what felt like a crushing hangover.

Shaky and sick, Gladys dressed. It was a gorgeous day outside. The swaying trees, the singing robins, they all mocked her.

Accepting only a mug of coffee from her daughter, Gladys slid into her chair with a whimper. Amelia buttered toast and readied for school. She left for the bus stop without a word. Gladys was glad when she was gone. She could better nurse her misery alone.

To distract herself, Gladys decided to drive into Lilac City for a shopping expedition. She deserved a respite. Perhaps she would buy something lovely for Amelia. A new hair ribbon, maybe. A new tie for her husband. Sometimes a new tie could fix everything. She laughed, madly and loudly, and the sound of her laughter seemed to cut a hole into the fabric of the world. *God,* she thought. *How alone I am! How abandoned!*

The steering wheel vibrated against her palms and she thought for a moment that it was an inner quaking, a breaking apart. She parked beside a short avenue of shops and stepped onto the sidewalk. *I'm dying,* she thought. *I'm about to die.* This revelation satisfied her. *I will die and then he'll see. That will end the argument.* She pictured her funeral, her gorgeous black gown and gleaming ebony casket. Beside it, Eli would weep. Amelia would beat on his back with her fists— *How could you do this to her!*—and he would moan his remorse into the relentless sheets of rain.

Gladys parked in a garage downtown and took an elevator to the street. On the sidewalk, she tried to enjoy the cheery atmosphere, the bustling bodies around her, the salesclerks and the occasional passerby telling her hello, recognizing her as the good doctor's wife. They allowed her the elevated status that she had always carried among them. *Hello,* they said to her reverently. *Hello, Mrs. Dr. Roebuck.* She smiled at them. Then she lifted her gaze to the awning above her and read the cursive writing painted there.

Odds and Ends
Queerities, Confoundisms and Strangelings

Well, Gladys thought. *A new shop! I'll go in and welcome the owner.*

She pressed inside through the French doors, triggering a bell. Despite the teeming sidewalks, the store was empty. It was cool and dim but not at all unpleasant or gloomy. Rather, it was an immediate feast for the eyes, an exploding bouquet of color and flair. Items were piled everywhere, cluttered on the floor, sitting on tables, leaning against one another haphazardly as though they might, at any moment, tip over. The shop gave Gladys an immediate sense of euphoria.

The shopkeeper was not present, although Gladys could hear someone shuffling around in a back room. At first, Gladys wandered the store timidly. She eyeballed some of the peculiarities: a chair that rocked sideways rather than front to back, a statuette of a nude woman with a beak and wings, a kite that quivered on the wall as if in mid-flight. Bolder now, Gladys picked up a normal-looking wooden box and turned it over in her hands.

She opened the latch.

Out flew a live yellow bird.

Gladys screeched. The bird fluttered wildly about the room. Looking for a way outside, it threw itself furiously against the glass windowpanes. Terribly embarrassed, Gladys tried to follow the bird and recapture it, but it flew through her fingers like a feathered missile. Gladys dropped the box, panicking. The box hit the floor, clamped shut, and the bird disappeared in a puff of purple smoke.

Gladys cried out for help.

"Yes?" a voice said. "How can I help you?"

A long, shady slip of a woman stood behind her, regarding her with wide round eyes. She wore a full-length velvet dress, buttoned tightly at the throat. Two sparkling red globes swung from her heavy earlobes.

"Your bird," Gladys said, pointing to the wooden box, too unnerved to pick it up again. "I've killed it."

The shopkeeper bent and retrieved the tiny receptacle.

"The bird?" the shopkeeper said. "Dead, you say?"

She opened the box and out flew the bird again, twittering, flashing yellow against the windows.

Then, glowing with a private, satisfied smile, she clamped the lid shut. Again came the puff of purple smoke. The bird disappeared.

"As right as rain," the woman said. "Really, it's impossible to damage any of our goods. They are"—she gave a careless wave at the shelves—"invincible."

"I'm so relieved," Gladys said. "You have no idea. With the week I've had, I just couldn't have added a murder to the list."

Gladys laughed too loudly. An awkward silence fell. The shopkeeper watched her carefully. Gladys found the shopkeeper's face ravishing, so waxen smooth and pure, although she seemed by her stiff carriage tremendously old.

"Please," the shopkeeper said, her hands primly clasped before her waist. "Look around. Enjoy."

"Oh," Gladys hurried to say, "I just wanted to step inside and welcome you to the area. I hadn't noticed your shop before! How long have you been here?"

"How kind of you," the shopkeeper replied in her calm, steady voice. "We've been here a good forty years now."

"Forty years?"

"A little over."

"Funny, I've never seen you," Gladys marveled. "I've shopped this street for half my life."

"People pass us by until they need us," the woman said.

She gave Gladys another charming smile. It cut through the wan darkness of her face like lightning. And then she walked over to the cash register, bobbing up and down like a large chicken. She bent behind it to withdraw a wide blue feather duster, which she began to wield around the dustless room, passing from aisle to aisle with her awkward gait. The feather duster shook and giggled like a tickled child.

"What a marvelous thing that is!" Gladys said.

"Yes, isn't it?"

"How does it work? Batteries?"

The woman shrugged. *Of course*, Gladys thought, *she doesn't want to reveal any secrets.*

"The wooden box, too, is miraculous. And the bird was like flesh and blood! It's a trick of the light?"

But she remembered, as she said this, how her fingers had grazed the bird's feathers. Maybe her imagination, she considered. After all, she hadn't been feeling well today. Quite dizzy and out of sorts.

"Not a trick, no."

Gladys felt, standing in this strange shop beside this paradoxically old and ageless woman, that she herself had regressed in years. The hard shell of her body was lighter now, filled with energy. She felt excited and open to the world.

"It's as though," she said, "these things are enchanted."

The shopkeeper hummed to herself as if she hadn't heard, working the giggling feather duster around the room. Gladys stopped trying to converse and began, again, to wander.

What marvels the shop carried! A stuffed frog that belched gold coins when she patted its head. A baby's mobile that, when wound up, issued not only song but also enticing aromas of roasting meats and stews. In a cage tucked near the back, a live weasel stared at her with deep-red eyes. It had glossy black fur and an uncanny way of chirping; it sounded as if it were speaking French. It occurred to her that her husband would enjoy this shop, and she thought how she would bring him here the very next weekend if he returned, and maybe they could take a picnic lunch in the countryside if the weather permitted and how rejuvenating that would be for them, how such a splendid afternoon, a splendid moment, could make them feel deeply in love again. Oh, how she wanted this to happen.

This was when Gladys found the patchwork cap.

It rested on a mannequin's head, a wooden mannequin whose half-carved features were familiar to Gladys, although she could not quite place the face. She reached out and touched the cap. *There is nothing enchanted here,* she thought. If anything, it looked old, overused, the patches dull in color, the stitching coming undone on one side—but when her fingers grazed the fabric, she was electrified by a surge of confidence. She pulled her hand away. The shopkeeper moved beside her soundlessly, looking at her with the same unreadable expression, her head bobbing very slightly up and down.

"It's a wonderful cap," the shopkeeper said. "Very powerful."

"It's an ugly sort of thing," Gladys said, although now, she saw, there was a lovely shine to it. Perhaps it was not so dingy and worn, after all.

"My grandmother made it years ago. Stitched it herself from her favorite garments. It has sat on many heads—some quite famous, others not." The shopkeeper gazed at the cap affectionately.

"And what," Gladys laughed, finding herself inexplicably jealous of these previous hat wearers, "are its special powers?"

"Whoever wears the cap is irresistible to her heart's desire."

Gladys grew very serious. What a silly thing to say about a cap. What nonsense. But she could not wrest her eyes from it.

"The thing is," she began, more to herself than to the shopkeeper, "I'm a doctor's wife. I say it as a fact, you see. I'm not trying to gloat. I'm only saying it to prove how very odd it is that I want this cap. I've never been compelled to buy a used cap before, especially one not so very . . . well . . . used."

But she smiled at the cap as she said it, her eyes flirty.

"Try it on," the shopkeeper encouraged, carefully releasing the cap from the mannequin's head, which instantly became unrecognizable now that it was naked. "See for yourself. It will fit beautifully. It always does."

Gladys wrinkled her nose at the fabric's musty smell, but it dissolved quickly, and she felt the cap tighten itself around her skull. It wrapped around her head the way a warm, affectionate cat might curl itself onto its owner's lap. The smell became pleasant, reminding Gladys of her grandmother's house when she was a small girl, the soft smell of laundry, of fresh-cut herbs, of old settling wood, even of Eli's musk. For the first time in years, Gladys felt relaxed and handsome.

"How much is it?" she asked, opening her purse.

The woman told her she would sell it for twenty-five dollars.

She handed over the money immediately.

"Now," the shopkeeper said, her tone suddenly fierce, "there is one simple rule you must follow to achieve the best effect from our product."

Gladys snapped her purse shut.

"You must never, ever, take it off."

Gladys's head shot up, meeting the woman's bright and serious eyes.

"If you do, the spell will be broken, and you'll find your love greatly compromised."

"Are you saying I must never, ever, remove this cap from my head?"

Gladys's head radiated a pleasant warmth, as though the sun were caressing her bare scalp.

"Exactly. As long as you want its powers to work, do not take it off. Not for bathing. Not for hairstyling. Not for eating. Not for anything you might wish to do without it."

"And is there a return policy?"

"All sales," the shopkeeper said, "are final. As it states on your receipt."

How cheap to not allow returns, Gladys thought. *Ah, well.* She bid the shopkeeper goodbye and exited the shop, returning to the bustling avenue. She remained, despite the admonition of the shopkeeper, very pleased with her purchase. The patchwork cap fit her head wonderfully. It fit her better than any item she had ever before worn, as though it had been forged specifically for her skull. It rested on her ears not like a cap but like a good friend who had only nice things to tell her. What confidence it gave her! She held her shoulders back as she ambled to the parking garage, her chin riding high.

She passed a group of other doctors' wives. There they all were, her friends and enemies: the cardiologist's wife, the neurologist's wife, and the slender, stylish wife of the gynecologist. They sat outside at a café, drinking coffee and eating croissants. It did not bother Gladys that she had not been invited to their outing. She congratulated herself for not being too sensitive about the matter, as she normally would have been. She told them good morning sincerely and then continued to her car.

(After she passed, the wives giggled to one another about the silly cap, which was a horrid little thing and clashed with Gladys's fine blouse and skirt. And hadn't she smelled strange? The gynecologist's wife mentioned the stench of overcooked bacon. And yet, after the laughter had subsided, the cardiologist's wife admitted—and all of them were quick to agree—that Gladys hadn't looked so well in years. She carried herself like royalty, as though what sat on her head was not a patchwork cap at all but a bejeweled tiara. Yes, the neurologist's wife concluded, she must have had some work done on her face. She must be using a good cream. The gynecologist's wife said that she would seek Gladys out and ask what, exactly, was her secret. The cardiologist's wife remembered how Gladys had once been a beauty queen in central Washington. Here they were, eating croissants, drinking coffee, and discussing again, as they once had, Gladys's beauty secrets. The neurologist's wife said they should have invited Gladys to brunch. "Stupid cap and all," she said. *Yes,* they all agreed, laughing, *next time we will invite her, stupid cap and all!)*

Gladys, meanwhile, had found her car and was gliding home. When she pulled into the driveway, she saw her husband's car parked before their stately brick house, rather sloppily, as if he expected only to run inside, grab something, and return immediately. Gladys parked in front of the garage and touched the patchwork cap, just so, before rising to find him.

He was in his study, fumbling through the files and cursing under his breath as though running very late.

"Hello, dear," Gladys said. "What are you doing home?"

"I've gone and forgotten my notes," the doctor said hurriedly, "and I just wanted to pick them up and head back out for the woods. I can't find them here. So the day is not going well."

"I'm sorry," Gladys said. "Can I make you a sandwich?"

He glanced up then. "What is that *thing*?"

Gladys touched her cap reverently.

"Did you lift it from the Army Surplus? From a Dumpster? Really, Gladys. Your taste is slipping. The smell! God! It's like burnt flesh."

Gladys was crushed. How stupid she was to listen to that mendacious shopkeeper. She had a thought to tear the cap off her head, but when she moved her fingers to her scalp, she found that she could not bring herself to do it. Her arm dropped to her side. She was overcome with pure rage.

"How dare you," she told him, straightening. "How dare you insult me, Eli. I'll dress however I please. After all, my taste should not be in question. *You're* the one. Leaving us for an ape. Leaving us for an *imaginary monster.* Hominid or hominin or whatever you call it. Shame on you, Eli."

The doctor gaped at her. Then he cocked his head. His wife, he thought, looked markedly different, and he found the difference alluring. She reminded him of her aloof younger self, the self he had met and married all those long years ago, the young beauty queen from Omak, Washington. Even her skin had taken on a youthful ruddy hue.

"Perhaps," the doctor said, putting down his papers, "I will take a sandwich, after all."

"Then make it your damn self," Gladys said, turning on her heel and stalking away, the scent of burning meat trailing after her.

That was all it took. The doctor—if not exactly in love again— was intrigued. He followed her down the hallway like an old dog, all the way to her room, where she had slept alone for several years now, per his request, and stood at the door in substantial agony when she slammed it in his face.

In her room, ignoring her husband's whining pleas for entry, Gladys sat before her vanity and admired the sight of the patchwork cap. It was working! She wrapped her palms around it and gave it—and her head—a squeeze. She would kiss her cap if she could, but then she would have had to remove it. *No,* she thought, *I won't ever remove you!* She found it odd that earlier in the day she had balked at the very notion.

And so her new life began. She came to breakfast in the cap and arrived to dinner in the cap. She wore the cap in her car, in the shower, and in the garden. She appeared in it at social gatherings and at the hairdresser's. When the hairdresser began to remove it, Gladys gnashed her teeth and told her to leave it be.

"Just style the hair around it, please," she demanded, and the poor hairdresser complied, styling Gladys's sleek black tresses around the cap's faded fabric. In the end, the effect was a lovely one, like a plain of shining onyx beneath a pretty rainbow.

After this excursion, Gladys, feeling every bit as lovely as a goddess, walked down Main Street. The patchwork cap made her head itch, and she scratched at it absently as she walked. Odds and Ends stood with its French doors thrown open to the avenue, and yet, once again, it was empty except for the preening birdlike shopkeeper, who was mopping the floors with a lavender-perfumed liquid.

"Hello there," Gladys sang out, not wanting to catch the shopkeeper off guard.

The woman glanced up, her head bobbing slowly up and down, not at all surprised. "Mrs. Roebuck. You're looking well."

"Thank you. I've just been to the hairdresser."

The shopkeeper scowled. "I hope she didn't—"

"Oh, no!" Gladys said, touching the cap. "I've followed your directions perfectly. The cap hasn't left my head for even a moment. You know, it's funny, I can't imagine taking her off now. She's glued on to my head, as far as I'm concerned. Although I do sometimes worry about the smell."

The shopkeeper smiled. "There's always a drawback to the good things in life, wouldn't you say, Mrs. Roebuck?"

This struck Gladys as infinitely wise. "Oh, yes," she said.

"And how is your husband?" the woman asked. Her nostrils expanded as she spoke, a greedy hunger smoking her eyes. Gladys nearly recoiled, frightened by the shopkeeper's countenance, but the very next moment there was only kindness in the woman's face, a benign interest.

"He's better," Gladys said. "Thank you. I was a skeptic, I admit, but he seems vastly improved."

And he was vastly improved. Over the last few weeks, he had fallen in love with her again. He even stayed home from two cryptozoological conferences in the hopes of regaining her affections. He had stopped spending the night elsewhere. He even told her he was considering a full recommitment to podiatry, if it would please her. It pleased her, almost, but Gladys could not bring herself to respond to his entreaties. It was far too much fun to have him chasing after her. Bouquets of roses arrived daily, gem-studded gifts. He was wooing her again. And the more indifference she showed him, the more ardency he poured forth.

It was unintentional on her part, as Gladys felt little to nothing for him, not even when she tried. He was an odd, bespectacled little man. Fastidious and ambitious in his work, but so very tedious and silly! She was tired of him. If she never laid eyes on him again, then all the merrier.

She was relieved to no longer feel afraid of his lack of love, of his imminent failure. She no longer felt that if he flushed his career down the toilet, so she, too, would go. She and Amelia would be just fine.

Or at least she, Gladys, would be.

She lacked emotion for Amelia, too. All of her affection was given, instead, to her image in the mirror, to the image of the patchwork cap. How amazing it looked! As though it had sprouted from her skull, a thing born of her. It was a better, more loving daughter than Amelia; it was more helpful, more attentive, and more present. She loved the cap. She hardly even liked Amelia.

Amelia, for her part, didn't seem to care either way.

"And how is business?" Gladys asked the shopkeeper now.

The woman hitched up her long skirt to climb a stepladder. She was retrieving some books from an upper shelf.

"Business is booming, thank you. We made our first sale just a few weeks ago. The sale of your cap, in fact. Gramma was so pleased when we finally sold an item, she squirted ink everywhere."

"Your first sale?" Gladys asked, confused. "I'm not sure I . . ." But then she trailed off.

By drawing up her long skirt, the shopkeeper had unwittingly revealed her bare legs. She wore simple white ankle-high boots and no hose. Gladys squinted, unable at first to make sense of what she saw. The shopkeeper's legs were pocked and yellow, like rotting stalks of wheat. The knees were all askew; her legs bent backward like the legs of an ostrich. Gladys, disbelieving, rubbed at her eyes. Surely she was imagining things.

No. It was true. The shopkeeper had long, terrible bird legs. No wonder she walked so strangely, up and down, up and down, like an oil pump stabbing the earth. Gladys felt an immense pity for the woman, and then an intense fear. The shopkeeper glared down at her.

"Would you like a closer look?" the woman said angrily.

"Oh, I'm very sorry," Gladys said, flushing. Then, sympathetically, she went on: "What do they call your condition? Is it a form of rickets? My grandma had rickets. She was quite deformed."

The shopkeeper's anger receded. She finished selecting the books and then descended the ladder, allowing her skirt to fall again to her heels.

"There is no name for the condition," she told Gladys, arranging the books into an empty box. "My grandmother has a form of it. As does my mother. It affects us all differently." Seeing Gladys's withdrawn face, she added carefully, "None of us suffer. There is no pain. It is how our Maker formed us."

"You mentioned your grandmother earlier," Gladys remarked, although she could not remember what exactly had been said. "Did she pass long ago?"

"Pass?" The shopkeeper laughed, showing her sharp white teeth, small and clean like a baby's. "What a thought! No, she's alive and well. She lives here, with my mother. With me." She motioned to a door at the back of the shop.

That even this ancient woman's mother could be alive was

a shock, but to think of her grandmother thriving made Gladys grimace. *She thinks I'm a fool.* Gladys, irritated, gazed around the shop for a new topic. It looked very different today.

"So many boxes! Are you packing up?"

"Yes. There's quite a lot we have no need for."

"And where will you take them?"

"To the lake."

"We've always wanted a lake cabin, Eli and I, but there's no time for it. He's always so busy with his patients."

"We'll drown them in the lake. Each item. One by one."

Gladys, surprised, said, "Even the little yellow bird?"

The shopkeeper slowly blinked, the lids sliding like a latch over the wide circles of her eyes. Like two perfect coins in shape, and as silver as nickels. Gladys suddenly wanted nothing more than to leave the shop.

"Well," she said, turning to the door. "Thank you again for the patchwork cap. I do love it. I really need to get going. I hope you enjoy your trip to the lake."

"But don't you want to meet my mother? My grandmother?" The shopkeeper looked over her shoulder at the door to the back room. It gave a harsh shudder, as though someone had flung a heavy body against it.

Gladys, terrified, shook her head.

The door creaked open an inch. A tentacle wrapped around the door's exterior. The next moment it was gone.

"I've got to go," she said. "Amelia will be home from school at any moment. Tell your family thank you. And goodbye."

She sailed past the open boxes sitting on the shop's floor, practically falling out into the bright street, relieved to be among the traffic and the people, who cruised by and gave her an amused look, as though she had materialized from nowhere. Gladys glanced over at the shop and saw the shopkeeper standing at the window, gazing at her with a dark smile. Gladys straightened and shook herself and smoothed her jacket against her waist. She waved at the shopkeeper, embarrassed now for her rushed departure, and was glad when the shopkeeper returned her wave in a friendly manner. Gladys returned home feeling as if her outing had been, overall, a pleasant one.

Her husband waited for her in the foyer. He helped her off with her coat and peppered her with questions, which she answered politely enough. He asked if she wanted anything.

"Only to be left alone, dear," she replied. "It was a nice day but busy. Now I'd like a nap."

"Can I take your hat?" he asked, and his tone struck her as sinister.

She covered the cap protectively with her hands.

"Gladys," he continued, "you don't want to nap in your hat, do you?"

"I won't have you bossing me around, Eli. This cap will leave my head when I am good and dead."

The doctor argued that he meant no offense.

Amelia flounced in from another room, wearing a pretty dress. In another lifetime, a lifetime before the patchwork cap, Gladys would have helped make her daughter more stylish. She would have folded her arms over her chest and considered the girl with a critical eye. She would have advised Amelia on shoes and jewelry, on the correct ribbons and coiffure for her hair. She would have pinned the dress there, and here, to better flatter the girl's plump figure. She would have urged Amelia to pull back her shoulders, to look elegant, poised. And Amelia, expecting this, would have told her, half sarcastically, half gratefully, "*Thank* you, Mother dear."

But now Gladys took no notice of her, only saying in a tired tone, "Hello, Amelia."

"Hiya," Amelia said. She twirled. "For picture day on Monday. Do you like it?"

"It looks well enough, dear."

Eli overrode his wife's indifference. "How beautiful you are, Amelia!"

Amelia, unaccustomed to receiving glowing reports from her father, and even more unaccustomed to her mother's lack of criticism, silently looked from parent to parent before saying, "Well, I hate it! It makes me look fat! I won't wear anything to picture day! I won't go at all!" And she stomped off, her irritation punctuated by the rifle-shot slam of her bedroom door.

With their daughter gone, Eli said to his wife, "Have I told you, Gladys, how lovely you look today?"

Gladys yawned. "Yes, Eli," she said. "You told me this morning, at breakfast. And now, really, I'm beat. I'm going upstairs for a nap."

She moved away from him, and he said, "But, Gladys."

He did not follow her this time, and she was glad for it. She was tired of having to shut the door in his sad little face. She did, however, shut the door in Pookums's sad little face. The smallest of the dogs—the only dog she actually liked and pampered—received no attention from her now and was nonplussed by her disinterest. (He whined outside her door before giving up and taking out his wrath on a jade plant settled near the mudroom.)

It was true: Gladys was very tired. She sat before her vanity, scrubbing off her makeup and taking off her jewelry. She did not feel as lightweight and carefree as she had been of late. She thought of the surreptitious tentacle sneaking out of the darkness of the shop's back room. In her imaginings, it would continue to snake around the doorway—multiple doorways—until it finally wrapped around her ankle and dragged her away, no doubt into a drooling bloody mouth. She glanced anxiously at the closet door, afraid the tentacle sat inside, ready to split the wood in half, hell-bent on its pursuit of her.

"No matter," she said. Her hands were very busy, flying here and there as though of their own accord, wiping her face clean, applying hand cream to her dry elbows, tugging off her earrings. "I need to rest. I'm just anxious, and for good reason, because I'm so tired."

And so she stopped fussing at the mirror and rose from her vanity. She rolled onto the bed and fell asleep quickly. At the threshold of her dreams, she noted that the top of her head felt odd, as though it had blistered beneath the hot blade of an iron. It was not a painful sensation. If anything, the resplendent heat sped her into sleep more swiftly.

Then she was awake, sitting up, heart hammering. Something was wrong. It was not just the dream she was having, in which she had the short furry arms of a raccoon, but also that her confidence—the confidence that she had worn so mightily these past few weeks—had vanished. In its place was a restless, damaged version of her hatless self. She reached up to touch the patchwork cap, expecting it would restore her poise, but her hand grazed something else, something leathery and bumpy and oozing. She cried out in pain. Her fingers came away covered in pus and blood.

And then she saw it. Sitting on her vanity, curled up there like an ugly dead cat, was the patchwork cap. In her exhaustion, in her distraction, she had removed it along with her makeup and earrings, forgetting, for once, to leave it soundly in place.

Gladys did not blame herself or her pathetic human nature. She blamed the shopkeeper and her family. She ran from the house with a shawl tied over her head, waving Eli away when he tried to get in the car and accompany her. She drove downtown, parked haphazardly, and stormed down to Odds and Ends with the stinking cap clutched in her hand. The doors were locked. She pressed her face up to the glass. The entire shop was empty except for the giggling feather duster, which lay on the floor as though drained of its powers. Gladys took a step back and noticed a little handwritten sign posted above the mailbox. It read, *Closed forever due to the economy. Our sincerest apologies.* Gladys shrieked, and a few of the children walking with their parents in the street shook with terror.

Her shawl had come free, and the children stared at her oozing burnt head. *An ugly lizard witch,* these children would call her, and she would appear in their nightmares for years following.

Later, after her return from the institution, Gladys would roll down the window of her car and toss the patchwork cap into an alfalfa field. (It would be picked up by an alfalfa farmer during the next harvest. He would wash the cap twice and then give it to his awkward daughter, who formed a bizarre attachment to it that the rest of the family struggled in vain to accept.)

But this all came later.

Right now, on the street in front of Odds and Ends, Gladys removed her scarf and tried to reaffix the cap to her head. She tried and failed. It hurt to even graze her skin. Her scalp was raw and blistered. She returned to the car and opened her hand mirror. All of the prettiness she had gained, all of the color and flush to her cheeks, was gone. She was sagging and greenish and sickly. A round circle was punched into the top of her head, a hairless and fleshless red beacon. Her beautiful black tresses—her best quality—had melted away.

Gladys returned home and took to her room, bellowing in pain and wretchedness. Amelia and Eli rushed to her bedside.

She looked up into her husband's face, afraid of what she might find.

His eyes were filled with concern. But it was not the concern she wanted. He pitied her not as a woman he loved but as a sick person he had been put in charge of, simply because there was no one else in the world who would care for her now. He sat with her and took her hand into his own and made shushing noises. He told her all would be okay. Amelia stood in the corner, wild-eyed, looking from parent to parent with a panic-stricken expression that made Gladys hotly angry with the girl.

He won't leave me, she told herself, moaning on the bed. *He wouldn't dare.*

Not a moment later, Eli dropped her hand and went to the phone to call for help. Doctors arrived, colleagues of his who owed him favors, a burn specialist, a head shrinker. They whispered about the hospital on the lake, Eastern State Hospital. Their wives had come with them, and Gladys could hear them outside the door, clattering about on their heels, chattering excitedly. Eli entrusted Gladys to the doctors' care. Before he vanished, he reassured them that he'd be back to assist with her removal to ESH. Gladys begged him to stay, but he explained that he could not.

"I'm so sorry," he said. "I'll only be in the way here today. The doctors will examine you. The women will take turns sitting with you. What you need to do now is rest."

And so he left her alone with the doctors and their wives, the dogs, faithful Pookums, and their daughter, Amelia, who eventually grew bored with her mother's moans and disturbances and went to her father's den to play "secretary" with his letter knife and envelopes.

Gladys fell in and out of a wretched slumber. In the torture chamber of her dreams, her husband's monsters were more beautiful than she had ever allowed. They made better wives, better mothers.

Better women!

They were all so very grand and regal and kind.

1972

THE STUDY HABITS
OF DEDICATED CREATURES

HERE CAME THE LITTLE MAN, PICKING HIS WAY UP THE DEER trail: fussy, measured, painstaking. Waiting for him, hidden in the thicket, Mr. Krantz grunted softly to himself. This was now his favorite part of the day. He delighted in the man's arrival; he admired his bright-red spectacles and delicate skull. How funny this studious little man was! How out of place he looked here in the forest!

These were the remote north woods, the timberlands of the Inland Northwest. There were hiking trails a mile or so east, scarcely used. The forest was dense with undergrowth, shuttered with soaring ponderosas, lodgepoles, and white pines. Mr. Krantz could go months—whole seasons, even—without seeing a person here other than his own wife, but now the little man arrived almost daily. He fingered leaves, spooned up samples of dirt, examined the smallest fragments of marred bark. He came for several weeks in a row, through the wet spring and into the dry heat of summer. What was he looking for? Sleet and rain never deterred him.

Mr. Krantz scratched at a tick behind his right ear and then plucked it loose and flung it away. The man looked familiar. More so, he smelled familiar, but Mr. Krantz could not place the smell.

As much as Mr. Krantz enjoyed watching the little man, he

wasn't going to march out and start a conversation. He wasn't going to ask, *Can I help you?* He wasn't going to squat next to him and squint at leaves all day, not if the leaves weren't edible, not if they weren't covered in fat tasty bugs. Mr. Krantz was not a conversationalist. He rarely spoke, not even to his own wife. But he liked this man, whoever he was, and he continued to watch him, day by day, as the man returned again and again.

With the exception of Agnes, Mr. Krantz had no friends. He had always lived in these woods, isolated from the towns and people of the Idaho Panhandle. His father had been a simple-minded man, ugly, with black teeth that pained him until he howled. He was hit by a train and killed when Mr. Krantz was quite young. His mother—towering, rank-smelling, and hairy, with craggy shoulders and cheekbones—raised him to be wild. The only words of English she could muster were the name of his late father, *Mr. Krantz*. When old enough, Mr. Krantz accepted the name for himself. It fit him well, he thought. It was dignified.

Like his mother, and so very unlike his dad, Mr. Krantz was enormous, muscular, hirsute. He was also, like his mother, a hunter and a thief. He preferred to hunt and gather in the dense woods, away from the stink of civilization, but now and again he would descend to town to steal a chicken or a loaf of bread. In the dead of night, he lifted articles from backyards, patios, unlocked garages or shops: clothing, a crate of oranges, sometimes a larger item like a wagon or a picnic table. He moved silently, with precision, his senses battered by sights and sounds and smells of a world he did not understand: vibrating televisions; drunken conversations; unchanged diapers; spilled gasoline. What animals these people were! He liked to watch them from afar, to see how oddly they moved and behaved. He could smell their laziness like he could smell pine sap. He could smell sulfuric anxieties and honey love. He would return home to his wife and gaze on her. Was she happy here in the woods with him, living with him in their little shack? Wasn't it better than being crammed into one of those cement boxes, sur-rounded by unnatural stench and buzzing neon lights? *Yes*, she assured him.

Mr. Krantz spent most days sleeping or wandering the forest. He fished in the creek and ate thimbleberries and huckleberries and mushrooms and bugs. If he felt like it, he washed himself in Lost Creek. If not, he just lay in the sunshine next to the creek's unspooling, glimmering thread. In the winter he slept almost con-stantly, dreaming deeply, rising only to relieve himself and eat tiny servings of whatever food his wife offered to him. His dreams in the winter were of mountain lions, of hunters with loaded rifles, of predators who chased him and murdered him, much as his mother had been murdered. But then spring would come and those deep dreams would leave him, and he would sleep less soundly.

It was a mostly peaceful existence, except that Mr. Krantz suf-fered from unpredictable murderous rages. When a rage struck him, he needed to kill something. Not just kill it, but consume it. Lift it in the air and shred it limb by limb and feast on the bloody remains. Usually he found a deer or an elk, but once he had killed a person. A chubby hunter, lost in the woods, bumbling along the deer trail with bow and arrow slung on his back, squinting at an expensive compass. Mr. Krantz appeared on the trail in front of him, loping westward, and then rose to his full stature while the man shrieked and fumbled for his bow. Mr. Krantz pounced, taking hold of the man's padded shoulders and shaking him, then slam-ming the screaming jaw closed and deftly snapping his neck. The hunter dropped. He poked at the hunter's dead form with his hairy foot, turning him over before the feast began. He always looked into his victim's face before eating him; it was a proper thing to do. But when he studied the hunter's face, his appetite dulled. Despite the lack of resemblance, he was reminded of his father.

He ate him, but the taste was off, like meat beginning to turn.

After, Mr. Krantz sat on the forest floor, filled with self-loathing and regret. Blood matted his hairy chest; the raw red meat tasted like silver on his tongue. If he could, he would reach down his throat and stitch the man back together again, a patchwork nightmare of his prior self. Depressed and disappointed, he sank into the glacial creek bed and lay there until the cold made his powerful jaw ache. He moaned, and the trees above him shook. The birds went silent.

What of Agnes? Would he kill her next?

Agnes, calm and fearless, would never flinch. But he worried for her. After destroying the hunter, he could hardly imagine looking her in the eye. He reluctantly returned to the shack. Seeing him wet and shivering, Agnes ordered him into the bed and brought him warm blankets. The creek had mostly washed him clean, but she sponged off the caked blood around his mouth. She never questioned what had happened. She accepted his barbarity as part of her chosen life.

The days passed. Sooner rather than later, washed clean, purified by an all-berry diet, groomed and lean again, Mr. Krantz emerged from his depression, but with an expanded anticipation of his next murderous urge, a dense velveteen swath of worry that hung like a black curtain behind the beauty and lightness of all things. He feared when it would draw open again, but he knew better than to expect change. It was part of him, this dark nature. It was the most certain part of him, more certain than his bones.

The fussy little man did not have such a nature. Was this the difference between them, then? Intellect versus emotion? Brain versus brawn?

He studied the little man carefully.

The little man studied the forest.

Inevitably, Mr. Krantz worried that these urges would affect the one-sided relationship he shared with the little man. He wished him no harm. He even wanted to help him, if he could.

He felt genuine affection for the man. He liked how gentle he was with the leaves when he overturned them, or how motionless he became when studying a bit of trampled mud. Most persons thumped about the forest violently, talking loudly or just walking loudly, disturbing the wildlife, but this man was downright reverent. He had none of the silly paraphernalia that the other persons carried: no expensive backpack, no ornate hiking boots. Anything he brought with him had a true purpose. Sometimes he carried a small, sharp instrument or a clear glass vial, and other times he would shake open a plastic bag and, with gloved hands, drop a stick or stone or leaf into it. He wore a brightly colored bow tie and clean leather shoes. Now and then he lunched in the forest, eating from a brown paper sack that held a banana and a foul-smelling sandwich, likely assembled from a can. Agnes liked these foods, too, although Mr. Krantz could hardly stomach their processed aroma. He wondered if the man ate red meat.

Even when lunching, the man worked. He scrawled notes into a small black composition book that, when not in use, rested in his shirt's breast pocket. When he finished writing something particularly satisfying, he said, faintly, "Yes."

The man loved the forest, Mr. Krantz felt. He was at peace here.

So when the urges arose, Mr. Krantz smothered them. He took a walk, or ate berries, or dove into Lost Creek's deepest swimming hole. It calmed him. Mr. Krantz killed nothing—not even a deer or a rodent—for a long time.

His stomach, protesting, rumbled.

"You might try a good steak," Agnes suggested one evening, noting her husband's peaked color.

He made a face.

"I'll make it very rare," she told him. "I'll make it exactly how you like it."

She understood and accepted him for who he was. He was a hunter by nature. A hunter and a gatherer both, but it was difficult to do one and not the other. There was bound to be some withdrawal.

"I could throw it up in the air for you," she joked. "A moving target."

He tried to laugh. She was an easy woman to please, and that was a good thing. He admired her, appreciated how little she demanded of him. She was like him now more than ever: She wanted to be left alone. She was getting older and stringier. She winced with pain during sex. She shortened her daily walks, citing her bad knees. Mr. Krantz was older than she was, but he was "better preserved," as she said. There were other women in other places, he knew, younger women with fake fingernails and breasts like hot-air balloons. He spied on them as they teetered, drunk, outside the Rathdrum taverns, talking in shrill voices and smoking cigarettes. He enjoyed watching them from the dark trees.

One night the boldest of these women approached his hiding place and pulled her panties down and crouched to pee, cussing when the stream nudged her pink shoes. After she returned to her companions, who were now attempting to light a bonfire from a bag of garbage and a bottle of lighter fluid, Mr. Krantz put his nose to the wetness. It smelled like beer and hairspray. He felt a surge of lust.

One day soon, he knew, he'd seek out a new woman. But for now he was happy enough. A friend was probably what he ached for most in the world, and now he had perhaps found one in the little man.

The steak his wife gave him was not a perfect success, but the cooked meat did appease him. When he saw a deer or elk or moose, he managed to avoid killing it. He felt more civilized, more respectable. His urges were under control. Mr. Krantz watched his new friend in relative peace and looked forward to the day when they would formally meet. He waited for the right moment to stride up to the man and extend his huge, hairy hand.

I'll shake the man's hand carefully, he told himself. *I'll make sure not to squeeze too hard.*

(Agnes always teased him about not knowing his own strength.)

He practiced over and over again on an elegant branch of dog-

wood. He had smashed the branch on his first try, but now he could
shake one of its limbs so gently that the leaves barely shivered.

ONE BRIGHT SUMMER day, the man arrived with another person.

A woman.

She was taller than the man, and louder. She spoke constantly,
nasally, and asked the man endless questions. Her footfalls were
noisy for such a thin creature. She tottered through the forest, tripping every now and again on a root or stone, cursing as she caught
herself. The man blushed whenever she spoke, raced to her side
when her clumsiness nearly felled her, and admired her secretively
whenever she turned away to exclaim over the furtive (and apparently miraculous) appearance of a squirrel or woodpecker. It was
easy to see that the man was in love, although Mr. Krantz could
only guess as to why. To him, the woman was too clumsy for a
proper mate. How could you properly mount a woman who had no
sense of balance?

Perhaps it was her youth. She was younger than the man. Mr.
Krantz could smell the youth coming off her in big, bright waves. It
aggravated his carnivorous urges. How sweet she would taste, he
thought; how easy it would be to pluck a supple limb from a socket.
And the silence following, what a vast improvement! But the little
man would disagree with this: He swiveled his head toward her
whenever she spoke, as if she issued not words but music. He was
in love with the woman. She could do no wrong.

Out of respect for his new friend, Mr. Krantz vowed not to kill
her.

After all, she was only here for the day. He assumed that she
would not return the next day.

But she returned, clutching a large yellow notepad. She waved
the notepad around as she told the man about her writing. Poetry,
she said. Mr. Krantz did not fully understand what poetry was, but he
took from her long rambling description that it was something both

silly and self-important. The words she used to describe her work were strange and meaningless to him: *semi-autobiographical; lugubrious; tempered, but aiming for transcendence.* She was, he realized, trying in her own way to impress the man. With a sweet smile, she called him "Doctor." She fluttered her eyes and then went silent, stooping over her notebook and etching out words onto the page. She wrote like that for a good minute or so, swaying on her gangly, clumsy limbs before accepting the doctor's invitation to sit on a boulder beneath the white pines. The doctor told her to write all that she wished—he would be nearby and would check on her throughout the next hour—and then they could lunch together beside Lost Creek.

"How lovely," the woman said. "What a lovely name for a creek."

"I brought wine," the doctor said, and the woman broke into applause.

Mr. Krantz had concealed himself behind a line of jagged rock, in a thicket of bridal wreath that obstructed the view of the forest. Despite his great heft, it took very little for him to remain hidden. He, even more than the doctor, knew how to be motionless; even his chest remained still as he breathed. The woman gazed off in the opposite direction, and Mr. Krantz, watching her profile as she bent over her notebook, saw for the first time that she was pretty. Much prettier, he thought, sitting than standing. Standing, she seemed about to collapse at any moment. But now he could see why the doctor was so enamored of her. The sun sluiced through the tree limbs and dappled her legs, and she smiled up into it as though giving thanks. He tried to smile, too, but all that came out was a lopsided snarl. He touched his lips with his hands and tried to drag the mouth upward, but he could only bare his teeth in a sinister grin. The muscles just weren't there. His elbow collided with a branch from the effort, and the white blossoms trembled.

The woman turned then, startled by the movement in the brush.

He froze, looking like a wide, fuzzy tree trunk, a brown chunk of earth. The woman brought her hand up to a blossom and cupped it.

"What is this?" she asked no one. "Lilac?"

He almost sighed. She was a sweet if ignorant woman. She returned to her poetry. After several more minutes of scribbling, she gave a satisfied hoot. She leaned back and wrapped her hands around one leg, then lifted the notebook to her face. She recited what must have been her most recent creation.

It was called "My Lover Walks." It was about the doctor and his studiousness, about how he was married and how his wife was crazy and cruel. It was overwrought and florid, too emotional, Mr. Krantz felt, and too (if he could use one of the new phrases he had picked up from her) *semi-autobiographical*. It was as though she had indiscriminately vomited out her thoughts onto the page. He was embarrassed for her. At the same time, he wished the evil wife would join them in the forest, too, so that he could lift her into the air and snap off her limbs one by one. He would enjoy feeding on her wicked flesh. Because then the doctor would be happy and so would this young woman, and all would be well. And perhaps they would do something nice for him, like bring him wine and food. And he would invite his wife, and the four of them would go to Lost Creek and enjoy a nice picnic in the dirt. After all his long years in solitude, Mr. Krantz would welcome a cheerful luncheon with friends. Perhaps he could write a poem of his own, and he could share it with them while they were digesting the meal. Although it would likely contain a few shrieks and fist jabs, the poem would greatly please the young woman. She was, after all, a sensitive sort, the kind who appreciated a sincere effort. She would see his burgeoning talent and wish to cultivate it.

He crouched back on his haunches, ruminating. A millipede uncoiled itself from the dirt. He snatched it up between forefinger and thumb and tossed it into his mouth. As he chewed, he watched the small shoulders of the woman bend and unfurl. She continued to write and speak aloud the words and stare off into the trees. Writing was clearly not the wretched, arduous task that she had earlier said it was. No, she seemed to flit along in it like a butterfly, brainlessly, not taking it seriously at all. When they became great friends, Mr. Krantz decided, he would try to coax her toward a darker outlook. It would give gravity to her words.

It occurred to Mr. Krantz that he was an artistic being. *Most solitary creatures are,* he mused.

The doctor emerged from some dimmer corner of the forest. He had a mad look on his face, a look of exultation. He was not one to skip, but he practically did so, bounding up to where the woman sat on her wide, short stone.

"Vanessa," he said. "You must see this. You must come. Now."

She held up a finger to him without raising her head. Then, smiling, she tucked her pen into the notebook's spiral and shut it and set it aside, next to one of the tawny stalks of her legs, which she now crossed in a gesture of transition. It was a flirty game she was playing, a game of feigned unavailability.

"I want to share a poem with you," she said.

The doctor was turning red with impatience and ardor. He was practically stomping on the earth. "Vanessa, please," he said. "I'll show you. Come with me. Now."

The woman (*Vanessa,* Mr. Krantz noted, a name that sounded like the hiss of a snake) pouted. "We always do what you want to do. The famous doctor. The famous cryptozoologist. God forbid anyone listen to me. God forbid anyone listen to a very short poem." She rolled to her feet and stood tall and thin and awkward before the doctor. The movement jostled the silk scarf tied loosely at her throat. "I'm just asking you to listen to a few meaningful words. It's so difficult for people these days to listen. They're like zombies now, I swear, sitting there like morons in front of their televisions."

The doctor's brow furrowed. He tugged at his bow tie. For the first time, he perspired, the sweat rolling off his ears and down onto the normally perfect collar of his white dress shirt. Mr. Krantz had never seen the doctor perspire before.

"That's unfair," the doctor said. "I don't watch television. I wouldn't own one even if I had the choice."

"Ah, but your wife does own one," Vanessa said. "Your wife has two large, expensive televisions. I could live inside one of those televisions. I could sit in it and eat crackers and just blink at all of the pretty lights."

"You'd be like my little fish," the doctor replied. "Trapped in your little box."

Mr. Krantz smelled the woman's pure anger coursing from her scalp to her shoulders. It sent out a shock wave of acrid heat. Mr. Krantz wondered if he should kill the woman now, before she killed the doctor.

But in the next second she was laughing. "*Glub glub,*" she said. "That's me." She put her palms next to her cheeks and spread them wide like gills. "*Glub glub.*"

The doctor, clearly relieved, put an arm around her waist and drew her close. He kissed her ear.

"If I could leave her today," he said, "you know I would."

The doctor breathed in the woman's artificial-strawberry scent and seemed to enjoy it. Mr. Krantz thought of the woman outside the bar, the woman whose pee smelled like beer and chemicals.

"Lead me onward," Vanessa said dramatically, tossing her hair. "Only no more mention of the wife. The vile wretched wife. And no more mention of the daughter, either, the poor thing. Only us. Only us."

"Only us," the doctor agreed joyfully, leading her up the narrow deer trail. "Only us and your poems and our Sasquatch."

She whooped in delight.

Mr. Krantz sat upright. What had he said? "Sasquatch," he'd said. Why had he said that?

"Our Sasquatch."

The term was familiar. When he'd seen the hunter, for example. "Fuck me!" the man had shouted. "A goddamn Sasquatch!"

He'd heard other names, as well. When his own mother was shot by a different hunter, the hunter had cried, "I bagged Bigfoot, man!" but had begun to shriek incoherently when she peeled herself from the earth, stomach gushing blood, and barreled toward him, fists blazing.

Mr. Krantz had listened to those exclamations and smelled the mingling fear and fascination in the words.

No, he wanted to tell them, *I'm human, like you.*

I'm the same as you, only bigger, stronger, quieter, lonelier, scarier.

I am you, intensified.

It dawned on Mr. Krantz: The doctor was looking for a monster.

He is looking for me.

So THIS WAS why the doctor scoured the forest floor. This was why he collected broken branches and torn leaves. This was why he'd been returning, again and again, to this same square room of forest, this wilderness that Mr. Krantz inhabited with his life-hardened wife. It was not a coincidence.

Beneath all of his rich brown hair, giant goose pimples rose.

I haven't been watching him, he thought.

He's been watching me.

Stunned, he crept noiselessly through the forest, occasionally swinging up into a tree to get a better view. He followed the love-struck couple to where the item of the doctor's excitement resided. For a moment, the item was hidden from view by the long bare legs of the woman, by the immaculate pressed khakis of the man. But then one of them moved aside and Mr. Krantz saw what it was that the doctor referenced.

It was shit.

It was Mr. Krantz's very own shit, lying there like a dead turtle for everyone to see.

The woman clamped a hand over her mouth, turning rather green at the sight, or maybe at the smell. For it was true that it smelled pungently. He had built a small lean-to outhouse for his wife next to their tiny cabin, but he never used it. He preferred to shit in the woods. He liked to share the smell with the forest and all of its creatures. It was a smell that said, *I am here. I am here and, yes, smell how powerful I am! Only a thing as big and powerful as me would deposit such a smelly shit here! I am amazing!*

But he saw Vanessa react, disgusted, and he saw the funny way the doctor poked and prodded at it, and Mr. Krantz blanched.

He was ashamed.

He'd felt regret before, loads of regret, great steaming heaps of regret. Especially over the rages he had succumbed to, regret for his baser animal instincts.

But never shame. Shame had been unnecessary and useless here in the guts of the boscage. But now it riddled him. It made him quake.

Vanessa shrank away and giggled nervously. Wasn't she a poet? Wasn't she supposed to take even the smallest article of nature seriously? Wasn't she supposed to be jotting this down with some reverence?

Mr. Krantz understood that everyone—every living animal—shat. That these two shat. This small fastidious man and this gawky radiant woman. Although he could not recall the doctor shitting here. He was too neat for it, not unlike Agnes. So where did he go? Did he hike all the way back to the campground, find his car, drive home, and then sit gasping with relief over his pristine toilet? And the woman, did she poop like a deer? Little pebbles, *plunk plunk plunk,* falling in fast succession like hail? He wanted to wipe their faces in it, humiliate them as he had been humiliated.

God, the shame of it. So this was what separated him now from these gorgeous, clumsy persons. He saw that they were studying him, studying even the most simple, crude details of his diurnal existence. He was a thing to be looked down on, a thing to be discussed in a vast lecture hall. A thing to revere and fear, but not a thing to befriend or love or even hate. A two-dimensional being, at best. Mr. Krantz had always been a creature of solitude, but his loneliness, his otherness, was now unbearable. His entire life had been flowing toward this moment, when two lovers pointed and laughed at his shit pile.

He could kill them. Easily. They were caught off guard, completely defenseless. Red rage billowed up before him like a storm. He smelled their sweating, ignorant stench, noted their soft, thrumming throats, their tender white wrists. What joy it would give him to bash their heads together, to watch their gray skulls collapse into each other like two old hornets' nests. He would taste the man's cleanliness and the woman's rich youth, and then he would bathe in Lost Creek and be whole again. This time, no regrets.

But when he began to move toward them, a large monarch butterfly floated across his line of vision, and the movement distracted him for a moment and made him take a step backward, and what happened to be directly behind him was an enormous, rusted metal spring trap, a trap that had been there for so long that it shared the color of the leaves and surrounding shrubs, covered as it had been with the forest's detritus. The teeth sank like a bear's fangs into the flesh of his heel and ankle. The Sasquatch bent back his head and gave an earthshaking cry. He saw nothing in the bright light of his pain, but when he surfaced from the blindness of it, he observed the tree canopy encircling a coin of sky, a sky so red that he could see the blood dripping from it, and then he fell into blackness again.

1974

LIVING LARGE IN THE
ELECTRIC CITY

YOU CAN'T CALL IT STEALING IF YOU TAKE IT FROM FAMILY.

This is what I tell Marion when we crest the hill to Grand Coulee. The air conditioner is broken and my palms sweat on the steering wheel. All four windows are down. The wind is loud and we're shouting just to talk. The earth is dry and cracked, but the lake below glows cool and blue. It's long and solid and shaped like an ear. It widens and shimmers as we plunge downhill.

We're borrowing, Marion agrees. Stealing is for assholes.

The hood of our car is sleek and shiny, the hood of a black Jaguar. I took Eli's newest, best car on purpose, but I would have changed my mind if I'd known about the air conditioner. It's hot as hell in central Washington. Marion has been moaning about the heat since Davenport. He says being hot makes him cranky.

Jesus Christ, Amelia, he shouts. It's the fucking desert here. Did we cross into northern Chile? Are we in the Atacama? Where are the goddamn trees? Where are the fucking camels? Pull up to that lake, honey. Let's dunk.

Marion knows about places like Chile and the Atacama because he's been around the world with his dad, an ex–naval pilot who now flies private jets. How the two of them wound up in Lilac City is a funny story. That's what Marion says. I don't know if it's funny or not. From what I gather, it's because of a woman his dad fell in love with, the wife of an air force pilot stationed at Fairchild Air Force Base. Marion says it's a funny story because the ending is tragic. He says tragedy makes things funnier.

Another coupla miles or so, Marion says. There's a turnoff. I'll wash my armpits in the lake. I'll lick yours armpits clean.

Gross, I tell him. No way, man.

But when the turnoff comes, I take it.

Marion's been my boyfriend for five months. I met him in the smokers' section at our high school. The smokers' section isn't really a section; it's just a plot of dirt about a quarter mile from the school campus. That's where I meet my friends at lunch or when we skip class. There's a truancy officer who comes by and slits his eyes at us, but we lie to him and tell him we're seniors and that we've got an off hour like a lot of seniors do. I'll be a sophomore in the fall. I'm almost fifteen.

Marion's too old for school but too young to work, he says. He looks like he could be seventeen or thirty. His dad gives him whatever money he wants so he'll stay out of trouble. Before me, he didn't have any friends in Lilac City, so he used to go on these long drives in the crappy car his dad bought for him, going nowhere, just driving around the South Hill, where his dad rents an apartment, bored to near insanity, bored to the point, he once told me, that he wanted to kill someone. Instead, he just drove, usually down Regal Street to the Palouse Highway, cruising a bit in the rolling green farmlands before turning around and driving back. Once he made it all the way to Pullman. He said those drives were cleansing, but they didn't stop the killing feeling. Then on a whim one day he turned down 37th Avenue and looked to the right and saw me standing there, smoking with my friends, and he stopped the car. He bummed a cigarette and we talked. He told me he planned to shoot Nixon in his fat guts when he came to speak in Lilac City in June.

All presidents are liars, he said. All presidents are dicks. They all need to be shot in the leg, at the very least, but Nixon needs to be shot in the balls.

I laughed. My girlfriends stamped their feet, nervous like big-faced horses, but I wasn't nervous at all. He wasn't like the ugly goons we hung around.

Marion knows stuff. He's interesting, has opinions. He's good-looking, too, skinny but tough, with searing black eyes and plush, girlish lips. His mother is South American, he says, or maybe Portuguese, but he has no idea where she is now. His dad is just a gringo.

The way he approached me was half crazy, his gaze locked onto me like I was something to be conquered and vanquished. I liked that look. No one ever looked at me directly. Not Gladys. Not Eli. Definitely not Vanessa. Not my teachers or my friends. No one. After that day, he returned every afternoon to meet me on lunch break and smoke with me and eat half of my banana-and-honey sandwich and bitch about the world. It was the best part of my day.

After school we would drive to the Palouse. Once he kept me out all night and made me lie down with him in a dirt field. He kissed my bare stomach beneath the flickering starlight. I had never seen the stars so bright, like they had fallen out of a crate and spilled across the sky. I returned home in the morning expecting police cars, expecting an angry speech at the very least, but Eli hadn't even noticed I was gone. He was sitting on the couch with his new wife, Vanessa, and their baby girl, Ginger, and they were all blissed out on one another, and all he said was, Hi, there, Amelia. Not *How was your night?* Not *Where the fuck have you been?* Just, Hi there. I wanted to tell him that I'd almost lost my cherry to an older boy, but he wouldn't have cared, anyway. He'd already turned away to change Ginger's diaper.

And then I wished very seriously that I had given in and let Marion do me, and so the next night I begged him for it, even if it wasn't as magical as that starry field. We were in the back of his car, and a pop bottle was pressing against my back, and I could hear his knees crushing a bag of chips, and the car smelled like cat piss, and when it was over I just felt glad that it was over. It wasn't mystical or earth-moving. I hadn't crossed over into some glorious new womanhood. I was just me, only pawed and tired and disappointed.

Marion sat up and saw me frowning at him and said, What?

It was no good, I told him. It didn't feel good and it sucked.

I opened the car door to let in the fresh air. I breathed it in and felt better.

It's the first time, honey. It's always bad the first time.

I like it more when we kiss.

There are other places to kiss, he said.

Not right now. I pulled on my underwear and pants and lowered my shirt.

Okay. Marion sat back against the seat.

We sat there for several minutes, silently. Marion put a warm palm on my thigh. His knees began to jump. I could have just stayed there, doing nothing but watching the valley, the peaceful twinkling house lamps of Lilac City, but Marion was always restless. It was his restlessness that had found this quiet place, the top of a hill called Tower Mountain. It was called that, stupidly enough, because it was covered with electrical towers, high steel structures tipped with ugly flashing red lights. There was nothing else on the mountain but forest. The view was copacetic. It was illegal to be here but no one cared, not really. No one was there to notice.

Let's do something crazy, he said.

I shrugged. Sure.

Get out of the car, he ordered.

I got out.

Leave the doors open, he told me.

I left the doors open.

Push, he told me.

I clutched the open driver's side door and pushed. He pushed from the passenger side. His shitty little car glided easily enough over the grass, toward the boulders and the darkness below the cliff face.

The world opened up before us like a cruel black mouth.

I asked, my breath labored, Marion?

He grunted. Keep pushing. Faster.

And then the car was really moving. I started to panic.

Dive! Out of the way! Dive! He was yelling and laughing, and then I saw him fling himself away and I screamed in terror and did the same.

Some part of the car or some sharp stone slapped my ankle, but I barely felt it or cared, and I watched in absolute breathless glee as the car careened over the cliff and into the darkness, and then the forest below received it with a shuddering crash that seemed like it would never cease, but then suddenly it did, swallowed up by the trees.

You're fucking crazy, I shouted at Marion. I was happier than I had ever felt.

A sacrifice for you, he said. He ran to me and wrapped me up in his arms, and I smelled the sweating musky smoke of him. Despite his affection, he sounded furious.

Listen, he said. My car for your love. For your love always. Now you'll never leave me. You and me are always.

You're fucking crazy, I repeated, and I kissed his mouth just to shut him up, but there was some weird shift in me, a lightness blooming like wings. If I'd taken a running leap off the cliff, I'm sure I would have flown.

Instead, though, we walked. My ankle swelled. I wrapped my arm around Marion's neck, and he guided me steadily onto the forestry road and down the hill. It took us nearly three hours to walk all the way to my house.

I asked Marion what he was going to do for a car now.

He said, You'll get me one, honey.

Then we hatched the plan to borrow Eli's car and to leave Lilac City for good.

When I finally limped into the house, it was morning. Vanessa was cooking breakfast and Eli was knotting his bow tie.

Eli saw me and said angrily, What the hell is happening here? Finally he was pissed, like a normal dad.

Nothing, I said. I'm dating this guy and we're together. That's what the hell.

You're ruining your life, he said. Your life was like this—and he splayed his hands wide—but now it's turning into this—and he narrowed his hands into a little funnel. Why are you doing this?

It's just a phase, I said. My bored teenage-angst phase.

You have to find what you love and apply yourself to it, he said. That boy does not count. Are you trying to hurt me? Is that what you're trying to do? Because it's not working. You're only hurting yourself.

Vanessa stood in the corner, poking at the stove, pretending to cook an omelet. I could see the leer in her brow, even if her face was blank. She was so fucking smug. I mean, what a bitch. She didn't even leave the room.

This is a private conversation, I said to Eli. I crossed my arms and glared at Vanessa.

Goddamn it, Amelia, he said. This is her house as much as it is yours. Even more so, in fact. She's the mom here. You're going to have to get used to it. However much it bothers you.

I should shoot you both in the balls, I said. I heard Vanessa drop her spatula, but I wouldn't look at her now. I wasn't even angry, just embarrassed. I didn't want to be screaming and crying like a baby, but there I was, my hands crimped into little fists.

Both of you! I screamed. Shot to hell!

I hurtled past him for the stairs. He called after me—ever so calm, ever so repetitive, my father—that if I wanted to squander my life, so be it; it didn't hurt him any. I stayed in my room all that day, sleeping on and off and crying on and off. Sometimes while I was crying, I would hear Ginger crying, and I thought it was funny that we were just a couple of babies living under the same roof. I refused to come down for dinner, which was the worst time of day in our household, when Vanessa would drink too much wine and blab in this weird flighty way, radiating this plastic happiness that made me want to barf, and Eli would ignore her behavior and pretend everything was hunky-dory, and Ginger would watch me from her high chair and grin, and I would accidentally smile back at her and then hate myself for it.

When Ginger cries, it's not long before Vanessa is there, cooing to her, changing her diaper or readying a bottle, telling her it will all be okay.

She'll be a much better mom to Ginger than Gladys is to me, but that's not saying much, really.

Finally, the house went still. The baby was down for the night. Eli and Vanessa's bed creaked and then settled. I heard a rap on my window. I was already pulling on my jeans, planning a late-night fridge raid, having eaten nothing all day, and I went to the window and opened it and there was Marion. He'd pulled a ladder over from behind the garage and had climbed up to my window. It was cheesy, but I sort of swooned. I removed the screen so he could climb through, and we embraced and kissed and rolled around together on my bed.

We should leave tonight, he murmured into my hair. I think we should get married.

What are you talking about?

I've made sacrifices for you, he said. I destroyed my car for you, honey. What have you done for me?

I rolled my eyes. I gave you my virginity, I said sarcastically. I gave you my innocence. My wonderful squeaky-clean innocence. That's what I sacrificed.

We both knew I didn't think of it this way, that what I really thought was that the whole virgin/non-virgin thing was a bunch of ridiculous hooey. So Marion laughed.

What I want, he said, is your life.

I don't know what you mean.

We'll take your dad's car. The fancy one. We'll take it and we'll drive to Seattle. And when we get there, we'll get married.

I laughed, loudly. You've got to be fucking kidding me.

I'll buy a ring, he said, grabbing my hand and kissing it. We'll have dozens of little babies.

And what will we feed them? I asked. Dirt?

I'm serious, Amelia!

You're a serious spaz.

He threw my hand down.

Ow, I protested, even though it didn't hurt.

You're always telling me I'm crazy, insane, stupid. He rolled off the edge of the bed and sat cross-legged on the floor. I'm sick of it, Amelia. I'm the only serious person in your life. Don't you see that? Why can't you take me seriously?

I shushed him, worried he would wake Eli.

I'm sorry, I told him. You're right. I'm the stupid insane idiot. Not you.

He rolled up on one knee and wrapped his hands together. Marry me, honey, you tall goddess of a girl. Marry me. Please.

Well, I said. Are you serious?

I smiled a little, amused. Mrs. Marion Grimes. I liked the sound of it, even. It was funny. I would be the only married girl among my friends. They would think it was super weird. I would move away from Eli and Vanessa and Gladys and go somewhere with Marion. To Seattle. To the West Side.

Okay, I said, I'll do it.

Marion grinned and slapped his thighs.

But you have to get a job, I warned him. I want to be a fat rich wife who doesn't work.

You could never be fat, Marion said adoringly.

He didn't know, like all the kids at school knew, that I had been fat for years, until I sprouted suddenly and the fat stretched away into nothingness. I loved that he didn't know this about me. Although I didn't want to be tall, either. Vanessa was tall. And now people thought she was my mom, as though two tall women must be related.

You could never be fat, he repeated, not if you ate Twinkies and drank Cokes all day. You are my beautiful tall goddess. You'll always be just *her*.

Marion had traveled the world, had seen all sorts of women. He'd been on nude beaches in Spain and Italy and Thailand. And he thought I was the most beautiful girl ever in the history of everything.

There were worse husbands to have than that.

But you can't marry me to get back at your dad or anything shitty like that, he said. You have to marry me because you love me. Unconditionally.

Unconditionally? As in, you mean, shampoo only?

He punched himself in the leg and looked like he might cry. Stop fucking joking. This is not a joke. Tell me you love me. Mean it.

I felt sorry for him. I was such a mean girl, I knew. It wasn't fair that he was so nice and so stuck with me.

Fine, I told him. Okay. I love you. Happy? I fucking love you. Unconditionally. More than the stars. More than the moon. More than my beautiful sweet self. More than anything on this whole stinking planet.

The smile that broke open his face was a bright and beautiful thing, and I thought how easy it was to say something and make it true, no matter what you really thought deep down.

Come on, he said, pointing out the window to the star-swept sky. Let's do some shit. Some dynamite shit.

And we snuck downstairs to make sandwiches. We shook my dad's keys out of his wallet. We stole all the dough out of it and out of Vanessa's purse. We backed my dad's Jaguar out of the garage, out of the driveway, into the street. We put it in gear and shot out of that shitty town like it had been set on fire by a thousand atomic rockets. I was ready for us to drive all night, but Marion stopped at a motor lodge just past Airway Heights. He wanted to be naked with me, he said, one more night before our nuptials. And I was in such a glad mood I didn't fight him on it even slightly. The woman at the front desk looked at us nervously when we gave her cash for the room. She asked if we were minors. Marion showed her his ID with a proud grin.

This is my little sis, he said to the woman, shucking his thumb at me. We're going to Alaska to see our dad.

I liked this story. Alaska sounded like a great place to live. I felt a strange longing to have an older brother, a doting Alaskan father. We could go fishing, maybe. Bear hunting. What a better life that would be.

I asked Marion if I could see his ID. The woman had laughed at his picture, called it goofy. He shook his head.

No way, he said. You'll make too much fun of me.

We took our backpacks to the room, and I let Marion touch me all over and have sex on me. I didn't fake anything or moan or do any of that crap. It felt less uncomfortable than the last time but not at all amazing. Not like things I'd read or heard rumors about. I smiled and patted his head when he finished, as though to tell him good job, and he went right to sleep. He always said he was really skilled at sex, but he wasn't. Or maybe it was me. Or maybe he was lying when he said he'd done it lots.

Just like we all lie to seem better, cooler, tougher.

I like it when people lie. I like how vulnerable it makes them.

I stayed awake for a few hours. I ate a peanut-butter-and-jelly sandwich and watched TV with the sound dial turned completely off. Eventually, I slept. When we awoke, it was near ten and already hot in our room. The TV was still on. A sudden terror rose in my throat. Eli would know his car was missing. Vanessa would notice her empty purse. The police could be after us already.

We have to go, Marion. Now. Get up.

He moaned. He grabbed at me and tried to pull me down.

We're fugitives, he said. That makes me horny.

Too bad. I'm leaving. You can come with me or not.

He stumbled out of bed, grinning. He had a boner that stuck straight out. I tried not to laugh at it, but I did.

You think it's funny, huh? Funny? And he poked it into my thigh as a joke and I screamed in mock disgust, which was really real disgust. We grappled with each other, and I enjoyed being kissed. And then there was no choice but to let him fool around with me again.

Finally, we made it out to the car. We were already sweating. The heat made us groggy. And then the air conditioner spat out more hot air at us, stinking and raw like onion breath, but it was sort of funny that my dad's fancy car had this bogus side, just like everything else in life. We were laughing at it by the time we pulled into a diner for breakfast and coffees. After coffee, our grogginess receded and we felt like we could drive all the way into the guts of the sun. Not that we needed to: it straddled our car with its big hot legs, dripping onto us.

Marion drove us the first hour or so but then said he was bored. He pulled over in Davenport and told me, Your turn.

I don't have a license, I told him, and he said he didn't much care if I didn't.

So I took over. It was thrilling to feel the wheel against my palms, to press the ball of my bare foot hard on the accelerator. I turned up the radio and crooned along to a song I didn't know, making up the words. Marion complained about the heat, but when I glanced at him, still singing, I saw that he was smiling.

My silly honey, he said, putting his long skinny fingers in my hair. He leaned over and kissed my cheek before releasing me. My silly gorgeous honey girl.

This, I thought. This is what it's like to be loved.

I WANT TO park on the boat ramp, I say.

The boat ramp is a lovely gravel road sloping into the lake. It would look wonderful underneath the car.

We can't, Marion says. It's for people with boats.

I don't care. I'm parking here. What are these assholes going to do?

Arrest us, he says. Check my ID and call me a kidnapper.

But I ignore him and park on the boat ramp anyway. Not enough to block it, but just enough so that I can get out of the car and see what my first parking job looks like.

I'm pleased. The Jaguar looks important, its nose pointed downward, toward the lake. It looks beautiful in the sun, sleek and shining.

We get some of our stuff from the backseat and dump it on the sandy shore and then race into the lake. Marion follows me as I splash in the water. I'm still limping a little, but my ankle is much improved. I'm wearing a bikini top and my jean shorts, which I don't even bother to remove. One of my cheap sandals floats forlornly to the surface, and I throw it at Marion's head. Somehow I've become the reckless one. I'm shrieking and splashing and wanting all of the attention. I make more noise than the children present. They paddle away from me, wary, looking for their moms. The moms lie on their big towels on the sandy beach, gray and fat like dying porpoises. One of these women rises up on her elbows and gives me a look. I dunk under the water and swim to Marion and pull at his trunks. The white worm of his dick appears and I emerge from the water, laughing.

You're embarrassing me, Marion says. Settle down. You want us to get caught?

I scowl at him. It's no fun to laugh alone. I stomp out of the water and collapse on the beach, sulking. Marion stays in the water, swimming here and there. He is a deft swimmer. I had no idea he was an athlete, but I'm transfixed now, watching his long arms carving out smooth lines of water, propelling him forward. He reaches a raft far away from us and stands on it and waves. Despite my wanting to punish him, I sit up straight and eagerly wave back. He's a total fox, the sun glinting off his skin, his bright white teeth grinning at me over the lake, and I want to be close to him. I want to kiss him again, to be in that dirt field with all of those stars overhead. I want to do everything with him. Get married. Have babies. Always. All of it.

It's funny how the distance from him makes everything seem possible.

And then someone touches my back.

I jump, thinking it's a snake at first, so cold and slimy. It's rattlesnake country here. Things can bite you and then you die.

But when I look behind me I see it's an older man, crouching there in the sand, dressed head to toe in black. He has a derby hat on his head and looks to be some kind of minister.

Sorry to bother you, young woman, the man says. I'm wondering if you've seen my grandson?

He has a kindly face, older and wrinkled and soft to the touch, not that I would ever touch it. Despite the heat and his heavy black clothes, his skin is dry and powdery.

I don't know, I say. I haven't been looking for anyone.

He's about your friend's age, the old guy says, though not as beautiful as your friend. The man looks across the water to Marion. He's a beautiful young man, isn't he?

I feel an inflated pride at this comment. We're going to be married, I say. We're in love.

Really? You're awfully young for marriage, aren't you?

I shake my head and say, I'm a nurse. At Deaconess, in Lilac City. And he's a doctor. A famous one. That's his car.

I look back at the Jaguar. I'm sort of realizing how awful this story is, how stoned I sound, but I love telling it.

He's leaving his wife for me, I say, and I think of Vanessa, how powerful she must have felt when my dad decided to leave Gladys for her. We'll be married soon. In Seattle.

I guess I want to try this life on, twirl around in it, and see if someone approves of its fit.

The man does seem impressed.

You are both so beautiful and young, he says. He gives me a profound smile. I wish you all the very best in life.

He speaks formally, as a preacher might. I see how strange his thumbs are, locked around his knees. They bend backward and not forward. They must be double-jointed. Something about these hands makes me fidget, as if they're touching me without touching me. I look quickly over my shoulder, hoping Marion is coming, but he's talking on the raft to some older men. One of them has a cigarette that he bums. I wonder how that man swam out there with dry cigarettes.

My grandson would love to meet you, the man says. He would simply love it.

I look around the beach. I don't see anyone else our age. What does your grandson look like?

You wouldn't miss him, the minister says, his eyes all over me, like he's memorizing every inch. My grandson has a fish's face. He has the legs of a rooster.

I laugh and say, I don't think I've seen him. He sounds like a bad joke.

The minister smiles at me broadly. It's odd; he had seemed so old a moment ago, but now he looks semi-young, no older than forty. He says, He does, doesn't he? I hadn't thought of that before.

He sits down beside me, very close, so close that our legs touch. I scoot away to give him more room. His legs fold strangely at the knees, like he's made of rubber. I consider his hands again. A whole body of creepy liquid joints.

Anyway, I say, growing uncomfortable. I haven't seen him. Sorry.

Don't be. You don't mind my sitting with you, do you? I won't be a nuisance. I'd like to meet your mister.

My what?

Your mister. You said you were going to be married, right?

Suddenly I know what's happening. This man is on to us. He's a cop of some sort. He's a weird cop, but this is a weird area. He's Electric City's Finest. I look in a panic over at Marion. He's sitting there, smoking, not even glancing at me. He's telling some story and moving his hands in the air like small birds. I stand up and try to wave.

The man says, sadly, You're not leaving, are you?

No, I say. Well, I thought I might swim out there. You know. Get some exercise.

I don't know if you should, the man says. You left your car unlocked.

I look down at the man where he sits, his hideous hands wrapped tightly around his hideous knees. I ask, How do you know that?

My grandson is in your car, he replies. He shakes his head sadly. I saw him just now, crawling up from the water. He's in there, waiting for you both.

I laugh awkwardly. *Come on, Marion. Come the fuck back.*

Gosh, I say (a word I never say). I'm going to—

Oh, don't go out there, he says mildly. My son will just follow you, you see. He's a remarkably strong swimmer. We all have our strange talents, we do, all of my family: my sisters, my nieces, my son, and I. He's a world-class swimmer.

I wave my arms at Marion. He sees me now and waves back, grinning. The raft is millions of miles away. I beckon to him frantically. *Come! Come now!* He pumps his arms in the air, mimicking me, laughing. He always says that he loves to feel wanted. Maybe he senses now that I want him more than ever. Not him, but someone. Someone safe. He turns back to some of his new friends and shouts something unintelligible. I hope it's *goodbye*.

You poor children, the man says, rising to stand beside me. So eager to grow up. My son was the same way. Only he grew smaller and smaller, you see. He grew backward.

I have an image in my head from my biology book at school. The fish that crawled out of the water and became the first mammal. The fish with the flesh mustache and the muscular yellow arms.

Around us the chubby happy bodies of children float, overseen by the larger, looser bodies of their moms. They all seem headless to me now, decapitated; brainless forms strutting brainlessly from one activity to the next; unfeeling and stupid. I reach up to touch my own head, to make sure it's there. It is, but just so. A small vein throbs in my throat. Life drips away from me with each beat, every moment surging toward non-life, whatever that is. My hair is hot to the touch, soaked with sun. Marion swims toward us now, slowly and smoothly, face down one moment, lifting to the side the next, his arms rotating, stroking. The danger ahead of us has calmed him. He has, without knowing it yet, become a hero.

Here comes your young mister, the man whispers. Here he is now. So much to look forward to, isn't there? I can't wait for you to see what's in store. It's so beautiful. So crushing.

Something catches my eye. Something in our car, some dark form pressed against the windshield. I can't quite make out what it is. Part of it is suctioned to the glass.

The man is right. Something is there, waiting for us. It has been waiting for us all along. We've been hurtling straight toward it since that first day when Marion set eyes on me.

The man notices my stare. He puts his broken fingers on my forearm as if to say, *There, there*. His fingers are icy cold. He makes a sound that is guttural and comforting, a sound Eli might make to Ginger.

Marion comes out of the water, extends his hand to our stranger. For a moment there, I wanted to be with Marion forever, but what a crock of shit.

Forever. I should really know better. After Eli. After Gladys.

There is no such thing.

The man, beaming, bends in for a kiss.

ALL'S WELL

Gladys had lost her husband. Also: her hair, her self-respect, much of her already fragile sanity. But mostly she thought of her husband. Of all that she had lost in life, this loss pained her the most.

Even after he'd left her for Vanessa, she still had funny dreams of him sleeping with his monsters. In some of these dreams he came home with gruesome red claw marks on his back. In some of them he opened his mouth to speak to her and produced, instead of words, a string of knotted gray hair balls. In all of the dreams she looked away and said nothing, letting it ride. As she had tried to do in her waking life.

Once the word *divorce* came up, she fought. She fought hard. She lost. Again with the loss. Always, always with the loss.

Following the divorce, she suffered another nervous breakdown. She went to Eastern State Hospital again, convinced the staff that she was well, and returned home to her daughter after a week. She took Amelia, then sarcastic and petulant at age thirteen, to Omak for a month or so but believed her doting and rural parents were a poor influence on the girl, and so they returned to Lilac City and the big empty house that Gladys adored. She was glad she hadn't lost it along with everything else.

Gladys's father died soon after that, and then her mother died, followed by both of her sisters, all of cancer, one after the other like balls shot from a cannon. Gladys could not find a proper way to grieve. She returned alone to Omak for each and every funeral. Amelia stayed with Eli and Vanessa, which she hated. Gladys was glad she hated it there, but where else could she go? She was practically the age where she could stay by herself in a house, but she wasn't quite there yet.

At each of the funerals, Gladys wore a different pair of expensive black gloves, a new black dress, and a fresh hat with a drawn veil. She was careful not to touch anything with her bare fingers and to lean away when anyone spoke to her too directly. She stayed just long enough for a cup of strong tea. Then she would throw the used garments in the trash can and drive rapidly back to Lilac City. The ghosts of her sisters and her mother crowded into the car, too; they chattered away at her about nothing. Simpletons, all of them, even after crossing over to the afterlife.

She picked Amelia up, unable to keep her hands off the girl, fussing over her hair and clothes and figure. She noted how much Amelia hated her stepmother, and she encouraged the hate. Every Wednesday and every other weekend—the days when Amelia was supposed to stay with Eli—Amelia complained of stomach pains.

"Let me call them," Gladys would say. "I'll say you're not well."

Eli's anger was palpable on the phone, but he was too indifferent, really, to fight it. He threatened going to court but never would. Amelia went to their house less and less. Soon she would see nothing of her father at all, Gladys hoped, and she almost felt triumphant.

"Did he say anything?" Amelia would sometimes ask after Gladys hung up.

"No, dear," Gladys would reply. "Only to get well soon."

Amelia would stare into the floor, gnawing at her lip. "I feel better already."

So she and Amelia were a team, Gladys saw. When Amelia returned from her rare nights with her father, she reported on their disgusting habits.

"Vanessa licks her fingers when she serves us dinner. She'll lick the butter from her fingers and then pass me a knife! It makes me want to barf."

"She's an uneducated harlot," Gladys would say, pleased. "She's a menace."

"You should hear her talk to the baby. The way she carries on, the baby will never learn to wipe its own ass or feed itself. It's really bogue."

"Language, dear," Gladys would say, but then she would hug Amelia and promise her a new dress, something pretty for a date with her fine young gentleman, whose name, Gladys had recently learned, was Marion.

OF COURSE, THEIR relationship wasn't perfect. Amelia sassed her and rolled her eyes, went to bed pouting, struggled to communicate and then stopped as though disappointed. At times she went so still that Gladys wondered if she was having a stroke. But she was a good girl and a good daughter, and Gladys was grateful for her loyalty.

Then Amelia disappeared.

Gladys braced herself for the inevitable. She was likely gone, like everyone else Gladys loved.

Amelia was missing for three days, and the news was grim. They found her boyfriend's car at the bottom of a ravine near Tower Mountain, but no bodies. Eli's car was also missing, stolen, apparently, along with some money.

All of this had happened under Eli's and Vanessa's watch. They cared nothing for Amelia, just as Gladys had always suspected. Gladys wondered if she should sue.

She told this to the police.

"They seem pretty bent out of shape," an officer said. "Do you know why she would have stolen her father's car?"

"My daughter is not a thief," Gladys said. "She would not take a car without asking. Not without good reason. I'm sure he's a bit confused."

The police asked if Amelia was a bit of a troublemaker.

"Not at all!"

They mentioned her grades.

"She does her best."

They mentioned her truancies.

"She's a beautiful girl. And curious."

They mentioned her older boyfriend. Last year he had been arrested for destruction of property, for crashing one of his young girlfriends' cars. And did she know that he was too old to be dating a teenage girl?

Illegal, they said.

Kidnapping, they said.

They said, *Rape.*

"I've met him," Gladys said. "He's an upstanding young man. His father, you know, is a decorated war pilot."

A pilot, they confirmed. Not decorated. Navy-trained, yes, but not a veteran of any war. Gladys tried to think if she'd been told that detail or if she'd made it up.

"The boyfriend's a shit," one of the larger cops said. "High school dropout with a slew of young girlfriends. Been arrested for petty crime but his dad always bails him out. Probably wrecked that car of his for fun. He could've really hurt somebody. Could've hurt your daughter."

Gladys tensed. "I don't appreciate that sort of unruly language in my home."

"Huh?" The cop's big dumb mouth hung open.

"Your diction, Officer. The word you chose to describe my

daughter's young man. Is this something your supervisor would appreciate, befouling a citizen's home with such rude language? Is this how you comfort a worried mother?"

The officer looked over at his colleagues in confusion.

One of them laughed. "You said the word *shit*, man. She's calling you out."

All of them laughed now.

"Apparently I'm a source of amusement to you gentlemen," Gladys said. "I think it would be best if you got back to work and found my daughter." She went to the door, opened it primly, and stood to the side to usher them out. "Please. She's all I have left in the world."

They shuffled toward the door, feigning humility, but once they were outside she heard them laughing again and cussing. One of them even spat on her rose bed.

"Monsters," she cried into the thick panes of glass, watching them fold themselves back into their vehicles. "Monsters, all of you!"

Her husband studied monsters, she thought, and grimaced. He had left her not for a Sasquatch, after all, although his new wife was nearly as tall, nearly as awkward and uneducated as one. He had left her for a poetess. Imagine! A poetess! Gladys had known many true artists in her time, and it amused her to think of how poorly Vanessa spoke—like an uneducated woman, a woman who had never been to college, which, obviously, she had not.

No, Eli had fallen in love with Vanessa because of her verruca plantaris. Gladys had scraped the lurid details from him the night he finally admitted to the affair. A longtime patient of Eli's—one of the few he continued to see after selling his podiatry practice to his partner—brought Vanessa to the house during one of his own appointments (the two had been dating casually but not seriously, which only strengthened Gladys's notions of Vanessa's general whoredom), and Vanessa had mentioned, as an aside, that she had barnacles on her feet.

"Barnacles?" Eli had asked her, amused.

"Yes. I've had them for years. They ache."

He instructed her to remove her stinking yellow socks, and Vanessa shyly complied, revealing what Eli described as the worst case of plantar warts that he had ever seen.

Only he, Gladys raged, would love the truly disgusting.

Eli had ordered Vanessa to return for a private consultation. Their tryst began, certainly, at that next appointment, in Gladys's own home. While she was there! Walking overhead! Cleaning or cooking for her husband! Having recently returned from a nightmarish "respite" in a filthy hospital!

There was no fairness in the world.

And the worst part of it: She had enjoyed Vanessa initially. She had approved of Vanessa being chummy with Amelia. She had even encouraged it. Here was a beautiful young woman, she had assumed, who was desperate for a family of her own. She had found Vanessa's attentions touching. She had even invited the younger woman to dinner.

If only she had known!

Maybe, Gladys thought, Amelia's disappearance would return Eli to her. That would be something, wouldn't it? They would be at the funeral together, holding hands, consoling each other, and Vanessa would be dry-eyed and ignored on the other side of the casket. It could happen. Not that she wanted Amelia dead. She would die if the girl were dead! But she wasn't dead. A mother knows. She knows in her bones.

Frequently after these vivid mental outbursts, Gladys would feel sick and need to lie down.

Three days passed in this electrified manner. The police phoned almost hourly with updates. *No word on your daughter,* they would say, until suddenly they had news: *Someone spotted the car up by Coulee Dam. We're combing the area. We'll be in touch. Stay strong.*

"I'm as strong as an ox," Gladys said. "Just as strong. Don't worry about me."

The officer on the other end of the line promised he wouldn't.

Finally they found the car. It was submerged in Lake Roosevelt. Again, no bodies.

Things didn't look good. Gladys worried: Should she call Eli now? Should she seek his support? Her daughter! Amelia! Likely dead. Drowned! Possibly dismembered!

As Gladys sat by the phone, brooding, her hope for Eli turned to rage. Why hadn't he phoned her? His daughter's mother. His wife of nearly twenty years. She imagined the funeral, the scene she would make. *We did nothing but love you,* she would tell him. She would beat on his chest elegantly. *And now she's gone! My baby! My one and only lost little girl!*

Gladys put a pillow over her face and screamed into it. This final loss, she knew, would wreck her forever.

The skin on her scalp burned. She stood under the rays of a cold shower and wept from the heat. Then she went to stand in the living room and stare out over the immaculate lawn.

It was twilight. (The raspberry bushes had bloomed, and their asymmetrical fuzzy heads were haloed with empurpling sky.) A shadowy figure moved quickly across the lawn, and Gladys felt less afraid than curious. The chicken-legged woman from the old shop, she remembered. The woman who had sold her the devil's cap. Here she was, tall and lean and menacing, returning to finish her off. She was the one of the three Fates who would bring her to the cutter, and then her life would be shorn.

When the doorbell rang, Gladys bravely went to it. She was ready. She threw open the door, her heart thudding in her chest.

It was not the chicken-legged woman.

It was Amelia.

Amelia!

Her baby!

Gladys was frozen with joy, holding the door open, gaping.

Amelia was thinner, tall as ever but smaller somehow, and she was shaking and weeping and saying wonderful things like, *Mommy, I'm home. Mommy, Mommy, I'm home.*

She collapsed into Gladys's arms, and Gladys stroked her back and head. She breathed through her mouth to avoid smelling the child's putrid filth. She triumphed, thinking over and over, *She chose me. She came back to me. Not him. Not her. Me.*

She had won. Here was proof: Amelia loved her more than the others. And, Gladys knew, she must never lose that love. She wanted to take up her daughter's arms and dance with her around the living room, rejoicing, but Amelia was a poor limp creature, barely able to stand erect, and so Gladys brought her over to one of the leather couches and sat her there before the fireplace, stroking the girl's wan cheek.

"You'll have some dinner," Gladys said. "No. First, you'll have a shower. Then some dinner. Then we'll tuck you into bed for some rest. How does that sound?"

The girl was a mess. She clawed at Gladys and glanced nervously around the room with wild, wet eyes. She babbled incoherently about a horrible old man she'd met, about her trip to be married ("Married?" Gladys murmured, but then she told herself, "No matter"), about a lake monster ("You sound like your father," Gladys scolded), about how she was sure Marion was dead.

Gladys shushed the girl, retrieved for her a glass of ice water. "Calm down, sweetheart. I'm sure it's been a terrible adventure, but you need to get cleaned up, and you need food and rest."

Amelia upended the glass of water on the floor.

"Don't worry about any of that," Gladys said. "I'll take care of it."

"I was upset," Amelia said. "Loopy! I walked back to the beach for the backpack. It took me hours. I was exhausted and slept there."

How had the police not found her? *Those idiots,* Gladys fumed.

"The backpack was there! A miracle! I had enough money for a bus ticket."

Gladys, incredulous, said, "Why didn't you phone? Why didn't you go to the police?"

Amelia gnawed on her lip, a habit Gladys hated. "I don't know," she said. "I tried you both, but the phones were busy. Then I thought . . . I guess I thought maybe no one cared. Or that's not it. I didn't want to get in trouble until I was back here. You know, like I could walk back in and start all over? Sort of like none of this had ever happened? Like in *Where the Wild Things Are.*"

It was so ignorant and sweet that Gladys laughed.

Amelia picked at a cuticle. It bled.

"You've had us in knots, Amelia," Gladys chuckled, handing the girl a Kleenex for her finger. "Absolute knots. But"—and she sang this last part—"all's well that ends well."

Amelia did not laugh. She regarded Gladys for one serious moment and then rose unsteadily to her feet. Gladys followed closely on her heels, humming.

Gladys helped her daughter undress and shooed her into the bathroom.

"I'll call your father. Just get clean now, dear. Everything feels better after a shower." And Gladys smiled to herself and traipsed to the den to make her phone calls.

She called the police department first. None of the detectives working the case were available, so she left a happy message with the receptionist. "My daughter's come home! All's well that ends well! Case closed, I suppose."

The receptionist asked her, please, to hold for the detective.

"No, thank you, it's all over now."

The woman replied with some incredulity that the detective would likely wish to speak with her.

"It's just fine. Don't you worry. She's right as rain. A silly teenager, you know? Rebelling! These things happen."

Then, hanging up before the woman could respond, Gladys dialed Eli's house. Vanessa answered. Vanessa always answered. Gladys could never bring herself to speak to Vanessa, so thick was her hatred.

"Roebuck residence," Vanessa said again. "Hello? Hello? Anyone there?" Vanessa's tone changed, lowering just enough to indicate her discomfort. "Gladys. Hello, Gladys. Hold on a moment. Eli's right here."

She passed the phone along.

"Hello?" he said.

"Hello, dear," Gladys said.

"Gladys."

"I've been meaning to call you, what with all of the week's excitement."

"Well, yes," Eli said. "Thank you. How are you holding up? I meant to call you this evening myself. I'm thinking of hiring my own private eye to do some real investigating."

"It's so kind of you to suggest, dear," Gladys said. "I'm doing very well. It's been emotionally exhausting, but I've chosen to look on the bright side of things."

"I'm sorry," he said. "I know how hard this must be for you. I just—we just, Vanessa and I, that is—I'm not sure what to make of it. All I can do is hope for her safe return, but now I'm worried—"

"But, oh!" Gladys interrupted. Bathing in the warmth of his kindness, Gladys had forgotten the reason for her call. It came rushing back to her, and she wanted to share the good news with him, to rejoice with him, together, as a mother and a father should. "But she's here, my darling! Things are splendid. She's here! A little rattled, I'd say, and stinking to high heaven, but right as rain. All's well, as they say!"

There was a sharp intake of breath and a shuffling sound. No doubt Eli had leapt to his feet, beginning to pace back and forth as widely as the phone cord would allow.

"Amelia's there? She's safe? Thank God! Thank God! She's all right? What happened? Have you phoned the doctor?"

Gladys heard Eli shushing Vanessa, who had begun to ask excited questions herself.

"Yes, Nessa," he was saying. "Yes, she's all right. She's with Gladys." He returned the phone more squarely to his mouth and repeated, "Has she seen a doctor?"

Gladys had not done such a disgusting thing as wheel her to a doctor, but she did not deny it, either.

"She's in the shower now. As I said, she's right as rain." Then, waiting a moment, "She'd like it if you came and saw her."

"She should see a doctor if she hasn't already," Eli pressed. "The police mentioned rape. That boy is no boy, Gladys. He's a man. Nearly thirty. He preys on kids. I know they told you all of this. There may have been abuse."

Had they told her about this? Gladys didn't think so, not exactly. She thought of the submerged car. Had Amelia been in it when it sank? She could hardly remember what her daughter had narrated to her. And the cops had not liked Amelia's young man. No, they'd called him a bad word. She remembered that horrible fat cop with the disgusting mouth. But they hadn't told her his age. They'd said *older,* yes. They'd said—

"I'll meet you at the hospital," Eli finished.

"What she needs," Gladys argued, "is a good, hearty meal. A good home-cooked soup. And rest, Eli. She needs a long nap and a—"

"Can you please stop, Gladys?" Eli fumed. "Can you please live in the real world for just this once? She's been missing, for cris-sakes. That criminal stole my car. He kidnapped her. God knows what they've been doing!"

"The *real world,* Eli?" The scars on her head burned. She felt she wore a wig of fire, and she spat the fire through the phone at Eli. "Is this the world with your monsters—ha, your *hominids* or *human-oids* or whatever you call them—is this the *real* world you mean? Isn't the real world the one you abandoned when you abandoned me, when you abandoned Amelia? Clearly this is your doing, your—"

"Don't make this about me, Gladys. This is about Amelia's health and well-being. She needs to see a doctor. Immediately and no later."

"I agree. She needs to see a doctor. Dr. Roebuck, her father. If only he would be so kind as to leave his harlot wife and illegitimate baby for a few hours. We understand, however, if you are not so disposed, being as we are older and more tiresome than the false family you now choose to love."

He slammed the phone down with such force that Gladys winced from the pain in her ear.

Oh, she thought. *Oh, oh. That isn't how I wanted that to go. It isn't. I wanted him to come over and be with us. I wanted us to be a family again, if only for a few hours.*

But he had been so very cruel, so very accusatory, as if to say that she didn't know Amelia well, that she didn't much care about her daughter's—how did he put it—*health and well-being.* Well, of course she cared! What sort of cruel father would accuse her of such a thing? Why did he think she had fought so hard against the divorce? She had known his leaving would damage Amelia permanently. He had argued the opposite: Their marriage was setting a bad example for her. But Amelia had been a happy, wholesome child before the divorce (hadn't she?). Now she was changed.

And now here came Amelia, clean if still haggard, her auburn hair darkly wet, wearing a torn black T-shirt and shorts that were quite a bit too short on her long legs—more like underwear than shorts, in fact—and her eyes were tearstained and her voice scratchy when she muttered hello, but she looked more like herself, calmer and even pretty now. She perched right beside her mother on the couch, as though afraid to be alone. Gladys wrapped an arm around her.

"I made fried chicken last night," she said. "Do you want it warm or cold?" She knew her daughter would want it cold, but she asked just to confirm that Amelia was, after all, quite right in the head.

"Cold," Amelia confirmed, and Gladys, satisfied, patted her daughter's knee and went to prepare the food.

Amelia followed. She hung against the doorframe like a long, crooked crack. Gladys was a bit shocked at how tired the girl looked. So wrung out. A little food, she knew, would do wonders.

"You called Dad?"

"What?" Gladys sang back innocently, rattling things around in the refrigerator.

"Dad. I thought I heard you talking when I was in the shower."

"Oh, yes, dear. He was beside himself. We had a wonderful conversation. He's filled with excitement."

"Excitement," Amelia said. "Yes, how very exciting."

Well, Gladys thought. *She must be feeling well enough if she's speaking to me in* that *tone.*

"I thought he might be freaked out," Amelia added, more hesitantly.

"Your father? Oh, he's the picture of calm, always. You know that."

Gladys set a plate down on the kitchen table and patted a chair.

"Here, dearest. Put some yum yums in your tum tums." She had said that when Amelia was a young girl. It always made her smile. Even now Amelia curled her lip.

The teenager came to the table and plucked the chicken off the plate, chewing it indelicately. She started for the living room without even a napkin.

"I'd rather you eat here, dearest," Gladys told her. "I'd rather you not get grease on the nice couches."

Amelia gave her mother an annoyed look but turned obediently and collapsed into a kitchen chair. The whole table shook from the impact. Gladys feared the plates would break. She was not worried about the plates, per se, but certainly about the mess it would make, the danger it would wreak on her nerves.

"Gently, dear! My goodness, it constantly amazes me how such a scarecrow of a girl can pound around the house like a rampaging elephant. There's no excuse for it anymore."

Amelia ignored her. She chugged her milk and set it down and wiped her mouth with the back of her hand. She sucked the meat off the chicken so that there was nothing left but slender gray bones. After she had belched and asked for more, which normally Gladys would not have allowed, Gladys willingly served her again. No doubt the girl had been starved enough. If anything, she needed more fat on her. She was as slender and gray as those chicken bones, Gladys saw. *Yes,* she resolved, *for a while—a short while only—we'll work to fatten her up.*

When Amelia's feasting slowed, Gladys sank into a chair and patted Amelia's wrist.

"So tell me, dearest," she said gamely, as though she were not the girl's mother but a close friend. "What happened, exactly?"

Amelia slumped back in her chair. "Like I said. I was with my boyfriend. We drove around. It was pretty cool for a bit. But then it got"—her eyes flitted around the room for a moment, searching for a word—"weird."

Gladys made a pitying sound in her throat. Weird was not good. Weird was . . . bad? Uncomfortable? No, it was simply what it was: weird.

"I have to ask you something," Gladys said, so softly that Amelia leaned forward, hugging her sharp elbows to her body. "I have to ask you something about the word *rape.*"

"What?" Amelia said.

Gladys felt a surge of anger that she had to repeat such a terrible thing.

"*Rape,*" she said, louder this time. "Has there been any raping? The police mentioned—"

"God!" Amelia said, equally horrified. "Stop!"

Gladys sat back in relief, ready to let the whole thing go, but the girl buckled forward in her chair and gagged violently. Gladys rose in alarm, believing Amelia was about to vomit.

"Oh, my dear, oh," she said. "Oh, oh. Mommy didn't mean to upset you. I'm sorry, dearest. They told me to ask, they made me—"

But when Amelia managed to work herself upright again, Gladys saw that the girl was heaving not from nausea but rather from a crippling bout of laughter, a laughter so encompassing that Amelia could hardly catch a breath. Tears rolled down her cheeks, and her mouth worked silently, filled with spit and teeth. She tried to speak but kept falling apart into fresh bursts of hilarity.

"I don't see what's so funny, Amelia," Gladys said crossly, but now she, too, felt like laughing. It occurred to her that she had not seen Amelia laugh for several months. Or was it years? She laughed when she was with friends sometimes, but even then it sounded forced, like the short honking retort of a goose. It was not pure like this, overwhelming and cleansing.

Amelia wiped at her eyes. She hooted one last time and let out a deep, almost happy sigh. "Oh, Mom, it's not funny at all. That's what's so funny about it."

"But—" Gladys began to press awkwardly.

"No. No rape. No raping. I promise."

Gladys brought a heavily jeweled hand to her heart. "What a relief. You should have told me how old your young gentleman was. Thirty, they said! I thought he was young, no more than eighteen. Now, I don't mind your lying to me about it, dearest. Girls will lie. I did things like that, too, when I was your age. I dated older men. It was normal when I was a girl. Intelligent girls crave maturity. I understand completely. What amazes me is how nobly he comported himself. A fine young gentleman, like I told the police, his dad a pilot and all. The sort of young man who impresses one the instant—"

"Thirty," Amelia said.

It was a repetition, a statement, but Gladys answered it as a question. "Well, yes, dearest. Isn't that right? Your young gentleman?"

"Please don't call him that."

"Oh!"

Gladys leapt to her feet. Through the deep bay window, she watched a car pull into their driveway. A familiar car. Not the fancy Jaguar that had been dumped into Lake Roosevelt, but Vanessa's car, which was an old sedan, an eyesore. *The car of a poetess*, Gladys thought with disdain, *the car of a low-class woman*. Happily, she saw only one head floating in the car's interior: Eli's head. Vanessa, Gladys rejoiced, had stayed home.

What bliss Gladys felt then! What hope! He had come home to them, after all. What a wonderful evening this was turning out to be. The return of her daughter. The return of her husband.

"Your father's here, dearest. Straighten up. Straighten up your shoulders. And here . . ." She leaned forward and pinched the flesh over the girl's cheekbones. Amelia winced and pulled away roughly. "That looks better. Adds a little color to your face."

She couldn't have Amelia looking like a victim. Not now.

Eli had never believed she was a good mother. He had told her, not infrequently, that she was selfish and material and cloying and demanding. But once, when Amelia was younger, after she'd had a bad fall and had come reeling from the carport to present her mother with the vicious wound on her elbow, which Gladys had quickly washed in the kitchen sink and bandaged and cooed over soothingly, Eli had commented that she was excellent in a crisis. Years and years had gone by since then, but Gladys believed that once something was said it could not be unsaid and that somewhere in Eli's heart he felt that way for her still. That she was excellent in a crisis. That she, above all, could weather the bad times.

It was not as though she expected him to love her again. In truth, she doubted they'd ever really loved each other in the ridiculous, knock-kneed manner you read about in books. But if he could just *admire* her once more . . . why, that could change everything. Love was a paltry, insignificant thing: There one day, gone another. But admiration, respect: From those could sprout great trees, towering redwoods, that could reach and reach and almost touch—

And then he was at the door, knocking violently, and the trees in her reverie shook and tottered. Amelia sat before her, withdrawn, hugging herself again. Gladys touched the girl's shoulder and then rushed to the door in her expensive pumps, smoothing her skirt, telling herself to *calm down, would you, calm down!* He was here. She opened the door.

Here he was.

"Please," she said grandly. "Please. Come in." She beamed. She didn't mean to look so happy, so psychotically happy. But she was! "She's here, darling, and she's doing *wonderfully.*"

She stepped back and spread one arm open like a wing, directing him into the house. Eli was not smiling. He was frowning the way he did when concentrating, the way he did when he looked over bills or read one of his dense scientific journals. Oh, but she admired that face, even that smart, unhappy expression. It pleased her to no end the way that he strode into the house as though he still lived there, as though it were still in his name. *Some part of him believes it's still his,* Gladys knew. *Some part of him understands this is home.*

Amelia tiptoed into the foyer behind them and stood off to one side, biting her lip. Her father came toward her and embraced her. The girl smiled—pleased or amused, Gladys was unsure. Eli snapped away from her then and held her at arm's length, looking her over.

"You've lost weight. You're pale. Are your hands shaking?"

The girl opened her mouth but said nothing.

He plucked up one of her hands. "Yes," he confirmed. "Shaking."

"Low blood sugar," Gladys said cheerfully. "She was ravenous.

Just sucked down some of my chicken. The shaking will stop any moment, I think. Would you like some chicken, darling? A little bite of cold chicken while we sit and chat?"

"I hate cold chicken," he said.

Horrified, Gladys brought a hand to her throat. How had she forgotten? He'd always hated cold chicken. He liked it straight from the oven, so hot that it would blister the roof of his mouth. Gladys couldn't believe her lapse of memory. Surely he could forgive her something like this, considering what they'd all been through in the last week? Surely he wouldn't hold this against her, too? After all, had she ever forgotten anything before, ever? No, she had not.

But when she started to speak, he hushed her. "Gladys, not now. I'm taking Amelia to the hospital."

Amelia shook free of him. "Like hell you are," she said.

"Amelia," Gladys protested. "Language!"

Amelia rushed from the foyer and pitched herself onto a couch in the living room. Eli went after her, tried to sit with her and hold her, but she sprang upright and wriggled free of his grasp. She moved to the recliner instead, which had room for only one person, and then she drew her knees up to her chest and buried her head in her thighs.

Eli angrily turned on Gladys. "Is this what you call healthy behavior?"

"Let me heat up the chicken. The oven heats up in a jiffy. I'll give you the thighs and we'll sit in the kitchen and have a chat while she relaxes. She just needs to unwind, Eli."

Eli's jaw worked. His eyes glared out at her from behind those large red frames, two blue raging stars. "I will not tolerate this, Gladys. She needs to see a doctor. We have no idea what that man has done to her. Or whatever other creep she ran into out there."

"That young man—"

"Gladys, do not fight me on this. I'm a doctor, I—"

"Does anybody care what I think?" Amelia wailed from the

recliner, lifting her head from her knees. " 'Cause I don't wanna go. I'm not gonna go. If you take me, I'll leap from the car. I'll scream. You know what I'll do? I'll run away again. 'Cause that's what I did. I stole your car and I ran away. To get married, if you wanna know."

And then she returned her head to her knees and sobbed. Eli stood there for a moment, caught in the headlights of his daughter's sorrow, unable to move. Gladys could feel his anger evaporating. He went to console his daughter. By the slant of Eli's shoulders, Gladys saw that she—the mother, the ex-wife—was uninvited. She left the room and went into the kitchen and stood next to the softly thrumming refrigerator. She bit down on her hand, into the soft flesh between thumb and forefinger, and tasted her own blood.

She was not upset. She was joyous. The three of them, however estranged, still formed a little Bermuda Triangle of familial love. Events had, in fact, transpired tonight exactly as they did during the marriage—their miscommunication, their useless arguments, their daughter's bleating solidarity with her mother, Eli's shift from anger to compassion, her own quiet retreat. It was all so familiar, so wonderful. She bit herself to keep from screaming with joy, from laughing out loud and ruining the moment. Too soon, Eli would remember his new wife and his new daughter and he would leave them again. *The eternal return,* Gladys thought. *Isn't that right? The eternal return?* Gladys had not paid much attention in college to her professor's ramblings, but she had remembered that phrase. The eternal return. The happiness and the sadness of it.

Gladys did not want the moment to end. Not yet. She understood that it would end, but if she could manage to make it linger . . .

Through the window she saw Vanessa's ugly sedan. She had heard from Amelia that Eli had wanted a new sports car, but Vanessa had called it an inappropriate purchase for a man with an infant. Gladys thought with some pleasure about Vanessa's disapproval, of how it must have irritated Eli. Vanessa was not the sort of woman who could appreciate the finer things. Not the way Gladys appreciated them.

Next to the butcher block rested the dirty cleaver she had used to cut apart the raw chicken. Gladys took it up and washed it carefully in the sink. She was used to being her own cook and housekeeper now, and it suited her fine. She had thought she would miss the help, given how she could no longer afford it, but it turned out to be comforting to clean again, to cook with her own hands.

Clean and bright, the blade shone. It was like a magical thing, a thing that could change a mere moment into an hour, a night, even an eternity.

She heard her daughter speaking in the other room. Eli was slowly bringing her around again.

Still clutching the cleaver, Gladys slipped out of the kitchen and into the garage, walking trancelike out the side door and into the driveway. She stood there before Vanessa's car as the stars twitched around her, the frames of her neighbors' homes snapping in the ebbing light. The crickets started up in the grass, rustling it with their impatient wings. The trees winced. Then the cool air kissed her bare scalp and caressed the raw red line of her burn, and Gladys felt a great calm.

It was hard to remember when the good life ended and the worst life began.

But she could change it back. The cleaver gleamed and winked beneath the flickering streetlamp.

Hacking at the tires didn't work. She had to poke into them instead with the sharp edge of the blade, little tiny holes, dozens of them in each tire, and at first she worried that they wouldn't make much of an impact. But then came the whistling sound and the car drooped to one side. She couldn't stop with one tire (no doubt he carried a spare) and she couldn't stop with two (for fear he would borrow her spare) and by the third tire she knew she would do the fourth, just to complete the work. Oh, it felt good. Marriage work.

The sort of daily, repetitive work a wife did to make sure that her husband and children were safe and sound and content.

He would not be able to leave now, not exactly when he wished. Her own car was trapped in the garage behind the sedan, so there was no giving him a ride herself. Phone calls would be made. He would have to return to retrieve the car, most likely, or maybe he would send a mechanic. Either way, she had bought herself—and she had bought Amelia—more time alone with him.

She went back into the house and into the living room and found the two of them sitting there, watching Johnny Carson, kicked back and comfortable. Eli had gone to the kitchen and retrieved the rest of the cold chicken, and they sat snacking on it contentedly, as though some big conflict had been resolved.

"Where were you?" Eli asked. He had not seen her outside, shredding his tires.

"Bathroom," she said.

She stood there watching them, looming over them, drunk with pleasure.

"You two," she said affectionately.

Amelia peeled her eyes away from the television and looked at Gladys, at first lazily, and then with concern.

"Mom," she said, sitting up. "Mom?"

Gladys looked at her hands. Her fingers were bleeding. How had she not noticed? A small bloody trail followed her from the kitchen. She still held the cleaver. Why hadn't she set it in the sink, as had been her intention? Why had she not washed it and slid it back into the wooden cutlery block? Why had she brought it here, to stand before her husband and daughter, bleeding and guilty?

Both of them were holding chicken thighs, which they now returned to the plate, half-eaten. The television droned. Eli rose to his feet, approaching her warily.

"Mom," Amelia was saying. Gladys could barely hear her through the fog of her own thoughts. "Mom. Put down the knife."

"It's a cleaver," she corrected.

Eli's arms went around her then, soft as a lover's embrace, and Gladys closed her eyes and smelled his familiar musk (one of her yearly Christmas gifts to him, which, she noted tenderly, he still used). She sank to the floor beneath him, surrendering herself to the knees that pinned down her shoulders, the bony hands that held down her wrists. She moaned.

To Amelia, he cried, "Quick! The knife!"

Amelia came forward with a dead look in her eyes. Some light there had been extinguished, although Gladys wasn't sure when. The girl pried the cleaver away from her mother's bloody fingers, digging in with her stubby nails.

She'd been misunderstood.

Her luck hadn't changed at all.

Or had it?

It had changed! After all, there was this *togetherness*. Look at them, the three of them, struggling together here on the floor, embracing and shoving and crying and grunting. *Togetherness*.

Gladys allowed herself this, then, despite the biting pain in her shoulders and wrists and fingers, despite the barking demands of her husband to call an ambulance, despite her daughter's robotic senseless knuckle-cracking and stony uncertainty: *togetherness*.

And that, in the end, was all Gladys had ever really wanted.

STAY DOWN

MARION KNEW HE WAS A CREEP. HE HADN'T ALWAYS BEEN THIS way, but he certainly was one now. He was a creep, as pure as they came. He liked teenage girls. He didn't rape them (not exactly), but he did cajole them into sex. They were, all of them, good girls, if a little bored, attracted to his meanness. He loved the feel of their velvet stomachs and their knifelike hipbones. He loved it when they pouted or whined. He loved it when he dumped them and they called him on the phone and cried. *Get over it,* he'd say. *Get a life.* He loved it when they spat and clawed at him. He loved it when he saw them for the last time. He loved their messy crying eyes, their swollen protesting lips. *Those stupid girls,* he thought. He loved them all so much.

He was nearing thirty now, aimless. *Heading nowhere special,* his dad said, and then his dad would laugh and pull out a wad of cash and shove it at him and tell him to get lost, to have fun. Marion would drive around, looking for girls, and inevitably a girl would appear who was intriguing and intrigued, and he would take up with her for a while and pretend he was her age, or somewhere close to her age, to avoid any sort of nonsense with parents or authorities. Some girls snuck a peek at his wallet or just naturally caught on. They rarely gave him grief about it. They liked it. Girls wanted to grow up. He helped them figure it out. It was, he joked with himself, his charitable contribution to womankind.

Then he met Amelia and everything got fucked.

She was better than the rest of them, maybe because she was a wreck. God, how he loved her. She was already broken, already mature, hard to make laugh, hard to hurt. He'd never been with a girl so tall. Her height embarrassed him. She was unashamed of it, or maybe just unaware. He teased her about it and she rolled her eyes. He wished he could shame her like the other girls. She gave him no power. Amelia treated him with some affection and some amusement, but her heart was off-limits. The role reversal, for Marion, was painful and baffling.

I am the adult here, he wanted to tell her. *I decide who gets to be amused, who gets to be scared.* She would roll her eyes if he said that to her, or groan in deep annoyance, so he kept quiet.

She was the reason things got fucked.

They had just met the old man, the old man with the strange, familiar face that Marion could almost place. Something was off with the old cat. He kissed Marion on the cheek and Marion recoiled, blinded by sunlight, confused. Amelia gasped. In a better state of mind, Marion would have hauled off and punched the old fucker, but something about the man's face unnerved him. He wiped away the kiss with the back of his hand and then touched Amelia's arm, saying to her, "Let's go." Normally, Amelia might have laughed at him for being a sissy, but she was terrified and silent. She drew herself into his shoulder, and Marion wrapped an arm around her, charged by her need.

They walked together to the Jaguar, the old man following them, speaking to them in a low, foul voice.

Marion opened Amelia's door for her before moving to the driver's seat. Their swimsuits were wet and uncomfortable against the fine leather. Marion, for the first time in his adult life, was stupid with nerves. They had left some items scattered on the beach, but to go back for them now seemed ridiculous. The old man followed Amelia and babbled at her incoherently through the open window. Despite the intense heat, despite the broken air conditioner, Amelia rolled up the window in his face.

Marion feared the man would get into the Jaguar, maybe crawl in and drape himself across their laps. Instead, he touched Amelia's window and looked at her for a long moment. He was still leaning there, staring at the spot where her face had been, when Marion drove away.

"What the fuck was that?" Marion asked.

"Pull over," Amelia said, clawing at the door latch.

"What the fuck, Amelia? Who the fuck was that?"

"Pull the car over, Marion. I'm freaking out. Something's wrong."

"You're goddamn right something's wrong. There's a shitload of water in here. And no towel. We left our towels back there. My fucking backpack with the weed in it. Not to mention twenty bucks."

There was a loud slurping sound. Marion assumed it was Amelia's wet jeans shorts sticking against the leather seats.

"Pull over," Amelia shrieked.

Marion pulled the Jaguar tightly against the narrow shoulder of the byway. Amelia opened the door and tumbled to the ground, falling hard onto her knees. "Marion," she cried from the side of the road. "Get out. There's something in there. I saw it. A monster. A lake monster. Get out. Come with me."

She's hysterical, Marion thought uneasily. *She's totally lost it.* Cars honked and sped by them. They could die out here on this narrow road.

Marion loved Amelia, but he wasn't going to play her childish games.

Not out here, not like this.

"Get in the car, kid," Marion said smoothly. "We'll be in Leavenworth by three. We'll be in the fucking mountains."

"Marion," Amelia said desperately, her voice cracking. "Come with me. We'll take a bus. We'll go back home."

"You've had too much sun, girlie. You're talking crazy."

"Please," Amelia sobbed. "Not the car."

God, Marion thought. Was he going to have to get out and drag her back into the Jaguar? Drag her by her hair, like a caveman? Passing cars slowed, the people in them gaping. Surely a cop car would follow. Marion did not want to be picked up for statutory rape, for kidnapping.

Fucking Christ, what had he been thinking? He was such a creep. He could have punched himself in the face for his own stupidity. He deserved all of this.

"I want to go home," Amelia wept. "Please. Please. I want to go home."

She was a child now, a tall, sunlit child, screaming by the side of the road. There was nothing mature or impressive about her. She was just some spoiled kid and the fun had run out. Marion felt cheated.

"You little bitch," he said. "You little spoiled rotten bitch. Go die on the side of the road. See if I care." He leaned across the passenger seat and slammed her door shut. Then he peeled out, grimly satisfied to see her coated with the Jaguar's kicked-up dust.

He flew along the side of the lake, cursing angrily. He pressed his foot down on the pedal. He knew that in a few minutes he would give up and turn around and go back to her. This made him grind the gears more vigorously.

He was cresting a scenic road overlooking the water when the slurping sound came back.

Lake monster, he laughed.

Then it happened again and he knit his brow.

It was coming from the glove box. Without slowing down, with one hand on the wheel, he reached over and snapped the box open.

An enormous dark fish—mouth like a suction cup, opaque

eyes—flung itself from the interior of the glove box. It was mostly dead and flopping. Marion screamed and swerved from the byway.

He was still screaming when some calmer part of his brain told him, *It's not a lake monster, asshole: It's a walleye. An enormous dead walleye, crammed by that goofy old fucker into your glove box.*

He had caught walleyes with his grandfather in a similar lake, back in the days before he became a pervert, before he became a creep. His grandfather, he remembered, was a bit of a creep himself, if not a pure asshole like Marion's dad. But no one was a creep out there on the water, not when they were fishing walleyes in the early fall. In those instances, they were just an old man and a boy; they were simple fishermen. Marion was a decent kid. Not an amazing kid, but also not a creep. What would it take, he wondered, to get back to some better, simpler life? A life where he owned a small rowboat? Where he fished on the weekends? Maybe where he had a grandson all his own?

But it was too late now.

He was an adult, jobless and floundering. His grandfather was dead. His father cared little about what he did.

You're a loser, his father would say as he opened his wallet. *Always have been. It's the Latin in you. Your goddamn mother. Well, might as well have a good time.*

What if he spoke back to his dad? Called him a racist piece of shit? Called him a rich useless asshole?

But it was too late now.

Marion was a sex addict and a statutory rapist and now a kidnapper. He had stolen a car. He had stolen this teenage girl and then abandoned her on the side of a dangerous road.

Too late.

The Jaguar had already crashed through the guardrail and plunged nose-first with great velocity into the lake. Water poured in through the open windows, pushing at him with powerful hands, the palms thick and cold, the palms of his dad.

Stay down. Stay right where you are.

It would be so easy to give up, Marion thought, almost like giving in to a generous kindness.

You were heading nowhere special, anyway.

He sank.

At the bottom of the lake, the walleyes converged. They came to him with their somber faces, their opaque eyes. They regarded him balefully in the murk. Marion's own face changed, drawing in on itself, rapidly aging. Detached as he now was from his body, oxygen-deprived, near insanity, Marion saw his own face: It was not the youthful handsome face of his recent years. It was the face of the old man in Electric City, the old man who was also a creep. Marion saw all of this and was thrilled. He felt he was dancing with all of the lost possibilities. He danced and twirled.

The walleyes gathered in the water patiently, waiting with their endless dull hunger for Marion to stop thrashing.

1978

SNARE TRAP

It was September, dry and warm, when Eli returned to Lost Creek. It had been a few years since his last visit. He was returning for abandoned equipment—a sonar piece of crap that had never really worked but that he wanted back, regardless, simply because he was trying to make a fresh go of things. The sonar detector was missing, but, fumbling through the underbrush, Eli uncovered a different treasure nearby.

It was a bone. A foot bone. Long and lean. To Eli's trained eye, it was clearly a metatarsus.

It was caught in a rusted snare trap, pierced by a sharp metal tooth. It had been here for some time; the bone was ivory but filthy and almost, in the sunlight, yellow. There was no flesh and no other bone—all evidence had been stripped bare, chewed up, dispersed, or consumed by natural elements. All that remained was this long, lone bone.

Even from above, squinting down at the thing, Eli could see that it was not the metatarsus of a typical woodland mammal. It was, at first glance, human. But it was far too large, too fat, to belong to a normal man.

Eli's heart raced.

He knew exactly whose bone this was.

It belonged to Mr. Krantz.

ELI REMEMBERED KRANTZ's feet very clearly; he recalled perfectly the impressions they'd made in the dirt outside his home, when Mr. Krantz had fled with Agnes. Eli's obsession with the footprints, so monstrous beside the dainty footprints of his mother, had led him down pathways geographical, emotional, professional; they led him into the woods, into loneliness, into podiatry and beyond. In the days following Agnes's disappearance, Eli had stood in the yard, staring down into those mismatched tracks. His father had stood with him, incredulous, grief-stricken, faking cheerfulness for the sake of his young son. At first, Greg liked to insist that she'd left against her will, dragged into the woods by her tormentor or even carried, but they both saw the willing path she'd left in the dirt. Soon a rain came, bringing with it thunder and lightning and erasure. The prints were gone. Greg could pretend whatever he liked now, but Eli had memorized the feet. Their imprints would be on the backs of his eyelids forever, flashing in neon pinks and purples and reds and yellows, whenever he closed his eyes.

Eli was a cautious man. Despite his desire to bend down and touch the foot bone, even sniff it, embrace it, he held back. He'd need to suffer through long days of testing to prove that the bone was not from a deformed bear or a giant human or an escaped zoo animal. Then would come the abstract, the scientific paper, the rejections at various scientific magazines, the inevitable jeering response of the scientific community. No matter how careful he was, how thorough, he would be thwarted by nonbelievers, so it was of utmost importance not to get too ahead of himself.

But, look! The metatarsus was flat and sleek, despite its hairline fracture from the snare trap. It was clearly the bone of a flat-footed, flat-sauntering apelike creature. Humans walked more on their toes, creating a metatarsus that was more crushed, punished, by the force of gravity. Not so with this bone!

Not that he needed proof.

This was Mr. Krantz's foot bone. Of that, Eli was sure.

The problem now was to prove it to the world.

Eli fingered the foothold snare, turning it over delicately, careful not to disturb the bone. Grass and moss clung to both the metatarsus and the trap. He considered depressing the levers to release the foot bone into his hands but then decided it might be best to take the entire specimen with him.

He lingered for several minutes, wondering.

It was Sunday, he remembered, and the SNaRL office was closed for the weekend. He had founded SNaRL—the Sasquatch National Research Lab—around the time when he married Vanessa, and it was one of the best moves he'd made as a cryptozoologist. It had become a thoroughfare for news of sightings and rumors regarding not only Sasquatch but a host of other Northwest beasts: the Pend Oreille Paddler, a man-sized tick outside Cle Elum, a three-headed Chinook in the Columbia (the latter was written off as an environmental disturbance caused by the nearby Hanford Site). Its focus remained on Sasquatch, however, and Eli refused to receive any information, no matter how promising, without forcing it through his gauntlet of serious scientific process. While this limited the availability of useful data, it also bolstered Eli's reputation in the academic community. Despite his unconventional interests, he was a dedicated, respected researcher. The office was mostly peopled by interns from Lilac City's community colleges, who signed on with SNaRL for a semester or two to fulfill credit requirements. Some of them were smart, ambitious kids, but a lot of them were lazy shits. Eli enjoyed giving them a challenging workload, and a few of them whined or quit. Eli wanted these naïve students to realize that he was not performing circus acts here. He was engaged in hard science. He hoped that each of them would leave with their belief system shaken to its core. Tomorrow, for example, he would school them on the rigors of scientific analysis.

Eli touched the bone gingerly. He wondered if he should stay the night here, sleep with the bone, make sure that it didn't up and hop away.

And then, shaking his head, he decided to release it, to protect it in the lab. He depressed the levers. The trap groaned but held its grip. It was rusted shut. There was no choice but to take the entire snare trap with him, lest he disturb its precious cargo.

Cradling the large trap and its fragile contents in his hands, he hiked back through the forest to his car and then drove to the closest gas station.

He stood at a pay phone for a moment, fingering the coins in his pocket, and then phoned Vanessa.

If his wife was excited for him, it was tempered by what he assumed was her usual mother-hen concern.

"So," he said. "I'll be at the lab tonight. I want to prepare the metatarsus for testing. It's going to be a long day tomorrow."

Vanessa was silent.

"What?" Eli asked. "What is it?"

She reminded him of Ginger's piano recital. Had he forgotten?

"No," he said.

She waited.

"Okay. Yes. I forgot."

And, by the way (Vanessa reminded him), he had promised Ginger that even if bombs fell and blew up the church, even if it rained fire and brimstone, he would still be there, ON TIME, DADDY, to watch her and other tone-deaf preschoolers plunk away on the keys as the world burned around them.

Christ, he thought.

Yes.

He had promised.

Ginger was an earnest, dramatic little creature. Every emotional pinprick was like being attacked with a chain saw. After he had missed her tumbling routine the month before, she had sobbed on and off for a week, all the while saying in a sweet little voice that broke Eli's heart, "I know you didn't mean to miss it, Daddy. I know. I don't know why I'm so sad," and then she would cry afresh.

Eli's other daughter had never been so sensitive. In fact, Amelia was insensitive. Why was it children were always the exact opposite of their siblings? What sort of chaos or balance did that explain about the world?

"Shit," Eli said to Vanessa, frustrated. "Tonight of all nights."

She would be destroyed if he didn't attend. Not merely annoyed or even angry; no, it had to be total. Eli hated having that on his shoulders.

And what could possibly happen (his wife suggested now) to the bone in one night?

"I mean, you took it, right? You've got it with you? Can't you just shove it in the glove box or something?"

Eli winced. "It's quintessential evidence, Vanessa. You don't go throwing it around like a pair of old shoes."

"Well, you're the scientist. I'm just a mom looking out for our kid."

She was not trying to be a nag, he knew. She was trying to be practical. But didn't she see that this was it? Not it, but IT? His life's work, finally vindicated? All of the laughter and finger-pointing he'd had to endure would now be silenced. Short of an actual corpse, this would be the necessary evidence he'd long sought. Mr. Krantz would be disclosed to the world for what he was. Didn't she get that this was both a miracle and his destiny?

"I am really happy for you, Eli," she said now, reading his silence. "This is what you've always wanted. You'll get the recognition you deserve now."

He forced himself to calm down, to take a long breath. She understood how much this meant to him. Somehow this allowed him to turn a corner emotionally. He could go home for the night. He could enjoy Ginger's recital. It might even calm down the shaking in his hands, the twitching in his eyes.

"Okay," he said, "how much time do I have?"

"Not much. You'll need to head directly to the church, or else you'll be late."

Eli agreed that he would meet them there. He could hear Ginger in the background, practicing her scales on the hallway piano— the same piano that Mr. Krantz had played all of those long years ago. Ginger played her scales unevenly; it sounded like a soprano alternating singing with coughing. It was a cheerful if discordant tune, and Eli felt happy enough as he buckled his seat belt and drove the thirty-some miles west to Lilac City.

HE MADE IT to the recital with few minutes to spare. The parking lot was crowded with cars and overdressed children and fussing, smiling parents. Eli considered the trap and the foot bone. He had rested it on the passenger seat, which was now flaked with dirt and brittle leaf remnants.

What would he do with it? Lay his coat over it and close it in the car? Wrap it in fabric and place it in the trunk? He hesitated. It was a sunny Sunday in the early fall. He did not like to think of Mr. Krantz's metatarsus sweltering alone in the hot dark. He was not paranoid about car theft, either, but still: What if? It would destroy him to return to the car and find the specimen missing.

He decided to take every possible precaution. He would carry the foothold snare into the recital, bone and all. He took care to wrap it in his coat. Even so, it appeared bulbous and awkward in his arms, as if he were holding a stillborn horse.

As soon as he entered the church, he saw Vanessa, standing taller and straighter than anyone else there, her wild hair framing her handsome, relaxed face. She saw him and brought a hand to her heart, grateful. He maneuvered through the crowd and noticed

that some people were making room for him as he passed, eyeballing his laden arms.

"You're here," Vanessa said with relief, and she leaned into him
and kissed him. "Ginger will be so happy."

Ginger was, in fact, peeking through the dense red curtain at
the front of the room. She beamed when she saw Eli, and he smiled
back at her with what he hoped was encouragement.

Vanessa noticed his coat. "Eli," she said, "what are you doing?"

"I couldn't leave it in the car," he said. "I just couldn't. It's too
important."

She was more amused than horrified, and he was glad for it.

"Ew, let me see," she said. "Show me, show me."

He partially unwrapped the coat and she peered into his arms,
smiling. "Good God, Eli," she said with delight. "It's positively
gruesome!"

Eli rewrapped the foothold snare proudly.

Another set of parents approached them. They greeted Eli and
Vanessa warmly, and Eli returned their greeting.

"Whatcha got there?" the dad asked. He was a slim, overly
tanned dentist with perfect teeth. His wife stood squat and white
beside him like a freshly painted lighthouse, grinning broadly. "Some
fancy camera or something?"

Eli shook his head.

"Eli is a cryptozoologist," Vanessa explained. "He found a bone
today."

"Crypto-what?" the dentist said.

"He studies diabetes," said the wife.

"You're thinking of an endocrinologist, Nora," said the dentist,
rolling his eyes.

The wife said, "I was close, right?"

"He studies Sasquatch," Vanessa said. There was no shame in
her tone, but Eli sensed a dry amusement. "He knows all about them.
Ask him anything!"

"Sasquatch," the dentist repeated. He was puzzled, his orange forehead furrowing. "You mean, like Bigfoot? You believe in that shit?"

Eli shifted uncomfortably. "I wonder if we should sit now? I think they're about to begin."

"Listen," the dentist said, leaning forward, "my brother-in-law saw Bigfoot once. Said he looked like a giant turd with legs. Over by Snoqualmie Pass. Almost hit him with his car. Of course"—and the dentist laughed hugely here, showing all of his perfect, white teeth— "he's the drunkest bastard this side of the Rockies. Damn idiot swears he saw the Loch Ness monster, too, swimming in Puget Sound!"

"He's not a drunk, he's a schizophrenic," the wife said. "And he has diabetes. So, you know, if you have any advice for him?"

"He's a damn monster-stalker, Nora," the husband cried. "He doesn't know shit about diabetes. I *told* you." The dentist bent toward Eli, shaking his head, and Eli smelled the man's minty breath, a combination of Scope and whiskey. "She's deaf in one ear, I swear to God. Denies it, but I swear on my life. Hears half of what I say, if I'm lucky. Or if I'm unlucky, ha!"

Vanessa put a palm against Eli's back, pressing him toward an empty pew. Eli hoped to escape, but the couple followed them, the wife squeezing in against Eli's legs.

"Funny, though," the man said, leaning over his wife's lap. "My Matilda told me you were a foot doctor. A pee-ologist, she called it. She's as deaf as my wife, I swear. 'Podiatrist,' I told her, and she was like, 'Yup, that's it. Pee-diatrist.' "

"Well," Eli said, "I am. I'm still a licensed podiatrist, it's true."

"Your daughter is the sweetest little girl," said the wife now, sincerely. "She just raves about you both." She turned to Vanessa and said, "She told me you're a professor?"

"Oh," Vanessa said. "No. I teach some creative writing classes through the extension program, but, no. I'm a poet."

"A poet and a monster-stalker!" cried the dentist. "Your sex life must be amazing."

"Oh, my," the wife said, reaching up and nervously tugging at an earring. "Christopher, the things you say."

"Big imaginations," the dentist said. "That's all I'm saying."

"Well, it is," Vanessa said.

"What is?" the wife asked politely.

"Amazing. Our sex life."

The dentist laughed and the wife stammered and Eli wanted to shush his wife but refrained. The curtains drew back then and a child emerged from the recesses, sitting stiffly at the piano bench and beginning to struggle through a simple Mozart sonata. Eli tried to relax and enjoy the show.

He did enjoy it, almost. He wanted to stand up and sing and dance and drown out the cacophony of the children, to show these little wonders what joy *really* looked like, but he remained seated, blazing from within, straining not to wiggle too noticeably on the uncomfortable wooden pew. The foothold snare grew increasingly incommodious on his lap.

Finally, it was Ginger's turn. She was one of the youngest performers, too young yet to read or even learn a real song, but the crowd applauded her anyway. The teacher came onstage and informed them that Ginger would be performing a very short piece, called "Dad," in which she played only the D and A notes for about one minute. She stood at the edge of the stage for a moment, looking out and, finding her parents in the crowd, happily waving. Eli and Vanessa waved proudly back at her.

"She is too precious," the wife said to them approvingly, and Eli saw that his daughter's sweet goodness had restored their standing in the world.

Her performance began, and Eli noticed that his thighs were sweating horribly, droplets of sweat running from the backs of his knees, behind his trousers, and into his socks. He tried to open up the folded coat a little to allow better air circulation, but in the attempt he unfolded it too wide and the couple beside them gasped, catching sight of the menacing device and its contents.

"My God," the dentist said to his wife. "He's got a goddamn weapon in there. It's not a bone at all. Just a weapon."

The dentist's wife hushed him. "Christopher," she said. "The children."

The dentist scowled for a moment, crossing his arms over his chest. His beeper sounded. He checked the number, resettled it into the back of his waistband, and re-crossed his arms. Then, after a bit more of listening to Ginger play, he stood and shuffled away from them.

"Excuse me," he said, as people slanted their knees, making room for his passage. "Sorry. I have to make a phone call."

A few moments later he returned, taking his wife by the elbow and pulling her to her feet.

"Nice to see you," Vanessa whispered, and the woman bade her a friendly goodbye. The dentist kept his eyes averted, tugging his wife along.

"Must have been an important call," Vanessa whispered to Eli, and he shrugged indifferently.

Ginger had finished playing. They whistled and cheered for her, Eli loudest of all.

It wasn't a bad evening. Eli felt fine as they left the church and filed outside with the other parents and children. Ginger came to them and accepted their congratulations and hugs. Eli had to set his trap down on the sidewalk to hug her, but he did so willingly.

"Eli," Vanessa said then, her tone tight. "I think this man would like to speak to you."

Eli turned. A policeman stood at Vanessa's side.

"We received a call about a weapon," the officer said. "Would you like to show me what's in that jacket?" He pointed at the trap, where it sat on the sidewalk.

"It's nothing," Eli said. He lifted the trap and opened his jacket, presenting it to the officer, who wrinkled his brow in confusion. "It's not a weapon at all. It's a trap. See this bone? I'm a scientist, and this bone is very important."

"I wonder if you shouldn't hand it over to the authorities," the officer said.

"I am the authority here," Eli said. "I'm a scientist. This is what I do for a living."

"That trap is illegal in this state, you know."

"I didn't set the trap," Eli said. "I only found it. Besides, it was in Idaho, not in Washington."

The officer sucked on his teeth. He stared off into the cloudless sky for a moment, thinking, or pretending to think, very hard. "I'm gonna let you go with a warning. But next time you want to frighten a church full of kids, you're gonna have to answer to *moi*."

"Okay. Yes, I see. Thank you, Officer."

The officer looked over at Vanessa and Ginger, who were playing hopscotch off to the side of the parking lot. Ginger threw a stick and then bounded—*one leg, two legs, one, two, bend, pluck!*—and the officer softened and said, "Cute kid."

"Thank you. Yes. Thanks."

Eli was angry with Ginger. It was an irrational anger, but he couldn't shake the feeling that her recital had dampened a triumphant day. Why did children always force themselves into the center of everyone's attention? Why did they demand the sum total of one's affections and abilities? Sometimes he wondered why he'd agreed to another child, when he'd known how much work it would be.

He forced himself to smile as he approached his wife and daughter.

"Ready to go?" Vanessa asked, and Eli reminded her that he had his own car and that he planned to stop by the office so that he could lock the trap and the metatarsus safely into it for the night.

Vanessa looked ready to argue with him, but she stopped herself and then said, a little petulantly, "Fine. Whatever. As though it hasn't caused enough trouble tonight. We'll save you some pizza," and Ginger shrieked in pleasure at the word *pizza* and skipped eagerly over to Vanessa's car.

Eli, frustrated, guilty, returned to his own car.

He drove with the trap in the passenger seat beside him. God, was he insane? Everyone else seemed to think so. How many years had passed since he'd seen Mr. Krantz? He remembered it all so clearly: the hulking shoulders; the tufts of reeking hair; the cold, simian eyes. But doubt ate away at him, nonetheless. How was it that he had been the *only* witness to Agnes's lover? How was it that even Eli's own father could never bring himself to believe his son's testimony, would assume only that Eli was an imaginative and traumatized little boy? What was true? It was quite possible, as the family doctor had said, that he had made the whole thing up, an elaborate fantasy that deadened the pain of abandonment.

"To you," the doctor had said, "it is very real. But, I assure you, it's not real."

Couldn't that explain life in general?

Because, look, there is the bone! Proof! Lying right there! As clear as day!

But other voices spoke to him, too. *It belongs to a man, stupid, a man with a hereditary disease such as Marfan syndrome. It belongs to a bear. It is purely faked evidence, not even real bone.*

You were searching, endlessly, for this one thing, Eli told himself. *And your mind cracked and then . . .*

Eli stopped himself. He had reached the SNaRL office. He unlocked the door and went inside, feeling numb. The lights were off. It was cool and quiet. It was peaceful.

He put the bone, snare trap and all, in the cooler in his office, and before he locked the cooler for the night, he stood over it and looked down into it and saw reflected in the clean metal the hazy outline of his own face.

The next day would be a flurry of excitement around the office. The trap would be opened, evidence would be carefully examined and reported, news media would be contacted, funding would begin pouring in from intrigued parties, and the doubting Thomases—far from being silenced—would cry foul.

But for now the world was quiet and waiting. There was a patience in the air that was mimicked by the hum of the cooler, and Eli tried to enjoy it. He locked up the office and headed home, wishing only to be left alone, wanting to see no one, especially not his wife and his sensitive young daughter, who invested so much in him emotionally. He was drained.

When he entered the house, Ginger was waiting for him. He could not have been more disappointed to see someone. She sat on the couch in a matchlessly bright mood.

"Come read with me, Daddy," she said, and patted the sofa violently beside her so that a sparkling flower of dust bloomed at her side.

Eli wanted a drink. He wanted to take a long walk. He wanted to sink into his own dark heart, to shutter himself up with his hope and his exhaustion.

He opened his mouth to tell her, *Daddy's exhausted, sweetheart. Another time.*

But then he looked at her, this little fragile creature, really looked at her, and he found himself moved by her wide, pleading eyes, which had already begun to glisten with fresh tears. He saw, horribly, that her hurt and her hope could be as wide and oceanic as his own.

"Okay, sweetie," he said, and then watched with breathless pleasure as her mercurial face lifted skyward, so easily infused with joy.

Ginger was, Eli acknowledged, the most wonderful thing he'd ever seen. She put even Mr. Krantz to shame.

The good doctor set his own longings aside, hanging them up with his coat in the hallway closet.

He sat down next to his daughter.

He took up the book she shoved at him, a boring tome about a family of pigs, and he began to read.

1980

THE MOUNTAIN

It was a lovely May morning in the Selkirks, an hour or so after sunrise. Eli parked his wife's beat-up old sedan in the small town of Rathdrum, next to Lakeland High School's modest football field. The hiking trail threaded from the outskirts of town up Rathdrum Mountain, overlooking Highway 41. The woods smelled of lilac and water, fresh and still cold. Eli hiked away from town, uphill and then down and then up again. The trees swallowed up any signs of human life, but Eli could still hear a plane overhead, could make out the distant hum of the highway and the freeway to the south.

He was sure he was alone, but he was not.

Agnes Roebuck, who now called herself Agnes Krantz, recognized her son immediately.

She was returning to the shack from the creek bed, where she had enjoyed a zesty, teeth-clattering bath. Her clothes were over one arm and she held her tattered shoes in her left hand. She was an animal walking in the forest now, as quiet as a young elk—she moved silently, unseen, stepping with care but without being conscious of it.

Mr. Krantz was off on one of his expeditions, gathering food. Sometimes he would disappear for days, but usually he returned within a few hours. In the old days, he would gesture lustily for her to remove her clothes. The hunt excited him. He didn't make these urgent requests of her any longer; she had changed too much, and he had perhaps grown bored with her, but still he was enthusiastic about sharing his harvested goods. He would take her hand and drag her to the pile of stuff, gesturing at it excitedly, and she always made sure to thank him profusely. She truly was grateful. He returned with assortments of food, never paid for, only taken or stolen. Potatoes, berries, fresh fish (trout, usually, but sometimes, if they were lucky, a fat pink salmon), groundhogs, rotting loaves of bread, bleating lambs—once, to her horror, a large, handsome horse. She dressed and ate almost all that he brought to her, but the horse she refused. She released it with a spank on its rump the moment her husband fell asleep. When he awoke and found the horse missing, he was angry. He punished her by keeping his back to her for two days, but he never brought her another horse. He was a good, if aloof, husband. She didn't mind the aloofness. If anything, she loved him more for it.

On the best days, he broke into a local grocer or gas station and brought her hot dogs, bags of potato chips, fresh, cold milk. He usually dragged cold goods to the shack in a stolen cooler, filled with miraculous chunks of ice. Over the years he had presented her with other random gifts: wicker chairs, a patched leather recliner, even an oven, which she used only for storage, because of their lack of electricity (it held chipped, mismatching china and a plastic bucket she used to collect water from the nearby creek). Before their first winter, he gave her a woodstove. She had gathered his large, bearded face into her hands and kissed him passionately.

Agnes was approaching old age now, and her life with Mr. Krantz grew more physically demanding by the year, but she remained content. She was even grateful for the difficulty of it. She fashioned their rattletrap home together energetically, and its constant wear and tear distracted her from past grief. It was a lovely if makeshift little house in the woods. When times grew hard—when she nearly froze to death, for example—or when she was almost suicidal from loneliness, Mr. Krantz would return to her with the perfect offering: a fancy down sleeping bag, for example, or a tiny, mewling kitten. That they ate the cat one night after being snowed in for twelve days was irrelevant. She had wanted this: an escape from the human, from boredom, from routine. Krantz gave her that, and she thrived.

And, besides, even with the unpredictability of it all, they managed their own routines. Here she was, for example, returning from a springtime bath, as she would every other morning for the duration of the warmer days. She was glad it was spring. The days were longer, the leaves thrusting from the blossoms in a way that seemed to Agnes both pleasant and painful. Food would be easier to come by now. Her bones would no longer ache from the cold. In the evenings, she would comb Mr. Krantz's matted fur with a broken brush, picking him free of ticks. She would chatter at him as she worked, and he would cock his head and listen sleepily. When she fell asleep, he would rouse himself and go out into the night, and she would be able to stretch her limbs fully and enjoy the private bed. He never slept longer than two or three hours at a time, but he napped throughout the day.

Agnes tried her best to placate him. Sex had lost its pleasure for her. She was muscular and lithe but also lined and drooping. Her breasts and ass hung low now, and it seemed there was always a pain in her belly when he penetrated her. Lumps there, maybe, she thought, or just dryness. She felt she would live forever, but in what way? As a bag of floating bones? As an old bat in the woods? She liked the bats. She knew it was not such a bad life.

The sex didn't matter, she told herself. They were happy, in love. They enjoyed each other. Their own simple rhythm would always include the other, she believed, even though she noted with some alarm that she continued to age quickly while her husband—despite a slight, uneven whitening of his brown hair—more or less remained the same.

No regrets, she told herself. None whatsoever. Not even about her son. If she thought about Eli at all, it was usually with relief. Leaving him, she believed, was not even about her own freedom. She had freed Eli, too, cut him loose from the leash of her own unhappiness.

But when she saw Eli now, moving through the forest at an ambitious clip, she felt disappointed. He looked well: healthy, fulfilled, graceful if not exactly handsome. He wore fine clothes, pressed trousers, an expensive button-up shirt, a whimsical bow tie, and big red spectacles. He radiated self-care. Her first thought was: *Well done, Greg.*

Her second thought was: *Well, so. He was better off without me, after all.*

It was a puerile disappointment. She relished it bitterly, shrinking into the underbrush with a pouting lip.

He hadn't seen her. He didn't know she was there.

She wondered, irritably, What is he doing here?

She wanted him to leave.

Still naked from her bath, Agnes shivered. She quietly hurried into her clothes and, overcome with curiosity, followed her son deeper into her familiar wood.

ELI STOPPED IN a small opening of trees and unzipped his backpack. Clouds were piling in from the east, which was odd, because the weather report had described a clear, perfect day.

Damn weathermen, Eli thought. *Always wrong.*

It was light enough to film, however, so Eli pulled out a Canon 310XL loaded with Super 8mm film. It was a shaky and grainy medium but reliable in decent light and ultraportable, used by many of his colleagues. Eli set the camera to one side and then polished his spectacles. This same spot was where he had located the metatarsus, and he had returned to it again and again, always with a growing sense of Mr. Krantz's elusiveness. The foot bone had received its fifteen minutes' worth of fame, but its exact origins remained dubious. Was it a hoax, people wondered, or real evidence of Bigfoot? Even the fascinating genetic evidence failed to prove its origins without a doubt. No, it was not exactly human, tests seemed to suggest, but it wasn't inhuman, either.

Eli thought he would spend the morning recording video footage of the area. He was not expecting to see an actual Sasquatch— they were mostly nocturnal, he believed, or at least preferred dawn or dusk, like the other arboreal wild—but you never knew. In those days, Eli was filled with hope. He'd found the metatarsus, hadn't he? More impressive evidence was sure to follow.

Calm, enjoying the morning air, Eli put the camera to his eye and began to record. The world through the lens was slightly foggy, limited. Eli filmed for a few moments, aiming at nothing in particular.

Then a figure moved in the trees. Eli's heart stopped.

Had it happened, finally, just like that? Had the creature been waiting here for him all this time? He kept the camera trained on the figure, his hands shaking from excitement.

But the figure continued its approach, and Eli, disappointed, calculated the figure's proportions: too small and too slim, tallish but only just so, like a juvenile bear. Certainly not Mr. Krantz.

But it was not a bear. Eli lowered the camera.

It was a woman stepping toward him.

The sky went black.

It was blacker than a storm. It was like a blotting out of all light, like an eclipse, suddenly midnight.

It smelled like burnt sawdust.

It began, impossibly, to snow.

"WHAT ARE YOU doing here?" she said to him.

"Mom," he said.

White flakes fell around them. When she stepped on them, smoke rose. Looking up, Agnes could make out the rounded black heads of the clouds that hung over them like bent knuckles, like punching fists.

"Something's not right," she said. She squinted. "The sky is falling."

"It's snowing."

"That's stupid. It's a warm day." Her nose burned, her lungs. She laughed. "The world is ending."

It was dreamlike, wandering to her son like this, in the dark in the middle of the day, with the smell of sulfur around them, with the gray smoke of her footfalls. The birds stopped chirping, the bugs burrowed desperately into the earth. The flakes fell heavier, a thick blanket that made her cough.

"We need to get inside," she said. "We need to get out of this."

Her son seemed unaware or indifferent.

"The air is poisoned," she pressed. "Come with me."

"Where is he?" Eli said.

"What?"

"Where is Mr. Krantz?" Eli said. "Is he with you? Are you with him now?"

She shook her head. She had no idea where Mr. Krantz was. He was no doubt searching for her, worried for her with the foul air.

"It's raining hellfire," she said. "Come along, now."

"Will you take me to him?"

Her son's face was no longer recognizable to her, cruel now, filled with ache and murder.

She could not bring her son to meet her husband. Not now. Not ever.

The two males would cancel each other out.

"You should go," she said. "Your car is close by. We shouldn't breathe this in. It's raining acid."

"You look horrible," Eli said. His face was pale, unnerved. His small pink mouth squirmed. "What happened to all of your red hair? It was red, wasn't it?"

Agnes reached up absently and touched her hair, still wet from her bath. "Auburn," she told him. "That's what your dad called it. It's gone gray now. White."

"Do you know where he is?"

"Greg?" she asked, confused.

"No." Eli's face hardened, and she saw in his expression that Greg was dead.

"I'm sorry, Eli." She cleared her face of all betrayal. "I'm alone now," she lied. "I've been alone for years."

Eli didn't know what to make of this. He repeated his question.

"Really, I don't know. He could be anywhere. I don't know. It's been years. I've been here, all alone, for too long." It was easy to lie. It felt natural, what she said, as if she truly had been alone. Had she been? She felt almost confused as she spoke, light-headed.

Eli's face fell. He still trusted her, she realized with some amusement, the way a young boy trusts his mother. Even after all she had done to him, all she had not done for him. She felt a sharp triumph at this.

She took advantage of his trust and hurried on to say, "Your car. You should go. Your family? Surely you have a family?" She gestured at the terrible sky. "They might be stranded somewhere. They need you."

She winced as she said it. It was silly to chide him for possibly abandoning his family in a time of need. She braced herself for a stock answer. *I needed you*, she expected. *How could you? Why did you leave me all of those long years ago?*

But Eli, always so resolute, said nothing of the sort. He had never been one to whine.

"If you see him," he told her, "please call me."

He handed her a business card. *Dr. Eli Roebuck*, it read, *Crypto-zoology. Podiatry. 509-905-3660*. His address was written there, too.

"Eli," she began, uncertain of what to say but stumbling toward some sort of apology, however banal, "If I don't see you again—"

"If you see him," he said firmly, "please call."

I won't, she thought, but Eli was already charging down the pathway, toward his car, the smoke rising with each step, swirling up and around his shoulders as if he were a demon himself.

ELI MERGED ONTO Highway 41 and crawled south to the interstate. He could hardly see ten feet in front of the car. The world was nothing but ash and smoke and gray fog. It was noon, as dark as midnight. Darker.

He pulled over at a gas station and waited in a long line to use the pay phone.

Ginger answered, gasping. "Volcano, Daddy!" She screamed it so loudly that it hurt his ear. She was beyond elated. "Aunt Helen's blown up!"

So that's all it is, Eli thought. He felt relieved. "Give the phone to Mom, Ginger," he said.

Ginger passed the phone to Vanessa. "Thank God. Eli. Where are you? Come home now."

"I'm near Post Falls. I'm on my way."

"Mount Saint Helens blew," she said. "Please hurry. I'm worried for you." She waited for a moment and then added, "They're closing the interstate."

He cursed.

"Can you make it back?"

Eli thought of his morning in the forest, of his discovery of his own mother living like a wild woman in the woods. The Super 8 camera sat in his car. He would show Vanessa the footage of his mother later. Otherwise, how would she believe it? It seemed he would have to prove her existence with as much painstaking diligence as proving his Sasquatch. It was as though he could not quite prove it all to himself.

"I'll make it back," he said. "One way or another."

"We love you."

Eli began to respond, but a man waiting behind him cursed and said, "Come on, buddy. We've all got wives to call."

Eli mumbled his goodbye and hung up.

"There you go," he said to the man, moving aside.

"It's the end of the world," the man said. "Eat shit."

Eli hurried to his car, frowning. When he got inside, he brushed the ash from his head and shoulders and coughed at the bulging brume. His eyes watered. It hurt to breathe.

"Screw you, asshole," Eli muttered to his steering wheel.

He wished he could have said it to the man's face.

He wished he could have said it to Agnes.

And yet, as he drove, he wondered about her. Where would she go in the woods? Would she cower under a tree somewhere? Her hair had been wet, like an old water nymph. He pictured a cave behind a waterfall. Likely, though, she lived in Rathdrum, mooching off the government, eating canned peaches and growing older and thinner by the day.

She was still an imposing figure, taller than most women, broader-shouldered, he reflected. How much he had grown since he last saw her! So much so that it seemed as if she'd dramatically shrunk.

Life had not treated her well, he thought. He wondered if she thought the same thing about him.

After all of these years, assuming Agnes was dead.

All of these years, not assuming anything at all.

He knew where she was now, and it struck Eli as more of an absence than her previous absence.

Red demon eyes—brake lights—snapped open in front of him, and Eli pumped the brakes with a shout. Visibility waned. Eli kept his eyes to the side of the road, just barely making out the white line, and he crept along beside it, blinking frantically when it flickered and vanished and then, sweetly, reappeared.

AGNES, BACK IN her little cabin, listened to the nothing outside.

Her husband had been there, waiting for her, when she returned. He had been relieved to see her, had gestured for her to sit and eat, had stroked her hair as she chewed her food. Now he slept in the patched recliner, his mouth hanging open, his large purple and yellow hands draped over his bare genitals. His good leg was up on the recliner footrest, his crutch resting against the floor.

Agnes stood at the window, listening. There was no sound. The nothingness expanded and grew.

The next morning, when she awoke, Agnes tiptoed out of the cabin, curious, and saw the tiny squiggling paths of insects that had fallen, struggled, and then died in the soft gray ash. These little deaths were everywhere.

In their place was born a queer soundlessness: no wind through the trees, no birdsong, no bugs buzzing by, no distant traffic from the highway or the interstate.

Agnes wandered farther through the moonscape, the silence stuffing her ears. Her husband, stooped over his breakfast, lifted his head and called for her to return.

She didn't return, not yet. She remained rooted to the preternatural quiet.

It was possible to believe then: No one else was left. The world was emptied of all life. It was just the two of them. The only survivors. What remained was yours and yours alone.

ELI WAS FORCED to leave the interstate and navigate dark back roads, but he did, eventually, make it home. After dinner, after discussions of the volcano and its aftermath, he unpacked his camera and saw that the ash had sifted into everything, into his shoelaces and his watch face and the gears of his car, and he knew immediately that the film, like much of what the volcano touched, was destroyed. Even the trustworthy blue sedan would refuse to start up the next day.

"Something major happened," he told Vanessa, fingering the ruined camera.

"It sure did," she said, meaning the mountain. "I'm going to write a poem about it. It's so inspiring."

"I saw my mother today," he said.

Vanessa fingered her lower lip. "That's a good line," she said. "I should write that down."

"In the woods," he added, and Vanessa picked up a pen and wrote that down, too.

He suddenly wanted to be alone. It was not his wife's misunderstanding that floored him, but his own.

He had often wondered: If he found his mother, would all of his other searching end? Wasn't Agnes what he had been looking for all along? He had suspected that his search for Krantz was, beneath it all, a search for Agnes.

The day had shown him how simple an answer that was; it was simple and wrong.

So maybe the best answer was this: that no matter whom he found—Agnes, Mr. Krantz, a three-headed alien magician—he was still stuck with his past. It was unchangeable. There was no panacea for those memories. Even if his mother had run forth, thrown her arms about his neck, cried into his chest, and begged his forgiveness, his younger self was still frozen in time, heartbroken.

He left his wife to pen her poem on the divan and went into the living room. Ginger was there, asleep in front of the television. The news was on, showing images of Mount Saint Helens' ashfall across Washington State. It was a monumental event, but all Eli could think about was that he had failed somehow.

He poured himself a drink. The house was quiet. He went to the window and peered out into the darkness and wondered if his mother was doing the same, having a drink, peering out into the impermanent midnight, thinking of her son. He wondered if her loneliness followed her everywhere, as his did.

Or maybe she lay dead on the forest floor now, suffocated by ash.

He could have saved her. She was an old woman. My God, he marveled, she looked so much like Amelia. He had not remembered her face correctly at all.

Why had he left her out there, without even offering her a ride, without accompanying her home?

But maybe he was being too hard on himself.

Maybe she was a ghost.

Or, more likely, he'd imagined her entire existence, Eli told himself. Krantz existed, certainly, but not Agnes. She was the greatest figment of his imagination, his life's creative work. It could have been any old hag out in the forest today. He had no proof, no reason to believe she was alive out there at all.

These thoughts comforted him.

A reporter on the news program began to list the names of people missing or killed by the lava flow. Eli went and sat beside Ginger's knees and listened. There was an octogenarian who refused to leave his lodge in the woods. He wanted to die right there where he'd always lived, and so he did.

Eli thought about the man and his lodge. He imagined the roar of the explosion, the interminable wait. Would the man just sit patiently in his chair, maybe shuffling an old deck of cards, or would he go and stand and face the mountain? Would he pace back and forth on his porch, only to begin to suffer regret as hot mud filled his shoes? Was he stubborn or silly or idealistic or noble or all of it or none?

What would I do? Eli wondered, safe and sound in his comfortable home, with his kindly daughter stirring lazily beside him on the couch. *What would I do with that last hot, excruciating minute? Would I think of Mr. Krantz?*

God, would I?

Would I still care?

1982

RELEASE THE DOGS

"I'm not surprised, is all," Ginger's mom said.

Ginger's dad checked his watch, then rested his light, warm palm on Ginger's head.

"It doesn't bother me," her mom continued, "because it's not my event. If it were my event, I would have called that Katie girl. The one your intern recommended. She's reliable. I'm not going to bring up what happened the last time. I promise I won't bring it up."

Ginger's dad dragged in a deep breath and held it.

"I won't. I'm sorry. You're right. I won't bring it up." Her mom fell silent. The hand on top of Ginger's head relaxed.

The only sound now was the hum of the refrigerator, a new refrigerator with nice Shaker paneling. It was the nicest refrigerator in the whole store, her mom had said. Nicer than anything she'd ever bought in her whole life. Ginger liked the refrigerator just fine. It matched the cupboards. That, Ginger supposed, was a good thing. She liked things to match. For example, her socks. Or the pink bauble in her hair and her pink sneakers. She also liked to try on her mom's lipstick, to wear the same color her mother wore. That, too, was matching.

Ginger's lips were bare now. Her mom's were outlined in red

and filled in with a lighter shade of red; her short hair was teased into a flattering shrub. She was very tall; she towered over both Ginger and her smaller-framed father. She wore a black dress, and her nude shoulders were sharp and shining from recent sunbaths.

"You look so pretty, Mom," Ginger said.

Her mom came forward and embraced her, giving her a wet kiss on the cheek. "Oh," she laughed. "My lipstick."

She went to the counter to get a wet cloth and returned to scrub Ginger's face. Ginger closed her eyes and inhaled her mom's warm perfume. It smelled sweet and metallic, like flowers and melted gold. It gave her a headache.

"Is that Amelia?" Ginger asked, seeing someone slow down before the driveway.

But then the vehicle accelerated and disappeared.

Her mom sighed. "Look how excited she is, Eli. I hope, for her sake, that Amelia shows up."

They waited next to the window for what felt to Ginger like a long time. They lived on the very outskirts of Lilac City, where the suburbs met the hillsides of Palouse country. Her mom wanted character, her father wanted land, so they bought an old farmhouse on a ten-acre plot and began slowly remodeling it. Ginger loved where they lived and loved staring out the windows at the pasture and animals and trees, but right now the only thing she wanted was for Amelia to arrive.

Her mother waited with her for a bit, but then threw up her arms dramatically and left the bedroom, and Ginger heard the television snap on in the den. Her father had already tuned out, but he remained nearby, collapsed in a chair with a book that he was very intently reading. Ginger asked him what the book was about. He shrugged. "Sasquatch," he said. And that was all. Ginger turned back to the window, fretfully tugging at her bangs.

But then a maroon car pulled slowly around the street corner, disappearing for a moment behind a grove of lilacs. It drew past the neighbor's large lawn and then slowed, kindly, Ginger felt, before their driveway. The driver nosed the car onto the gravel and then stopped abruptly, as though unwilling to drive the rest of the way. A passenger door popped open and out stepped Ginger's sister.

Amelia was in college now at the local university (and had been for "too long," according to Ginger's mom). She had recently returned to live with her own mom, just for the summer. Amelia had lost her license after what Ginger's mom called "another troubling incident." Ginger waved frantically at Amelia, grinning. She tried to get a look at Amelia's mom. Gladys had once been married to their dad, but now their dad loved Ginger's mom instead. Ginger had met Amelia's mom once. She'd been invited over to Gladys's house for a birthday party for Amelia. Her mother had warned her that Gladys was a very cruel person, but Gladys had not been cruel in the least. When Amelia and her older friends ditched Ginger to play games in the backyard, Gladys invited Ginger to watch television and handed her a bag of rock candies. She had chatted amiably with Ginger as they watched a cartoon and mentioned several times how pretty Ginger's mom was.

"She's nice!" Ginger had told her mom. "She likes you! She gave me rock candies!"

Ginger's mom had said, "Oh, right, she just loves me," and then joked that the rock candies were probably poisoned. Ginger, still young enough to take all things literally, had cried.

"She's here!" Ginger said now, running for the door. "Amelia's here!"

She threw it open and stretched her arms wide to embrace her older sister, but Amelia took no heed of her, only strode through the foyer and into the living room, looking this way and that, as if wanting to pick a fight. She tossed her attractive black purse onto the floor, and Ginger admired it soulfully for a moment before saying shyly, "Hello, Amelia."

Now Amelia looked over her shoulder. "Hello yourself, Kumquat," she said. "Where's your *padres*?"

"My . . ." Ginger trailed off, confused.

"*Padres*. The 'rents. Where are they? Speak now or forever hold your peace, Kumquat."

"Amelia," Ginger's mom said, materializing from the kitchen, ferrying a drink in each hand. "Thanks for coming. We weren't sure, you know, if you could make it."

"Well, I'm late," Amelia said. "Not my fault."

Ginger's mom nodded as though she understood, but it was a fake nod that hid how annoyed she was. Their father joined them silently, coming forward smoothly, as if on wheels, to give his eldest daughter a kiss on her cheek. Amelia smiled at him warmly.

"Dad," she said. "Sorry I'm late."

"Why?" he asked.

"Why am I sorry?"

"Why are you so late? We've been waiting for you for almost two hours. My presentation is at eight o'clock. We missed the dinner."

"Oh, dear," Ginger's mother said, handing him his drink. "We had better run. It's nearly seven-thirty now." She waggled her drink in the air. "For the road."

Amelia ignored Vanessa. "If you must know, Dad, it was Gladys. She didn't see why you needed me. She wants Vanessa to stay home with Ginger. You know how she gets. She's pigheaded. I had to get down on my knees and beg her for the ride. Practically." Amelia's frown deepened. She was clearly annoyed with the memory. "As though it was so important to me."

"I'm sorry, Amelia," their dad said. "It's not fair, her behavior."

"Well," Amelia said, "at least she treats me at all. I mean, how long has it been since you've invited me over? Or visited me on campus? You've never seen my dorm room, you know."

Ginger's mom grew pale. She began to respond, but Eli lifted his hand and silenced her.

"You're welcome here whenever you wish," he said. "It's an open invitation, Amelia. I shouldn't have to explain that to you. And as for your dorm room, well, we've been very busy with my work."

Amelia stood very still. Ginger went up to her and touched her hand. The fist was curled in on itself like a tortured bird.

"Have a good night," Amelia said. "Have gobs of fun."

Ginger's mom giggled, the nervous way she did when drinking. "We really need to leave, Eli. You'll be too late. They said six, and—"

"Come on," Amelia said, taking Ginger's hand into her own and yanking her toward the den. "Let's go watch TV, Kumquat."

Ginger surrendered gratefully. When she looked over her shoulder, she saw her father setting down his drink, putting on his coat, taking the drink up again. His face showed no emotion whatsoever, but her mother was grinning, with a smile that was painted on like a clown's.

Amelia threw herself down on the couch and took up the remote. "We're watching *Dallas* later. No arguments." She groped around on the side table for a moment and then pulled the phone onto her lap. The door to the garage swept shut. Ginger was delighted to finally be alone with Amelia.

"I'm so glad the other babysitter was sick," Ginger confessed. "This is so much fun!" Then, when Amelia didn't say anything, she added, "I *love Dallas.*"

That was a lie. She didn't follow *Dallas*—it was just a lot of adults talking about money and lying around in bed together half naked. Amelia said it was glamorous, but Ginger didn't really know what that meant. Beautiful, she supposed. Secretly, she preferred shows like *Looney Tunes*. Or, especially, *The Muppet Show*. But that was baby stuff now. Stuff that Amelia hated.

"Sick babysitter," Amelia said, bemused, gazing off into the white space above the television set. "So that's why they called me. Those dicks."

"Should I make popcorn?" Ginger asked.

"No," Amelia said. Then, beginning to dial, "Yes. Popcorn. Good. Lots of salt and butter."

Ginger jumped to her feet, squealing and clapping.

"*Silencio,* Kumquat. I'm calling my boyfriend."

And Ginger fell silent.

THEY HAD BEEN outside for over an hour now, and Ginger, coatless, began to shiver. It was early summer, but the day had been rainy and cool.

"I'm cold," she said, tugging on Amelia's jacket, which wasn't really her jacket. It belonged to the larger of the two boys, the boys who were now punching each other on the shoulder, harder and harder, a game that Ginger thought was stupid.

Ginger didn't like these boys. She hadn't liked them ever since they'd arrived, hauling with them a wide silver case of beer. The beer followed them everywhere like a loyal animal. They—Amelia, too—kept fishing around in its mouth for a fresh can. The empties lay all over the lawn and pasture, like so many dead silver fish. Ginger thought she might have one, too, but then she became too cold. The idea of drinking cold beer in the cold air sounded awful to her. They should be having hot chocolate. Apple cider. Something warm and comforting. But she knew better than to say this aloud.

"I'm cold," she repeated.

"Stop whining, Kumquat," Amelia said. "Good grief, kid."

"How old are you, sweetheart?" the larger boy said, giving his friend one last punch. His name was Rudolph: a reindeer's name. He was tanned and half naked in a tank top and shorts. He was big, solid, and the shadows of his muscles winked with every small movement. Ginger thought he was probably considered very handsome, but she liked the shorter one more, whose smile seemed less wolfish and whose thin, graceful body seemed less inhuman—at least he was wearing jeans and a windbreaker. The shorter boy's name was John. A simple, likable name.

"I'll be ten soon," she said. "I'll be in fifth grade."

"Good," Amelia said. "Stay in elementary forever. Junior high sucks." She reached over and ruffled Ginger's hair. "But you're not a tub of lard like I was back then. It'll be easier on you."

"Give me a break," John said. "You were never."

"She was," Rudolph confirmed. "Plump as a piglet. Fingers like sausages. We called her Fat Arm-Elia. She hated it."

"You were an asshole," Amelia said affectionately.

"Were?" John said.

"But then she got all beautiful and mean and weird," Rudolph said teasingly.

"Yeah, that old man you dated in high school," John said. "What a creep."

"Oh, fuck!" Rudolph said. "I totally forgot about that dude."

"He was handsome," Amelia said.

"Wasn't he like forty-five?"

"He was older, but she didn't know how old," John said. "I mean, who knew? Guy could pass for one of us." He wrinkled his nose, growing thoughtful. "Hey. Didn't he die or something?"

Amelia stared into her shoes. "Ask *her*," she said with a nod at Ginger. "She'll tell you. She knows every last detail."

Ginger blushed. She had been listening carefully; she, like the boys, wanted to know the story. She shook her head.

"You don't know?" Amelia asked, eyes narrowing.

"Mom won't tell me the whole thing."

"What about Eli?"

Ginger almost said, *He never talks about you,* but it wasn't that exactly; it was that her dad didn't really talk much, period. Normally when they sat together there was a comfortable silence, or he just listened to her talk. Any news or stories came from her mom.

"No," Ginger said.

"Huh," Amelia said, baffled. "I can't believe Vanessa wouldn't tell you. She usually leaps at the chance to slander me."

Ginger rushed to her mom's defense. "She says it's a crazy story." Her mom had also said: *It was a good thing it happened. She was self-destructive before that guy died, but it woke her up. She stopped hanging out with the wrong people. She started taking school seriously again. She's still a wild one, but not like she used to be.* Ginger knew she shouldn't mention this to Amelia. "She says she'll tell me when I'm older."

"Why, 'cause you're such a big baby now?" Amelia said. Then, straightening, she said, "Look. I'll tell you guys what happened. The short version. I met this guy. I dated him, for fun. We stole Dad's car. We had sex." Ginger squirmed uncomfortably here, and Amelia continued, "Lots of it. He was gross. We drove toward Seattle on Route 2. I knew it was stupid, even then, but I thought, why not? Hilarious! Then he drove Dad's car into Lake Roosevelt and drowned." She shrugged. "They found his body weeks later, washed up at Grand Coulee Dam."

"That's a fucked-up story," Rudolph said.

"It's not a story. It's true." Amelia looked off into the trees, tall white papery poles with black shifting coins for leaves. Then, turning suddenly to Rudolph: "And don't say *fuck* anymore, you dick. My little sister is right here."

"I liked you best when you were a fatty," Rudolph said. "You were nicer."

To Ginger's relief, Amelia laughed.

Ginger laughed, too, mostly because she could never picture Amelia as fat or unattractive or vulnerable. Amelia could cut anyone down to size. Ginger's mom and their dad withered before her. Weren't all of her enemies obliterated in such a fashion?

The wind picked up and Ginger shivered.

"I need a coat, at least," Ginger said.

"Well, go get one. Do I need to hold your hand?"

"No. I mean, I can go get it. I just . . . Will you be here when I get back?"

"No, we'll be riding camels into the rocky Himalayas." Then, after Ginger's silence, "Jesus, yes, we'll be here. Go. Go now, please, before I tell you to piss off for good."

She already sounded pissed, so Ginger hurried. The truth was, she didn't trust those boys, or Amelia, really, with the animals. There were rules about letting the dogs out of the kennels, for instance. And Rudolph had already thrown an almost full can of beer at one of the goats. Ginger had screamed at the impact and then watched sorrowfully as the poor beast limped off toward its companions, which had wisely sprinted for the far end of the property. John and Amelia had laughed—laughed!—at the poor goat limping away.

When Ginger's beloved cat, Peter, sprinted by, Rudolph had tried to snatch him up, saying he wanted to "feed it some beer," but Ginger came forward angrily and pushed at him, hollering, "Leave Peter alone!" and he had stood back with his arms raised in surrender.

"She's annoying," Amelia had said.

"It's cute," Rudolph had replied, and he grinned at Ginger as he said it, but it was not a nice grin. It was a grin filled with blunt white teeth and bulging, mocking eyes. The eyes of a wolf, Ginger thought. She hated Rudolph.

Ginger considered all of this as she raced to fetch her coat, as she thrust a hat on her head and even considered—and then abandoned—a pair of warm woolen gloves. Why had Amelia invited these two boys over? And which of them was her boyfriend, anyway? To both of them, Amelia was as indifferent as she was affectionate. It made little sense to Ginger. If she were Amelia, she would choose John. She would choose John in a heartbeat. And she would tell Rudolph to go home, please, and to take his crazy grin and stupid muscles with him. That's what she would say, if she were Amelia.

But it seemed to Ginger that she would never be Amelia: tall, pretty, independent and adult, flip and serene. She would forever be "Gentle Ginger," as her mother called her: dull, unimposing, soft-hearted, childish, and afraid. Boys at school liked girls in much the same way that these older boys liked Amelia, but they did not like Ginger. They made fun of her brown mop of curls ("Mushroom Head," they called her) and imitated her when she gazed out the window, lost in a reverie while the teacher repeatedly called out her name. But Amelia had been teased, too. Maybe she would grow up to be like Amelia, after all. This knowledge put a skip into Ginger's step.

But when she returned with her coat, the garden plot where she had left Amelia and her boyfriends was empty. Ginger looked around in alarm. She told herself not to panic. They couldn't have gone very far. And sure enough, there they were, heading for the dog pens. Ginger sprinted after them, calling out in warning, "We're not allowed over there. We'll get in trouble." They only laughed. Ginger pumped her short legs.

It seemed even as she raced toward them that she would never reach them, no matter how hard her legs pushed against the compact earth. Their bodies shrank. The ground stretched before her like a conveyer belt, so that Ginger ran in place, so that she ran backward, so that her sister and her sister's companions became no more than dark scrambling ants. From this great distance, Ginger's screams of protest meant nothing. The latches to all of the kennels were released. The dogs unfurled from their hovels and scattered in all directions, fast and random as smoke.

It was dark. Amelia had not bothered to put her to bed, the way the other babysitters always did, but instead gave her a large bottle of pop and allowed her to settle, exhausted, before the television set in the den. Ginger sat there for a good hour or so, pleased enough to sip her pop and watch heretofore-taboo programming, but before long the house became too dark and too still. Ginger began to feel awash in a gaping, raw sadness. Where had her sister gone? Where were the two boys? She could hear laughter from somewhere upstairs, but mostly it was quiet, and the quiet disturbed her more than the rude guffaws.

She floated through the house uncomfortably. None of the lights were on, and she wanted them to be on, but she felt that if she ignited them, something horrible would be illuminated, some ghost or monster, and so she left the world extinguished. Outside, the dogs howled. Eventually, after much shrieking, after much laughter and chasing, they'd been collected and returned to the kennels, but the wrong kennels, Ginger knew, although Amelia didn't seem to care. Ginger had felt terrified about her parents' reaction. They would come home and see the dogs in the wrong cages and the beer cans on the lawn and they would know that Amelia and Ginger had not followed orders, and they would be so very upset, and Ginger was on the verge of tears as she had explained this in earnest to her older sister.

"So what?" Amelia had said.

Ginger started. It had never before occurred to her to upset her parents just for the sake of upsetting them.

"Well," Ginger stammered. "Well, for one, they won't have you babysit me again."

"Geesh," Amelia said, rolling her eyes. "Bummer."

Ginger's shoulders drooped. John, seeing this, hurried to say, "Ouch. Harsh, Roebuck."

Amelia made a face, annoyed, but then gave her sister a pitying look. "Not because I don't like being with you, Kumquat. Just because"—she stopped here, struggling, looking up into the air as though surfacing from a deep river—"because they never ask me. Plus, you know, I'm busy now with school, most of the time, anyway. So it doesn't matter. It's no big deal."

John seemed to approve of this answer. He squeezed Amelia's shoulder, and she, in turn, caught his hand and kissed it.

So they are *together,* Ginger had thought. She was relieved that it was the one and not the other. They were lying on the lawn, relaxing after their frantic corralling of the animals. Amelia and John sat very close, but Rudolph was not far away—he lolled on his stomach quietly near the hydrangea, knotting one strand of grass at a time into tiny silken green loops. He seemed to have forgotten about them all. Ginger sat crossed-legged near her sister. She wished the boys would go away.

"I suppose we should go in," Amelia said, standing and stretching, catlike. The boys began to rise, too, as though sewn to her limbs like large shadows. Ginger, however, remained seated.

"I thought we would be alone tonight," Ginger said.

Amelia laughed. "Come inside. I'll give you some pop."

"It should be you and me."

"You wish, Kumquat," Rudolph said. His voice was sad, even if his grin was not. "I wished that, too."

"Huh," Amelia said, striding toward the house. "The crickets are whining."

The crickets *were* whining, but Ginger knew that wasn't what Amelia meant. She rose, reluctantly, and followed the older people into the house. Amelia handed her a pop bottle—her mom's diet pop, something her mom never let her drink—and also gave her the remote.

"You're in charge of this television," Amelia had instructed. "Don't leave its side."

And for much of the evening, she hadn't. But now where were they?

Ginger floated through the house, silently, fearfully. She didn't recognize this place. It was another planet unto itself, a sinister home in a parallel world. She stopped in front of the door to her room and considered entering. She could turn on her rainbow night-light and snuggle with her stuffed unicorn, Charlie. She considered going to sleep. When she woke up in the morning, her parents would be there. Her mother would come in to lower the blinds and shut the window, to keep the room from growing too bright. Barefoot, wearing only her loose cotton nightgown, she would stop by Ginger's bed, bend over, and kiss her. She would smell of perfume and coffee: sweet and bitter. The sun would be up. The light would burn away all of the strange corners and shadows. It was so very tempting to just go inside and lie down in her sheets and hold Charlie and sleep until everything was normal again.

Strange sounds came from her parents' bedroom.

What are they doing in there? Ginger wondered. They shouldn't be in there.

She went to her parents' door and pushed it open. She meant to go in and tell her sister, firmly this time, *You need to leave this room. This is not your room.* But when she entered, she was too confused. All three of them—her sister, John, and Rudolph—lay in the big brass bed. They were wrestling with one another, grunting and groaning, but also kissing and fondling. And Amelia was happy— happier than Ginger had ever seen her—squealing and giggling and thrashing while Rudolph chewed on her neck and John touched her legs. Ginger stood very still, watching this lewd horizontal dance. She lost her nerve. She could say nothing at all. And she thought how very angry Amelia would be if she did speak now, if she did say something. She wanted to back out of the room but was afraid that any movement would give her away.

And then Amelia sat up, her hair flying, her shirt pushed up, showing her lacy white bra. Her jeans, Ginger saw, were unbuttoned.

"GET OUT."

Ginger gave a little cry of fright and obeyed. She left the room; she fled down the stairs; she ran to the kennels. Panting, she eased the dogs out one by one. She restored them to the proper cages. She picked up the beer cans and the empty beer case and hid them all at the bottom of the giant trash barrel, beneath the more innocuous garbage sacks. She made sure everything was as it had once been. When she finished, she was so very tired that walking felt more like oozing. She returned to the house. She rinsed her glass in the sink and deposited the empty pop bottle in the trash bin. She went up the stairs. Her parents' bedroom was dead silent. In the sinister hallway, its white doorway seemed to vibrate with disease and taint. She hurried into her room. She shed her clothes, put on her pajamas. For a long, painful moment, she wished that she could brush her teeth, but it was too late now, her bravery had ended, and there was no returning to the outside of things. She poured herself into her bed. Safe now beneath the pastel covers, covers she'd chosen with her mother while on a shopping expedition at the Bon Marché, Ginger closed her eyes.

Mommy, she thought. *Come home.*

A knock came on her door, lightly. Amelia's voice, quiet, curious, then insistent, and then, perhaps believing her to be asleep, receding.

Mommy, Ginger thought again, shutting her eyes very tightly, filled with a worry that her mother would never return. She pictured a car wreck, her parents' tangled, ruined bodies. *Oh, no,* she thought, and she hugged Charlie tighter to her chest and prayed.

And then, suddenly, her mother was there, drawing the covers back from her face so that she could kiss Ginger's cheek. Ginger was half asleep, her mind throbbing, uncertain.

"You're home," Ginger murmured, closing her eyes again.

She had been dreaming about a baby born without a head or limbs, just a torso from which a million agitated eyes sprouted.

Her mother murmured, "Did you and Charlie have a nice time?"

"Oh, yes," Ginger said.

"Good, sweetie," her mom said. "The house looks great. We'll have to ask Amelia to come back again." She leaned over and kissed

Ginger once more, and then the stuffed unicorn, too. "Night night, Ginger. Night night, Charlie."

"Okay," Ginger said, "good night."

But just as her mom began to rise, Ginger grabbed for her hand and clutched it so fiercely that Vanessa, rattled, cried:

"Ginger! Let go! You're hurting me!"

1990

STORYBOOK

ELI WAS STRESSED. FOR THE LAST SEVERAL WEEKS HE HAD WORKED as one of the five parent chaperones for the Comstock High Purple Days' Float Committee. It was unusual for him to volunteer for such an event. The parade was the next day, and while Ginger gushed to her mom about how cool the float was going to be, Eli was anxious to finish. He practically yanked Ginger out of the house, gripping her coat sleeve.

"Let's hurry," he said. "There's not a lot of time."

Ginger followed him out to the car. "Gosh, Dad, don't worry. It's going to look great."

"I know," Eli said. "We'll see."

Eli did not speak again as he drove. Ginger chattered at him from the passenger seat, telling him random, unimportant things about her classmates. While Ginger spoke, Eli considered the work he had to complete: attaching the bear hide, rigging the wiring, standing the damn thing up on the float, hiding the speakers. The electrician would be there the following morning. Everything had to be ready to go.

He had assumed this would all be a cakewalk, but now he found himself more obsessed with the float than he was about Mr. Krantz's whereabouts.

When Eli and Ginger arrived, they found the floor of the Meekses' barn freshly littered with purple crepe paper, poultry netting, and metallic fringe. The lowboy trailer sat groaning beneath the clumsy bodies of some dozen teenagers. It was messily adorned and rocking slightly from the activity.

"Where'd they move him?" he asked his daughter, and she motioned toward a dim corner where a girl squatted with a paintbrush, slathering glue onto a large papier-mâché figure.

"Oh, no," Eli said, but Ginger had already left his side to join her friends on the lowboy trailer, taking up a plum-colored garland and arranging it around her neck. She greeted her friends enthusiastically. She was in her element here, popular among dorks. Eli was proud of her in a distant, appreciative sort of way.

Eli approached the girl with the paintbrush and stood over her with his hands on his hips.

"Hiya, Dr. Roebuck," the girl said, looking up. "How's it looking?"

"Like a bear with mange. His legs are all wrong."

"Really? I redid them like you said. Exactly. I swear." She rose to her feet and considered the thing with solemnity.

"You put them on backward," Eli said, pointing. "See? His knees buckle the wrong way."

"Doesn't he look tubular, though?" she said. Eli could not remember her name. Carol? Karen? Kathryn? "He's really scary."

Eli grabbed ahold of a papier-mâché leg and tore it from the torso. His hands came away smeared with glue.

"Hey!" the girl protested.

"Realign them," Eli said. "I'll help you."

Eli had already wasted an entire month on this project, but there was no way he was allowing a less-than-perfect replica of Mr. Krantz to float down the streets of Lilac City. This was his chance to share a realistic Sasquatch with the entire Inland Empire. It was, he felt, an enormous responsibility.

Comstock High had recently chosen the Sasquatch as its new mascot, in part due to Ginger's influence on the mascot steering committee. Ever since the coronation, Eli had winced at the cute renderings of the creature. While Ginger thought she was honoring her father's cause, Eli was silently offended by the presence of the doe-eyed, weak-shouldered, smiling monster who now adorned all school stationery, sweatshirts, and signage. The cuddly beast paid no homage to Mr. Krantz. It was a mockery.

And this purple nightmare of a float was the icing on the cake. Mauve foam balls hung from its broad front like blood-filled testicles.

But he would fix it. The Sasquatch would fix it. High school mediocrity be damned.

"The knees will bend the correct way," Eli said loudly, "or not at all."

Carol/Karen/Kathryn applauded enthusiastically.

Ginger looked over at him now and waved. He forced himself to smile, to wave back at her, and then he leaned over and dismantled the other leg.

Carol/Karen/Kathryn made a sad sound in her throat, but then she was ready to work. Eli took up the task from the opposite side, monitoring the accuracy of the reattachment as they progressed. Every now and again he caught a glimpse of another Purple Days chaperone drinking a pop or laughing with a student and he thought, *You ingrate. Have you no purpose?*

Ginger, for her part, had been elated when Eli volunteered as Purple Days Chaperone #5. He was normally too busy to get involved with school activities. Unlike other dads, he'd never been an assistant coach or a classroom helper or an escort for a dance. He had other, more pressing concerns to address: the smooth operation of his nonprofit, SNaRL, which he'd founded and funded entirely by himself; the setting of traps and cameras in dense forests as close by as Riverside State Park and as far away as Snoqualmie Pass and the Olympics; retrieving and carefully scanning said traps and cameras; the research of purported sightings throughout the Northwest; the calculation and disbursement of funds received; the chemical analysis of purported evidence; the grueling editing process for his first book, *The Sasquatch Hunter's Almanac*, which Vanessa had ghostwritten (this, in itself, had been a difficult process— she had a tendency to write too floridly, so brutal editing was a necessity). Sometimes he went a week or two without seeing Ginger at all. He made every effort to at least arrive home in time to say good night but frequently failed. He was very busy. And, frankly, he liked it that way.

But for this—a citywide festival showcasing a mascot that embodied his life's work—Eli cleared his schedule. He planned on making sure that an anatomically correct version of Mr. Krantz rode the Purple Days float alongside this year's Comstock High Purple Days princess. The creature would be robotic, its movements on the float realistic and powerful. He hoped to educate all of Lilac City, to give them reason to respect, admire, and possibly even fear the presence of Sasquatch in their region. It was an added pleasure, too, to see how happy it made Ginger.

It was not, however, going according to plan.

Backward knees were just part of the problem.

The students meant well, Eli granted, but they had no respect for anatomical verisimilitude. They were more interested in flirting with one another, in reciting ribald jokes, in goofing around. They followed directions halfheartedly, expressing interest but growing insipid the moment he turned his back. The Comstock princess, a pretty if whiny senior named Lindsay Meeks, was a particular thorn in Eli's side. She worried that such a huge structure would overpower her. She worried that one of the papier-mâché arms would fall off and brain her. She worried that it would appear to the crowd as if she were getting humped from behind. She worried about everything.

Lindsay approached Eli now, massaging her hands together as though for warmth, wearing, as always, the glittering brass tiara on her head.

"I wanted to talk to you, Mr. Roebuck," she said in response to Eli's distracted hello. Eli had to stop himself from correcting her: *That's Dr. Roebuck to you, young lady.* "I don't know if you've noticed, but I'm *petite.*" She twirled for him, her pale skirt fluttering prettily as she did so. She gracefully rested on point and gestured at the giant papier-mâché ape. It lay facedown, hovering above its newly detached legs. "Look at this dude! He's a freak. You can't have some giant ugly freak standing behind me, you know? I'm *petite,* Mr. Roebuck. He'll dwarf me."

"He'll contrast you," Eli said. He appealed to the girl's vanity. "He'll make you more beautiful by comparison."

The princess seemed not to hear him. She anxiously masticated her bubble gum. "This is my float," she said. "It's my float, being made in my parents' barn. I mean, why have Bigfoot on the float at all? I mean, what's the deal-ee-o, Mr. R?"

"It's the school's float," Eli reminded her. "This Sasquatch here is the school mascot, representing the whole student body."

"What if we made it, like, two feet tall?" Lindsay suggested. "Like a cute little baby guy?"

"That would be really cute," Carol/Karen/Kathryn cooed.

"He could be holding a baby bottle," Lindsay said excitedly. "He could be in a sweet little Bigfoot diaper."

Carol/Karen/Kathryn squealed in delight.

Eli took a deep breath. "Our Sasquatch," he said, "is precisely seven feet five inches tall." He rose up to his knees, his hands on his thighs, and addressed Lindsay in a scholarly way. "This is a modest size for such a creature, Lindsay. Some hominids have been estimated at over twelve feet."

"God, I can so see it," she said, opening her palms before her, framing the lowboy trailer. "A tiny Bigfoot baby, right at my knees maybe, and everybody in the crowd saying, *Aw, isn't that so totally precious! They'd* be like, *Cutest little monster, EVER.*"

Carol/Karen/Kathryn cried out, "Yes!" She was clearly in love with the prettier, more confident senior.

"Pay attention to those gluteal muscles," Eli said to the younger girl, struggling to remain patient. "You're spacing them too far apart."

Carol/Karen/Kathryn flushed, bending back over the mascot's butt, working the crumpled newspaper into a more accurate position.

"It's getting late," Eli said now. "We'll finish up our work here, and then we can place him on the float."

"That's what I'm *saying,*" Lindsay said. "We could totally bust out a mini-Bigfoot. It'd be so much *faster.*"

"Linds," a voice said. "Linds. Leave the doctor alone. He's trying to work."

Eli turned and saw the girl's mother, a mannish middle-aged woman. She wore loose flannel pajamas and slippers shaped like fuzzy pink bear paws. She was smoking. They looked hardly at all alike, the one masculine and brooding, the other petite and bubbly, but they shared the same snapping eyes and the same defiant posture.

"I'm talking to Mr. Roebuck here about *ideas,*" the girl whined, but her mother persisted.

"Leave Dr. Roebuck alone. Go along to your friends."

Lindsay gave up and moved away, toward Ginger and the others, dragging her feet.

"God. These girls of mine. I swear. So perfect. Go *fuck up* once in a while, you know? Stop succeeding! It isn't healthy to be flawless at everything you do." She nodded toward Ginger and the tall boy who stood speaking together. "Your girl is nice. She's a sweet girl."

Eli agreed. There was not much else to say about Ginger. She was plain-looking—far from ugly, but not pointedly beautiful.

"You happily married?" the woman asked him then.

"Yes," he said. "Sure."

"Well, you know. I'm not. My husband hates me. They all hate me, in one way or another." She laughed at this, as if it were hilarious.

"I'm sorry to hear that," Eli said. He was amused by her frankness. "Maybe you could leave him?"

"I could. But I'm in love. And love makes us stupid. I'm just waiting for the other shoe to drop."

"That sounds painful."

"It's easy enough." The woman tossed her cigarette on the floor and ground it into the shit-strewn floorboards with the toe of a pink bear slipper. "I remember your first wife," she said.

He remembered then: This woman's eldest daughter had attended school with Amelia. "Gladys," he said.

"You hated her guts," the woman observed.

"It wasn't as extreme as that."

"She was an odd bird, Gladys," the woman said. "I remember that about her. Really odd. The scarred head and stuff."

"Well. You know. She's not well, my ex. Not well in the head, I mean. She has some mental issues."

"So you left her," the woman summarized, her tone disinterested.

"I fell in love with someone else."

There wasn't much else to say about it, but the woman stared at him, shifting her weight from one bear slipper to the other. The shine in her look made him slightly uncomfortable, so Eli turned back to the Sasquatch model. The legs were much shapelier now and were, at the very least, fastened to the torso correctly.

"Good job, partner," Eli said to Carol/Karen/Kathryn, and she beamed.

"Well," Lindsay's mom said. "Anyway. Thanks for the conversation. Sorry to chat your ear off."

He accepted her heavy, warm hand and shook it. "Pleasure to chat with you."

"Good luck with the monster," she said as she walked away.

"Hominid," Eli corrected under his breath.

"God," Carol/Karen/Kathryn said, "Lindsay's mom is *so weird.*"

"We're all weird," Eli said, and it struck him as a wise and accepting thing to tell a child.

ON THE DRIVE home, Ginger asked him how it was going.

"It's better," he said. "Tomorrow looks good. We'll wire the dummy for ambulation. Anyway, the legs are accurate now, so his gait will be pretty realistic."

"You mean he'll be walking on the float?"

"Well, lifting his legs up and down. Swinging his arms. Walking in place, yes. I hope."

"Does Lindsay know this?" Ginger asked.

"Sure," he lied. "Does it matter?"

"It's just," Ginger said, "Lindsay's wanted to be Comstock princess her whole life, and, you know, she's supposed to be the centerpiece of the float. So if you're making this giant, moving monster—"

"Sasquatch are not monsters, sweetie," Eli reminded her. "They're hominid. Or hominin, even."

"Right, Dad, I know. The humanoid or whatever, got it."

"Hominid. From great apes. Or hominin. Meaning directly related to us. The debate—"

"My point is, Dad, you can't just put a giant moving humanoid up there behind Lindsay and expect people to think it's great. Lilac City loves its Comstock princess. She—not the monster—should be the center of attention."

"Hominid," Eli said. "I get what you're saying, Ginger, but we're talking about representing the entire Comstock High student body here. We're talking about respecting the natural identity of the Comstock High mascot. Lindsay is just a girl, a girl who wins things."

"The Comstock princess represents the student body, too."

"My impression of Lindsay is that she doesn't care at all about the student body. My impression is that she only cares about how pretty and popular she is."

"She's really, really nice," Ginger said, her voice growing nasal and annoyed. "She's like the nicest cool girl there is. That's why she won, why we all voted for her. 'Cause she says hi to us in the hallway and partners up with us in class. She's nice, Dad. She's not a mean girl like some of her friends."

He hated hearing Ginger speak this way. "I think you're just as pretty as she is, Ginger," Eli said to her, and he meant it. "You have a warmer beauty. She's like an ice queen. And she's too skinny. Guys like a little flesh."

"I think it's a good idea. The mini-monster thing. Instead of the big guy."

"Mini-hominid," Eli said, taking a turn too quickly. "She told you about her three-foot-tall Sasquatch idea?"

"She told everyone, Dad, and we all think it's a great idea."

"'We all'? 'We all' who?"

"You know. Me. Gary. The entire float committee."

"Is Gary the tall kid with the baseball cap?"

Ginger's face and neck blotched at the question.

"You like him," Eli said, steering onto their street now, "and I think that's great. He looks like a nice kid."

Ginger put her face in her hands. "Ack. Kill me now."

"But I agreed to help with the float committee on one condition," Eli continued, "and that was to create a fully functioning hominid/hominin model based on my research of Northwest Sasquatch."

"But, Dad—" Ginger protested weakly.

"That was my condition, Ginger," Eli said firmly, pulling on the parking brake and shutting off the ignition.

He turned to Ginger and put a hand on her left shoulder. She smiled at him for a moment and then pulled away, up and out of the car. He was glad to see that she wasn't mad at him, not really.

THE NEXT DAY was a Saturday. The parade was taking place later in the evening, so they had a full day to wire and affix the Sasquatch model to the lowboy trailer.

Eli shook Ginger awake at dawn and urged her to dress quickly. Once they were in his car, Eli offered her a bagel and a box of apple juice, as he would when she was a little girl. She accepted the food sleepily and leaned her head against the window. She wore shorts and purple high-tops and a roomy navy sweatshirt. She had matured faster than Amelia, had large breasts and a thicker waist. She looked entirely like a grown woman. This made Eli a little sad.

"Why are we up so *early*?" Ginger asked, sucking on her juice box.

"I need to stop by the office first," Eli said, and Ginger groaned.

"Couldn't you have woken me up *after*?"

"This saves time," he said. "Besides, you used to love coming to the office with me."

"Yeah, Dad, like, when I was six."

Her grumpiness rang false to Eli. He knew she was delighted with the time they were spending together. Eli relaxed his balding head comfortably against the headrest, stretching his forearms with his palms flat against the steering wheel. He spent so much of his time in solitude that it always surprised him when he enjoyed the company of others. Ginger's company was both unobtrusive and pleasant. Ginger was unlike any of the other women in his life: She asked little to nothing of him, accepted him simply for what he was.

But then she said, "Lindsay'll look beautiful in her gown today."

For a brief moment he saw Lindsay as Ginger saw her: the rightful heir, the rare and justified blessed, the effortless girl who Ginger admired from afar, beautiful and confident and excellent.

Ginger had once glorified Amelia this way and perhaps still did.

He made a face. "Those dresses always look like overworked wedding cakes."

To his relief, Ginger laughed. She wasn't taking the whole business *too* seriously, then. *Good,* Eli thought.

"You know something?" he said. "You'll probably have more fun than Lindsay. A kid like that—it's a lot of pressure. And you're good at so many things and involved in so many things. I'm proud of you, Ginger. I don't ever tell you that, but I am. I'm proud of you. Your mom and I both."

Ginger watched him from her side of the seat with large pretty cow eyes, her mouth slightly ajar, looking half amused and half flattered. She took a big bite of her bagel. It left a giant white smear across one cheek, which she made worse with a swipe of her wrist.

"Napkins?" she asked, and Eli shook his head.

Ginger took another bite of her bagel, chewed, and swallowed loudly as Eli parked the car at the SNaRL office.

"I'm not jealous of her, Dad."

He said, "Good," and set the parking brake.

"I mean, it would be cool," she said, "to wear that dress and wave to everyone and have everyone tell you all the time how great you are, but mostly it sounds boring."

"Exactly," he said, but he felt sorrowful then.

Eli knew he struggled with fatherhood. He wondered if it would have been different if he'd had boys. Boys could be mischievous and violent, but girls were vituperative, emotionally sensitive. It was always a shock to him when Amelia battled him on some misunderstood slight, or when Ginger suddenly burst into tears, hurt beyond reason over something so meaningless as a raised eyebrow. Sometimes he thought it was because women were so much smarter than men, more aware of implied meaning. Other times he thought it was because they were a little vain and a little crazy, all to varying degrees.

Not that he wasn't a little vain. Not that he wasn't a little crazy.

They stood together now in the SNaRL office, the lamps overhead flickering into fluorescence. For the office, Eli had rented a
small space in downtown Lilac City. It was the first floor of a his-
toric brick building that faced the riverfront. It had no windows,
only squat walls and ceilings. Despite the lovely view outside, its
interior was no more than a tidy cement box.

Eli had an elaborate filing system, a maniacally organized desk.
A chalkboard, recently washed to a black shine, covered the west
wall, and sturdy metal shelves lined the eastern wall. The shelves
bore the small but convincing evidence gleaned from Eli's most
successful fieldwork: a few foot molds from noted tracks, a narrow
card box containing envelopes of scant hair samples, two or three
vials of soil containing urine deposits, a glass jar of dried, loose
scat. Cabinets on the southern wall held paperwork from the region's
many sightings. Eli carefully documented each call or letter he
received, no matter how ludicrous. He approached every observation with a scientific mind-set, grinding into the smallest of details.
It was true that a few of the sightings were reported by maniacs or
attention-seekers, but most of them were from sincere, hardworking types who were baffled by their own encounters with the thing.
For example: an ophthalmologist who happened to see Bigfoot walk
out of a dilapidated, abandoned house from the forest-facing window of his clinic; a beautician living on the nearby Spokane Indian
Reservation, a self-described "very sane mother of five," who came
across a swaybacked hairy ape bathing itself one early morning in
Mathews Lake. Her oldest daughter, a straight-A junior-high student, was also there. The girl screamed so loudly that the creature
bucked and howled back at them menacingly before fleeing into the
forest. And then there was Eli. He, too, had seen the massive beast.

Sometimes, on the phone, the observer would begin by apologizing, stuttering, "I sound crazy, but I know what I saw. No one
believes me. My friends, my family. They say I'm nuts."

Eli always forced himself to remain distant, but what he wanted to tell them was, *I understand. Believe me, I understand. You can rely on me. We'll find him. We'll find Mr. Krantz together.*

How funny that would be. What silence he would hear on the other end of the line. God, an admission like that would terrify them. No doubt they would just hang up.

So he spoke to them calmly, asking only for a simple, detailed report, no apologies necessary, and they were comforted by his disinterest and professionalism.

The randomness of it all was disheartening at first. When he founded SNaRL, he had expected to narrow in on Mr. Krantz's exact location quickly, but the locations of the sightings varied greatly, from the Olympics to the Sawtooths to a highway sighting near Miles City, Montana.

Mr. Krantz could be anywhere.

After a few years, however, the ubiquity of these creatures made Eli happy. Did it even really matter anymore whether it was Mr. Krantz he found or some other ancient wood ape? Wouldn't humanity benefit, regardless? And wasn't that a good thing, that the heartbreak of his childhood had led to this interesting career, strange though it might be?

Why, he should be grateful to Mr. Krantz!

After all, one did not simply happen upon Sasquatch research. Cryptozoology was an inspired profession, if not a practical one.

And he believed this would be his legacy. He would better the world and make his family proud. It pleased him to think of it this way. He was doing this for his daughters.

He stood with Ginger now, his hand resting lightly between her shoulder blades as they took in the small, clean space.

"It smells the same in here," Ginger said. She was smiling. "It reminds me of childhood."

He went to the sturdy safe beneath his wide clean desk.

"What's the combination?" she asked as he toyed with the lock, scrolling from one number to the next.

"Amelia's birthday," he said.

"Aw," Ginger said, splayed out now in Eli's revolving office chair. "That's sweet. You should tell her that. She'd like that."

He didn't reply. Amelia required constant proof of his love. The most he could do was just stay patient. One day, he believed, she would understand everything: why he'd divorced Gladys, why he'd married Vanessa, why they'd shared a daughter together. (And, really, didn't she realize that Ginger's conception wasn't exactly planned? That it wasn't about replacing anyone?) It was illogical, Amelia's neediness. He should not have to explain his love. It was not a scientific phenomenon, although Amelia treated it like one.

"Hello, buddy," he said, opening the safe and taking out the precious metatarsus.

"It's a man's bone," the scientist had told him over the phone, almost a decade ago now, and Eli's heart had sunk. But then, after a slight hesitation, the scientist had continued, "Mostly, anyway, it's a man's bone. But some things don't quite match up, genetically speaking. This could be for a few reasons. Contamination, maybe, in my lab, or . . . I don't mean to sound spooky here. It's either from a man's foot or the foot of something very recently related to man."

"You mean there's evidence of interspecies mingling," Eli said. He thought of Agnes and Mr. Krantz's odd coupling. Maybe Mr. Krantz's own mother had been human. Or his father. Perhaps therein lay the attraction to Agnes.

"Yeah, sure," the man said. "Like an ape mom or grandma or something. Some men are real perverts! It's a possibility, genetically speaking."

He heard the scientist doubting himself on the other end of the line. Eli appreciated the seismic shift this nerdy lab rat was undergoing: A notion this rational man had never, ever believed suddenly seemed a distinct possibility.

"I don't know," the lab rat had said. "Maybe my interns fucked it up. My advice? You should get it tested again in a bigger lab."

But Eli was content enough after that conversation. Someone from the lab leaked the story to the local press, and a small collection of national papers took up the headline. The story sparked additional funding and international attention. Phone calls and letters arrived at SNaRL from around the globe, reporting their own hominid sightings. Eli enjoyed a healthy, skeptical fame. *This is it,* he thought. *The beginning.* He was financially comfortable again. He let his podiatry license lapse.

Through it all, he remained a thorough scientist. He meant to have the bone retested, but then in the mid-eighties the police came and took the metatarsus away from him, arguing that maybe it was the bone of a missing and/or murdered person. Their forensics department examined the bone and came away slightly baffled but convinced, in the end, that it was from a man's foot, after all, although there was no John or Jane Doe with a missing appendage. Eli threatened to take them to court to get the metatarsus back, and eventually, bored and indifferent, the police chief brought it to the SNaRL office himself.

"Bigfoot, eh?" he had said, offering the bone to Eli as if it were a large pen. Eli frowned as he accepted the metatarsus, noting that someone had written on it with permanent marker. He didn't like the police chief. He hated the word *Bigfoot.* The police chief grinned and said, "Thought I saw Bigfoot this morning, on my front porch. Huge, hairy. Had this big, fat back."

Eli looked up at the man, interested.

"Don't get your panties in a bunch, Doc. It was just my wife!" The man had roared at his own joke and Eli had turned away from him, his face flushing with disgust.

"Enjoy your fifteen minutes," the police chief had said, and slapped him so hard on the back that it stung. "Adios, Doc."

"Thanks," Eli had said calmly, but he wished he had the manliness to spit in the police chief's eye.

"Why are we taking the bone?" Ginger asked now as they drove toward Lindsay's barn.

"Final touch," Eli said. He looked out over the blackened fields, recently torched after the last straw harvest.

Ginger was looking in the same direction, at the scorched fields and at the rolling Palouse farmland beyond. "Beautiful," Ginger said, and Eli thought not of the landscape but of his Sasquatch model, and he agreed.

LINDSAY'S BARN WAS light-dappled, the dust swirling lazily through the air like flecks of gold paint. Lindsay's mother sat in an Adirondack chair on her back porch, facing the barn, smoking and drinking coffee, and she waved to them as they drove up the gravel road.

"Early start?" she called.

"Hope it's all right," Eli said as they exited the car. "Lots to do today."

"Don't I know it. Linds is showering. Has an appointment at the hair parlor at eight. Then the decorum coach comes to teach her the proper wave. What's that you got there?"

Eli looked at the metatarsus in his hand. He gripped it like a knife. It was white and pale and long. "Just something for the float," he said.

"It's the foot bone," Ginger announced, and the woman's eyes lit up.

Everyone knew about the bone. It was a source of pride in Lilac City.

Lindsay's dad stepped out onto the porch, his own steaming cup of coffee in his hands. Lindsay's mom said something inaudible to him, and he glanced up at Eli and Ginger and then strode toward them, spilling a trail of coffee onto his jeans and moccasins.

"The famous foot bone," he said. "You don't say!"

He stopped before Eli and thrust out his hand. "Joe Meeks," he said. "Pleasure."

He crushed Eli's small, nimble hand in his own, so that Eli winced from the pain.

Joe Meeks peered at the metatarsus. "What's she made of? Plaster?"

Eli was appalled.

Ginger said, "It's made of bone."

"Real bone? Must have cost a pretty penny, I'll bet."

"He found it. In the forest. It was in a bear trap."

"Bullshit," Meeks said, and then whistled. "Must be fun, huh? Cryptozoology? That's what they call it, right? You know what I do for a living, Mr. Roebuck?"

Eli was unsure, and he said so.

"I'm a banker. I work for Inland Empire Bank. Shiny glass building on Riverside? You've seen it."

Eli said that he had.

"Top floor. View of everything in the world from there. The whole valley, the river. Gorgeous." He took a sip from his mug of coffee, balling up his free hand against his hip. "Not that I get to enjoy the view. Too busy. Hunkered over the desk all day. I forget to look up!" He shook his head. "It's a busy gig, but I like it."

"Wonderful," Eli said. "Now, I hate to leave you, but if you'll excuse me . . ."

Ginger slipped away into the barn, heading for the lowboy trailer.

"Next week is vacation," Meeks said, not taking the hint and following Eli companionably into the barn, "and I'll be hunting just outside Pend Oreille. Last year I took down the prettiest stag, you wouldn't believe. I've hiked all over those hills."

"It's beautiful country," Eli said.

"And would you guess what I've seen in the forest? I mean, talking Bigfoot and all?"

Eli was silent, concentrating on aligning the bone to the bottom of the right foot. He muttered to himself about how perfectly it fit. He had calculated all of it so very beautifully. It would be the final touch, to have the famous bone as a part of the re-creation. It would give his Sasquatch an air of reality that Eli knew could not be faked. He would be very careful of it, to ensure that it was not damaged. He would ride with the model to the parade, keeping his hand on the real bone until the parade began. He would be there when the parade finished, to slide the metatarsus free again and return it to its secure location in his lab. And, in the meantime, the crowd would look on his Sasquatch and feel how very correctly rendered it was. They would be moved. It was the closest Eli had ever come to being superstitious.

"I've seen nothing," the man said. "Absolutely nothing. Not a trace of anything. I mean, I've come across deer carcasses. I've seen a mountain lion, even. I find elk antlers everywhere. Decorated my entire den with them. But there is not a single damn trace of any giant hairy monster like Bigfoot. And, believe me, if anyone were to see one, it would be me."

Eli checked his watch. The electrician would be arriving at nine to wire the Sasquatch to the float.

"I mean, wouldn't someone have shot one by now? Or hit one with a car? Wouldn't a guy like me have come across a dead Bigfoot in the forest and thought, *What the hell,* and phoned for help?"

Eli hated wasting his time on ignorant questions like this. He ignored Meeks as best as he could. He could see Lindsay's personality in her father, and it amplified his dislike.

Some students had wrestled the model onto the float the night before and now Eli jumped aboard to get a good grip on the head, to arrange it on the highest platform at the back.

Eli hoisted the thing to its feet, and Meeks scurried onto the float to help him.

When finished, they both stood back, looking admiringly at the giant brown beast.

"Looks great, Doc," Meeks said. "Real cute."

Eli wiped his face clean with the handkerchief in his pocket and then polished his glasses. He squared his shoulders at Meeks.

"With all due respect, Mr. Meeks, I'd like to address your concerns here as straightforwardly as I can."

"Please," Joe Meeks said, his insincere face puckering.

"Have you ever hit an animal with your car?" he asked.

"Yes. A few."

"Deer, I imagine?"

"Yes. A dog once."

"And when you drive down the road and see roadkill, what species is it, typically speaking?"

"Deer, usually."

"Stupid animals, deer," Eli said. "Poor things. They are also as plentiful as mice in this area. Really, almost like an overgrown varmint. Pretty, at least."

Meeks was silent.

"Have you ever hit a mountain lion with your car?"

"No."

"Have you ever aimed your gun at and shot a mountain lion?"

"No. Things are damn fast."

"Have you ever seen a mountain lion in the wild?"

"Well, like I said, yes, I saw one up at Priest Lake, hunting elk."

"And how long did it linger in your field of vision?"

Meeks stared at him, confused.

"I mean, did it stay there for a good few minutes? Did it sashay in front of you, posing?"

"Well, no, it was just a moment's sighting. I told you, they're damn fast, those cats, and rare."

"And, Mr. Meeks," Eli continued, "when you walk through the woods, do you stumble frequently over the bodies of deceased animals? Mountain lions, deer, elk? Anything?"

"No. Not frequently. I've seen a deer carcass, I guess. Once. I'm not sure—"

"And why do you think that is, Mr. Meeks? Is it because animals have never lived there? Is it because they have never died?"

Mr. Meeks made a show of returning to his coffee mug, of feigning amusement. "I can't wait to hear your conclusions here, Doc."

"Do you know what it means to biodegrade?"

Meeks scoffed, "Come on. Sure I do."

"Do you know how many mountain lions exist in the continental United States, Mr. Meeks?"

"A lot, I suppose."

"Yes, a lot, relatively speaking. Between twenty thousand and thirty thousand or so. Quite a few. Comparatively, do you know how many of these fellows, these hominids, are alive and thriving? Just an estimate?" Eli touched the belly of his Sasquatch. "And, to make it fair, let's include Canada and Alaska in this, as well."

Meeks laughed. "God only knows."

"My own personal estimates suggest between one thousand and five thousand hominids in all of North America."

Meeks's brow furrowed as he crunched numbers in his squid-like banker's head.

"All of your proof of the Sasquatch's nonexistence, then, is irrelevant. Bigfoot, as you so insultingly call him, is far more elusive than your average mountain lion and far more intelligent. Like other living and dying forest animals, he biodegrades quickly. He is not part of a dumb, overpopulating species like deer, who are too stupid to avoid our loud, bright roadways. His observability is practically nil. And yet he has a long-standing presence in North America. The country's original inhabitants made numerous sightings of him, long before the first white person ever walked here. There are numerous sightings even now. Eagle Scouts have seen him, doctors, Christians, atheists, scientists. And, yes, also the insane, the mistaken. You have not seen him, Mr. Meeks, but I have. I am, unlike you, a man with a medical degree and an illustrious academic career. I have seen him and have been trying to see him again ever since."

Meeks looked very small before Eli, a bug he could squash.

"You have a relationship with money and have built a career on it," Eli said, "but your money is more of a human fabrication than my Sasquatch. So, please, let me get on with my work."

Meeks swallowed more coffee. The barn had turned sour in the morning light, the manure warmed and stinking. The old boards on the walls were gray and splitting. Outside, Lindsay Meeks skipped to her mother's car, ready to visit the hair parlor and emerge as her own imagined thing: a beloved princess.

"Tonight is the parade," Eli said, turning away from Meeks. "I have a lot more to do."

Behind him, Ginger squealed. A few of her friends had arrived, and they swarmed together and began giggling and whispering. The tall kid, Gary, arrived, too, and Ginger kept her distance from him, coyly, Eli felt.

"Well, no one's going to argue with your intelligence, Roebuck," Meeks said. "But, you know, it doesn't mean you're not living in a storybook."

Eli shrugged. Men like Joe Meeks would never understand. They believed only what they were told in school: Everything has already been discovered; humanity is progressing fluidly; inequality and injustice are relics of the past.

The whole world is fragile, Eli thought then, and the barn became poignant with his daughter's laugh and the childish gluey smell of the Sasquatch.

Eventually, the electrician arrived to wire the Sasquatch for movement and sound. The beast could now kick out his very real-looking bony foot (with the metatarsus displayed front and center in it, settled delicately between two fiberglass bones, which were then attached to the stiff papier-mâché ankle) and raise his wide, long arms high into the air.

Ginger came and stood beside them as they played with the motions.

"He's going to kick Lindsay."

"No," Eli argued, "not if she stands right here, at the edge of her platform."

"Is he still going to howl?"

The electrician affixed a wire, and the paper-fanged mouth opened. Out came a soft, kitten-like meow.

Ginger and her friends laughed.

"What a pussy!" Ginger's would-be boyfriend quipped, and more people laughed.

This was his daughter's crush? A foulmouthed disrespectful turd?

"Gears are too loose, man," the electrician said, chuckling. He seemed annoyingly unconcerned. "Speeds it up. Twists the tape, too. Makes it sound like Alvin and the Chipmunks."

The Sasquatch flung up his arms and meowed.

"Fix it," Eli said.

The electrician tinkered with the simple gears in the Sasquatch's back, and then he ejected the cassette and laughed at the tangle of tape that exploded from the open deck.

A few purple-coated festival officials, known as the Purple Sleeves, arrived in a lavender limousine. The limousine would drive the princess to the parade and follow the float after she boarded it. The Purple Sleeves wandered into the barn. They were a few old men and a middle-aged woman; all of them sported lavender fezzes. They reminded Eli of performing monkeys.

The most ancient of the Purple Sleeves hobbled over to Eli and squinted up at the Sasquatch.

"Those arms are too high," he said. "There's a parade code, mister. No float over twenty feet."

The Sasquatch lowered its arms as the electrician worked on the gears.

Eli frowned. Why had no one told him the size requirements?

"It's only when he raises his arms," Eli told the Purple Sleeves, and, as if listening, the Sasquatch shot his arms skyward again, meowing.

"Shoot," said the electrician. "Now I have to unwind the tape again."

"So keep the arms down," the old man said, and the group of small, elderly Purple Sleeves squinted at Eli like so many angry raisins. "We don't want anyone getting hurt. Or scared. This is a family-friendly event."

"It's a *Christian* event," the middle-aged woman said. "It's a celebration of God and country."

Eli said, "I thought it was a celebration of Lilac City."

The Purple Sleeves exchanged concerned looks. "Yes, it is," the woman said, fingering a gold cross at her neck. "It's about God, country, city."

"And our public schools," Eli said.

The woman pointed at the Sasquatch model. "He's about as demonic as we allow," she said.

"Kids love monsters," Joe Meeks said, stepping up behind them with a fresh cup of coffee. "It'll scare the pants off of them."

The Sasquatch lowered its arms with a weak meow.

"Maybe not," Meeks chuckled.

Eli regarded his Sasquatch desperately. He wanted it to make an impression that Lilac City would never forget. And not the wrong impression, not a silly impression, but an intimidating one, one that would make all of the soccer moms and tennis dads quake in their sneakers.

But then the truck arrived, backing up to the lowboy trailer, and Eli, frustrated, realized that he would have to send an imperfect Sasquatch out into the world.

"I'll get it, old man," the electrician said lazily. "I'll get it. Just wait."

Lindsay bounded up to him, hair shellacked into a slick bulb atop her head, all excitement today, no regrets. "He looks neat-o, Mr. Roebuck—I mean, Dr. Roebuck! I'm happy to share the float with him today!"

Despite Lindsay's well-intentioned enthusiasm, Eli was annoyed. His shoes, he noticed, were dusty from the filthy floor of the barn, and he had a sudden urge to find a hose and wash them clean.

The electrician, bent over the wires, cussed approvingly and then rocked back onto his heels. "There ya go. All better."

The Sasquatch raised his arms again, slowly this time, powerfully. He bellowed a loud, terrifying roar.

Lindsay Meeks screamed and thrust her palms over her ears. The Purple Sleeves glared at Eli.

Eli pulled out his wallet and handed the grinning electrician a crisp one-hundred-dollar bill.

ELI AND GINGER were walking down Riverside Avenue now, threading their way through the thickening crowd. People sat in lawn chairs brought from home or reclined on hastily thrown picnic blankets. The whole area was tense as people bucked against one another for space.

Eli had left the Sasquatch's side only when forced to go by the Purple Sleeves. He tried to argue for the protection of the metatarsus, but they ushered him away, telling him, "It's fine, it's fine. We'll take care of it. Don't worry. High schoolers only now, mister."

He had refused to budge until Gary and Carol/Karen/Kathryn offered to stay right there with it until the float began to move.

"Okay," he'd said, taking a breath. "Okay."

He had then allowed Ginger to pull him away.

"There's Mom," Ginger said now, waving. Vanessa was waiting for them beside the library entrance, their agreed-upon rendezvous. "And, look, there's Amelia."

Eli saw Amelia with her fiancé, Jim. Jim had his hand protectively on her back, and they stood close together. It always looked as though they were about to make love or as if they'd just finished. It made Eli uncomfortable.

Jim, seeing them, came forward and offered his hand to Eli. "Good to see you, sir!" he said.

"Yes, yes," said Eli distractedly. "You, too."

The parade began. There were nearly two hundred participants in the lineup: the library, the fire department, all of the Lilac City schools (private and public), square-dancing societies, gardening clubs, various military orders, car dealerships, rodeo queens; there was even, oddly enough, a limousine-fan-club entry, which Eli found ridiculous, although he supposed they entertained the little children. His own float, carrying the princess and the Sasquatch, would be situated near the end. It could be hours before the float made its way to them. Eli eyeballed the crowd impatiently.

Ginger was chatting excitedly with her older sister, and Amelia cocked her head, half-listening.

"Can we find a place to sit?" Amelia said, speaking with the same tempered, impatient disdain she always seemed to use with them.

"Yes," Eli said. "Yes. Good idea."

Amelia took the lead. She found a small, cramped corner of pavement and claimed it. "Will you be all right standing, Dad?" she asked Eli. "Jim brought some chairs for you and Vanessa." She turned to Jim. "Get the chairs, Jim."

"Sure thing, babe. You'll be right here?" he asked, and Amelia said yes.

"I don't need a chair," Eli said, but Jim had already disappeared into the crowd.

"Might as well get comfortable, Dad," Amelia said. "We'll be here a long time."

A marching band thundered past, followed by a group of pretty horses, the largest of which took a dump not far from where the Roebuck family stood. A clown raced up to the steaming pile and shoveled it quickly away. The procession continued slowly. The

crowd cheered and grinned and twilight fell. Eli considered the
other floats: None of them were as impressive as the Comstock
High float.

"Our float's the best one, huh, Ginger?" Eli said to his younger
daughter.

"Guess so," she said. She was scanning the crowd, no doubt
seeking her friends.

Jim had returned with two chairs and a blanket and cooler. He
unfolded the chairs, and Eli did his best to avoid sitting in one but
finally decided it wasn't worth the struggle. Besides, he didn't want
to insult Amelia. He lowered himself into the chair and unwittingly
groaned—his knees had been hot to the touch from standing, his
arthritis kicking in, and sitting down was nearly orgasmic.

"You okay?" Amelia asked him, and he thought he saw judg-
ment on her face.

"Yes, sweetheart. I'm great."

"Thank you for these chairs, Jim," Vanessa said, happily seated,
opening a Coke from the cooler. "So thoughtful of you."

He saw Amelia roll her eyes. She thought Vanessa was a cornball.

If Vanessa noticed the eye roll, she did her best to hide it. She
reached over and pressed Eli's hand. "Isn't this fun?" she shouted,
and Eli, for her sake, agreed, but he was tired. He removed his
spectacles and cleaned them with his neatly folded handkerchief.
When he reset them on his nose, he could see that the streetlamps
were igniting, one at a time. Soon it would be dark.

"One seventy-five, Dad!" Ginger shouted, pointing to the num-
bered placard that was pinned to the front of a bright-green float.
"Five more to go!"

Then her friends arrived, one of them the tall kid, Gary, one of
them Carol/Karen/Kathryn, who Ginger enthusiastically introduced to her sister (Carol/Karen/Kathryn's real name, it turned
out, was Margot). It was not hard to see how proud Ginger was of

stylish, beautiful Amelia. Amelia accepted the introduction serenely, as if she understood that she was a treasure to be shared.

It made Eli happy for his daughters that they had each other, despite all of the tension within their family. He hoped that, after Ginger matured further, they could be close.

"Dad!" Ginger yelled. "There it is!"

And he looked and saw it: the impressive purple float with its two raised platforms, wheeling slowly up the road toward them. The Comstock High band preceded the float, energetically playing the theme from *Star Wars,* and the drill team danced athletically to the music. The crowd went nuts. The float was the most spectacular display of all.

Lindsay Meeks was admittedly very beautiful, waving happily from the lower platform, her enormous lavender gown sparkling like a star-studded gloaming. The evening light softened the over-eager angles of her face, Eli thought, or maybe it was just her smile, which, for the first time, seemed sincere and childlike. Her arms took turns waving, one after the other, the one lifting gracefully and then falling, the other lifting now, then falling, as though she were performing a one-woman ballet. It might be said that she was the star of the entire evening, until the Sasquatch slowly raised its own arms—bulging, powerful, intimidating arms—and bared its apelike mouth, its sharp white fangs, and roared.

Eli felt the roar in his shoes. The crowd screeched and applauded. Eli flushed with pleasure. Up on the lowboy trailer, standing just below the mechanized Sasquatch, Lindsay Meeks winced. She recovered quickly, redoubling her efforts, waving, smiling, blowing kisses to the crowd. The Sasquatch lowered its arms and kicked out its bony foot, the one with the real metatarsus. The kick just narrowly missed Lindsay's behind. She would have three more minutes before he roared again.

Eli turned behind him to gauge his family's reaction and saw

Ginger holding Gary's hand. She wasn't looking at the float at all
but up at the boy's mouth.

Oh, don't kiss him, Eli thought, but then told himself it wasn't
his business and turned away.

Vanessa patted his hand, cupped the other around her mouth.
She shouted so he could hear, "Looks great, hon!"

Eli was proud. All of Lilac City, it seemed, was admiring his
Sasquatch. It was anatomically correct, posturally perfect. It was
bipedal hominid perfection.

Then, alarmingly, the float shuddered as though it had rolled
over a pothole. There was a shrieking groan, and the Sasquatch's
arms shot straight up into the air.

"Oh, shit," Eli said.

"Meow," said the Sasquatch.

The crowd fell silent for a moment, listening.

"Meow," the Sasquatch said again, its arms shooting straight
above its head, unnaturally straight.

Lindsay Meeks playfully waved at the crowd. She was faking it,
pretending it was intentional. *Good girl,* Eli thought, but he wished
she would turn and give the Sasquatch a good whack to reset its
broken machinery. The crowd laughed and waved back at her.

The float crawled forward again. The Sasquatch's giant raised
fists were heading straight toward a low-hanging power line.

Eli rose uncertainly from his chair. Gary, too, had moved forward, still clutching Ginger's hand.

"It's been doing this on and off throughout the parade," Gary
told Eli. "He'll probably lower his hands soon." Then, consolingly,
he added, "He's pretty badass when he's not meowing."

"Stop the float," Eli said, concerned.

The fists approached the power line.

"Stop the float," Eli called out loudly now, yelling this insensibly
at Lindsay Meeks, as if she controlled the thing. She heard his sharp
cry but, above the sounds of the float and the crowd, didn't seem to

make out what he was saying. Nonetheless, she looked up. She saw what was about to happen and gave a bloodcurdling scream.

The Sasquatch's fists connected with the power line and then swooped down, tearing the line loose and sending sparks flying. The entire crowd seemed to suck in its breath, and when it exhaled, the Sasquatch burst into flames.

"Meow," said the Sasquatch, engulfed. Its arms shot skyward again.

Lindsay Meeks frantically unbuckled herself from the stand. The heat from the burning Sasquatch must have been unbearable. The float had come to a stop and the driver was lurching out of the truck cab, his eyes two white, fear-stamped circles. Lindsay stumbled forward, trailing smoke and flames as she moved. The entire purple train of her gown had ignited.

"The princess is on fire!" someone screamed.

Lindsay was running in circles, panicking, trying to shuck off her dress.

The crowd, too, was panicking, people pushing at one another, fleeing in droves. Sirens pierced the air. A fire truck honked its horn repeatedly at the parade participants, forcing them to the side. The Sasquatch was demonically braying and meowing, no more than a large, dissolving shadow in the flames. The street smelled of burning glue and scorched paper. Someone hurtled from the crowd and threw himself on Lindsay Meeks, rolling with her on the ground, tearing at her dress. The tall kid, Eli saw. Gary. A moment later, Lindsay was safe elsewhere, half naked but alive, eyes streaked with mascara, her two oddly matched parents crying with her off to the side, Gary keeping a hand protectively on her back. Ginger stared at them with a look of defeat on her face, but Eli's defeat was too enormous to register her own.

Those parents, Eli thought, *don't even like each other. They've stayed together, though, for the sake of those daughters.*

He looked at Amelia then and saw that she, too, was watching the Meeks family, perhaps thinking of Eli and of Gladys. He thought he could sense what Amelia was thinking as she eyed Lindsay Meeks: *Of course you would turn out well. Of course you would, if you had that.*

Eli looked away.

The float itself was now entirely aflame. The conflagration spiraled into the heavens like a hero's funeral pyre. Vanessa and Amelia and Jim and even Ginger were all pulling on Eli, telling him to run, to go, but he could only stand there, watching, feeling that it was not just the Sasquatch model but his entire career going up in smoke.

This would be the first of his darker days, when he would begin to seriously doubt that he would ever find Mr. Krantz.

The firemen and policemen were putting out the fire now, smoke billowing, and Eli finally allowed himself to be led away. He followed his family to the parking lot, too stunned to speak with them about what had transpired. When Vanessa offered to drive him home, he refused.

"I'll drive myself," he said. She put the back of her hand on his forehead, as if testing for a fever. He pulled away. "I'm fine. I'll drive. I don't want to leave my car downtown."

"I'll go with him, Mom," Ginger said. Eli didn't want the company, but he was too upset to argue, so he said nothing, merely opened the passenger door for Ginger and waited while she climbed inside.

"We'll come over, too," Amelia called to him from her own car.

"Okay," he said.

"See you all there," Vanessa said, and her cheerfulness, Eli sensed, grated on them all.

On the ride home, stuck in bumper-to-bumper traffic, Ginger giggled.

"What is it?" Eli asked.

"Nothing."

"Tell me."

Drawing her knees to her chest, Ginger propped her feet—encased in grubby sneakers—on the dashboard, something Eli typically hated but that he chose to tolerate this evening. "It's just . . . she was like the actress in *King Kong*—"

"Who?" Eli said. "Fay Wray?"

"Lindsay Meeks! Yes! Like Fay Wray! All like, *Ah! Help me! Help! Save me from the giant ape!*"

She flailed her hands around in imitation and then snorted and laughed.

"Ginger," he said. "Isn't she your friend?"

Ginger wiped at her eyes, both crying and laughing now. "And King Kong was like, *Ah! I'm on fire! Meow! Belching fire! Ack! Roar! Arms up! Meow!*"

She fell silent now, laughing so hard that no sound came from her, and for a moment he was concerned that she was about to pass out. But then she lifted her face and put her head back, gasping for breath, her face gone glossy with the purest happiness, so very happy and free, as only children can be. How young she still was, his littlest daughter, not a woman at all but just very young and very innocent, so very different from how Amelia had been at age seventeen.

There was a short window in life where she would be able to feel this way. It would close soon, surely. Eli wanted her to get a grip on herself.

"Ginger," he said, taking hold of one of her knees. "Ginger."

She shook with laughter. She erupted with it.

"Ginger," he said, trying not to yell. "She was your friend. Remember? You said she was nice."

Ginger sobered up, regarded him in confusion. "So what? I'm just laughing. Not at her. Just, you know, at the situation."

"This was her night," he said, "her big night, when the whole city admired her, and it was ruined. Set on fire, Ginger. Up in flames. Literally."

Ginger's lips quivered. She was trying not to laugh—trying—but the mention of the fire was too much for her. She crouched over her legs again and muffled the sound of her laugh with her arms, but it was no use; she couldn't hide it from him.

"It was her big night, Ginger, the night when all of Lilac City gathered to see . . ." And he trailed off here.

He was being a hypocrite, and he felt his hypocrisy keenly, and he was embarrassed about it and made all the more hungry by it.

Gary was now Lindsay's hero. Ginger couldn't compete with Lindsay Meeks, not now, not ever. *So let her have her laugh,* Eli thought. *At least she's not laughing at me.*

Ginger, meanwhile, continued to buckle and shake, stopping for whole minutes at a time before remembering some other hilarious detail and convulsing with laughter again. Eli ignored her. He saw himself as all of Lilac City no doubt saw him tonight: laughable, misguided. He thought of Mr. Krantz. He felt bested.

Eli took a hand from the steering wheel and wiped at his face. Ginger finally managed to calm down. For this, Eli was grateful.

They were home. Eli turned off the car's ignition and regarded the house for a long moment. There was no point, he told himself, in feeling such self-pity. Tomorrow morning, he thought, there will be a fresh pot of coffee and a thousand things to do at the office. He would engross himself again in his work. This was a great comfort.

Thus bolstered, he followed Ginger inside.

Amelia and Jim sat together on the living room couch, speaking in low voices with Vanessa. Eli greeted them and apologized. He was tired, he said, and he was going to bed.

He noticed the hurt on Amelia's face, the confusion on Jim's. Vanessa's face was a mask of anger and pity. And then there was Ginger, making excuses for him to everyone, as always.

"It's not like he doesn't want to see you," Ginger told her sister as Eli climbed the stairs. "He's tired. He worked really hard, you know? On his monster? His hominid, I mean? And the foot bone! It's nothing but ashes now. So it's a bummer. We can have dinner together, though. Maybe he'll come down later. I'm so glad to see you!"

But as Eli washed his hands at the sink and changed into his pajamas, he heard the unmistakable sounds of Amelia and Jim leaving the house, of Amelia and Jim's heated conversation in the driveway, of their car backing away and speeding from the neighborhood. Following came the predictable sounds of Vanessa finishing dinner, smashing dishes around, angry with him as she passive-aggressively cleaned. She wouldn't come to bed for hours, Eli knew, but would stay up, drinking wine and watching the popular television shows that she would later berate as artless.

And where would Ginger be? Talking on her phone? Thinking of the tall boy from the float committee? Or would she be scribbling the day's disappointments into her diary?

It didn't matter. Eli let it all go. He was fantastic at letting it all go. It was beyond him. He lay in bed, throbbing. He closed his eyes. At the threshold of the dreamworld, Mr. Krantz loomed before him, not made of paper this time but of flesh, and when the fire reached him, he could not be saved.

In his sleep, Eli screamed with delight.

1994

PEOPLE OF THE STREET

IT WAS GINGER'S SIXTH WEEK IN SPAIN. THE PANIC ATTACKS HAD ended. Now it was just the slow wretched acceptance of being away from Cort for another four months. On this sixth weekend, she called him from the Plaza Pelícano's public telephone. She used a phone card purchased from the nearby tobacco shop, a phone card that required she type in a twenty-digit number, her impatience swelling as her fingers trembled over the keys. What a relief when Cort actually came to the phone; what a relief that he was, unlike last week, waiting for her call. She listened to him talk, the phone pressed to her ear with such force that his voice gouged like a drill into her skull. She stared stupidly out at the world, ignoring the stray dogs glaring at her from beneath the tattered awnings, ignoring the children, many of them familiar to her now, tearing parentless around the plaza, stopping at her side to tease her and laugh at her: "*Americana, Americana, ¿con quién habla?*" Cort said he was glad to hear from her, and Ginger closed her eyes. He told her about nothing in particular: his microbiology professor's tendency to pick, mid-lecture, at the seat of his pants; his roommate's annoying habit of redistributing the unwashed dishes to Cort's bed ("What a dickwad!" Cort exclaimed, incredulous. "I pulled back the sheets and there was a rotting plate of lasagna. Such a cocksucker!"); the hangover he'd battled all morning, a hangover that made him miss having her around. At this moment, one of the glaring stray dogs deposited a slick wormlike turd near her feet. Ginger forced herself to laugh. Cort needed her, she reminded herself. He wouldn't leave her. He had just said, in so many words, that she bettered his life.

"So how's the rain in Spain?" he asked buoyantly.

"Not so much rain," she said. She winced at her voice's breathiness, at its high, tremulous lilt. She sounded girlish and sentimental, even to herself. "Just one day of it, really. I saw two mopeds crash. All the wet oil in the streets. So there are a lot of accidents."

"Cool," he said. "Anyone mangled?"

"This lady's leg was pretty effed up. Moped trapped her underneath. But she was okay."

"Bogue."

"Yeah. Totally." She waited a moment. "Have you been getting my letters?"

"The letters! Oh! Yes! They're awesome! Thank you!" His tone changed. "Although the fellas think it's funny. I mean, you send me one every day. Sometimes more than one. And don't get me wrong. I love it. It's like Christmas, kinda, when I get back from class and here are all of these letters and postcards waiting for me. It's cool, right? But, you know, they think it's weird." He exhaled loudly. "Not that I care what they think."

She swallowed with difficulty. "I really liked the letter you sent me. Your description of the river was beautiful. You're such a good writer."

"Yeah? Thanks. I was super inspired. Sorry I haven't sent you more. Been busy. Real busy. It's weird, you know, because I feel guilty for not writing more. Especially after how much you send me. But I think of you a lot. I really do, Ginger. I hope you know that."

Later, Ginger slowly walked toward the river, taking her time, watching her feet in their delicate espadrilles, avoiding the dog crap, ignoring the hissing, the catcalls. An old man rubbed his fingers together under her nose and put the fingers in his mouth as though tasting her. She scowled and drew her head down, parting her shoulder blades. She threaded her way from plaza to plaza until she reached the Guadalquivir, where her friends sat at a table littered with empty glasses, the sugary husks of recently drained *tintos de verano*. They were all—all six of them—the daughters of the wealthy. Like Ginger. Ginger told everyone her father was a doctor, too, a podiatrist, even though he'd given up his podiatry practice years ago. Sometimes when she visited a hospital and smelled the sterilizing chemicals and watched the orderly staff, she mourned her dad's chosen career. It was embarrassing, really. In high school, Ginger had considered becoming a cryptozoologist, too. It sounded like fun back then. Chasing beasts! But, like most things her parents did, it no longer made sense to her. She wanted to be an artist. A famous painter or writer. Maybe a musician, although she didn't know how to play an instrument and she couldn't much sing.

Cort wanted to be a doctor. A real one. He, too, found her father amusing, a droll little man.

Her friends pulled their chairs over to make room for her. They were awaiting a pitcher of sangria and a plate of Roquefort sandwiches. When they finished eating and drinking, Ginger rose, lightheaded, less somber if not exactly happy, and followed her friends into the heart of the city, toward the cathedral, the Gothic towers rising like a dark stony cliff before them.

This was how she spent her days here, drifting along sadly with her bubbly compatriots. She forced herself to eat and to drink. She forced herself to drink too much, to fake enjoyment. Every now and again she noticed something beautiful that briefly captivated her: a tiny fountain on an empty street; a hidden avenue with salmon-pink walls; a school of ancient Spanish women, huddled together in an old church, finally learning how to read. But these moments came to her as things happening to someone else. She wasn't there. She was back in Seattle, with Cort. Back in his bed, wrapped in his red flannel sheets, listening to Leonard Cohen and talking about James Joyce. She wasn't here in this beautiful sun-blanched city, this city that was both Roman and Moorish, Gypsy and modern. She wasn't here with these wealthy American girls from all over the United States, from the Midwest and Texas and California and Maine, from large lawn-dotted suburbs in random cities. She was now a satellite self, discharged to orbit a remote planet. She stared out at everything with a robot's eyes, merely collecting information, no emotional attachments forged. Like a good robot, she counted down every precise moment to departure. The return to Seattle. To Cort.

Her friends snapped photos and gossiped. They pitied themselves for their language program's lack of attractive American males. *Why is it,* someone mused, *that the boys stay home? Why are we girls the only ones studying abroad nowadays? Isn't that wrong? Aren't men,* one of the other girls said, *the more adventuresome sex, stereotypically speaking?* Ginger listened to the argument with a sick heart. She had her own opinions on the matter: that women were weaker somehow, less satisfied with the present; that the baubles and styles of Europe attracted them with shallow promises of beauty and fashion. Ginger hated the reasons that brought her here. Except that she couldn't really remember what any of them were. Maybe to learn Spanish? Or maybe that she had heard that it was something intellectual young women did in their third year of college? After all, she saw herself so very much as an intellectual young woman. It was how she wished for Cort to see her.

Someone tugged on her arm. *This way,* they urged. The girls were quite drunk. It was midday, crazy hot, and the alcohol made Ginger hotter. She rustled in her pockets for her change. She had stopped carrying a purse or a backpack—too many girls had fallen victim to thieves that way—and she carried almost nothing with her, finding that most of the time the bill was collected and paid for long before she even thought of asking for it. That was the thing with people her age who had lots of money: It was easy to be generous, so easy that it made all such gestures worthless. No one said thank you and no one noticed the lack of gratitude. Ginger did feel grateful, especially that these girls continued to humor her despite her clear misery. Some of them even listened with patient, kind eyes to her effusive monologues about Cort. Sometimes she lost control of herself, when she drank too much or her ache for him overflowed.

Mostly, Ginger tried to keep to herself. She hid from them her stuffed unicorn, Charlie, which she'd packed to help her through the difficult nights. She spoke to Charlie nightly, cried her fears into his matted, dissolving white fur. And she tried not to take it too personally when the other girls teased her about Cort, although it really did hurt.

The young women stepped together now beneath the high clean awnings of Calle Sierpes. A man painted entirely in gold stood perfectly still, regarding the world with the same empty robot eyes. Every now and again he shifted position, wondrously, mechanically, as though he were made not of flesh but of gears and gadgets. Ginger watched him for a long time, her friends slipping in and out of the nearby shops to try on shirts and dresses and shoes, and finally she gave him one of her few coins, depositing it in a hat at his feet. He rolled suddenly into a bow of thanks and remained frozen there, staring at the ground as if he had finally broken down. Ginger smiled briefly and then moved forward, looking for her companions, who had now gathered before an *heladería* a bit farther down the avenue.

A woman materialized just as Ginger began to order her ice cream, a beautiful older woman with dark hair and skin like boiled gold. Ginger shrank away, unnerved by the woman's closeness. She reeked of some sort of herb that Ginger could not place—something rustic and earthy. Rosemary? The smell was overpowering if not unpleasant. The woman took up Ginger's hand and stroked her palm, gurgling low in her throat, and Ginger tried to pull her hand away but could not. The woman gripped her wrist too tightly.

The woman began to ramble in Spanish about Ginger's future. Ginger understood parts of it but not others: *You'll have two children, blondes—*rubio. *You'll find wealth. You will live a long life but not one without sadness. Your one true love—the man who will love you the fullest—will be a* moreno. *You will make—*

Ginger began to speak, too, with more-rapid Spanish than she had ever spoken.

"No," she argued. "No. My one true love is a *rubio*. A *rubio*. Please. Look again."

The woman lifted Ginger's hand up higher, peered down into her palm.

"*Moreno*," she confirmed, and dropped Ginger's hand roughly.

She extended her own long, bejeweled fingers for money.

Ginger reached on impulse into her pocket and then stopped herself. No. This woman would receive no money. Not for misinformation.

"He's a *rubio*," Ginger repeated. "*Rubio.*"

The woman laughed and shook her head.

Some of her friends approached, licking their ice cream, listening to their argument.

"Palm reader," one of them exclaimed. "Gypsy!"

They shoved money into the woman's hands and presented their own palms. "Who will love me?" they demanded, laughing. More coins appeared, more palms. Ginger stood by, heartbroken, abashed, as the woman listed what color of hair to expect from their life's true loves. *Moreno, moreno, moreno.* In one instance, laughing, *calvo.* Only one girl was allowed a *rubio*, and she was ironically the one who wanted to stay in Spain forever, hoping to marry a native and live by the sea in Cádiz.

Ginger slipped her palm into the mix again, as though to come up with a different outcome, but the woman slapped her hand away.

Moreno, she said firmly, and made a severe chopping motion with her fist, as though to say, *Enough.* She left the girls standing there, laden now as she was with their pesetas. Ginger watched her go, destroyed. Her friends giggled to one another, but soon their attentions wandered to a bar they'd never noticed before, a bar that likely served fried calamari and pale beer. Ginger faced away from the bar, watching as the woman slipped into a blue doorway across the avenue. She read the sign overhead. A *zapatería:* a cobbler's shop. The door snapped shut. Ginger waited a moment before allowing her friends to guide her inside the bar.

"Don't tell me you're taking that woman seriously," one of them— the girl from Georgia with the small, perfect nose—said, noting her stricken expression.

"She said *moreno,* but Cort is a *rubio,*" Ginger said.

"God," another of the girls cried, a more courageous girl than Ginger, a girl who had already banged a *sevillano,* "one more word about Cort and I'm going to shoot myself. In the guts. With a rifle."

The other girls laughed. Then some of them cooed, saying, *Ah, Ginger, it's just a joke! Don't take it so hard!* All the while, the courageous girl flared her nostrils in annoyance. Ginger, flushing, bowed humbly over her small glass of beer. She stared into the golden liquid. Its warm tint matched a certain fleck of discoloration in Cort's right iris.

When the attention fully shifted to some other laughable subject, Ginger rose and mumbled something about going to the bathroom. She left the crowded bar and, with a quick look over her shoulder, crossed over to the blue door of the cobbler's shop. She stood anxiously before it for a few moments before trying the latch.

Inside was a display room of shoes. They looked comfortable and hand-sewn and uniquely fashionable—urban but sporty. If Ginger had been in a different state of mind, if she had been at all calm and content, she might have tried the shoes on. Instead, she ignored the beautiful shoes and pressed toward the back of the room, where a red velvet curtain hung over a doorway. She called out timidly, then more strongly, and rocked back on her heels, waiting. There was a rustling sound in the back, a slight wavering of the velvet curtain as though the air had changed, and then nothing. Ginger pushed the curtain aside and passed uninvited into the back room.

As charming and refreshing as the showroom was, the workroom was airless and cheerless. An old door lay flat on two paint-splattered sawhorses, forming a crude worktable. On it rested several metal tools that were stained a deep reddish brown. The concrete floor was murky with dust and strips of leather and empty tubs of polish and even more dirty tools. Ginger waded through a mess of discarded shoes, half-finished articles abandoned due to some small annoyance on the part of their creator. She could tell that some of these carcasses had been here for years and years. It seemed that this back room had never been tidied. She thought of how every person had a back room to herself. Only a few beautiful, well-adjusted details were allowed in a glittering front room.

Ginger suddenly felt that she was in love with this cobbler. She pictured the cobbler with Cort's face. She wanted to find where he was, to crawl into his lap and expire there, crooning.

But then a door opened at the back of the workroom, a door she hadn't even noticed in the dusky half-light, and in came the palm reader, a man following closely at her heels—a man who was certainly not Cort and certainly not anyone Ginger would ever love.

The woman saw her and smiled knowingly.

She said in rapid Spanish to the man behind her, Spanish that Ginger just barely understood, "Look here. It's the girl who loves the *rubio,*" and the man smiled kindly and approached Ginger to kiss both sides of her face.

Ginger accepted the gesture and then stood back to address the palm reader again.

"This is what I wish to speak to you about," Ginger said in her halting Spanish. "About the *moreno*. Is this an act? An act you perform?" Then, in English: "How do you say *performance*? Do you know what I'm saying?" She sputtered a brief apology for her poor Spanish, and then continued: "Because it would comfort me if it were. If you could just admit that to me."

"*Oye, chiquitita*," the man said to her. He switched on a small lamp over the makeshift worktable and took up one of his tools. He began to work it along a wide swath of leather, the sound like tearing flesh. Goose bumps rose on the backs of Ginger's arms. The cobbler continued in decent English, "My mother is very talented. She does not read a palm wrong. You do not ask her to give you a lie. It is underneath her."

"Beneath her," Ginger corrected miserably.

"You love this *rubio mucho*," the man said. "I do not see other *chiquititas* chase my mother so."

"*Mucho*," Ginger confirmed. "Yes."

The man carved into the leather with fluid movements. The object in his hand did not resemble a shoe. It was stranger than that, shaped like a horseshoe, too large. Ginger wished he would make her a leather plane, a plane to soar home in, so she could forget about Spain and her fellow *extranjeras*.

"*Pobrecita*," the palm reader said. And then she rattled off something about silly young women in love, something Ginger couldn't quite understand.

Ginger wondered at the cobbler's age. His mother was a lovely woman, but he was stooped and ugly and almost crippled, as though he had been thrown from a great height at a young age. Yet his kind face was wondrous to behold, especially considering the cruel fierce swiftness of his mother's expressions. Ginger believed that he would tell her what she wanted to hear, even if his mother refused.

She asked him timidly, "Does he love me, do you think?"

He turned to her, holding his little knife in the air, a surgeon of delicacy. "You are beautiful and good. You are rich. Your family is rich, no?"

She shrugged.

"Yes, he loves you. Who would not? Anyone here would die for a *chiquitita* like you, smart and *muy linda* and good and rich. It is a rare thing. To be all of those things. Very rare."

He turned back to his work, humming.

Ginger was not easily satisfied. "So she's good at predicting outcomes?"

"La mejora," he said apologetically.

"Can she also change outcomes?"

He shook his wide toadlike head. "Nah," he said. "Do not ask that of her."

"What is she saying?" the palm reader asked him in Spanish, grinning.

He explained. His mother looked back at Ginger. "You love this *rubio* so very much," she said in Spanish to Ginger, slowly enough that Ginger followed. "Why?"

Ginger was used to the question. She had been asked it by many people: her classmates here, even her own mother, who met Cort and did not at all understand why Ginger glorified him so. She had an answer to it, as she had an answer to everything involving Cort. She was not proficient enough in Spanish to give her answer in full, so she offered the short response.

"He has sad eyes," she said, and then stopped, as though the explanation would suffice. She did not go into how Cort's own brother had died of testicular cancer a few nights after their first drunken hookup or how she had traveled at first hesitantly and then passionately with him to what was a gut-wrenching and beautiful funeral. She did not say that Cort was majoring in both physics and literature, indicating a general well-rounded intelligence. And she didn't mention that he was very kind, even if he refused to ever mention the word *love,* a word that would cure Ginger immediately of all of her deep woe. No, Ginger did not mention these details. She felt very much that her simple words—*tiene ojos tristes*—said everything.

The cobbler and his mother sat silently, watching her for a few moments. *"Qué lindo,"* breathed the cobbler. "I would like a girl to love me this way."

"You love him," the woman said. "For his eyes. For his eyes you would do anything."

"Oh, yes," Ginger said. "Yes, yes."

"You would endure great pain and suffering."

"Yes," Ginger said. "I have been. I have been doing this."

"You would kill yourself for him. All for this *rubio*." Her jaw tightened, her eyes challenging, punishing. "You would do anything for him in the world."

They were not questions. They were simply statements that Ginger fluidly agreed with, no hesitation, not even at the word *kill*.

"You would kill your family for him."

Ginger stopped nodding. She stared balefully at the Gypsy woman, at her sleek dark hair and cruel eyes.

"Basta ya," the cobbler said angrily. He stopped working the leather and frowned at his mother.

She glanced at him witheringly, and he fidgeted and stayed silent. Then she turned back to Ginger. "You have parents? Loving, rich parents?"

Ginger admitted this was true.

"You have a brother?"

"A sister."

"And you would let them suffer for your love, too, no? You would let them suffer and die. All for this *rubio*'s sad eyes."

"Mamá," demanded the cobbler, rising to his feet. *"Déjala sola."*

"Just say the word. Tell me yes, tell me you love your *rubio* and would see them all suffer great pain. Tell me this and he will always love you. I'll change the avenue in your palm, the avenue of your *vida*. You will be with your *rubio* forever, if you want it so."

Ginger brought a hand to her throat, considering. It suddenly seemed to her that she was the only person in this room who breathed, sucking in great breaths and letting them out. Of course, she told herself sensibly, they are speaking, so of course they are breathing. You have to be able to breathe to speak. This was what her father had told her when she was struggling with her panic attacks.

"I'm going to die," she'd told her dad, sobbing, phoning him on her third day here. "I'm going to suffocate."

"You can speak," he'd said calmly. "Can you sing?"

"I think so," she'd said, and had hummed a few bars of "Twinkle Twinkle Little Star."

He'd laughed, and she had been relieved to hear his laughter. "Then you have plenty of breath. You're hyperventilating, Ginger. It's a simple panic attack. Next time the panic attack starts, sing a little song. If you can sing, you can breathe, and you'll be just fine."

And from then on, when the panic attacks would begin to take over, when she felt that she might suffocate and die, she would sing softly to Charlie the unicorn to prove that she was just fine, that she was not at death's door but alive and young and well. She chose the songs her mother used to sing to her throughout her girlhood, twinkling stars, or the one about the cradle falling and the poor baby with no one below to help her. And slowly in the coming weeks the panic attacks disappeared.

But why, then, were her companions' chests not rising and falling with the same ferocity as her own? Why were their nostrils so still, their nose hairs so undisturbed, their mouths clamped shut, watching her, one face challenging and cruel, the other soft and compassionate?

She saw now that these weren't real people—they were the ghosts of people. Not real people at all but demons.

God, to be with Cort again. To rest her head on his chest, to listen to his strong noble heartbeat. She would give anything, anything, for that comfort.

"Do not do it," the kind man warned her in English. "She plays with you. Do not do it."

She did not want him to see, did not want him to hear. Ginger leaned in to the cobbler's mother and cupped a hand around the woman's bejeweled ear. She whispered her answer and then withdrew. The woman cackled.

"Sí, sí," she said, looking triumphantly over at her son. "It is done already."

Ginger waited for the woman to say the word. She did. Then Ginger whispered her thanks and returned to the street, avoiding the terrible reddened eyes of the cobbler, which groped after her like a pair of bloodied, scrabbling hands.

In the street outside the bar, her friends had gathered, drunker now, ready to dance. They noticed her dazed expression and asked what was the matter.

"Nothing," she said. "I have to make a phone call. I have to go back."

She ignored their reproaches. She ignored the courageous girl's mocking, "Off to call Cort. Figures."

Ginger ignored them all and followed the meandering cobblestone streets back toward La Macarena, leaving the throngs of tourists behind, glad to be somewhere quiet again, or relatively so. The streets, after all, were never truly empty. Mopeds rocketed past, motors shrieking and then receding. Children played with one another or with their dogs. Entire families gathered together, dressed in fine clothes, parading their clan, digesting their late dinners. A young girl grasped the arm of her grandmother, and they bowed their heads at Ginger as she passed them. They were enjoying their evening stroll, the same stroll they enjoyed every evening at this time. The grandmother watched Ginger carefully with black eyes and a firm mouth. The young girl gave her a shy smile, a smile almost of forgiveness.

In the Plaza Pelícano, Ginger dialed the long number with

shaking hands. She murmured to herself quietly while the ringing gonged in her ear, a strange and wordy prayer. What relief she felt when the man picked up, when he said lazily, "Roebuck residence."

"Daddy," she said. And she began to cry.

Her father was awkward with this immediate onslaught of emotion. He fell silent for a moment, then asked her if she was okay.

"I'm fine," she lied through her sobs. "Are you guys okay? Are you well?"

Her dad skipped over her question, worried. He passed the phone along to her mother, who, no doubt registering her husband's tone, answered with a bright flurry of concern.

"Ginger," she said urgently. There was so much love in her voice that Ginger sobbed harder. What a disappointment she was! What a wretched daughter she had become!

"Tell us what's wrong," her mother was saying. "What's the matter? Have you been hurt? Are you safe? Do you need us there with you? We can be on the next flight."

Through her sobs, Ginger burbled that she loved them.

"Well," her mom replied, relieved, "we love you, too, sweetie. I wish you'd tell me what's wrong."

Ginger's panic began to subside. *See?* she told herself. *Nothing is the matter. Nothing is wrong. It was all a ruse, all a performance. Everything will be okay.*

"I'm okay," she said. She had control of herself now. "Just missing you guys. So much."

They talked a little bit longer. Everything was so normal back home, so boring, and Ginger relaxed. The palm reader had been toying with her. That was all.

"I almost forgot to tell you," her mother said, just before the call ended. "Cort called a few minutes before you. He would like to pick you up at the airport. Instead of us."

Despite her mother's disappointment, despite the dark thing that she had done to them, Ginger was overjoyed. It was unlike Cort to make such an effort. But now, yes! *He loves me,* she exulted. *Here, again, is proof!*

"Oh, yes!" Ginger said. "Please. He'll get me, and I'll see you later. Soon. I promise."

On the other end of the line there was a long pause.

Then, abruptly, came a loud and violent sneeze.

2003

THAT WILL TEACH YOU

PUT YOURSELF IN CORT'S SHOES.

Imagine returning home from work to what you assume is an empty house. Your wife's car is missing from her spot in the garage. There is no toddler tearing up the place. All of the rooms are dark and quiet.

Imagine that you have been working in a hospital obstetrics unit for the past twenty-eight hours, caring for patients and struggling to impress your new colleagues, and imagine that you have been existing, like all medical residents, in a twilight coma of exhaustion and excitability. Imagine that the silence is like a warm, silken rain falling on you, cleansing you of the hospital's bright and terrible otherness. Imagine sinking into the couch, beer in hand, mind empty, leaning back, and putting your feet up on the ottoman, which appears newly anointed with smears of purple crayon. Imagine that you have taken but one sip of your smooth, black, cold beer and that the tight bands in your neck have just begun to release, when you hear, coming from the first door in the hallway, a long, low wail.

Imagine your surprise.

Why, it sounds like a baby crying. *Your* baby. Your newborn, the one who was born seven (or eight?) weeks ago, a pretty little girl named Ruby, who, compared to her wild cyclone of a sister, is usually quite serene. But it can't be the baby, you think, because your wife is not here. And who, in her right mind, would leave a newborn all alone in the house? Not your wife, who is normally frantic and responsible, so overzealous in her watchdog approach to motherhood that you feel both jealous and critical of her impenetrable scrutiny.

Then again, Ginger has not, of late, been her normal self. She has been extremely haggard, unnaturally quiet, both wide-eyed and numb. She has always suffered from internalized, irrational guilt issues, but she now seems crippled by them. She blames herself for everything: her mom's pneumonia (easily cured, once diagnosed), her dad's mild heart attack (he fully recovered), Blythe's fall in the driveway (more your fault, really, as you were watching the kids when it happened), her sister's many sinus infections ("Sinus infections can kill you, you know," Ginger told you, and you struggled not to laugh).

"We've caused all of this pain," she tells you, and she is tearful, glutted with regret. "It's because of me, of what I did in Spain. Because of us."

You don't know what to say to this. You try to remind her that she's always felt guilt, always, only now she has something concrete to pin it on.

She tells you she needs help. You assumed, at first, that she meant a babysitter or a nanny, but what she meant was therapy or drugs or both. You agree.

Imagine considering all of this, with the knots retightening in your neck, as you set your smooth, black, cold beer aside and journey to the nursery, where your daughter lies kicking and sweating in her swaddle, looking somewhat like an electrocuted burrito. Imagine your anger and frustration at seeing the poor baby abandoned and alone here. Then, perhaps, you'll be able to understand Cort, to forgive him, for what he did next.

He is like us, after all: only human.

Cort packed the baby up and carried her outside. It was a beautiful day in an uncommonly cool June, when the rains had just ended and the clouds had parted and the sun was warm but not uncomfortable. The trees were greener on a day like this, the lawn sparkling, newly anointed. The sky, radiant blue and bright, appeared freshly scrubbed. Cort was even delighted to see a large eagle—a rare if not implausible sight—sitting on the telephone pole near their neighbor's yard. The eagle was watching them with a noble posture, as though approving of Cort's train of thought. And Cort's train of thought—despite a distant sort of appreciation for the fine sort of day it was—clattered along a track of revenge. It would have been a wonderful day for a walk, and Cort even considered retrieving the stroller from the garage and ambling about the neighborhood with his tiny charge (and how excellent that walk would be if he had been able to finish his beer, if he had worn, like a soft helmet about his head, a comforting and expansive beer buzz), but his incredulity and anger with his wife had yet to pass, and he decided, instead, to teach Ginger a much-deserved lesson.

What use was it, Cort thought, to be so guilt-ridden if you were also going to be so irresponsible? Why set yourself up, he wondered, for future episodes of guilt? It was maddening.

Cort opened the swaddle on the grass in the backyard, close to the house, and let the baby lie freely on top of it. Released from her confinement, Ruby became cheerful, and she kicked and gurgled appreciatively.

Ginger's car pulled into the garage then, and Cort, after bending over to give Ruby a kiss on the forehead, straightened and slipped back into the house, unseen. He returned to the couch and resettled his feet on the ottoman and took up his beer and quickly chugged half of it down before his wife entered the room.

She held their large toddler—their older girl—against her chest. Blythe was fast asleep, her plump mouth hanging open, her legs swinging freely. Ginger widened her eyes at Cort in greeting and whispered something he couldn't quite make out, and he smiled and lifted his beer to her as though in solidarity. She disappeared into the hallway and then into Blythe's room, and Cort could hear his wife settling the child into her bed, the springs shifting, Ginger's soft voice clucking, the slow removal of the toddler's shoes. Not a moment later his wife returned to him, wiping at her forehead, holding the shoes in her opposite hand.

"I could not get her down today," she groaned. "I finally had to just drive around. You know how she is. Fights it tooth and nail."

He made a small sound of sympathy in his throat.

She eyed him sleepily for a moment and then said, "I think I'll have a beer, too."

He leapt to his feet to accommodate her. It had been several months since they had enjoyed a beer together. It almost made him forget his rage. But as he snapped the cap off with the bottle opener, his frustration returned. How could she leave their baby alone in the house? Was the door even locked when he returned? No, it hadn't been. He was sure of it. Something was wrong with Ginger, to abandon the girl like that. Postpartum depression, malcontent, whatever. But it was not good parenting. That much was obvious.

He peeked out the back window to make sure his daughter was okay. She was there, considering with intense concentration one of her little fists. She seemed perfectly happy to be outdoors. The fresh air was no doubt doing wonders for her. Regardless, he knew he should hurry his little lesson along. Babies were content for only a few minutes at a time before they overturned a new grievance.

He returned to the living room to find his wife collapsed on the recliner, a forearm thrown over her eyes. She accepted the beer from him with an almost-happy grunt.

"God, I hope she keeps sleeping."

"Where is she?" he said casually. "Where's Roo?"

"I left her in her crib." She stopped here, taking a long pull of her beer. Then she said, "I know I shouldn't have done it, Cort. I know. It was horrible of me. I won't do it again. The whole time I was driving, I worried about what she might be doing, but I just had to take care of Blythe first. I just had to. And I started to take the baby with me, but then she would be awake, and I would be, I don't know, more flustered. My energy lately, Cort. My mind. I don't know. Something's not working."

Your heart, he wanted to say. *Your heart is not working.* To leave her there alone like that: *How could you?*

Still, he did sorrow for her, his wife. He pitied her. She was exhausted, he saw. She was a wildly emotional person. He liked it about her, in fact, but it meant that she was prone to irrationality, to terrible mood swings, to paranoia. Clearly, this had been a deeply irrational moment. Dangerous. He wandered over to the window again and checked on Ruby. She was still there, straight-lipped, alert. Content enough. The eagle was still there, too. He thought of showing the eagle to his wife, but then surely she would see their daughter, and the lesson would be spoiled.

"Should we check on Ruby?" he said.

"Go ahead," his wife said. "She'll cry if she needs us."

He sat back down on the couch. He was growing anxious. Much longer and Ruby might grow cold.

"Tell me about the hospital," Ginger said. "More assholes? More d-bags?"

He told her, quickly, that nothing much had happened, that the day had been, overall, a pleasant if busy affair, and that he was really just happy to be home.

"I'm happy, too." Ginger smiled. "I feel like it's the first time we've been able to just talk to each other. Without the kids, I mean." She looked around herself, as if gazing at new surroundings. "Isn't it nice?"

It was nice, but he was becoming anxious, so he avoided a verbal response.

It was as if Ginger knew, as if she were toying with him.

How was it that she always managed to win their battles? How was it that she always, despite everything, triumphed?

But then she said, rising suddenly, her maternal instincts flaring, "Ruby doesn't usually sleep this long." She went toward the hallway and disappeared into the infant's quiet green room.

Cort held his breath, waiting. What would she do when she saw that the child was missing? Walk into the room, pale and speechless? Sprint for the phone to call 911? What would happen? He feared and desired it equally. It suddenly occurred to him that she might immediately accuse him. Her wrath would fall on him and the lesson would be for naught. If that happened, he decided, he'd play dumb for a few moments, feigning panic himself.

She returned then, unsmiling. "She's fine," she said. "She's glorious. What a good baby. Sleeping away."

She collapsed back onto the recliner, threw her forearm over her eyes again, and sighed contentedly, drawing her beer up to her lips.

Cort stood and began nervously pacing. He wanted to check the nursery, too, to see what it was that Ginger had seen, but he dared not. He remained with her in the living room. He sidled up alongside the window and looked outside. There was Ruby, still on her swaddle blanket in the grass, beginning, he could see, to flail about and whine.

Had Ginger seen the child on her way into the house? Maybe she had peered over the gate and noticed her lying on the grass, deciding then and there to boomerang Cort's lesson back to him? Maybe there was a bear or a pillow or a blanket in the crib that looked like a sleeping baby's form? Or did she see a corner of the baby's blanket from Ruby's bedroom window, realizing immediately what Cort had done? Cort wanted to ask, wanted to yell, really, to scream at his wife, and it occurred to him that he had wanted to scream and to yell at her for days now and that he finally had found a good reason to do so.

His eyes lifted from his daughter to the telephone pole. The eagle was gone.

And then the eagle was there again, falling, diving murderously toward the open yard. Cort moved to the back door, filled with an intense concern. He had just stepped onto the stairs when the eagle nearly struck him with her wide black wings. She drew the infant in with her ugly ancient talons and, with some difficulty, lifted her into the air, swaddle blanket and all.

Cort shrieked, leaping for the child. The eagle danced in mid-air, finding it difficult to rise with her heavy purchase.

"My baby!" Cort yelled. "My little girl!"

Ginger joined him, still grasping her beer. She seemed neither worried nor startled by the episode but only watched the scene unfold with a sort of mute resolve, as if she had expected it all along. *This, too,* she seemed to be thinking, *this, too, is my fault.* Why had he tried to blame her, when she already blamed herself for so much? Cort hated himself for it, and he focused his hatred on the eagle.

He grabbed the baby's chubby legs, bloody now, and he pulled against the eagle with all of his might.

The eagle flapped her wings. The baby wailed. The eagle turned her big head toward Cort and pecked at his fingers.

"I'm not letting go, you fucker," he cried.

"Don't," Ginger said. She came forward and put her thumbs in the eagle's eyes. "Don't let go. Whatever you do, Cort, keep fighting."

She could have been talking about anything. The baby. His career. Their marriage. Her voice was calm and clear.

Cort obeyed his wife. He fought. He had never fought so hard for anything in his whole life. He was determined, just this once, to win.

2004

THE GLUE FACTORIES

"S OME OF YOU ARE REQUIRED TO BE HERE," THE MAN AT THE PODIUM said. "Some of you are here voluntarily. Whoever you are, why ever you're here, welcome. Showing up is the first step. So I congratulate you. We welcome you with open arms to our little ZSG family."

The man applauded himself loudly. A few women lifted their palms and clapped them mechanically together, like toy monkeys. A large chalkboard behind the man was filled with his name: MR. DONALD.

Mr. Donald—flushed, narrow-faced, heavily eyebrowed— continued, "We're the Zoophilia Support Group's first women-only Inland Empire chapter, and no doubt some of you have come from as far as Banff or Missoula to seek help. To all of you: Welcome! This is a safe place. We're all here to help one another. We're here to stop loving beasts. We're here to begin loving ourselves!"

The women sat in their metal chairs, arranged in various postures of disquietude. The chairs were in a lopsided semicircle so that everyone faced the creaking black podium. Mr. Donald spoke directly into the microphone, although there was no clear need for amplification. The room was small and smelled of burnt toast. It was the dead of winter, and the air flowing from the vents was scalding hot.

"Can you say it with me?" the man said. "*Stop loving beasts! Start loving myself!*"

Half of the women responded in kind. Half of them did not.

Introductions began, moving clockwise. Some of the women wept as they spoke. Many of them spoke hesitantly, softly, so that everyone had to lean in, cupping their ears, to hear the exact confession.

There was Morgan, who repeatedly used her cat to massage her loins.

There was Hilary, who made love to her horse, not just once but over and over again, until her husband discovered them and threatened to send them both to the glue factories.

Next to Hilary sat Flannery, plump and bashful, who had married her dog in a stunning lakeside ceremony, an event that had horrified her parents to no end. Flannery was pregnant. She was unsure of what to do with the impending litter.

And then there was Agnes Krantz: the lone nonagenarian; wrinkled and slim; wearing a small wooden ring on her thumb, which she twirled nervously as she spoke.

"I'm not sure I'm in the right place," she said. Her voice was hoarse. "I don't know if I belong here."

The women stared at her blankly.

"But I need a change," she said. Speaking was difficult. She was unused to addressing anyone but her husband. The words fell from her mouth like dull filthy rocks. "I can't go to my son. My son wouldn't understand."

Oh, yes, the faces watching her said. *Oh, yes.* The sons especially. The sons especially did not understand.

"My husband is a man, you see, but my son would call him a woodland ape. He studies these things, I've learned. My son would skin my husband alive. He would use chemicals to melt the flesh from the bones and then hang them in a glass box at the university."

The women had stopped nodding along with her. They glanced at one another, alarmed.

"But I love him. My husband. Truly I do." She rested her sore, arthritic wrists on her knees. She was wearing her husband's old top hat. She wore clothes that she had fished out of the ZSG charity box: an oversize hunting jacket (so wonderfully warm!), a man's white tank top, a slightly scuffed pair of jeans. The new clothes felt strange on her, luxurious. It made her realize how sick she was of her old sweaters and dresses—the ones she'd had for years and years, stolen from backyard clotheslines in Rathdrum—which she washed once a week in the creek. "I love him so much," she continued. "I gave up everything for him, even my son. And he repaid me by being the best husband a woman could imagine."

Mr. Donald—their group leader—touched his bow tie. He regarded her with firm but encouraging eyes. He leaned into the microphone. "And what happened to this 'man-beast' for which you sacrificed everything?"

Mr. Donald's voice was loud, hollow. He asked as though he already knew the answer, which he did.

The day before, Mr. Donald had come across Agnes in the forest. She had been walking toward the swimming hole, wearing enormous boots and a giant sweater and not much else. She was carrying a load of laundry. He had been coming back from the creek himself, dressed warmly against the winter weather, whistling a sunny tune. He wiped a hand off on his pants before offering it to her. He noted that she was living like an animal, and he encouraged her to attend a meeting. *There is a better life,* he had told her, *an easier life. A Christian life,* he said. Agnes normally would have spit in his eye, but with the way things had turned recently, she was curious. She accepted his business card and the crude map he drew for her. She kept the meeting a secret from Mr. Krantz—not that he would have judged her. There were no restrictions in their relationship, except for those that she gave herself.

Agnes looked away from Mr. Donald now, away from all of them, out the window, toward the distant woods. "He has a new wife," she said. "A young wife. A silly thing. Pretty and naïve. Not that I can blame him. Compared with me, he's hardly aged. He's still beautiful, you see. He's still strong. And look at me. Look at how I am now."

She spread open her hunting jacket and opened her arms to them. Even that was an effort. Her arms shook. The flesh dripped from her throat and eyes. She was spotted, gray and brown, like an owl. The women regarded her sadly. She closed her arms, pulled on the hunting jacket, shivered despite the room's oppressive heat.

"So I came here, I guess. For a change."

"We're here to help you," Mr. Donald said. "We love you and support you. We want you to start loving yourself."

He clapped thunderously into the microphone, and the bedraggled women around Agnes eventually joined in, applauding shyly. Then, with an apologetic smile and a tap of his watch face, the man shifted his gaze to the woman seated to Agnes's left. Her name was Wanda. She had an unnatural interest in her pet ferret, who, she said affectionately, was named Carl.

Agnes didn't understand what these women saw in their stupid pets. But, she knew, it wasn't her place to judge.

What Agnes wanted to say, what she really, really wanted to tell them all, was that all love is natural love, so long as it's invited, and also that the woods are terribly dark and cold when you're lonely.

AGNES WALKED SOUTH down the busy street, away from the brick Unitarian church, through a small pretty neighborhood, toward the bus depot. Her son lived on the hillside, she knew. She had spied on his house before, had watched him emerge from its thick stucco walls with his wife. She liked this wife. She liked how tall and awkward she looked, pretty and wild-haired, like an overgrown tree. She looked like someone who could easily bend with the wind. Those sorts of women, the flexible ones, made excellent wives. Agnes had never been flexible. She was as strong as a flint stone, with a will just as unbending.

Spying on the house, she had seen that there were daughters, too, and even little grandchildren. Her great-grandchildren, she recognized with a twinge of unfamiliar feeling. *I could snatch one of them away,* Agnes thought. Lure the littlest girl with candy into the forest. It would be so easy! The girl would miss her family at first, but in the end, when she learned how much simpler life could be in the woods, she would be pleased, even grateful. Humanity was a shitstorm. The woods were just as cruel, but unapologetically so.

It was the apologies that killed you. Forgiving and asking for forgiveness were exhausting work, the worst chore of all for a woman. Mr. Krantz, thankfully, never apologized, never sought forgiveness. There was a beautiful freedom in this.

They both did what they wanted. If either of them disapproved, well, then, so be it. They could continue living in the shack together or, hey, there was the door. A shabby door, yes, lined by a dirt threshold that Mr. Krantz routinely sprayed with his urine, but it was a door, nonetheless. You could leave whenever you wanted.

She had never passed through that door with the intention of leaving him, not once, not even when blisteringly angry, not even when the new wife arrived, not until this very day, and even now she was unsure about her departure. She didn't know if it would be better for her in the end or if it would be, at this late date, entirely stupid. But she could no longer watch Mr. Krantz fuck his young wife, not without clawing out her own eyes. It was unbearable, even after he returned to Agnes's bed and held her in his arms as she wept, cooing to her softly. No, it was too much. Not even she, so unbending, so strong, could handle it. She might have been able to when she was younger. She might have been able to step in between them, supple and fierce, and roar in the young woman's face. She had certainly done it before, a scene that excited her husband and made him ignore the other lover entirely. Now, dry as an old leaf, brittle-hearted, she could only weep from her bed as the lovers pushed and pulled at each other. She could only cover her face with tattered, moth-eaten blankets until, in one final explosion of noise, their coupling ended.

She climbed onto the bus, hating its mechanical stink, and handed the driver a few of Mr. Donald's coins. The bus rumbled and roared and traveled along the interstate to Idaho. Then it turned north, with Agnes tired from the day's loud sights and sounds, and deposited her in Rathdrum.

Agnes hiked out of town, thinking of the new wife. She followed the familiar deer paths of the forest, letting the branches scratch at her face and entangle her hair without putting up her hands in defense. Here was the creek—its edges frozen—in which she bathed. Here was the pile of rocks she used to wash and pound her clothes clean. Here were her husband's carefully laid droppings, a warning that made the mountain lions and bears roar in contempt before they slunk away.

Here was the little shack in the woods, once her happy home.

Here, inside the shack, was the new wife, sitting in the dingy recliner, looking balefully at her fingernails. She glanced up at Agnes. She'd been crying.

"I need a manicure," she moaned. "I'd kill for just a nail file."

Her hair was growing out but was still shorn in a shaggy, fashionable bob. She wore sparkling silver ballet flats and a pretty navy sweater. Agnes thought she should tell the new wife about the color navy. *Don't wear it in the summer. It attracts mosquitoes and black flies.* But summer was a long ways from now. Let her be.

Agnes came forward and touched the girl's shoulder. She wordlessly handed her a rock. When the new wife stared at it, nonplussed, Agnes took the rock back and drew it across her fingernails.

The new wife followed suit, taking up the rock and filing her nails with it. Her face brightened. "Thank you," she said.

Agnes noticed then that the new wife's wooden thumb ring lay on the side table, recently removed.

"I said thank you," the new wife repeated. She was not annoyed, Agnes saw, but desperate.

Agnes felt sorry for the new wife, but she avoided, as much as possible, speaking to her. She was only trying to help the new wife grow accustomed to their silence.

"Will you cook dinner?" the new wife asked her. "Should I?"

"You will," Agnes responded shortly, and then went to lie down on her narrow bed and rest.

BACK IN THE semicircle, sitting stiffly in her simple metal chair, Agnes told the group that she both loathed and admired the new wife.

"She's nothing like me," Agnes said. She worked at the wooden ring on her thumb as she spoke. "She wants to talk—all the time—and she misses city life. She spent all night filing her toenails. She can hardly boil water. She buses to Lilac City to buy toilet paper and new shoes—shoes with heels that look pretty but are worthless in the forest." She stopped here, took a breath. "The point is, I don't understand her. I never went back. Not for toilet paper, and not even to visit my son. My own son, for crissakes, who I loved more than anyone in the world—even more than myself—until I met my husband."

"Maybe that's why you stayed away," Mr. Donald suggested. He stood at the podium again, but he looked tired, sort of slumping over it as if he might collapse onto the floor. Agnes could smell alcohol on his breath. She thought he might be hungover. She wondered, pitying him, if he wasn't depressed, like the rest of them.

Why was there a man overseeing their women-only meeting? Why did leaders always need to be men?

"I don't understand," Agnes said.

"Maybe you stayed away because seeing your son would wound you? Make you question your choices?"

Agnes shook her head. "No. I stayed away because I wanted to stay away. Motherhood didn't suit me."

"Motherhood suits all women," the man said. He lifted a pen and jotted something down on a clipboard that lay before him on the podium. "I think we're reaching the heart of your suffering here. You abandoned your son, your duty to him, and now you find yourself alone. Tell me: When was the last time you saw your son?"

"I saw him," she said, "a few years ago."

"When?"

"The volcano," she said. "When the volcano blew."

Mr. Donald laughed. "Mount Saint Helens? That was twenty-four years ago!"

Twenty-four years! In the forest, time was both mercurial and phlegmatic. God, how old did that make her now? How old did that make Eli?

"If I may ask another question," Mr. Donald said. He said it so low, so dramatically, that she almost couldn't hear him. "Was he happy to see you?"

Agnes wasn't sure, really, but Eli hadn't screamed at her or pushed her away or anything like that.

"And would he be happy to hear from you now?"

The simplicity of this question was like a kick in the face. She sat up straighter, swallowing hard. *Does he know the answer? Does he think he would know the answer to this, if I don't know the answer?* She felt a moment's anger toward this man, then an insipid jealousy.

"Yes," she said. What she meant was: *Yes, of course you would ask that, you stupid man.*

The man did not take it that way. "Yes," he said. "He would be elated. Which is why you should reach out to him. Family is salvation, Mrs. Krantz."

Agnes felt hope then. It was inexpressible and discomfiting.

Flannery, the woman pregnant via her dog, put her hands on her belly and gave a happy little sound, halfway between a sob and a laugh. She was, like the other tortured souls in the room, touched. It also gave her hope, Agnes saw, the assumption that the love between a child and his mother never dies. Flannery must have hoped the same for her dog babies, that they would stand at her bedside as she grew old, that they would all love one another unconditionally, no matter what.

Agnes did not want to dash the pregnant woman's hope. She smiled and touched the woman's knee and said sincerely, "I've always loved him. That's the thing. You always love them. Even when you don't."

She wished she could say that the reverse were true, that children always loved their parents, no matter how horrible the parenting, but she could not.

It takes a certain sort of woman to leave her young child for a new husband, for a whole new life, and Agnes was that exceptional sort of person. She had assumed, upon leaving: Once a mother, always a mother. The truth, however, was not so simple. Out of sight, out of mind was more like it. But it was true that even after long stretches of not thinking about Eli at all, he would return to her, rising up from the dry soil of her heart like a noxious weed. And then, just as certainly, the weed would be plucked up or would wilt, the soil smooth and unmarred again, usually for long stretches of time.

Mr. Donald moved on to Flannery. "And when is the due date?" he said, his tone serious.

"It's hard to say," she said shyly. "We're not certain. You know, because of the species."

"And you've heard," he said, "that we'll help with the adoptions."

"Yes, I've been told."

Agnes wondered if Flannery had had an ultrasound, something that hadn't been around when she was pregnant with Eli. She'd heard the other women asking about it, and thought it sounded eerie and wonderful to peer into one's own darkest space.

"I'm wondering," the woman said meekly, "if I can keep at least one?"

Mr. Donald's smile flickered but his voice remained upbeat. "What an excellent question. I'll speak to you privately about this. Let's think about what would be best for the babies, and for you."

The pregnant woman looked quickly over at Agnes, as though begging for help.

Agnes thought carefully before she spoke, about Eli, about Mr. Krantz.

"He's probably right, you know," she said. Her voice sounded hollow, despite her best intentions. "It will be easier on you to just give them away."

"Well, it's only a notion," Mr. Donald added. "A point of entry." He narrowed his eyes at the women in a way that was supposed to denote respect but was really, Agnes felt, quite insulting.

Agnes, annoyed with Mr. Donald, said loudly to Flannery, "What, exactly, do *you* want? It's your choice."

Flannery stuttered for a moment and then fell silent.

"Now, now," Mr. Donald said. "Let's not make this about choice. That's too easy. Sometimes we don't know what's good for us. Our emotions get in the way. Sometimes we must have faith and trust in others."

Agnes reached over and grasped Flannery's hand. She squeezed Flannery's swollen fingers with as much force as she could muster, the arthritis shooting painfully up her own arm as she did. She was trying to communicate, *Have strength. It's not his life. It's your own.*

"Now," Mr. Donald said. "Let's talk about our emotions. We

women are emotional creatures. Let's talk about our emotions today. Let's explore!"

Agnes grimaced. As if emotions just sat there, static and obvious, like unchanging monoliths, perfectly defined.

Agnes knew: Emotions were like the moss on the forest floor, trampled, fluid, hidden.

Try to put your finger right on the moss, and its form spreads and changes.

"Let's begin with you, Agnes," Mr. Donald said.

"Okay," she said. "I'm annoyed."

The room laughed, and Agnes was happy to see that Mr. Donald seemed worried.

IN THE SHACK, Agnes and the new wife awaited the arrival of their husband.

The new wife flitted from one task to another, all things that Agnes had never done: pouring coffee, plucking her eyebrows, reading magazines that she'd brought from the local library.

Eventually she heaved a large sigh, cocked an eyebrow at Agnes, and asked her, "How can you stand it?"

Agnes was lying on the woven gray rug Mr. Krantz had stolen to celebrate his union with the new wife. She liked to put her face against the rug and smell its newness, so foreign to this familiar room. She uncurled her limbs and stretched and turned toward the new wife, confused.

"I mean," the new wife said, "how can you just sit there, doing nothing all day?"

"I'm not doing nothing."

"You've been lying there, dozing. Resting. I don't know. I can't stand it." The new wife plucked a small silver tube from her pocket. She opened it and applied a fresh coat of lipstick to her already-sanguine lips. "You know what he needs? A television set. I think he'd like a big flat-screen TV, right there." She put up her hands in a frame and looked through them, picturing the television against the shack wall. "I mean, we'd need a generator. But he could get one of those easily enough."

Agnes almost smiled.

"I know you're old, but are you sick?" the new wife asked, genuinely concerned.

Agnes shook her head.

"God, can't you even talk to me? I mean, I know he's great and all, but how do you handle it?"

Agnes considered the question. "I wasn't lonely," she said finally. "Or maybe I had already been lonely. For me, it was exciting and adventurous. There had been a big void in my life, and Mr. Krantz entered and filled it."

"Ha," the new wife giggled crassly. "Yes, he's certainly gifted at filling holes."

Agnes ignored her and said, "I was made for this life. You, though, I'm not sure. You're too"—she wanted to say *normal,* or *ditzy* maybe, but instead she said—"glamorous."

As expected, the new wife took this as a compliment. Clearly not one to absorb a compliment without immediately doling out one in return, the new wife rushed to say, "I bet you were beautiful. Just beautiful. When you were younger."

Agnes was stiff and sore. She thought of the pamphlets about facilities for the elderly that Mr. Donald had forced on her. She had buried them outside, beside the creek, and had marked their burial with an old gray brick. The facilities were large buildings with faux-feather beds and unlimited toilet paper. Against her will, Agnes found herself salivating at the thought of the hot foods they would serve—soft oatmeal with raisins, maybe, or fried chicken. *Fuck me,* she thought, drooling, *fried chicken!*

What would it be like to say hello to the other old people bobbing through the high-vaulted hallways? It wouldn't be so bad, that life. She would be the eccentric one, the odd one out. But, then, when had she not been? The only place she'd ever fit in was here, in Mr. Krantz's shack.

She thought of the recent zoophilia meeting, the suggestion of finding Eli and becoming a part of his life. Would he care for her now, as she had once cared for him?

Mr. Donald said she had nothing to lose, and she supposed this was right. She decided, sitting there with the new wife, that she would march up to Eli and open her arms and say, *Hate me or love me, I've returned. I've returned, like it or not.*

Mr. Krantz entered then, bellowing his greeting. He patted Agnes chastely on the head before scooping up the new wife and nuzzling her neck. Agnes lowered her chin and went out into the icy forest. Even from outside the pine walls of the shack, Agnes could hear the moaning and shouting that ensued. She went to the creek bed and followed its slow stream upward, toward the mountain. The sounds receded behind her, until she could hear only the gurgle of the creek, the wind sweeping through the canopy overhead, the creaking icicles. She startled a family of deer and watched them, dazed, as they crashed like lightning into the underbrush and then disappeared vaporously, like a wish.

She was alone again. Only now there was no grace in it.

She turned around, passed by the shack (now silent), and moved along the well-worn deer paths, all the way to the bus stop. She waited for an hour and then boarded the bus for Lilac City. She walked to the Unitarian church and sought out the man, the zoophilia group leader.

"I wish to speak with my son," she told him. She was unsure of where to begin. She did not trust this man, but he was more man than she was, more akin to her son. "Can you help me?"

He could, he said. Anything, he added, to help her overcome her bestial cravings, to get her away, finally, from Mr. Krantz.

She did not correct him. She listened.

"Meet him at his place of work," Mr. Donald instructed. "Not at his home. Things are too personal at home."

It seemed like wise advice.

"Do you know where he works?" the man asked her.

"Well, I'm not sure. He's famous for studying Sasquatch."

"Fitting," Mr. Donald said. "Clearly, your poor choices affected him."

That was too simple, Agnes thought, but she did not argue. She had once believed that Eli's search was all about finding her, but now she sensed it was something more damning: It was more about destroying her new life, destroying Mr. Krantz. There was rage there. It had nothing to do with love.

The man sat down at his computer and typed. He clicked the mouse. Agnes watched him, unsettled. She had never used a computer. She feared that the brightness of the screen would melt her face off, so she stayed as far away from it as possible.

The man hooted softly and then wrote something down on a piece of paper. "Jackpot," he gloated.

It just so happened that Dr. Eli Roebuck was taking part in a zoological conference that very afternoon. He would speak at one-thirty at the convention center downtown. Mr. Donald could not believe their good fortune.

"God's will!" he exclaimed. "God himself is urging you forward!"

Mr. Donald even offered to drive her in his little yellow car to the nearest parking lot, and Agnes gratefully accepted.

He left her off at the parking lot with a friendly chuck on a shoulder, a fresh Ziploc bag filled with coins for bus fare, and an annoying, go-get-'em smile. Agnes stumbled along the frozen stone pathway, feet aching in her shabby shoes, still wearing Mr. Krantz's hat and the same warm clothes from the ZSG donation box. She was keenly aware of how out of place she was amid the bustling crowds, but no one took notice of her. She arrived just as the doctor was finishing up his lecture. The entire expanse of the room was filled wall-to-wall with people, stinking of cheap perfume. She saw her son at the front of the room, shaking hands and smiling with members of the audience.

Off to the side of the stage, nestled on a velvet pillow atop a wood podium, was a foot.

God, Agnes thought, horrified. The bones were polished and sharp and long, both human and not human. *Whose foot is that?*

Then she realized: It was her husband's foot. Agnes recoiled. So, she thought. Her son had almost killed Mr. Krantz, after all.

Her husband had changed so much since the loss of that foot. He had become restless, impractical. He had become obsessed with the young drunk women of Rathdrum. He had begun, although he would never admit it, to despise her.

A crowd had gathered around Eli, around the foot, admiring both, it seemed. He looked intelligent and self-satisfied before them, well dressed as usual, sharp-eyed. He looked like Greg, and she even felt affection for her first husband then, that hardworking man who had foolishly devoted himself to their unlikely marriage.

It didn't matter whose fault it was. Living in the woods had taught Agnes this much: Fault was useless, as useless as apology. Life spiraled out from life, and death, too. It was random, it was constant. It was faultless and unapologetic and real.

She didn't have to forgive him, because there was no such thing as forgiveness. So he didn't need to forgive her, either.

Agnes waited for the crowd to disperse before she approached Eli. It took nearly an hour for him to finish signing books. Then he was alone, dismantling the items on the stage.

It was now or never.

She urged herself toward him.

"Hello," she said, touching him lightly on the elbow.

He was wrapping a cord about his elbow and hand, and he continued wrapping it as he turned to face her.

It was the moment of truth, the moment when Agnes would know, for certain, what would become of her.

Her little boy faced her, no longer a little boy but now a little man, very stressed, very bothered. He wore large, round red glasses that dwarfed his blue eyes (so beautiful, those eyes, like two perfect agates! She had nearly forgotten their color and intensity). His hair, almost gone now, had lost the sum total of its youthful blond luster; its thin remnants were dirty brown, streaked with gray.

He had aged since their last meeting.

But still—*oh, yes*—this was her little boy. The same apple-shaped shoulders, the same skinny frame, those same large, tender ears, that same open, curious expression that seemed both shocked and pleased.

Pleased? Was he pleased to see her?

She opened her arms to him.

He recoiled. No. No, then, he was not pleased.

"Eli," she said. "Eli, hello."

"Yes?" he said.

"Yes," she repeated. "Eli, it's good to see you again."

Eli glanced down at his watch, then up, and she felt that his expression was generous, affectionate even. "Can I help you?"

"Yes," she said. "I hope so."

He looked down at the floor and noticed her worn shoes— slippers, really—and then his eyes lifted and fastened curiously onto her face. He peered into it, at a total loss.

Then he said, and she would never forget it for the rest of her life, "Do I know you?"

Her smile faded.

Do I know you?

It was a strange question. Agnes understood its basic meaning, but it was so very loaded. God, he didn't recognize her! Had she changed so much in the last two decades? She wanted to explain to him, *I'm your mother,* but suddenly she wasn't sure that she wanted to be his mother. Had she ever wanted to be his mother? What would happen to her if she accepted the role now?

"No," she said. "No. I don't suppose you do."

"Did the newspaper send you?" he asked.

"No," she said. "No, I'm not with the paper."

"Ah. Well. They had said they might send someone. Although they weren't sure. They were busy, they said." Eli wiped at his face. "My career. What a shithole."

"You seem popular enough," Agnes said. "There were hundreds of people here when I arrived."

"Popular. Well. Yes." He looked around the room, at the scattered chairs and deflated balloons and remaining merchandise. "Yes. I suppose so. But I've never found him."

"You found part of him," she said, and gestured to the foot.

He smiled at the foot, waved his hand at it. "Oh, the real one was incinerated. I only had a single bone from it, anyway. That's just a replica."

"Well," she said, "could have fooled me. Looks like the real thing."

It helped her somehow to know the foot was a fake. She felt suddenly that she was a fake, too, and that this man in front of her was a fake. If they were all fakes, then none of this was worth crying over.

"So. How can I help you? Are you a fan?"

She was silent for a moment, staring at him searchingly.

"Yes," she said. "Yes. I am a huge fan."

He reached forward and took her hand into his own and squeezed it. "One moment," he said, and went over to a cardboard box sitting on the merch table. When he came back, he held a small wooden skull in his hand—a dog's toy, really—a fake Sasquatch's head. A joke of a thing. She noticed that he had signed it with a permanent marker, a careful, fussy penmanship that spanned the entire cranium.

He pressed it into her hand. "Here you are," he said. "It's one of the few I have left. Good thing you came when you did."

"Yes," she said. "Good thing. Thank you."

"Ah," he said. He motioned to two women entering the wide

room. "Here are my daughters. They'll help me clean up this mess."
He turned back to her. "What was your name?"

"Agnes," she said.

He took up her hand again and shook it firmly. "Agnes," he
repeated. Then, matter-of-factly, without a thread of affection or
vitriol, he added, "That was my mother's name."

Was.

He smiled at Agnes politely until she moved aside, and the figures from the hallway approached, one short and dark and plain
and the other light and tall and muscular. Her granddaughters. She
smiled at them and lingered for a moment, giving everyone more
time to recognize her, but their faces remained blank. They spoke to
her robotically, polite and inhuman. Like androids, maybe. Naked
gesticulating apes. It didn't matter, then, who was related and who
was not. It made her ache for Mr. Krantz.

She hurried for the exit.

The trio thought she couldn't hear them, but her hearing was
still sharp, and the sound was amplified in the cavernous room.
She could hear every word.

The taller daughter said to her dad, "Do you know that old bird?
She's a weird one."

The shorter woman added, "She looks crazy."

Agnes opened the door, trying to flee before she heard what Eli
said next, his tone no longer phony and polite but sincere, admon-
ishing.

"She's nobody," he said. "And dangerous. Stay as far away from
her as possible."

Agnes was outside now, safe from their words, but she put her
palms up against her ears, anyway, as if to keep them warm.

THE SHACK WAS empty when she returned. It reeked of cooked veg-
etables and Mr. Krantz's ripe body odor, but it was as hollow as an
old gourd.

A small piece of paper was left for her, with an address written on it: an apartment in Lilac City. Somehow the new wife had convinced Mr. Krantz to move with her there, no doubt funded by her wealthy parents.

Come visit! the new wife had written, dotting the *i*'s with hearts. *We'd love to host you!*

Agnes sat on the new rug. They hadn't taken it with them. She stared at the note for a long time before taking up a pen and scrawling her own words across the top. She folded the note carefully and put it into the pocket of an old housedress. She would hold on to the note for almost two more years, fingering the thinning sheet of paper every morning and every night at Gertrude Elms until she received a pink, lacy announcement one cold January morning that Mr. Krantz and the new wife were expecting a baby.

This was when she took the Gertrude Elms shuttle to the post office to buy an envelope and a stamp, when she finally mailed the faded apartment address to her son.

It was more an act of closure, Agnes told herself, than an act of revenge.

AT HER LAST meeting with the Zoophilia Support Group, just before she moved into Gertrude Elms, Agnes reported that she had decided not to seek out her son, after all.

Otherwise, what would she have said? That she was reviled? That he had recognized her but had feigned otherwise, refusing her even the simple kindness of acknowledgment? That she, an old woman, had disgusted her own granddaughters?

So she said she'd never seen him at all.

She was free. Now she could do as she pleased. After the meeting, she would tell Mr. Donald that she was cured. *I'm leaving my husband,* she would say. She would take him up on his offer to place her in a retirement home, Gertrude Elms or Silver Gardens. *Whichever one has space for me,* she would say; *whichever one has a view of the trees.* She very much looked forward to the pristine toilets, to the hot showers. She especially looked forward to the plates and plates of soft, warm food. Her teeth were ruined. The softness would make her weep with joy.

But for now she just smiled and let Mr. Donald pass over her without comment to the pregnant woman seated on her left.

Flannery chose this seat because, as she had earlier confided, she felt a kinship with Agnes. "One mama to another," she had said sweetly.

Agnes had nodded as though in approval, but she was merely being kind. A mama? She was no such thing. Neither was Flannery. The very word was revolting.

"Everything's worked out splendidly with the adoptions," Mr. Donald told Flannery pointedly.

Flannery was as plump as a cow now, bovine in both heft and manner. "I'm going to keep them," she said. She turned to Agnes for approval. "I'm going to keep the puppies."

The man mumbled his objections. Agnes wanted to slap the pregnant woman's dull, fat face.

"Flannery, honey," the man said. "Think of your future. Think of your children. Fatherless, strangers to this world."

"He's right," Agnes agreed. Her voice was loud and harsh and infinitely wise. "He knows what's best for you."

Flannery—uneducated, easily swayed—gazed back at Agnes with a look of stupid incredulity. Troubled, she murmured, "Really? I thought you said . . . about choice?"

"Choice," Agnes scoffed. All of the women in the room were watching her, their faces attentive and trusting. "There's no such thing." She crossed her arms, could feel her bony, weakening chest through the dense hunting jacket. "Shit in one hand, make choices in the other. See which one fills up faster."

Mr. Donald was pleased with her change of heart. He grinned

at her. "Well, yes, Flannery. Don't fret. We'll figure it all out," he said. "We'll figure it all out very soon."

They did figure it out, and quickly.

Flannery went into labor with her dog babies the very next day. Mr. Donald was there. Later, Agnes learned that the puppies nursed from Flannery's breasts with their soft dog's heads, their unopened eyes. Mr. Donald assured her that he would find a good home for them, that they would be loved and cherished; then, after securing her signatures on the necessary paperwork, he swept the puppies away. Flannery wept as they were taken from her, but Agnes liked to imagine that her relief was enormous, too, filled with inordinate sadness but also with boundless hope.

Agnes knew the truth. She had heard rumors of how the ZSG handled their adoptions. Mr. Donald tried to convince them otherwise, but Agnes saw right through him. She could spot a liar as easily as she could spot her own reflection in a flat pool of water.

She knew where he would take the babies. She remembered him striding through the forest, away from the swimming hole at Lost Creek. As soon as she heard about Flannery going into labor, she went to the trail and hid off to one side of the stream.

He kept her waiting long enough that she began to shiver uncontrollably. She could feel the frostbite tingling her nose.

But then he appeared, holding three wriggling potato sacks. He knelt beside the creek and filled each of the sacks with wide, heavy stones from the creek bed.

He, too, was shivering, but he was also whistling a sunny tune.

Agnes watched, hidden in the pines, as he threw the sacks into the deep swimming hole and waited until they sank. Then, brushing off his palms on his pants, he journeyed back the way he had come, whistling all the while.

Agnes raced to the creek's edge. She peered into the icy water, heart hammering. The puppies were down there, submerged. Drowning. Dying.

There was no time to think.

She dove.

2005

ANTIDOTE

On the way to one of her three weekly therapy appointments, Ginger hit a unicorn with her car.

Incredulous, racked (again) with guilt, Ginger relayed the story to her therapist, Gordon.

"Wow," Gordon said. He was a positive guy. He believed any deviance was a sign of progress. "A collision," he marveled. "What a great way to battle your passivity!"

"I creamed it," she continued. "Came out of nowhere. One second there was nothing, black road, and then—*blammo!*—unicorn."

She could still see the poor animal before her: its ivory flesh and noble head, the long, tapered candle of its horn. Her car barreled toward it as though plunging into ecstasy.

"So much beauty in the world, isn't there?" Gordon said.

"It happened on the way here." She showed him her trembling hands. "Just before Glenrose."

"Glenrose," he noted. "Lovely neighborhood."

"There's silver blood on my windshield."

If he thought her crazy, his face belied it. "I hit an elk on Snoqualmie once. Crumpled the hood of my car. God, what a mess! I imagine a horse is similar?"

"Unicorn," she corrected.

"Unicorn," Gordon repeated. He re-crossed his legs. He took no notes. Ginger loved him for that. Her last therapist had typed every word she'd said into a laptop, and the typing had made Ginger very self-conscious. Gordon remembered—or pretended to remember—every detail perfectly well without ever transcribing a word.

Now he asked her, "I wonder what your father would say about this?"

"Dad? Oh. He would be skeptical. He's a scientist, you know. A medical doctor. He prefers hard facts."

Gordon smiled. "He's spent his life pursuing Sasquatch."

"He believes they are real. He would say, *Conclusive evidence*."

"But he's never found one. Not really."

Ginger shook her head sadly. It was embarrassing to her, her father's obsession. She didn't want to be embarrassed by it anymore. It was unfair to him after all of his efforts.

"I'm not blind to the parallels here," she said. "But it wasn't Bigfoot. It was a unicorn."

"Sounds like a ghost. There one moment and gone the next."

Recalling the animal's moonlight flesh and graceful liquidity, Ginger agreed.

"Do you remember what you told me about your father? The dream you had where he was dying?"

Ginger waited, uncertain. She had said so much to Gordon about her dreams. They were horrible, almost always involving a family member's death or dismemberment.

"'Gaunt,' you said, 'pale.' Seeing him dead in the dream, you said he looked like a horse."

"Those teeth." She remembered the cruel bony thrust of them. "He looked inhuman."

"'He glowed,' you said. 'He shimmered.'"

"I was relieved when I woke up," she remembered. "That he was alive. Anyway. I see where you're going with this—"

"It's just an observation, is all, Ginger. I don't want to upset you. It's just, the choice of a unicorn—"

"Choice," Ginger repeated dully.

"—means you're considering your own healing. Hear me out. The magic horn. The restoration of innocence. I believe you've stumbled on your symbolic antidote. See? I think we're at a major crossroads here."

Ginger reached up and played with one of her earrings, a tiny dangling skull. "Antidote for what?" she asked, even though she knew.

"The Gypsy curse," Gordon said.

Ginger wanted to believe him. She wanted to be free of it.

"It's really beautiful how this happened," Gordon said. He tented his fingers together and held them up to his lips, thinking carefully. "You literally *ran into the truth*. Isn't that outstanding? I mean, look at you! Taking matters into your own hands again!"

"I struck it dead with my car," she said doubtfully.

"A confrontation."

"I killed the unicorn, or hurt it, anyway, just like I hurt everyone in my life."

My presence, Ginger had once told Cort, her ex-husband, *is an imposition on the world.*

She was no good for anything now. Her girls needed her, she understood vaguely—they somehow loved her despite her general cheerlessness and forced smiles—but it seemed that goodness, like youth, had fled her permanently. She was thirty-two now, thicker-legged and softer-bellied, decent-enough looking, but uninterested in sex. She was just beginning to understand how average, at best, her talent at painting was. They had recently moved back to Lilac City, at her insistence, and Cort had joined a practice at Deaconess Hospital. Their separation began a few months later. To give herself some autonomy, she began to work at a local grocery store. At present she was the butcher's assistant. Her favorite task was grinding the meat. She tried to remember when she had wanted more from life, but it was hard when you felt so undeserving of any of it.

"I don't even know what I saw," she said now.

"Believe in yourself." The therapist had a wide forceful brow and a clean white beard. He watched her, concerned, and then confided, "I saw Jesus in an Arizona Pizza Hut. He was eating a banana. No one else could see him."

Ginger raised her eyebrows.

"I mean, we were all super high."

"An acid trip is different—"

"Immeasurably different," Gordon allowed, "but it's a type of delusion, isn't it? Drug-fueled, perhaps, but a delusion nonetheless. And powerful. Your belief in the Gypsy curse is also a powerful delusion."

Ginger heard him but as though through water. Gordon harped on the Gypsy curse. He wanted to exorcise her. If she could just "let it go," he said. No more guilt when someone got a cold! No more believing that the curse was to blame for her severe postpartum depression, for the failure of her marriage! No more anxieties about her dad's imminent death! No more fearing that her two girls would one day very soon fall ill, irreparably, because no doubt the curse would destroy them, too!

"The unicorn saw me," she said weakly. "It knew who I was. It was afraid. I see what you're saying, but—"

"Your homework," Gordon said, tapping on his watch to indicate the late hour, "is to find the struck animal. Pull over on your way home. Look for the horse."

"The unicorn. It limped into the woods. Its leg was hanging behind it, like in a war movie. There was a trail of silver blood."

"Pull over." He rose, opening his palm to the door. "Follow the horse."

"Unicorn," Ginger corrected again.

"Unicorn," he said. "Follow it. See what you find."

She left feeling hopeful, more grounded. Her therapist was amazing.

IT WAS THE middle of spring, wet and cold. The forest was strange at night, and Ginger, too long a city dweller, had a difficult time following the trail of iridescent blood. Despite the forest's relative sparseness, she crashed and tripped clumsily over branches and debris. Limbs clawed at her as she walked, and every now and again she panicked, sputtering, as she careened through a spiderweb or an inexplicable wetness. Even the unevenness of the forest floor caught her off guard. A rat's hole sent her sprawling. Picking herself up, bruised and scratched, bleeding, she stumbled on. She nursed a long-dormant anxiety about ticks. She opened up her flip phone and held it before her like a torch. The effect was a terrible one, giving birth to dark shadows that lurked against the trees. She clicked the phone shut and pressed on, half blind, led forward by the thin starlight glow of the unicorn's blood.

Her dad also loved the forest, considered it a second home. She thought of him now and felt for him a deep regret. He was a misunderstood man. Ginger had tried to explain him to Amelia, but Amelia had her own version of him, and Ginger's version rang to her as supremely false.

"He loves you, you know," Ginger had told Amelia a few months ago.

"Yes," Amelia had replied tiredly, "sort of, he does. But not like he loves you. Or Vanessa. Not even close."

Ginger had tried, weakly, to argue, but how could she? How could she explain how sensitive to criticism he was, how afraid he was? How could she say anything truthful without implicating Amelia herself? Ginger surrendered, letting Amelia have the last word, and then privately mourned her own incompetence.

Ginger sensed she should not blame herself for this, either, but she did.

The blood trailed up the mountain, toward the radio towers. Ruby had always been afraid of those towers. "Scary!" she would yell, seeing the towers as they drove home in the dark. "Scary, scary! Wanna go home!"

"They help keep airplanes safe," Ginger would explain. "They aren't scary, not really."

But seeing them reaching into the sky now, thrusting high above the tree line, blinking their red, angry eyes, she saw they were, indeed, scary. *I mean, shit,* Ginger thought, *they are meant as a warning! Of course they are scary!* Why hadn't she allowed Ruby that one honest truth?

Ruby, even with her scarred eye and cheek, had grown into a pretty toddler now. Her imagination was vivid and crushing, capable of conjuring great joy or great despair. She was an enchanted one, that girl, attractor of eagles, granter of wishes, a vessel for magic. The children! Ginger's oldest, Blythe, was pragmatic and willful, as physically strong as twelve men. Or so it seemed. Ginger's heart swelled, tripping through the forest, smelling the life and the rot of the earth, thinking of her girls. She had done wrong by them.

They'd been devastated by the separation. They manifested it in weird ways. Blythe refused to sleep in her own bed, afraid of the "bad men" in her closet. She bunked with Ginger nightly. Ruby began chewing on her fingers, sometimes until she drew blood.

It was hell, but how could she stay with Cort? How could she, when he'd inspired her life's greatest betrayal?

The truth, she saw now, was even simpler: She didn't love Cort. The Gypsy had been correct. He was not the love of her life. Not of her mature life, at least. He was a good man but wrong for her.

She was a horrible person. She loved the girls. That they continued to love her, too, was both a miracle and an injustice.

She did not exactly wish herself dead, but she continued to think that everyone else would benefit from her departure, and, really, what was the difference? Dead and gone were the same thing.

Here the trail ended. Ginger was relieved to find the unicorn alive. It lay on its side, breathing laboriously. Hearing her noisy approach, it lifted its head and regarded her with calm black eyes, too drugged by its own blood loss to fear her and flee.

The beast adjusted its legs. The hind leg, connected by a wide throbbing vein, lifted and drooped. Ginger winced at the opening it revealed: She could see the unicorn's pink innards, the hint of white fractured bone.

"Poor girl," she said to it. "Poor love."

She came forward and knelt beside it. It was smaller than a horse, more deerlike in its delicacy. Ginger stroked its velvet-soft nose and cooed to it. She moved her hands to its ears and rubbed them, and the unicorn relaxed its head onto her thighs and snorted in pleasure. The heat from its nostrils warmed her. The air smelled of fresh grass.

She touched its horn and almost recoiled. It vibrated, scorching her fingertips. The horn was a living, breathing thing. *Healing properties,* Ginger remembered, and she wrapped her palms around it and closed her eyes.

She could feel it moving through her, the salvation.

The relief was extraordinary. The great unburdening! Ginger cried out in surprise.

Then, overwhelmed with joy, she sobbed.

She did not want to let go. She held on for a few more moments. Maybe the feeling would stay with her, if she let go?

She let go.

The darkness returned. After its absence, it hung on her thicker now, its weight nearly unbearable.

Ginger longed to return her hands to the horn, but she worried that having to remove them again would kill her.

The unicorn blew warm air through its nose. It seemed to be moving into its own black twilight. Ginger's heart broke for it. She bent over the animal, half-hugging its ropy neck. Burying her nose in its hide, she let loose the loud, hiccuping sobs of her distant childhood.

When she finished crying (hours later, seconds?), the forest was brighter. The moon had risen. The unicorn no longer seemed at death's door. It breathed calmly, steadily. The blood had coagulated around the wound. The unicorn's eyes were closed as though it meant to sleep. It ruffled its ears. Ginger stood and brushed the dirt off her jeans.

Magical healing properties, Ginger remembered again. Even the unicorn's leg was reattaching itself, sewn back together with the sparkling silver blood, the giant scab drying in a silken swatch.

"I'll be back," she told it. "Don't move. Rest. I'll check up on you."

The unicorn remained motionless, maybe concentrating on healing itself, or maybe just willing Ginger away.

WHEN GINGER GOT to her house, Cort told her the girls were asleep. He offered her a glass of her own beer.

"No, thank you," she said. She felt like she should go on a run. She felt like she should fly to the moon.

"Right," he said. "Hope you don't mind if I had some."

"Of course not," she said, smiling at the open beer bottles, but it irritated her, as everything he did irritated her. "Thank you for watching the girls. I know it's uncomfortable. I appreciate it."

"I love seeing them," he said. "It's no trouble."

Cort looked good. She had to admit it. He looked better than she looked. He was happy, in shape, successful. He was also apparently in love.

"So," he said, leaning proprietarily against the kitchen counter. "How's it going?"

"Oh," she said, waving her hand through the air, "it's great."

"Therapy is good?"

"Great."

"Yeah, Gordo's a good guy."

Cort had recommended Gordon to her, an acquaintance from his residency. Cort had wanted her to see him when they were still together, but she had refused. The problem, she had said, was *them*, and no therapist could help with that.

"Well," Cort said, moving to the sink with his beer glass, turning on the water, "I should go. Meeting Mandy at the bistro."

"Can you stay?" she blurted. "Can you stay a little longer?"

"Tonight? Now?" He shut off the water. He wasn't angry with her—he was never angry with her—but, she saw, he wanted to leave.

"It's just, and I know this sounds like nothing, but I hit a deer with my car tonight."

She couldn't tell him it was a unicorn. She could never express the fantastic to him without confronting her own silliness.

Cort was concerned. He gave her a once-over, even reached forward to jiggle her arm, as though to check if it was broken. "Are you okay? Are you hurt?"

"I'm fine," she said, pulling her arm away. "It's just, it was still alive, lying there next to the road. I want to go check on it. I'll take it a blanket or something. It's lying there in the dark, and it's in shock and cold."

"It'll probably die," Cort said, and she turned away from him. He added quickly, "I'll stay. I'll call Mandy."

"Thank you."

She pulled out her keys. She hadn't removed her coat. Cort was a pushover. She had known he would stay, had never doubted it for a second.

"You can invite your girlfriend over if you want," she said, and he shook his head.

"Will it take long?" he asked her a little helplessly, following her to the back porch.

"Nah. I just need to get the blanket out of the garage and go. I'll be back in thirty minutes, easy."

Cort smiled affectionately at her, coming forward and giving her a light squeeze. "Ginger," he teased. "You've always been a softy."

As though to prove him correct, she stood on her tiptoes and kissed him on the cheek.

"You're a lifesaver," she said, and he beamed at her but casually wiped the kiss away with his shirtsleeve.

It reminded her of what he'd once said to her: *Your unhappiness is contagious.*

BACK IN THE forest, Ginger threaded her way to the unicorn.

There was no doubt about it now: The unicorn was healing itself. It glowed softly on the forest floor, bright enough to cast shadows. It raised its head to gaze at her sleepily, calmly, before lowering it again and shutting its eyes. It was still too weak to fight. It didn't seem to believe she was a threat.

Ginger knelt beside it, cooing, and slowly unwrapped the blanket.

"I brought you something, sweetheart," she told it.

Inside the unfolded blanket was her hacksaw. Ginger drew it into her lap and took a deep breath. Then, reaching up and clutching the unicorn horn with one hand, she grit her teeth and began, despite the sudden fury of the animal, to saw.

AN HOUR LATER, Ginger stood in Gordon's office, smelling of sweat and mud. She clutched the blanket to her chest. She glowed.

"Ginger," Gordon said. "I was just leaving for the night. What are you—"

She unfolded the blanket and pulled out the horn. One end was jagged and broken, smeared with silver liquid. Wet tatters of the animal's torn flesh hung from it.

The other end pointed skyward, a perfect taper.

"Ginger," Gordon said, and brought his hands up as though to touch it. He stopped himself, wiped at his face. He asked her, "What have you done?"

"I'm cured," Ginger said. She thought of the unicorn's corpse in the forest, how it had, without its horn, melted into the ground like spilled water. "The curse. It's broken."

For a moment, Ginger could not tell whether Gordon was afraid of her or in awe of her. It didn't matter. Ginger wouldn't need him anymore. She would return to her children. She would meet a dark-haired man and fall in love. She would be brave for her family, even in the midst of great loss, even in the inevitable decline and death of her parents, whom she needed and loved and could not imagine life without.

The Gypsy had understood all of this. She had understood that people grew sick and died, that suffering and loss were inevitable, that she could blame it on Ginger as a big joke.

Ginger saw all of this for the first time. A joke! A terrible joke! She needn't punish herself any longer.

The unicorn horn pulsed, alive, in her palms.

Gordon stared at the horn hungrily now, his aspect wolflike. He tiptoed toward her.

Ginger backed slowly out of the office, tensing her legs, ready to turn and sprint for the stairs.

"Now," Gordon said, baring his sharp teeth, "*now* we're getting somewhere."

REMOVAL

MR. KRANTZ LIVED IN LILAC CITY WITH HIS NEW WIFE, EMILY, IN a fancy condo furnished by her wealthy parents. The condo was coldly beautiful, with its stainless-steel appliances and smooth marble countertops; it reminded him of a cave he'd briefly inhabited, a cave behind a waterfall. He thought of the noise outside—the interstate—as the noise of a big river. Which is what is was, really, a flat gray river teeming with fleet, metallic fish.

It was morning in late October, cold, smelling brazenly of dead leaves. He awoke as he often did, with his missing foot throbbing. The phantom toes ached; he knew better than to reach down and feel their absence. His steel and silicone appendage, a transtibial prosthetic, rested against the bedroom wall just beneath the window. He rolled toward it, reached for it, and attached it to his leg. The throbbing slowly ebbed. He remained prostrate, enjoying the cool feel of the sheets on his naked body. He enjoyed the privacy of the quiet bedroom and remained there for a long time, wide awake, his senses sparking with the world's intense smells and sounds.

Emily had scheduled a laser depilation appointment for him at the Glow Health Spa, just a few blocks south. A little before nine she hurried into their bedroom, pregnant but not yet showing

(Krantz could smell the change in her hormones the same way he could smell her gingery perfume), to kiss him flush on the mouth and remind him not to be late. She forced a mug of coffee into his hands. He sat up in their bed, watching her bustle. She owned a beauty supply shop near the river, also bought for her by her parents, and she did very well at her work. He rested the coffee on the side table, still finding its taste too bitter to enjoy. Emily insisted. He would never be fully human, she told him, without enjoying the taste of coffee.

"Now, don't be late for your appointment," she said, snapping on her pearl earrings. "I'll catch hell from Wendy. You know how Wendy is."

He didn't know or care how Wendy was, but he grunted his assent.

"Don't be so grumpy, sweetheart." She came and sat beside him on the bed, putting one of her tiny raccoon hands on the knee above his artificial foot. "This last year's been an adjustment. You're doing so well. I'm so proud of you."

He put his hand on her belly and held it there. He felt what he hoped was his son, bumping around like a blind sea horse in her gut, but it was probably just a bit of food, digesting.

"You'll be such a good daddy." Emily put her face close to his. Her eyelashes fluttered like a moth against his cheekbone. "Tell me you love me, bumpkins."

Sometimes he missed Agnes, who lacked all girlhood silliness, who never cared whether he declared his love or his need to take a piss.

But Agnes had never given him a son. Emily, fertile, selfless, was doing that.

He jostled his balls, rising from the bed.

He needed to take a piss.

"You big Goliath," Emily said.

He helped her rise to her feet again, even smoothing out her dress for her over and around her torso. She slapped one of his bare buttocks as he turned for the bathroom.

"You big stud, you," she said.

He could hear the horniness in her voice, and if he'd been more in the mood he might have answered it. But right now he had only one thought in mind: pissing. He went into the bathroom and stood before the toilet. He still hated pissing into this thing. Flushing his heavy-scented urine was such a waste.

"Make sure to raise the seat, sweetie," Emily sang from the bedroom. "Otherwise it sprays the wallpaper."

He raised the seat, annoyed, and then stood holding his dick for a few moments, trying to empty his mind. Finally he gave up, ran some water in the sink, rinsed out his mouth, and spat. When he left the bathroom, bladder still full and aching, his wife waved to him from the doorway and blew him a kiss. She had her purse and keys. She called out that she was running late. He lifted his hand to her and was relieved when the door clicked shut behind her.

There was the sound of the elevator as it sank lower and lower to the garage where she parked her car. Once he was sure of her departure, he opened the front door and looked out into the hallway. It was a boring, plain rectangle, painted in inoffensive tans, with a row of neat golden elevator doors in its westernmost corner. He sniffed the stale air and drew in the smell of detergent and fried eggs and dozens and dozens of people, all of whom he could nearly taste from their scent alone.

Then, satisfied, he put one elbow against the doorframe and pissed onto the hallway's carpet, moaning with pleasure as he did so.

Just as he was shaking out the last drops, the neighbor across the way opened the door for his newspaper.

"Good morning," the man said.

He put on his glasses with one hand and gathered the paper with the other, then glanced up at Mr. Krantz. Mr. Krantz smelled the man's shift from a state of calm to a state of fear. His face, however, betrayed no emotion. His eyes roved over Mr. Krantz's giant, naked body down to his feet—one metal, one flesh—and then landed on the puddle that dampened a good swatch of the tan carpet. He murmured an apology and withdrew into his apartment, and Mr. Krantz decided that the man wasn't such a wimp, after all, as he would have guessed of him from other encounters. Other men might have shrieked or fainted or worse. This one, at the very least, remained calm.

Mr. Krantz finished shaking himself dry. He reentered the apartment, pulling the door shut behind him. He could smell the heaviness of his piss even through the doorway. It pleased him, despite the inevitable consequences: phone calls from the condominium's board of directors, who always fielded residents' complaints about Mr. Krantz's "shocking" behavior; high-pitched, shrieky arguments with Emily, who would wonder why on earth he'd done such a thing when he knew how much it embarrassed her. Those arguments were always short, but her pitch hurt his sensitive ears. It didn't matter. It was worth it, just to know that the hallway was dominantly marked. Besides, his wife's parents owned much of downtown Lilac City, so there would be no kicking them out, despite their neighbors' protests. And, despite the small annoyances, he was glad for their security. Overall, he liked living here.

After a breakfast of rare bison steak and two fistfuls of berries, Mr. Krantz walked to the Glow Health Spa in his broad overcoat, his hat drawn low over his eyes, moving fluidly along with only the faintest of limps. Other pedestrians parted for him with nary a glance, but a small child stared and pointed in disbelief.

"Look at him, Mama," the boy said. "He's so big!"

Mr. Krantz didn't mind the attention. He could tell by the mother's scolding that she believed him to be a man.

"So rude, Horace," she cried. "Really!" Then, to Mr. Krantz, "I'm sorry, sir, he's very young."

Mr. Krantz smiled with his eyes, crinkling them at the edges. His mouth remained downturned. He nodded at the woman and then winked at the boy.

The woman tugged on the boy's hand. "Come along, Horace. Leave this nice man alone."

"Bye, big guy!" the boy cried as Mr. Krantz resumed walking. "Have a great day!"

The boy reminded Mr. Krantz of Agnes's son, that smart, kindly child he'd met all of those long years ago. He had wanted to take the boy with them, but Agnes had said no, that it would be too unkind to the boy's father. Mr. Krantz had reluctantly complied.

But what did it matter now? He was to have his own son! He was certain Emily would have a boy. Mr. Krantz felt that things were going very well for him. He was blending in nicely, urination transgressions aside. He could go wherever he wanted now. He even sensed that he was circling in closer and closer to the doctor's whereabouts. It would be only a matter of time before they met.

Somewhere in town at this very moment, Mr. Krantz thought, the doctor was going about his own day, unaware that Mr. Krantz was looking for him everywhere. Mr. Krantz liked to think about this as he took in the sights of the town. He liked to think that they inhabited the same place, that one day they would literally bump into each other while rounding a street corner, and he liked to think of the doctor's face brightening with recognition.

A part of him still believed the doctor had set the trap, but Agnes had disagreed with him. The trap was too old, she'd said, too rusted. It had likely been left there by someone else.

Maybe she was right, Mr. Krantz granted, but it was the doctor's face, spectacles and all, that he pictured as he gnawed through his own anklebone to escape from those oxidized teeth. By that utterly desperate point, he had not eaten in more than two days, had sipped at the dew from the leaves but was otherwise tunneling toward death. The gnawing was less painful than he'd envisioned.

Any pain was bearable after enduring the jaws of that rusted trap.

When the foot came loose, he dragged himself to Lost Creek and swallowed its glacial waters mouthful by mouthful. He managed to catch a fish. He sucked it down and believed in the moments following that he would die in relative peace.

But Agnes arrived. She'd been searching for him since dawn, walking slowly through the forest until she found him, drained and dying. No emotion—no disappointment or joy—crossed her face when she saw him. She merely dropped to her knees and began to address his wound. She did not ask what happened. She seemed to have her own notions about the whole business.

She urged him to stand and helped him to their cabin, which was not too far away. He limped there with her, gasping from the effort, leaning on her smaller frame. He was in agony but grateful.

He spent a week flailing on their cot. His wife nursed him as best she could. The rusty trap had poisoned his blood, or maybe it was the infection caused by the open wound, which she'd packed with handfuls of river mud. Beneath the dense grove of his fur, his veins blackened. Every infinitesimal movement pained him, from the blinking of his eye to the wiggling of his finger.

His wife disappeared for a full day, and he wondered if she'd abandoned him.

He didn't blame her. He would have done the same.

He thought for the first time how nice it would be to live as a normal man lived, in the city, with clean water that poured from faucets and a humming refrigerator filled with food. He could shave himself, he thought, could wear new clothes, could apply strong cologne. If he lived, he told himself, he would give it a shot. Urban living! Agnes had told him of a big city not far to the west, Lilac City, she called it, and he liked the name. He could move there and become a city dweller. The thought made him smile into the night of his pain. He closed his eyes and felt hope.

Agnes returned. She was wearing the shawl she always wore when she (rarely) descended into Rathdrum. She frowned over him, stuffing a foul-tasting pill into his mouth. She seemed to have aged ten years in the last week, and Mr. Krantz wished he had the strength to reach up and touch her lined face. She was a good wife. His friend, even if he didn't want her anymore. He accepted the pill and later, after sleeping, accepted another.

The antibiotics worked quickly. Mr. Krantz began to feel like himself again. He took short, awkward hops around the cabin, then deeper into the forest, and then down the hill to Rathdrum, gripping trees for balance. Agnes encouraged him. She lifted an old crutch from a pawnshop and pressed it on him. He shoved it under his armpit for support, and with practice he regained his speed. He was nearly as fast as his old self but much noisier now. The noise bothered him, but it also gave him something to focus on. He listened to himself moving through the forest, listened to his panting and shuffling as he descended from forest to town.

This was the onset of his restless phase, when he began studying the habits of everyday people.

He wanted to understand them and learn how to blend in with them. He knew Agnes would have nothing to do with his plan. He kept it a secret. He waited, and watched, and plotted.

Years passed. Eventually he met Emily, just outside town at a ribbon-cutting ceremony for Rathdrum's newest deluxe condominiums, which were owned by her parents. The condos boasted a view of the forest. She had wandered away from the crowd to the trees, where he presented himself to her, naked: crutch, healed stump, and all. Rather than run away screaming, she had smiled at him, impressed and playful. He drew her up under one arm then and there, ferrying her through the woods back to his cabin while she giggled and fretted. She was a nice enough woman, sheltered, pretty, and bored with life in Lilac City. She fell in love with what she called his "sense of adventure." She did not, however, love the woods or the little shack. She soon demanded that they live in Lilac City. He agreed. She demanded that he wear good clothes, learn some manners, eat with cutlery, live like a real man. He agreed to that, too. He appreciated the challenge.

They left a note for Agnes and went to live with Emily's parents while their new condo was being remodeled for them. The parents received them both with open arms.

"A real man's man," her father said, clapping him on the back. "Her last husband was a real talker. Couldn't shut the man up. But you, you're a humble sort. I appreciate a silent man."

"And attractive, to boot," Emily's mom said, waggling her glass of gin in the air in a sort of toast to him.

Mr. Krantz stood with them on their ample lawn, with its glittering fountains and cylindrical topiaries, enduring the attention. He wore a polo shirt and a pair of trousers, specially sewn for him by a local seamstress. The clothes felt clean and comfortable, and he really didn't mind them. Beside him, Emily snuggled against his arm and beamed; he could smell the fertility in her, and he thought about how well-fed his children would be.

Soon after that, Emily's parents told them the condominium was finally ready for them, and Mr. Krantz was relieved to regain some privacy.

At the depilation appointment, the dermatologist entered the room and stood over Mr. Krantz's prepped body. She warned him to brace himself.

"This is the painful part," she said, "although I probably don't need to remind you."

This was his second removal. The dermatologist had suspected seven or eight appointments might be necessary in total, given "the severity" of his "hair problem."

Emily had been with him then. She had said cheerfully, "Whatever it takes. He can handle it."

She loved him without hair; she said that she could now see "the real him." It was shocking to him to see himself in a mirror, smooth as a stone, and pale. The world was so much colder without his hair; he wore the clothes now not because it was expected of him but because he needed them to stop the shivering. Eventually, the follicles would be permanently damaged: The hair would never grow back. It would be a vanished part of himself, a premature death.

Agnes would hate to hear of this. She would look at him as if he were crazy.

What would Emily do about their son if he was hairy like his dad? Would he be expected to undergo the same laser-beamed torture?

The dermatologist pulled up a stool and pressed a few buttons on the machine beside her. She took up the wand and bent over him, preparing to laser his hair roots into oblivion. He hated the feel of the gooey cream all over him; it smelled terrible, too, of the most unnatural chemicals. His whole body tensed now, remembering the pain of the last treatment.

It was worth it, he reminded himself. That was his mantra now. It was all worth it.

The woods would always be there if he wanted them, once he finished what he'd come here to do. But the more he changed, the less the woods would accept him. He could feel both the pain and the comfort of this irrevocable shape-shifting, and he hated and lusted for it both.

He gritted his teeth as the laser wand approached the top edge of his thigh.

He closed his eyes and thought of the doctor then, much as he'd thought of him when he'd lain in the woods all of those years ago, bleeding to death in that rusted trap.

It was worth it, to create a better world for himself, for his son, a world without such a man.

He'd endure this pain, too.

He'd become a man, whatever it took.

Then he'd find the doctor.

I'll find him, Mr. Krantz thought, feeling his phantom toes curl. He breathed in the smell of his own scorched flesh. *I'll find him and I'll kill him dead, dead, dead.*

2006

PRODUCE THE MONSTER

NEARING THE END OF HIS LIFE, REALIZING WITH A FRANTIC CERtainty that he might never locate Mr. Krantz, Eli became disagreeable; he became, as Vanessa teased him, a grumpy old man.

He refused to speak at conferences anymore. He stopped trying to find funding for SNaRL. He paid for everything with his own retirement money, and Vanessa allowed him to do so. Crippled by a sloping spine and weak hips, Eli bought an ATV. It improved his mobility, but his visits to the woods felt more intrusive. He rattled through the forest loudly, wearing a headlamp, his father's rifle in hand. He glared into the darkness and waited for Mr. Krantz to appear. He never did.

After Jane Goodall expressed interest in Sasquatch research, there was a flurry of reluctant interest in cryptozoology. A few local journalists contacted Eli for comment. Despite his grumpiness, he did agree to an interview, if only to communicate his frustration with the whole business.

"And what will you do," a woman, some reporter from *The Lilac City Monitor,* had asked him, "when you find your Sasquatch?"

They sat in his pristine home office, facing each other over the neat surface of his desk. Cups of coffee steamed before them, untouched. He motioned at the rifle leaning against the wall, a beautiful mahogany Winchester 1894 lever-action .30-30, a beloved gift from his father.

"I'll shoot him," Eli said.

The journalist bolted upright from her chair. "Kill it?" she cried.

"Shoot him dead," he confirmed. "Irrefutable proof. An actual corpse is the only way to prove its existence. It's the only way."

The woman poked at him with a few more questions, but she was mostly finished. She primly tidied up her materials, her notebook and her unused pen and her recording device, trying to seem calm. Eli watched her gravely. He pictured her eager return to a miserable newsroom cubicle, where she would immediately type out her scathing, mocking, factual little article. She was so excited that she didn't even say goodbye.

Sure enough, the article appeared the following morning, placed, to his astonishment, on the front page of the paper.

DEADFOOT, the headline read.

Cryptozoologist Dr. Eli Roebuck has unexpected plans for his Sasquatch once he finds it: He'll shoot it dead!

Oh, the phone calls he had received after that.

PETA contacted him, sending him a faux pelt splashed with red dye and a note that read, *No creature will suffer!* His own bleeding-heart-liberal daughter, Ginger, left him a message about how the president should ban guns. Amelia called, laughing, to say that she thought the article was a riot. Gladys wrote him a long, careful letter saying that he looked handsome, if aged, in the photo taken of him. Also, since he was so famous, would he mind sending her a little extra cash? There were medical bills, so many medical bills! Signed, *your loving wife of nearly twenty years.* Even his *real* loving wife, Vanessa, who typically supported him in all things, blanched when she read the article, which he had shoved at her with what she maybe mistook as pride.

"You need to tone it down, Eli," she advised. "You sound desperate."

Eli nearly exploded. *Desperate! Wow! How astute! How smart you are! Way to go, Vanessa, you observant poet, you intuitive woman! How incredibly perceptive of you! Because who would have ever guessed? You've noticed that, after years and years and years of searching for this one goddamn thing, after tedious decades of research and catalogs and arguments and fieldwork and discussions and aching, throbbing desire, perhaps I've grown desperate! Well, I have! Thanks for noticing!*

He was not one for sarcasm, though, so he merely said, his face blank, "Ah. Well."

She was a good wife, a good wife who loved him. She patted his knee and gave him a sour smile. She cared for him. He sorrowed for them both.

The thing was, about the killing: He meant it. When he went on his excursions nowadays, he took the Winchester with him. He stopped searching for Mr. Krantz during the day, believing firmly now that he was nocturnal. He wore a headlamp and bounced along the uneven forestry roads in his new ATV, his dogs happily panting in the backseat, all of them enjoying the cool night air, and sometimes he drank a little whiskey. Sometimes he yelled at the top of his lungs, emitting a pained, elongated yodel.

It was a stupid plan: to drive an ATV, to wear a headlamp, to bring the dogs, to cry out in the night; why was he crashing through the forest like this, scaring away every living beast within a fifteen-mile radius?

It was, as Vanessa noted, desperation.

The Sleep of Reason Produces Monsters, Eli remembered, and so here he was. Maybe if Eli was irrational, his own monster would finally appear. Who knew? Mr. Krantz might just wander over to the road and stare at him as he passed. From his own research, Eli had concluded that Mr. Krantz and his type were shy, private creatures but also curious. If Eli made enough noise, if he seemed interesting enough, Mr. Krantz might just come up to the road's edge and peer at him. The key, the doctor believed, was spotting Mr. Krantz in the underbrush. And, if he saw him, he would stop the ATV, shush the dogs, raise a hand and murmur a soft greeting, then quickly aim the Winchester and shoot Mr. Krantz dead. Not because he was some sick killer, some horrible person, but because it was the only way to ensure both of their spots in the scientific firmament.

It was not a revenge thing, Eli told himself. It was not about bitterness. It had nothing to do with his mom or with his lost childhood. It was about human progress. It was about humanity, period.

Though he admitted to himself that he might enjoy the look of agony on Mr. Krantz's beastly face.

But nothing happened. The days grew colder and the nights longer, and then the days grew warmer and the nights shorter, and the cycle repeated itself, and sometimes Eli would go to his office window and look out over the forest and imagine moving, for the first time, away from Washington State, away from the north to warmer country, somewhere hominid-free, where time seemed to stand still. Hawaii, say. Jamaica.

He thought of his mother, the old hag. She'd come to him recently at a conference he'd spoken at, and he'd blatantly pretended not to recognize her. He wanted nothing to do with her. He'd been both pleased and slightly disturbed by her hurt face, her slow walk away from him. She'd made no attempt to explain herself. *Good riddance,* he'd thought then. There were wonderful women in the world, Eli knew—his wife, his daughters—but there were also women like Gladys and Agnes, depraved, loveless, mentally disturbed women who didn't truly know what they wanted from life. It was women like these who fucked up the world. It was women like these who hurt good men, who asked for too much, who slept with beasts. They made the pure impure: DNA; childhood; love itself.

Eli began to mourn his entire adult life. No one would ever

believe him until he emerged from the forest dragging Mr. Krantz's carcass behind him. It was the only possible vindication. As his life neared its close, it was the one thing Eli truly wanted.

READING *THE LILAC City Monitor* one day, Eli came across another article about Sasquatch, written by the same blond journalist. It focused on a middle-aged anthropologist and anatomy professor at the University of Idaho in Moscow, a man by the name of Eugene Ferm.

Ferm, too, believed in the Sasquatch, despite the dubious reputation it earned him among his academic colleagues.

Like Dr. Roebuck, he, too, was obsessed with the accuracy of existing evidence and floored by the scientific community's refusal to take it seriously.

For a moment, Eli believed that he had found an ally. He would drive to Moscow that very day, he decided. He would drive there and shake Ferm's hand and offer to assist him in his research.

"New species of apes have been found all over the world," Mr. *Eugene Ferm, Ph.D., said as he drank a strong-smelling cup of green tea. "Cryptozoologists, in fact, have played a major part in their discovery. The Sasquatch is not some ridiculous made-up legend, like a sea monster or a unicorn. Think of it as a missing link. Just imagine what it would mean for our natural history. It would be astounding! It's important research."*

Eli thought, *Yes! I've felt and said these very same things for several decades now!* He continued reading:

"You've gotta have a great sense of humor to do this," Ferm said, *laughing, when asked about his angry colleagues and overzealous fans. "You've gotta have tough skin."*

Again Eli thought, *Yes! I adore this man! He, unlike anyone else, understands!*

But then, toward the end of the article, he was alarmed to find himself mentioned, and not in flattering terms.

Despite the appreciation Mr. Ferm feels for his supporters, he admits that some of his most loyal followers are "a bit strange."

"These are people not looking at this from a scientific standpoint," Ferm said. *"They want Sasquatch to exist as a magical entity. They don't want to sit and hear me lecture about bipedal ambulation, about foot flexes. They want some crazy circus-sideshow act. And then you have quote-unquote scientists—hobbyists, really—who are threatening to kill the Sasquatch if they find it. This is a disservice to serious researchers."*

Such researchers include Dr. Eli Roebuck, once a prominent podiatrist in the Inland Empire, who has, in the course of the last three decades, garnered quite a following (and made quite a profit) with lectures and even a book, The Sasquatch Hunter's Almanac, *on Northwest monsters.*

"What if someone had harpooned the giant squid rather than filming it? What would that say about us?" Mr. Ferm grew teary-eyed as he spoke. "I'm interested in the potential life of these mammals. I'm not at all interested in their murder. It is a disservice to humankind to wish them dead."

Mr. Ferm went on to say that while he respects much of Dr. Roebuck's research, he believes that in recent years the older researcher has lost his way.

"We need to embrace the scientific method involved with such research. We cannot merely argue for one side without considering the other. The truth is, the Sasquatch simply may not exist. We have to be honest about all possibilities. It is possible, after all, that it is a fabrication."

I couldn't help but ask, "Is that what you believe?"

With a wink, Mr. Ferm concluded, "In my heart? No."

Clearly, Eugene Ferm is our best hope for finding this gentle, shy Bigfoot.

Eli finished reading the article and removed his red-framed glasses. He wiped at his eyes with his knuckles so that uneven bright splotches of light played on his shuttered eyelids. Then, leaving his glasses on the table, nearly blind with hatred and nearsightedness, Eli went to the utility room and retrieved his rifle. He went outside and sat down, *plop*, in the middle of his long wide driveway. It was late January, the earth frosted and cold. His haunches ached from the driveway's ice.

The Roebuck home butted up to a forested mountainside sloping away from the heart of Lilac City. Through the pastel blur, Eli could just make out the green smear of trees that indicated the edge of his property.

He aimed the rifle lazily and shot randomly into the trees.

Two figures came running out at him, waving their arms.

"Stop!" the taller figure cried. "Stop shooting! You'll kill us!"

The figures drew near. It was a man with a small boy at his side. Eli's heart hammered. *My God*, he thought. *You almost killed a damn kid.*

"What are you doing out there?" Eli demanded. He wanted to blame someone else. "This is private property."

The man and boy had blurry features, matching orange hunting caps shoved atop their heads. Eli rose to go back inside to get his glasses.

"You can't just shoot at things like that," the man said angrily. "You could have killed my son."

Eli began to walk toward the house, dragging the Winchester with him. He was not trying to be rude, but he wanted his eyeglasses. It seemed to him that this man was his father, that this boy was his younger self. He wanted to put on his glasses and destroy that impression.

"Don't turn away from me, mister. These woods have a public trail running through them."

The man stood there, lifting his arms in anger. Eli straightened at the door, horror-stricken. Although he couldn't make out the little boy's face very well, he could hear him breathing roughly through his small nose, and he could see that he wore large spectacles, just as Eli had as a child.

The man continued, raging, "Give me the gun. Give it here now."

Eli could only stand there awkwardly, gazing in their general direction with a sorrowful expression. *I'm sorry, Dad,* he wanted to say. *I let you down.*

He leaned the rifle against the doorframe, and the man stomped up the stairs and retrieved it.

"All right. All right. It's okay now, old man. Listen. Are you okay? You're not wearing a coat. Can you say your name? Do you need a doctor?" He looked toward the garage. "Do you have a vehicle here? I could drive you."

Eli shook his head. "I haven't had a stroke. Nothing like that. I'm lucid. I'm . . . I'm having a bad day."

"You do see the danger here, though," the man pressed.

"If I could go inside and retrieve my glasses—"

"You could have killed someone. Do you know how far these bullets travel?"

Eli said that he didn't, not exactly.

"Miles! You could have shot someone already and we don't know about it yet!"

Eli considered this. His shoulders slumped. Why was he allowing himself to be reprimanded? Had he really sunk so low?

"I've been very stupid," he said now. "I'm sorry."

"Well, I don't know," the man said after a moment, perhaps seeing how shocked Eli looked, how deeply frightened and regretful. "Bullet's no doubt lodged in a tree somewhere. Stuck in the dirt." How like his father this man spoke, so calm and so forgiving! "I'm sure it's okay. But . . . I'm going to take this. For today. Until you're feeling better."

He came forward and scribbled an address on the wood railing with a pencil stub he fished out of his breast pocket.

"Here's my address. I'm not stealing it, you know. You come

around and pick it up when you're feeling better. How's that sound?"

Eli wanted the Winchester back now. He didn't want to surrender it to anyone, not until he killed Mr. Krantz with it. Or until he killed Eugene Ferm.

He chuckled at the thought.

"I'm worried about you," the man said. "Okay? I'm worried. You seem off your rocker. So I'll take your rifle, all right? For the day."

It was easy for Eli to comply, to trust this kindly man, his own dead dad.

The man was comfortable with a rifle. He removed the cartridges and clicked on the safety. He hung it through the crook of one elbow and then nudged his son toward the woods with the opposite hand. The boy looked over his shoulder at Eli, just once, before falling into step with his dad.

"I'm sorry," Eli called again, and the man raised a hand without looking over his shoulder, and the boy stumbled, and then caught himself, and then stumbled again.

Eli hurried inside and grabbed his glasses and returned to the sun-and-ice-streaked field, the frozen molehills, the distant trees. The father and son were far away now, almost to the tree line. The little boy was running here and there, picking up sticks and rocks in his mittened hands and then, finding a better treasure, letting them fall, speaking in an excited way with his father. He was small and curious, mercurial as a deer mouse.

It was the ghost of his young self. There was no doubt.

VANESSA NOTICED THE missing Winchester on her return from the grocery store and asked him where it had gone. It had sat sentry for days in the utility room, and he could tell that its presence—and now its absence—made her jumpy.

Vanessa did not believe that she was a pushy woman, but she

was the pushiest Eli had ever met, however tacitly. His first wife had been pushy, too, although not as clever. Vanessa was excellent at playing dumb. Gladys would never have allowed herself to try; she would rather seem crazy than incompetent.

"Oh," he said. "I've put it away. I won't be needing it for a while, I don't think."

"Hmm," Vanessa said with forced insouciance. "I thought I'd make steaks for dinner."

This, then, was his reward. She was already cracking open the red wine. It was a pleasant dinner, and Eli was momentarily cheered.

But the next morning, stepping onto the front porch to smoke his cigar, he put his fingers against the railing and carefully studied the sloppy pencil scrawl of his dead father.

The Harms 9710 palouse hwy
comeby anytime.

He didn't even tell Vanessa. He just left: stubbed out his cigar on the top cement step and left it there in the way that she hated (*Use the coffee can, Eli! That's what I put it there for!*), got in his car, drove away. She had been rambling at dinner about Ginger, about her recently finalized divorce from Cort, about their sweet grandchildren. She was delighted with the prospect of Ginger moving back in with them. She argued for it daily. He had listened to Vanessa half-heartedly, pleasantly buzzing from the wine. *Sure,* he had said, *she can move in here. The kids, too. Sure. Why not? Might be a good thing—the noise, the chaos, the energized voices. Might be just the thing they need.*

He had asked Vanessa about her poetry. "Written anything lately?" he had asked.

She had frowned into her wineglass. "Well, no," she'd replied. "I've been so busy."

With what? What did they busy themselves with nowadays? What, after all of these years, was there left to do?

It seemed as if every day she came home with some large purchase from some distant store—never anything for herself but something for the house, or some new pants for him, or a present for the grandchildren, or a bag of exotic groceries, most of which ended up in the trash.

It was as though there were some large hole behind the house that she hoped to fill with acres of newly purchased crap.

We need this, she would say. *I need to go get that for us. They need this. You need this.*

But she never said, *I need.* And especially not *I want.* Wanting would be too unimportant.

The two of us are pathetic, Eli thought as he turned onto the winding gray ribbon of the Palouse Highway. They wanted major responsibilities, ways to be involved, but they were at the age where nothing further was expected of them. No doubt this was why Vanessa was practically begging Ginger to come and stay with them for a while, why she begged to babysit the grandkids. This was why he was firing rifle shots into the forest. Just to have an impact. Positive or negative. Inspire or destroy.

"You asshole," he muttered, and he was not talking to himself— he was talking, as he frequently did, to Mr. Krantz, that elusive, selfish piece of shit. He spoke to him the way an angry zealot speaks to God, desperately and bitterly. *Why have you forsaken me,* he might have said. It was a similar powerlessness.

He had been on the verge of proving his existence nearly a dozen times over, but the evidence would recede from him like a wave, and the reality of it would turn to water in his hands and drip away as cold useless possibility.

His wife indicated that she understood; she felt the same way about her poetry. *So elusive,* she would say, *just like your Sasquatch.*

She tried to relate to him in this manner, but it did not, for him, compute.

He poured himself into his work. She simply avoided it.

There was, he felt, no contest.

THE HARMS LIVED in a small pale-yellow home that had once been white but was now stained an unhealthy urine color from persistent wind and dust. It sat at the top of a tall bare butte, displaying an impressive view of the rolling Palouse farmland. It was winter now, the ugly season, when all of the bright colors had been drained from the world, but still Eli admired the icy brown earth, the white-laced sky. It was cold but snowless. The air was dry and sharp and smelled of cow shit.

An old lonely mare stood behind a beat-up fence. She was as brown and ice-streaked as the field on which she stood. Eli drew close and attempted to rub the furry plate between her ears, but she tossed her head and breathed heavily through her nostrils, and he sensed her disdain. He left her alone and went to the front porch.

The boy came to the door and Eli sucked in a breath. He stared at this vision of his younger self. Little Eli stared back at him with a wry mouth, as though he had been expecting Grown Eli's visit.

He pulled open the screen door and said, "What're you doing, mister? Better get inside. Don't let out the heat."

Eli withdrew his hat and entered, and Little Eli politely asked if he'd like to sit down.

"I'd forgotten how nice I was," Eli said to the boy. "I forgot all about that."

The boy smiled patiently and accepted the doctor's hat and went to hang it on the coatrack.

It was not Eli's exact childhood home—he had grown up near Stateline, some twenty miles away—but the similarities between the two were striking. The furniture was spare and masculine, the windows small but washed. The smell of burning wood and soap permeated the air, a smell so familiar that Eli wanted to lie down and press his nose into the cold wooden floorboards. The only warmth in the room—a thick, gathering blanket of it—pushed at him from the wide-bellied woodstove in the corner. Through a small charred window in the stove's belly, he could see the logs burning, cheerful amber twigs cracking and snapping. He thought of the color of his mother's hair, of Amelia's hair.

The boy returned to the dark-green couch and sat at its opposite end, his posture perfectly erect, his little fingers entwined on his lap. A dog padded into the room from what must have been the kitchen, and the boy lit up at the sight of him. Forgetting himself, he collapsed onto his knees and wrapped his arms around the animal's neck.

"I always loved dogs, didn't I?" Eli said.

The boy, smiling, patting the dog's head, said, "Me, too." He kissed the wrinkled folds of flesh on the dog's forehead. "This is Lethe."

"Lethe?" Eli said. "Like the river?"

"Like the dog," the boy said.

Loud sounds rang from the tail of the house, someone stomping the earth from their boots. A man emerged from the kitchen. The boy's father. Eli rose to his feet and offered his hand.

"Mr. Harm," he said. *Hello, Dad.*

"Hello again," the man replied, declining the hand, holding up his soiled fingers for inspection. "I was killing a chicken. I apologize for my clothes."

A wide random pathway of blood ran across his fingers and coat.

He continued, "I was distracted and did a poor job."

"I'm pleased to hear people still do that," Eli said. He felt silly as he said it. He sounded like a visitor to a foreign country, appreciating the native's exotic behaviors. He worried about being offensive.

"I mean, I did that, as a boy. I would help you—my dad, that is—I would help my dad kill our chickens. I hated it, but I did it."

"My son hates it, too," Mr. Harm said. "Still, he has to learn. Important to know where your food comes from, I say."

"Yes," Eli agreed. He looked at the boy, playing on the floor with his dog, and his eyes watered. "He's a beautiful boy," he said, and Mr. Harm glowed with pride.

"He is. And smart. Smarter than me. Kid could do anything one day. Be a lawyer. Be a doctor. He'll go places, this guy."

If Little Eli heard them, he hid it well, but Eli knew that he was drinking in every word, letting it settle into his bones, where it would sit until his last days, as warm and subtle as the woodstove's final embers. It would propel him to do those things, to enroll in university classes, to study hard, to become a doctor. It would become a nearly impossible place from which to rebel.

"It's hard for a boy," Eli said. "Hard for him because he's sensitive. But you're doing right by him. All a boy needs is his father, if the father's a good one. One day he won't even remember his mom."

"Is that right, now?"

"Oh, yes," Eli said.

"I always felt the opposite. A boy needs his mother. We men are . . . what's the word? Super—oh, good grief. I'm blanking on it."

"Superfluous," Eli said.

"Yes, that's it. We're beside the point. Yes. That's it exactly. Beside the point. That's what we are."

"You're doing a bang-up job," Eli insisted. If only someone had been there when he was a boy, to reassure his aching, uncertain father. "The boy is happy. Anyone can see that. You're all he needs, I'm sure of it."

A look of confusion again crossed Mr. Harm's face, and he opened his mouth as though to speak, but he grew distracted by the sound of a car door slamming. Eli wondered who in the world would be coming to *their* door way out here in the Palouse on a weekday morning, but then the door burst open to reveal a slender, plain woman with auburn hair, stamping the ice from her sensible shoes. She held a heavy grocery sack against her hip.

"Hello," she said to Eli. "How are you?" Then, turning to Mr. Harm, "The car is bursting. I overspent! I almost had to rent a trailer!" She laughed.

Mr. Harm hurried outside to assist her. Little Eli rose, too, but his father encouraged him to remain and entertain their guest. The boy returned with a little droop to his shoulders. Clearly it was a bit of a chore to speak to this older gentleman, who meant well, certainly, but who seemed to lean in a little too much, to speak with too much emotion, and to spit on his face unwittingly.

The boy, ever polite, smiled.

"That's not our mother?" Eli asked, his own smile having faded.

The boy crouched again beside his dog, rubbing at the animal's long, soft ears. He didn't respond to the question.

"Is that our mother?" Eli rephrased, and the boy nodded. The way he nodded indicated that he liked their mother—loved her— very, very much.

"Listen to me," Eli said, sliding with some difficulty onto the floor near the boy. "Listen to me. You love her and you don't expect it, but the bad day will come. She will leave you. She will leave you one day soon, and it will be too late. Don't let anyone in the house. No one. No strangers. Just the three of you, you see. Just the three of you, and you will—"

"What are you doing?" asked Mr. Harm.

The mother stood behind him, alarmed. Their arms were loaded with groceries.

Eli's hands were on the boy's shoulders, shaking him lightly. He pulled away, looking to his younger self for help, but the boy only jumped away from him, speeding over to his mother and burying his face into the thighs of her jeans.

She put a hand in his hair. "It's all right," she said to him, but she eyed Eli angrily.

Eli rose with great difficulty, his bones old and unwilling. He pardoned himself and walked outside. The man followed him, menacing now. He had set down his groceries and gripped Eli's rifle.

"I'm not sure what's wrong with you, old man," he said. "You've been acting awfully funny. Don't think I'll give you back your gun, after all."

Eli was seventy-one years old. He would soon be dead. He didn't know this outright, but he sensed it. He was dizzy, panting. There seemed to be flies buzzing at the periphery of his vision, a ridiculous sensation to experience in the middle of a bleak winter's day.

"Gonna keep your gun," the man said again. It was pointed at the ground, but it may as well have been pointed at Eli's heart. "For everyone's sake."

"Okay," he agreed. "All right."

"It's my gun, anyway," the man said, and Eli acknowledged this as the truth.

He got into his car and drove away, and he had no idea where he was going other than that it was south.

IT WAS SNOWING when Eli pulled into the avenues of the University of Idaho.

He did not have his rifle, as he had originally planned, but he had his fists. He would wound Eugene Ferm one way or another.

The professor was in his office, grading papers during his office hours. He was a huge, barrel-chested man with gentle eyes and skin the deep rich brown of those who live on the Indian Ocean. The size of him, the gentleness, surprised Eli, and at first he was speechless as he passed through the doorframe. He wavered slightly, and Eugene Ferm reluctantly pulled his gaze away from his work.

With his soft, precise accent, Ferm said, "Yes? May I help you?"

Regaining his composure, Eli introduced himself.

"Ah!" Ferm exclaimed, leaping to his feet and pumping Dr. Roebuck's hand. "The man himself! Of course I recognize you! What a delight to finally meet you. I've been very drawn to your work, as I'm sure you know. You've done amazing things for Sasquatch, have you not? Come, come, I've something to show you."

Eli was confused. "What?"

He had expected many things: tears, blood, invective, but not this.

"Come! I beg of you! My dear friend! I must show you something."

Eli followed Ferm, dazed. The larger man stomped like an elephant down the narrow hallway, every now and again looking over his shoulder to grin happily at his companion.

"What a good day this is turning out to be," Ferm said. His voice was contrary to his stature: lilting, light.

Eli walked uncertainly behind him. He did not want to trust this man, but it was hard not to, so friendly was he, so effusive.

"You're a great hero to our society," Ferm gushed. "As a young man, I followed your career rather enviously. Ah, here we are."

They had reached a doorway. Ferm opened the door and plunged into a stairwell's black narrow maw, igniting a light with a blind flick of his hand as he did so. Eli followed swiftly, with half a thought to push Ferm down the stairs.

The stairwell was gray and yellow and musty, its stairs short and uneven.

"What you said about the stride characteristics was spot-on," Ferm said. "You know, the whole Patterson-Gimlin video thing, about the size of her gluteal muscles. It was so illuminating, Eli, and it explained so very much." He laughed. "Her butt! That's what's so great. How do the kids say it nowadays? 'Baby got back'? 'Cause she does! She most certainly does!"

At the bottom of the staircase, Ferm pulled out an enormous set of keys and thrust one of them into a lonely door. He pushed on the door with one shoulder, the wood having been painted sloppily so that it stuck.

With a grunt, Ferm disappeared inside, then reappeared to bark at Eli, "Get in here, sir! Please, I mean."

He ignited another panel of lights.

Inside was a small, shallow room, no doubt meant as a janitorial closet, but it had been refurbished into a cryptozoological museum, filled with fur and bone samples and foot molds, all labeled meticulously with laminated name tags and arranged carefully behind locked glass cabinets.

Eli took a deep breath of air. It was dust-free. The room smelled of Lysol.

"It's amazing," Eli admitted. He had his own samples, his own foot molds, but they were packed away into cardboard boxes in the SNaRL basement, no use to anyone any longer. SNaRL itself was almost purely an Internet presence now, and not one he really had an investment in any longer; it was mostly run by unpaid college interns and middle-aged hobbyists. It was self-propelled by online interest and ads but not nearly as factual as it had once been.

Eugene Ferm stood there with his stupid grin, his knuckles resting on his hips. He was like a monarch surveying his kingdom.

"Had to beg the university for this space. Totally unused. They wanted to give it to some biologist for cereal storage. Cereals! Hilarious. Not that I can sneer at anyone's passions. I mean, we scholars must be understanding if we expect others to understand us."

"Us?" Dr. Roebuck said, and his sharp tone made Eugene Ferm's mouth thicken.

"Oh, I see. I wondered why you came. You're not upset about the interview, are you?" Ferm looked disappointed, and Eli felt a little guilty. "I thought you'd come to help me. Or maybe to ask for my help." Seeing Eli stiffen, Ferm raised one hand and hurried on: "Again, I only mean this respectfully. I know you've been at this a lot longer than I have been. I'm a pragmatist. So I fully understand that in another thirty years, I might very well want the Sasquatch dead myself."

"It's the only way."

"Do you know," Ferm said casually, "that the Nazis justified their actions by telling themselves that their victims were not human? Are you telling me, as a serious scientist, that you don't believe Sasquatch possibly shares many characteristics with man?"

Eli stared into his own foggy reflection in a glass case, rattled.

"And what if this is the last of the species? What then? You kill it to prove it does not exist? It's preposterous!" Ferm waited only a moment before continuing, with a friendly laugh, "No. I don't think you believe this. You wouldn't really pull the trigger on our woodland friend, not unless you shoot it in the back. You haven't thought through any of this, not really."

"You don't know me. You don't know my history with him."

"My poor man. Taking things personally is not our job." He had an arresting way of speaking that was brutally honest but not at all judgmental; he was completely devoid of subterfuge, made completely of logic. "I think you're so dead set on proving, you forget that there is just as much power in *dis*proving."

Eli straightened his small shoulders and frowned up at Ferm. "So that's what you're doing? Disproving?"

"Oh, no. I'm only saying, you put too much pressure on yourself. If you look at it more scientifically, less personally, if you put as much stock in *not* finding Sasquatch as you do in *finding* Sasquatch, then you'll be much happier with your results."

Eli looked around the room. The venom had been sucked out of him. He was a shell now, all used up. "So," he said. "You wanted to show me all this? All of this non-evidence?"

"This." Dr. Ferm steered Eli to a glass case near the doorway. The laminated name tag said HELLO MY NAME IS in orange print, followed by painstakingly neat handwriting, in permanent marker: *UMATILLA NATIONAL FOREST; WALLA WALLA #58: 35 CM*

(13.75 in) LONG AND 13 CM (5.12 in) WIDE. It referred to a giant plaster cast of a footprint that Ferm, after unlocking the glass with a tiny key from his enormous key chain, handed to Dr. Roebuck.

It was beautiful. It had been months—years even—since Eli had enjoyed the feel of a dense, irrefutable plaster cast in his hands. He ran his fingers along the intricate dermal ridges, the wide, inhuman toe gouges. It was too perfect to have been faked.

"I'm finishing up a paper on the functional morphology here," Ferm said, and for the first time Dr. Roebuck heard pride and excitement in his tone. "It's the most gorgeous print I've yet seen."

But Eli had seen better prints. He, too, had experienced the glow and excitement, but it had transpired long years ago, when he had been this man's age, late forties, early fifties. That time in life when you sense you are an old man but you are wrong, because actual old age is so very unknowable, so far more difficult, so far more taxing and terrible than you could ever have imagined—prostate cancer, for example, or an inability to truly stand up straight anymore, due to dissolving disks in your back, and pills, endless pills, so that you have to spend precious time organizing and swallowing them. Eli suddenly wanted to warn Eugene Ferm about all of this, but all he could think of to say was:

"Don't grow old."

And he did say it, murmured it, really, and Eugene Ferm nodded as though he understood, but he did not.

Regardless, Eli suddenly loved this large, doe-eyed dork of a scientist before him. He wrapped an arm around the larger man and squeezed feebly. As he expected, Eugene Ferm happily returned the gesture.

Eli, pulling away, handed back the mold.

"It's magnificent," he said. "Thank you for sharing it with me. And, please, when your paper is finished, mail it to me. I'd love to see it."

Ferm grinned, beside himself. Nothing would come of Ferm's

paper, Eli knew. It would be rejected at all of the major scientific journals. Foot molds were lovely, but they were useless scientifically. Ferm believed he had stumbled on something major, but he would soon learn that it wasn't enough.

Eli felt that he had seen two ghosts of his past now: the child and Ferm. They were both dazzled by the hope that would ultimately blind them, as he had once been. Eli was through warning them. Let them learn. Let them suffer.

Eugene Ferm locked the mold back into its pristine case, this perfect example of why people didn't just believe but *ached* for it, and then the two men journeyed up the dark staircase together and out into the light-bright world, where, Eli felt, no one knew or believed anything worthwhile at all.

BEFORE DRIVING HOME, Eli turned onto the long gravel road that led to the Harms' home. He was at peace now. He glided up the gravel driveway and turned off the car and thought about what he would say if Mr. Harm met him with the Winchester.

But the dad did not meet him there.

Little Eli did.

The boy sat on the front porch with Eli's rifle on his lap.

Eli approached the porch with his hands up, as if to prove he meant the boy no harm.

"My dad said to shoot you if you came back," the boy called out to him.

"Your dad is a fair man," Eli said. "He really does know best."

The boy raised the rifle and aimed it at Eli, but Eli advanced, anyway. Little Eli wouldn't shoot. He was too full of hope and love and youth. He was too far away from being emptied out and desperate and mean. Eli could remember how it felt, that purity. He could almost feel it again.

He strode right up to the boy and opened his hands to him. The boy lowered the rifle, seemed to consider for a long moment what would be best, and then rested the rifle in Eli's outstretched palms.

The dog, Lethe, wrinkled her nose up at Eli and growled.

"Do you remember what I told you earlier?" Eli said to the boy. "What I told you about your mom?"

The boy's eyes were tearing up from the cold wind.

"She loves someone else more than she loves you," Eli said.

He did not mean this to hurt the child, only to prepare him.

Then Eli turned and crunched across the snow to his car.

IT WAS NEAR evening now, and Eli sat with his dogs on his cold front porch. A small truck rumbled along the road, kicking up pearly snow dust. It reminded Eli of that day long ago, when Mount Saint Helens exploded, and he'd come across his mother in the woods.

It was time to let all of that go: his mother, Mr. Krantz, Ferm, the ghost of his boyhood self. His experiences over the last two days demonstrated this. He had his daughters to think of, his wife. He had neglected them all for far too many years. He could feel in his bones that he didn't have much time left. His eldest daughter needed proof of his love, his youngest daughter needed reassurance of her goodness, his wife—what did Vanessa need, exactly? Well, he would find out and give it to her. He was glad to be free of the rest of it. It had distracted him for too long.

The truck motored closer. Eli rose to his feet unsteadily, half-expecting to see the ghost of his dad again, but the truck was a white postal truck, and inside was the sprightly, energetic postman.

"Dr. Roebuck?" the man shouted, stopping his vehicle and stepping onto the ice.

The dogs swarmed around him, and the postman put out his hand hesitantly.

"They won't hurt you," Eli said, raising a gloved hand. "They're friendly."

"Yes, well. Cold evening to be outside."

"It is," Eli said, but he didn't offer an explanation.

"Rain or shine, as they say." The postman opened his pack and fingered some envelopes. "Here you are."

Eli accepted the mail and glanced through it.

"Blizzard coming," the postman said, and turned for his vehicle. "Looking forward to my wife's lamb stew."

He waved and Eli told him goodbye. Then, almost comically, the postman slipped dangerously on the ice and managed to catch himself on the hood of his car. Laughing, he turned back to Eli.

"I'm a bit embarrassed."

"We're only human," Eli said.

"Some of us," the postman said, petting one of Eli's dogs on the head.

"Some of us," Eli repeated.

"Well, good night."

"'Night."

Eli went inside, the dogs pushing at his knees, and stood in the foyer studying the envelopes.

"Anything good?" Vanessa asked, coming in from the kitchen.

"Junk, mostly," Eli said.

He held a white envelope up to his face, scrawled with unfamiliar writing, and then slit it open.

He read the first line aloud, *"He's here,"* and then went silent.

"Who's where?" Vanessa asked, but she was looking at the other envelopes, tuning out.

Eli looked up, first at Vanessa and then at the door. He thought of the Winchester, still in the trunk of his car.

Mr. Krantz, the letter said, was alive and well and living in an apartment in downtown Lilac City.

It was a marvelous coincidence, Eli thought. The simple math of it was, to Eli, an amazing thing:

Rifle + whereabouts = dead Mr. Krantz

"I thought we'd have a nice dinner tonight," Vanessa was saying, "and some of that Washington Riesling. Let's drink too much of it. Then we can light up the fireplace and make popcorn and watch the film I rented. *North by Northwest.* Hitchcock! I know you're sick of Hitchcock, but I love Cary Grant. He's such an uptight funny prig. Doesn't that sound romantic—"

"I'll be right back," Eli said loudly, woodenly, and then he went out into the night, slamming the door behind him, leaving his wife standing there in her pajamas, struck speechless, with the worthless envelopes still clutched in her hands.

ELI WAS WEARY by the time he arrived at Mr. Krantz's fancy apartment. The door was unlocked and he limped inside, wheezing. He found Mr. Krantz immediately, in the kitchen, naked but for a large white bathrobe, which looked funny, closed with an old leather belt.

Much of Mr. Krantz's hair had been shaved from his body, making him almost unrecognizable, except for his enormousness, his heft, and his primitive face. He leaned against the bright steel of the oven. On one foot he wore a prosthetic metal-and-silicone limb.

He noticed Eli but seemed unconcerned, only continued to chew slowly on a piece of raw meat.

As tired as he was, almost clumsy with fatigue, Eli managed to bring his father's Winchester to his shoulder. He took steady aim at Mr. Krantz's heart. Mr. Krantz brought the meat away from his face and sniffed the air. Eli fingered the trigger guard and pulled.

In his excitement, Eli had not braced himself for the kickback. It threw him against the wall. When he caught his bearings, he saw an unharmed Mr. Krantz leaping at him, wolflike, the robe coming apart, the muscles of his bare chest rippling, his wide cruel mouth open and snarling. For having only one real foot, the beast was impossibly fast. Eli yelled, lunging to one side, and Mr. Krantz smashed into the wall with a howl.

Kill him, Eli thought desperately, *kill him now. Finally. Kill him.*

Where was the rifle? Where had it gone? His giant red spectacles had been knocked across the kitchen floor. He groped for them frantically. He could feel nothing but the apartment's cold broad tiles. The dark blur of Mr. Krantz's enormous figure loomed before him. The beast was panting something to himself, over and over again, and it almost sounded like human language. Eli could smell the animal's foul tang.

It sounded like, *I know you, I know you, I know you.* And then the sound changed, and Eli strained again to hear.

"Wait, now," Eli said. "Wait, now. I need my glasses. At least get them for me. At least let me see you up close, just one more time, before you kill me."

And he realized, this was what Mr. Krantz had been saying: *Kill you, kill you now. Finally. Kill you.*

"And I was going to kill *you,*" Eli said, propping himself up against the wall. He put a hand over his stomach and laughed painfully. "And I was going to kill you! Mr. Krantz. The famous Mr. Krantz! You stole Agnes from me. My own mother!"

The creature's panting had slowed. His mantra had stopped. His dark huge figure swayed this way, then that. Eli braced himself for the impact, tried to be brave. His left arm had grown numb.

Mr. Krantz leaned toward him.

The earth changed. The nebulae shifted, the kitchen's features sharpened. Mr. Krantz had reapplied the glasses to Eli's face.

His vision restored, Eli looked right into the eyes of his monster. *God,* he marveled. *He hasn't changed! His eyes!*

Those eyes were like two dark, emotionless tunnels winding back into Eli's childhood. He followed them as far back as he could and then winced in pain.

"Thank you," Eli tried to say, but it came out ragged.

He was gasping for breath now. He was certain Mr. Krantz had stabbed him somewhere, but he could not pinpoint the location.

Eli's vision blurred again. He sagged toward the floor, and the glasses dropped off his nose.

The empty feeling in his arm expanded. He felt shot through, as though by a bullet. *He's killed me,* Eli thought, *he shot me with my father's own gun,* but Mr. Krantz had done no such thing.

Eli was having a heart attack. It was nothing like the tiny heart attack he'd experienced in his early sixties. This was the massive one. This one was fatal. He lay on the floor, clutching his arm to his chest, bleary-eyed, openmouthed.

Mr. Krantz loomed over him with his gloomy wide mouth, his empty eyes, his large, apelike brow. The mean, ugly face lowered, closer and then closer. *Finish me quickly,* Eli thought. Mr. Krantz brought his round heavy mouth to Eli's mouth with incredible force.

Eli faintly registered a woman on a phone somewhere, shrieking for an ambulance. "He's dying! A man is dying! Come now! Hurry!"

He's killed me, Eli thought dimly. *He's suffocated me.*

Then, feeling the wide mouth withdraw, feeling those powerful fists slamming onto his chest, he gathered that Mr. Krantz was trying to save his life.

What had happened? Only a moment earlier, Mr. Krantz had wanted him dead. Their rage had been mutual.

The mouth returned, covering his own. His vision had gone black, but Eli remained tenuously connected to the conscious world. He felt Krantz's putrid breath move into his lungs. The gray fetid smoke of him wafted into Eli's legs and feet.

Consumed! Eli was giddy with it. His body bucked and jerked. It floated upward, toward the apartment's chimney flue. He was going now.

The world left him, but not before he uncovered his last mortal thought. It was winter, and he flew through the night like a sleek missile.

I didn't even say goodbye to him, he thought. *Imagine! All those years and I never said goodbye!*

GHOST STORY

VANESSA

Two weeks after Eli's death, Vanessa listened to her step-daughter tell a room of mourners that her father was haunting her.

Someone asked, "Does he wear a white sheet?"

Amelia shook her head, perhaps missing the joke.

"He looks the same," she said casually. "Gloomier. He's wearing his old bathrobe, the robe he used to wear when he was married to my mom. He's just slightly more visible than a fart."

Vanessa winced. They were sitting in the den, reluctantly entertaining the latest round of well-wishers, who had brought Vanessa a lasagna and, inexplicably, an entire uncooked turkey. One of them giggled at the word *fart*, but the rest of the group sat in horrified silence, glancing meaningfully at Vanessa and then looking away. *She was always difficult*, these glances said, *and we're sorry for you.*

Vanessa had, at one time, appreciated these looks. Now they annoyed her.

What Vanessa felt toward her stepdaughter was not shame or anger.

It was envy.

She had a dozen pressing questions for Amelia: *Where? When? Is he here now? Can you see him? Can you touch him? How did he come to you? Why, oh, why, has he not come to me?*

Instead, tongue-tied, she turned for support to Ginger, who said thoughtfully, "I suppose we could barbecue it. There would be lots of leftover meat for sandwiches."

At first, feeling sick, Vanessa thought she meant Eli's corpse. Then, realizing, she stuttered, "Oh, yes. The turkey. Sure. We'll barbecue it."

"At this very moment," Amelia said, absently toying with her attractive white-gold watch, a wedding gift from her mother, "he's gesturing toward all of you. He's jumping up and down and yelling at the top of his lungs. He's waving! He's trying to say hello."

The crowd waited, holding its breath. A sweet if slightly dotty old woman who had, in her more lucid years, babysat Ginger, lifted her hand and waved hesitantly in return.

Vanessa's eyes roamed the room wildly. Where was he? She saw nothing; she felt nothing. She inhaled and caught no scent of him. *Eli,* she blazed, *Eli, where are you?*

"But what he really wants," Amelia said, "is my forgiveness."

Vanessa sat back against the couch, ruined. It was a profound moment, a moment of truth. A onetime colleague of Eli's cleared her throat in disgust. But Vanessa thought, *It's true. That is precisely what Eli would want: Amelia's forgiveness. Now of all times. Yes.*

He had never really sought it before his death. He was always downright carefree about it, in fact.

"There's nothing more I can do," he would say. "She'll either forgive me or she won't."

Vanessa had once fallen on her knees before him, begging him to give Amelia what she wanted, which she imagined was the most tearful sort of apology, an outpouring of his darkest guilt, a dramatic showcase of regret and woe for her difficult childhood. She hoped that it would put an end to the girl's wrath.

Eli had refused, as resolute as ever. "I don't regret a thing. I did nothing wrong, other than fall in love with you. Do you really think an apology would matter? The only thing I'm sorry about is marrying Gladys in the first place."

Unfortunately, he relayed this last sentiment to Amelia one evening after drinking too much vodka. Vanessa had cringed, watching Amelia (then a young woman, attending community college and piecing her life back together), whose expression had collapsed and then tightened.

"Well," Amelia had retorted hotly. "That would be the perfect solution, wouldn't it? Then I wouldn't be here at all. You could have your perfect threesome, and I'd be dead. Never even born." And Eli hadn't risen to stop her when Amelia sped from the house, seething.

"You're only making things worse," Vanessa had told him. "You're only making things worse for *me*."

How silly she was to involve herself with a married man! She should have known that his first marriage would plague her for their entire relationship and beyond, but her reservations about him were so stupid and naïve, revolving around his quirkiness instead of around the fact that he already had a family of his own. Christ, he was married! It had seemed so cosmopolitan then, so liberated. Marriage was an insipid institution, she had always felt. And she thought this now, too, sitting here with all of these people, who felt sorry for her because she had lost her husband, but not because she had lost her best friend, the only person who truly understood her and forgave her, the only person, other than Ginger, who she truly understood and forgave, too.

I should get dinner ready for him, Vanessa thought automatically. Then, pitying herself: *No. All of that's over now.*

She would never get used to this.

Amelia turned to her half sister then and said, bored, "I hate barbecued turkey. All the carcinogens. Might as well spray a can of aerosol down your throat."

The guests stood to leave, one by one. Vanessa tried to bid them farewell as gracefully as possible, but her mouth had gone dry. She felt relieved and exhausted when the last of their cheerful set departed.

"I can't see anyone else today," she finally said to Ginger. "I need to lie down."

The daughters watched her walk up the stairs. She looked back at them, her hand falling on the balustrade. Ginger's face was a soft pink balloon of concern; Amelia's face was a hard angular viper pit.

"We'll leave tomorrow," Amelia said sharply to Vanessa's heels. "We'll stay with Gladys tomorrow night. She's grieving, too, in her own way."

"Okay," Vanessa said, wanting to argue, wanting to beg her to stay a week, a month, a lifetime, lest she take Eli's ghost along with her.

"I'm surprised Eli hasn't haunted *her*," Amelia said. "If anyone needs to forgive him, it's Gladys."

Oh, bullshit, Vanessa thought. Gladys was a shitty person. She had done horrible things to Amelia and to Eli both. Nothing was beneath Gladys: self-immolation, slashing tires, wicked lies. She would do anything to make Eli and Vanessa unhappy, even if it meant her own daughter's discomfort. She deserved little kindness and was lucky enough to have Amelia's loyalty.

"It will be good for you to see her," Vanessa said. "Send her my regards."

"I won't," Amelia replied.

Vanessa nodded. She knew Amelia didn't mean this to be cruel. If Amelia passed along Vanessa's tidings, well meaning or not, she would be excoriated.

Alone now in the room she had shared for more than thirty years with Eli, Vanessa curled into his pillow and sobbed. It still smelled of him. When she was able to calm down, she asked the pillow, "Why are you haunting *Amelia*? Why *Amelia*? Haunt me instead. Haunt *me*. Isn't there something you need from me, even now?" She smacked the pillow with her hand.

After Eli's death, she had considered asking Amelia and Jim to stay at home, rather than with them. The couple had their own house in Lilac City, after all, and Vanessa didn't need the extra help. She had assumed that Amelia would be more than willing to comply. But Amelia insisted, and Ginger would have balked if she'd been denied—she always balked whenever Vanessa disagreed with Amelia. They had a complicated relationship, these two half sisters, one filled with jealousy and rancor and, somehow, admiration and love.

Ginger had such a good heart. Ginger, who was always apologizing for her parents' poor behavior: past infidelities, present-day drunkenness, perceived insensitivities. Ginger was a saint.

Amelia, too, was here out of good intentions. She was here because she wanted to support Vanessa and because, in her own twisted way, she loved her father. Her presence, however, pained Vanessa, as it always had; she could not look at Amelia without thinking of her life's greatest transgressions, could not speak to her without wanting to defend her most deleterious self. She tried to gloss over all of this with fake chatter and ill-timed compliments, a kill-'em-with-kindness routine that made Amelia's mistrust all the greater, but it was so much more comfortable for Vanessa than playing the part of the evil stepmother. She hadn't meant to hurt anyone. She hadn't. Why must she always feel the need to defend herself? Why did Amelia refuse to see her as anything but the venomous spider, the gold digger, the other woman? Why didn't Amelia accept that Vanessa simply loved Eli, that all she had ever done wrong was to love a married man?

Once upon a time, Vanessa felt that she, too, had a good heart. This was (she now knew) an estimable lie. Her love for her husband, her love for Ginger had nothing to do with goodness. Loving was about need and fear and commitment and survival. She would die for Eli and Ginger if need be, would eat their pain in order for them to remain painless, would cut off her legs for them to remain upright, would do anything in her power to protect them both—kill, maim, steal, lie, destroy—but these urges blossomed not from some tender soul-soil of goodness, like gentle beanstalks winding skyward, but rather lurched from a more primordial earth, tangled within her teeth and guts and bones, monstrous and dark and thorny, utterly powerful. There was no room for goodness there, no matter what others might say, no matter how many greeting cards she collected from Ginger exalting her generosity and affection.

To the best mom in the entire world, those cards read. Vanessa kept them all in a drawer in her bedroom and cried over them every few months.

But love and goodness had nothing to do with each other.

AMELIA

ELI IS HAUNTING ME LIKE A TOTAL ASSHOLE. HE'S THERE IN THE bedroom with Jim and me, he stands at my elbow when I'm on my headset with clients, he's with us in the backyard when we're building a snowman with the kids. It's been like this since the funeral. I've been showering less, making love less, because, what the hell? My dad is here. Even doing bills is embarrassing.

He hates it, too, I can tell. He turns to the wall when I undress or shower or shit, but he can't leave. He's waiting for something. An apology, a blessing, a curse? I try not to make eye contact. Most of the time, I pretend he's not there. The rest of the time, I'm asking him, What do you want, Dad? Come on! Speak up!

Eli can't speak but he can gesture, and he gestures at me urgently, as if he's trying to land an airplane. *OVER HERE,* he's saying. *KEEP YOUR NOSE UP. AVOID THE WATER, THERE ARE SHARKS.*

To this, I can only shrug. No idea, Eli. Does not compute.

When he's not gesturing, he's gazing at me in a mopey way. The mopey expression makes him look even older than he was when he died.

He died a typical asshole death. Heart attack. Too involved with his work to take care of himself. You'd look at a small, thin guy like him and you'd think, Wow, what a healthy person, but, really, his arteries were choked. When sliced open, they would have leaked cottage cheese everywhere. I know about this stuff. I sell pharmaceutical products to patients with calcium deposits in their hearts. All of these guys are the same.

This is what stress does to you, asswipes.

I sound unappreciative, like I don't love Eli. It's not that.

I'm even flattered. I mean, he could have haunted Vanessa (God knows she'd love it), or Ginger (who would be fucking terrified), or even Gladys (who is going be a hell of a ghost herself one day), but he chose me. This means he owes me something. Unfinished business, as they say.

But then I'm not sure. It's a problem for me, and it's a problem for Eli.

Maybe it's meant to punish us both.

VANESSA

IT OCCURRED TO VANESSA THAT AMELIA MIGHT BE MAKING ALL of this up, just to upset her.

But Amelia had never been a fantastical person. Ginger was another story. Ginger, even now, had the imagination of a small child, with her paintings and her unicorn obsession, although she'd never been very interested in Eli's Sasquatch. His eternal hunt for the beast—a hunt that had ended with a degree of humiliation and amusement—had not been seen by either daughter for what it was: creative, original, baffling, and inspired (as it was seen by Vanessa, who understood Eli's passion in terms of poetry, an equally elusive creature). Instead, they saw it as as misinformed, corny, confusing, and bogus. To Amelia, it was the career of a liar and a philanderer; to Ginger, the career of an adventurous if mistaken man.

But he believes in it, Vanessa had argued, in different tones, with both her daughter and stepdaughter. *He believes in it very much. And belief is everything. Don't you see that?*

Amelia, for one, argued that he did not believe. How could he, without being insane? He was in it for the money, she surmised, for the weird glory it provided. He was in it for the travel, for the long woodland trips away from all of them. Vanessa never argued with her, only listened to her rants with a sinking heart. Eli was happy, so Vanessa tried to be, too.

Eventually, Eli's confidence and dedication waned. The whole SNaRL program was taken over by younger cryptozoologists. They understood the Internet in a way that was beyond Eli, putting the entire business online, creating an informative if dense website, an online donations portal, and a comments section. The Internet meant far more sightings, but far less of them were sincere. Eli couldn't keep up with the speed of the thing. He became irrelevant. His book continued to enjoy healthy sales, but even he knew that it was purchased as a gag item, a funny gift to give a monster aficionado or skeptic at a birthday party.

It wore on him, Vanessa saw, and she tried to encourage him and flatter him and distract him.

In the end, it killed him.

Vanessa ruminated over the night of his heart attack. She liked to pick apart the details, as if somehow she would find the tiny key that, if twisted, would pop open the lock and bring Eli back to life. She would never forget the hospital where she was summoned, the sterility and brightness of it, so opposite the clutter and darkness in her heart. Eli was alive then, just barely, but they thought, or told her they thought, that they could save him.

That funny couple was there, too—Mr. and Mrs. Krantz. Mr. Krantz's presence was disturbing. He was gigantic, an eyesore, but he hung back from everyone, pressing against the wall as though trying to hide.

She had wondered to herself: Who were these people? Why was Eli with them when the heart attack struck? She eyeballed Mr. Krantz with a sense of urgency. He was a man who would seize anyone's attention. He was a man who seemed too mannish.

Mrs. Krantz had sprinted up to Vanessa in her tall heels, bubbling over, frantic with apologies, and relayed everything to her. She had arrived home with dinner to find Eli collapsing onto the floor and had gone right for the phone to call for help.

"Fell right next to his rifle, the poor thing!" She turned and opened an arm toward her brute of a husband. "Blue as a Smurf. Krantzy jumped right in. CPR and the whole bit! Learned it from watching TV, can you imagine? The paramedics were really grateful to him."

"Eli had his rifle?" Vanessa had asked. "Why did he have his rifle?"

"Oh, who knows?" Mrs. Krantz replied. "Men love to carry guns around."

It dawned on Vanessa then who Mr. Krantz was. She recalled what Eli had told her about the monster from his childhood, the creature who had stolen everything from him. And now she remembered the clunky, Germanic-sounding name: Krantz. Her face whitened.

"They know each other," Mrs. Krantz said, perhaps noting Vanessa's stricken expression. "Yes, I'm sure of it. Krantzy's silent on the matter, but I can tell they are old friends."

Vanessa could think of nothing to say. She knew what this stupid woman did not: Eli had gone to kill Mr. Krantz.

She caught Mr. Krantz's eye, and he stared back at her emotionlessly.

"Thank you," she finally said to him. "Thank you for saving his life."

She wasn't sure at first if he had heard her or not, but then he gave a slow, brief bob of his immense head.

"God, what a night," Mrs. Krantz said, fake eyelashes wet with tears, the splendid peach bulbs of her cleavage heaving above a pink camisole. She reached for Vanessa's hand and squeezed dramatically. "Krantzy did everything he could. The paramedics were so fast, I swear it, as quick as bunnies! I'm sure your husband will be right as rain by morning."

Mr. Krantz continued to lurk in whatever shadows he could find, limping from one corner to another. He was a dark, monstrous figure in a thin denim coat, shiny tuxedo pants, crisp white sneakers. He had recently shaved. His primitive face was all cut up from the razor, with tiny bits of Kleenex stuck to his skin by red tacks of blood. He was a massive, hideous man. Vanessa continued to stare.

"Thank you," Vanessa told the woman. It was in her nature to console annoying people. "Thanks again."

Mrs. Krantz looked lovingly at Mr. Krantz. He was watchful, contained, as though saving his energy for a sudden escape.

"Look at us two gals," Mrs. Krantz murmured. "Tethered to older men. And what for?"

"Love," Vanessa said. She toyed with her wedding band.

What was taking so long? When would she be able to see her husband? She had so many questions for him now.

"Well, we got more than we bargained for, didn't we? Couple of troublemakers, these guys."

Vanessa smiled tautly. She was through entertaining this diamond-studded hillbilly. She wished the young wife would go away. Her knees shook. She chose a chair next to a side table filled with magazines and sat down to wait for the doctor, to continue to observe Mr. Krantz.

Minutes later, ignoring the magazine spread open on her lap, she noticed Mr. Krantz reaching out toward the windowpane. His motions were graceful, athletic. Then he suddenly lunged, snapping up a housefly in midair, catching the insect deftly between his index finger and thumb.

Vanessa jumped. The reflexes alone were enough to startle her.

But then he brought the fly to his mouth and placed it on his tongue.

He *ate* it.

Vanessa put a hand to her mouth, not sure whether to laugh or gag.

By God, Vanessa thought. Eli's Sasquatch. It was him. There was no doubt in her mind now.

He looked up suddenly and locked his eyes onto hers. Vanessa swallowed but did not break the gaze.

The wind seemed to shift in the airless room. She thought she could smell him, a smell like burnt armpit hair. She wrinkled her nose.

They continued to openly watch each other.

Finally, Mr. Krantz looked away. His wife was asleep, crumpled over on an upholstered bench. Vanessa could see the soft hill of her stomach, its slope suggesting pregnancy. *There will be more of him,* she thought, and she told herself that she would alert Eli once he awoke.

Mr. Krantz, as though sensing this thought, decided to quit the waiting room. He lifted his wife effortlessly into his arms, half-loping, half-limping with his charge down the wide white hallway to the neon EXIT sign. Then he slipped through the door and was gone.

My husband's life's work, she thought, aghast. She almost wanted to follow them, and she half-rose to her feet, but how could she leave now, when her husband was so ill?

The doctor appeared then, shaking her head.

"Mrs. Roebuck," she began, and her tone was nightmare enough.

The doctor continued to speak, to explain, her hand on Vanessa's arm. She had purple nail polish, and the color reminded Vanessa of a bruise.

Why would you paint your fingernails that color? Vanessa wondered. *Why would you? I mean, considering you're telling people about dead husbands and all?*

"You have the fingers of a corpse," she said, interrupting the doctor, and the doctor took her hand away.

"Would you like to see your husband now?" the doctor asked.

"You should try a cherry red," Vanessa suggested, and half-giggled.

The doctor picked at a bump on her jaw with her purple fingers. She returned the hand to Vanessa's arm. Vanessa's giggle shifted to a low, heartbroken howl.

OUTSIDE THE HOSPITAL window, it had snowed, and beyond the stink of death, the world was sharp and clear and white. Vanessa shut her eyes and soared out the window, flowing through the glass into the icy sky, the wind slicing knifelike into her skin and nostrils and guts, and for a moment she felt vivified, ready for anything.

She opened her eyes and was right next to the bed.

"You silly old man," she told Eli, touching his lifeless forearm. "All this just to get out of watching Hitchcock."

He did not laugh. She pointed this out to him. "You never laugh at my jokes," she said. Oh, how'd they laugh together if he just woke up!

"I miss you, Eli," she said. "I already miss you! This isn't going very well, is it?"

But while she was here with him, it was something. Better than not being with him. She put her head onto his arm and let herself cry.

"I saw him, you know," she said finally, sitting up, wiping her eyes on her shirtsleeve. "I saw Mr. Krantz. Your Sasquatch. I saw him, Eli. He was spooky."

The world folded in and out of itself. *This is not real,* she thought. *This can't be real.*

"He wasn't worth killing," she said. "At least you didn't do that. I'm glad you didn't."

She leaned in to this head that was not her husband's head and whispered to it, "You did the right thing, Eli. Not by dying, you silly old fool, but by leaving the guy alone."

The strain of not killing Mr. Krantz had killed Eli. Vanessa was sure of it.

The night festered.

Ginger came and saw her father, too. Then Amelia. Amelia asked: Could Gladys? And Vanessa said, *Yes. After I leave.*

Eventually, she left. It was late morning.

The sky had warmed and the snow had hardened and there was no longer any striking beauty to the world. The sky was wrung out, gray.

It was morning. There was an entire day remaining.

Ginger drove Vanessa home. They went into the kitchen together. "I suppose I should make breakfast," Vanessa said.

Ginger didn't answer, just went to sit on the couch. She turned on the television and lay down.

North by Northwest began to play.

Vanessa hadn't eaten since lunch the day before. The untouched dinner sat on the table, and Vanessa swept everything into the garbage can, whether or not it was perishable.

Then she stared with some confusion at a package of Franz bread.

Eventually she opened the bag and extracted the heel and stuffed it into her mouth, the whole thing, and chewed it.

This would be her most vivid memory of the day. Even on her own deathbed, when she could no longer remember how her husband looked or sounded or smelled, she would remember the taste of the bread, so plain and good and filling, and she would ask her own hospice worker for it and they would bring her a slice and watch her gum it happily without being able to swallow.

But that was all in the future, and the rest of it was in the past.

*   *   *

VANESSA SPENT MOST of those first few days on the couch, greeting well-wishers, feebly eating from the paper plates offered to her, speaking with lawyers and funeral home directors and anyone else who managed the boring paperwork of the dead. The nights passed more garishly. She slept in fits and starts, her quietude crumbling without warning into a lurid, private panic, followed again by a catatonic calm. The darkness added to her grief; she pined for the mornings and was relieved when they finally arrived, however late and leisurely. The night after hearing about Eli's ghost was the first night Vanessa slept well. She woke to find morning waiting for her, streaming across the bedspread with its thin cold light. She could hear the houseguests stirring, Ginger in her old bedroom, Amelia and Jim in the guest room. She rose to find Amelia.

The guest room was on the first floor, and Amelia had turned it into her own personal pigsty, littered with magazines and drained tea mugs and plates of half-eaten sandwiches. Jim was there, too, Amelia's husband, a man whom Vanessa would have liked to enjoy less. He was a pretty fantastic guy. This was confusing for Vanessa. It suggested that Amelia, too, was fantastic.

Amelia and Jim's children were with Jim's mother, who lived slightly north of Lilac City.

Vanessa asked Amelia to step outside with her, and Amelia begrudgingly complied. Once there, standing on the back deck, shivering, Vanessa asked Amelia about Eli.

Amelia wrapped her arms around herself tightly. "I can sense what he's doing now. It's like he's part of my brain. Or like a prisoner I've brainwashed. For example, I don't need to look over my shoulder to know he's doing something disgusting."

"Disgusting? Like what?"

"Like dry-humping a tree. Like a dog. Panting while he does it."

Vanessa put her face in her hands, wanting to scream.

"I'm just kidding. He's just floating there, like an idiot. Floating and waiting."

"Waiting?"

"Yeah. Waiting for me to say okay. *Okay, you're free, Eli. You can go, little buddy.*"

"Why won't you?" Vanessa cried. "Why won't you say it?"

For a moment, Amelia put on her cruelest expression, and Vanessa braced herself for the next invective, but then something changed in her stepdaughter's face, and it was no longer Amelia the confident woman who stood before her, but Amelia the confused child, the brave-seeming girl who wet her bed into her early teens.

"I don't know," Amelia muttered. "I want him to be there. Just this once. I want him to be there, to be around. In whatever way he can be. You know?"

Vanessa chewed on her lip. Amelia trembled. Probably from the cold, but also maybe not.

Vanessa studied the grove of apple trees. Outlined in those fragile, hoar-frosted limbs was Amelia's life: how alone she'd been, how starved for her father's attention. Vanessa recalled the night of her wedding to Eli, when they dropped Amelia off at her mother's house; Vanessa had spotted Gladys standing sentinel at the upper window, her pale hand holding open the curtain, her bitter face glowering down at them all, even at her own daughter. What a horrible fate for any girl.

Thank God it had not been Ginger.

"He's not there," Vanessa found herself saying. "He's not." It was so very true what she said, and she saw the truth of it cross Amelia's face, saw the anger return, the embattled cruelty. "You made the whole thing up. He's with me." She felt him there. "He's always been with me."

Amelia clenched her fists for a moment, as though she had been bitten and was shocked by the pain. And then, exhaling, sounding exhausted or just plain bored, she said, "Okay. Whatever. It was only a big joke, anyway."

Vanessa muttered her thanks. She was relieved. Now she almost felt as if she could move forward. Eli was free.

She wanted no hard feelings. She owed it to Eli to be good to Amelia. She came forward with her arms open, intending an embrace.

Amelia recoiled.

"Fuck off, Vanessa," she said, and reentered the house.

AMELIA

THE TRUTH IS, ELI, I'M NOT GOING TO LET IT ALL GO THAT EASILY. I lied to Vanessa. You're not some big figment of my imagination, as she'd like to think, but that was my gift to her. She's happy now. She's humming away downstairs while Jim and I pack; she's humming away, "Que Sera, Sera" (God, I hate that song). Maybe she's humming it to you, drinking her wine, looking forward to having the house emptied. I'm glad for her. That sounds bitchy, sarcastic, but it's not. I'm glad for her and her future solitude.

I suppose she'll still be a part of our lives, but she's only ever been a small part and that's how she'll stay.

Ginger asked me one day, years ago, when she was still little enough to be forward about those things, You don't like my mom, do you?

I was taken aback by the question, and then thoughtful. I said to her, I don't know your mom, Ginger.

I was trying to be nice when I said it, but how true it was.

It wasn't about hatred, like I'd always thought. It was just that we were strangers.

Oh, Eli. You're jumping up and down now, throwing your arms all about, sitting on top of my luggage as though to keep it closed (which is useless, remember? You're still the consistency of a fart). You don't want me to leave here. You want me to stay here, because you want to be here, too. At your house with your wife and your other daughter.

That stopped you, didn't it? Here you are now, sulking. You're ashamed. I'm right, aren't I?

Thank you. Thank you for nodding.

It's nice to see this side of you.

But, Eli, I can't leave you here. It's been uncomfortable, having you around all of the time, but it's also sort of great.

I don't know you, either.

I know Gladys. Poor Gladys. She's unwell (says the daughter who is talking to a ghost, ha-ha).

I know Ginger, sort of. Poor Ginger. She's unwell, too. Not in the vindictive way of Gladys, but, God, so guilt-ridden.

You did a number on us all, didn't you, Eli?

Or did we all do it to ourselves?

Because I know you didn't mean it. Just like Marion didn't mean it.

I even know you loved us. You were selfish and stubborn about it, but you did.

Jesus, I hope I'm not accidentally forgiving you here. I mean very much for you to spend the next thirty years trailing me like a misshapen shadow. You owe me that much. Wouldn't you agree?

You're opening your arms up to me, offering an embrace. That's so unnecessary.

But. Fine. I'll hug you back.

Just this once.

Jim's watching me. His mouth is slightly open; he's off-balance. I shake my head at him, warning him not to come closer. In one of his hands is a tube of toothpaste. His medicine bag, in the other hand, is ajar, about to spill its contents onto the floor: my Xanax, my sertraline, our Ambien. He watches me wordlessly as I open my arms up to nothing, fold my arms around nothing, hug nothing hard.

Harder than I mean to.

It's humiliating, Eli, my crying like this again.

Your bathrobe is dry and scratchy. It smells like my childhood.

Jim says to me, Amelia. Honey. Are you okay? What are you doing? Who are you talking to?

I can't talk to Jim right now. I want to but I can't. My head is lolling on your shoulder. I can feel how there you are, how not there you are.

I'm so pissed at you, Dad.

I'm so glad you're here.

Just wait for one more minute, okay?

AFTERLIFE

LIFE SICKNESS

FOUR DAYS AFTER HIS DEATH, ELI ATTENDED HIS OWN FUNERAL service.

The Fates were there, too: the tentacled grandma, the apelike mother, the chicken-legged granddaughter; they were his escorts to the underworld.

Eli met the Fates at the instant of his passing. They sat together on the rocky floor of a misty gray hillside. The cliff face swelled over a large lake, also smooth and gray. Other ghosts sat on opposing cliff faces, either alone or with their own strange witches.

"Daughters of the Air, we're called," Ape Mom told him. "Fates, to the layperson. It used to be, before they changed our benefits, that we'd earn our souls back by doing good deeds, but *those in charge* decided to cut corners."

"The retirement package is total shit," Chicken Legs said.

"I'm sorry to hear that," Eli said, but he was neither sorry nor glad.

"Well, it gets worse," Ape Mom said. "You're our last job."

"Really?" Eli asked indifferently.

"It's true," Chicken Legs confirmed, bobbing up to him on her enormous speckled gams. "We've been laid off."

"We're not the first," Ape Mom said. "The whole underworld's in debt. We thought we were safe, having worked here for three billion years, but just when you get comfortable . . ."

"We're being replaced," Chicken Legs said. "Or they're just letting you souls police yourselves."

"I'm sorry," Eli told them again.

Ape Mom shrugged her wide, hairy shoulders. "Ah. You know. I like to look at the bright side. We've all got things we'd like to do."

"*I* don't have anything else *I* want to do," Chicken Legs grumped. The tentacled grandma growled deep in her wide throat. "Right. Neither does she," Chicken Legs added, thumbing at the bulging squid.

"We got a good severance package," Ape Mom reminded them.

"It's no golden handshake," Chicken Legs said.

Gramma grunted. She waved her tentacles around and then brought two of them together to make a malevolent cutting motion.

"Yeah, yeah, Gramma," Ape Mom said, rolling her eyes. Then, to Eli: "She's going to miss killing people off. Only thing she's good at, she thinks. She should take up knitting! With those arms?"

"I hope all goes well for you," Eli said mechanically.

"I forgot your emotions are shut off," Ape Mom laughed. "You'll feel like yourself again once we're reality-side."

Time passed, but aside from the random banter of his attending Fates, Eli was not aware of it. He was uncertain if an eternity had passed or only a moment when Ape Mom slapped him on the back and said, "Time to go, hombre. Up and at 'em."

Eli rose obediently to his feet. He blinked at the same gray cliff face he'd stared at for ages. Gramma slithered forward and put a tentacle on him, and he felt electrocuted.

The world snapped into focus. Sharp colors blinded him; the strong smell of fresh flowers made him want to retch. His senses, reborn, overpowered him. He dropped to his knees, cowering with his hands over his ears to muffle the loud sound of a ceiling fan. It occurred to him that, other than the detached, soft voices of the Fates, he had heard no sounds since his death.

The worst of it was that the return of his woe—everything from life that was undone, all of his ambitions, all of the people he missed—overcame him.

"Life sickness," Ape Mom told him pityingly. "It'll pass. Hang in there. In another minute, it'll be like you never left."

She spoke the truth. Soon enough the intensity faded, and Eli was able to pick himself up. He saw, with some embarrassment, that he was naked. Ape Mom noticed the pained expression on his face and told him not to worry.

"You're nude as the news, yeah, but no one can see you."

Chicken Legs sneered. "*We* can see you."

Gramma appreciated this and shook with what Eli figured was laughter.

Ape Mom rolled her eyes. "Don't listen to them. They couldn't care less about your dick and your unwashed butt."

Blushing, Eli tried to ignore the three attendants and concentrate on his surroundings.

He recognized the room. They were in the old Palouse grange. A few familiar people wandered around as though lost. The grange had three tables, laid with punch and food and, Eli saw approvingly, alcohol. An expensive silver frame housed a black-and-white photo of Eli's face. It sat prominently on the table, staring back at him with an important expression.

Eli the Ghost floated over to study Eli the Man.

Vanessa had chosen an older photo of him, the photo used by his practice back when he'd been a podiatrist, back when he'd been married to Gladys.

He looked young. Striking, one might say. In this photo, he looked exactly like a man at the top of his game, a man who would never die.

Wow, Eli the Ghost thought, *what bullshit.*

A car door slammed.

"More guests," Ape Mom announced.

"Does he even know what's going on?" Chicken Legs asked.

"Of course I do," Eli said irritably. "This is my funeral service."

"Saucy!" Chicken Legs said. "It's always fun to see their person-
alities come out, huh?"

Gramma waved her tentacles in agreement.

"Try not to bother him too much, dear," Ape Mom told Chicken
Legs. "He's got a lot to figure out this afternoon."

Chicken Legs sulked, picking at the wooden floorboards with
the claws of her feet.

Ape Mom explained to Eli then: He was here to finish his life's
most important business.

"My most important business? What is that?"

"Don't ask me," Ape Mom said. "Has nothing to do with us.
It has to be a resolution of your choosing. And, sorry to say, it
can't be a grocery list. *One thing only.* Just one thing you want
resolved."

"And then what happens?"

Ape Mom shrugged. "We resolve it. Sort of."

"How will I know what it is?" Eli asked. He could think of a
million things he wanted to do: make love to Vanessa once more, for
example, or publish a final paper about Mr. Krantz's whereabouts.
"How will I know if I made the right choice?"

"There is no right or wrong choice," Ape Mom said. "That's the
best way to think of it."

Chicken Legs guffawed at this, and Gramma clapped a few of
her tentacles together in amusement.

Acquaintances from Eli's life filed into the grange. They gathered before the punch bowl and the cheese plate and eyeballed
the alcohol but seemed shy to drink it. One of them approached the
silver frame and stood before it with a lowered face. Eli watched the

man carefully. It was a colleague of his—a biologist with halitosis—a man who had always been quite amiable.

"He's faking it," Eli said. He could sense the man's feelings as clearly as he could smell someone's perfume. "He doesn't give a damn about me."

"Yeah, a lot of them fake it," Ape Mom said. "Don't take it too hard. At least he's trying."

Eli was angry. "I worked with him for over thirty years!"

Gramma's tentacles lashed out to make their terrible cutting motion.

Chicken Legs touched Eli's arm. "Do you want him dead? She'd love to do it for you. Consider it a freebie."

"Dead? No, no. Nothing like that. No, forget about him."

Gramma's many shoulders drooped. She gazed sourly at Eli's colleague. He was stroking the picture frame now, mouthing the word *goodbye.*

"What a cocksucker, though," Eli said.

"It's wise not to humor her," Ape Mom said. "She kills off one dude and then a dozen more lie dead at her feet."

The corners of Gramma's long mouth sloped upward at the thought.

"If we had any integrity," Chicken Legs said ruefully, "we'd off the whole lot of 'em."

Gramma nodded emphatically.

"Right," Ape Mom said with a roll of her simian eyes, "and then we'd spend the rest of eternity lugging rocks up hillsides and being whipped by a grumpy Titan. No thank you."

Gladys Roebuck entered then, dressed in a stylish black tweed jacket and knee-length dress with black leather trim, over which she wore her valuable stole.

Eli recognized the stole. "I bought that for our fourth wedding anniversary." He sensed Gladys's thoughts as she stroked the soft fur.

"Finest sable imaginable. She still loves it," he noted. Then, squirming, he said, "God. She still loves *me*."

"Poor thing," said Ape Mom. "Look at her. Ugly as a plucked turkey. Her scalp's as bald and uneven as Gramma's."

"A terrible accident," he said.

"We remember," Chicken Legs said. "It was no accident."

At Gladys's side was a middle-aged woman, plumper and younger than Gladys, with a much friendlier face.

"That's her nurse," Ape Mom said.

"Her nurse?"

"She's unwell, as you've often said. She needs the assistance. She has no one else, you know."

"Gladys is the loneliest woman I've ever met," he said. "Always has been. She's alienated from Amelia, even."

"That might be to Amelia's benefit," Chicken Legs joked, and Ape Mom elbowed her in the ribs.

To Eli, Ape Mom said, "So. Here's something you could fix: Gladys's loneliness. She would love to be haunted by you, for example."

Chicken Legs stared at him eagerly, willing him to go ahead and be done with it.

"I don't think so," Eli said.

He had seen enough of Gladys already. He pitied her, but he had decided long ago to no longer be her caretaker.

Vanessa entered from the grange's back door. She stalked around on her big clunky heels, both klutzy and graceful, like an egret. Her hair—uncombed, curly, and enormous—was filled with flakes of white snow. She wore a trim navy jacket—Eli's own, he recognized— over a flowing black dress. Even with her drawn, exhausted face, she radiated warmth and care.

"She is beautiful," Eli said, close to tears. He felt that she brought him back to life.

Gramma motioned with a tentacle at his waistline. Eli covered himself with his hands, momentarily ashamed.

"She's right, you know," Ape Mom said. "We could do that for you, if you wanted. I mean, we could arrange for you to do *it* with *her*."

"Even just a hug," he said wistfully. He almost tried to read his wife's thoughts but decided he could not—it was too painful. "A kiss," he said.

"Whatever you want. But then, you know, it's vamoose. We're out of here after that."

Eli shook his head. "It's tempting," he said. "Doesn't seem very natural, though. Will we be alone?"

Chicken Legs hooted. "You're never alone. Not now. Not before, really, but at least you had the sense of it. But not now, no. Especially not now."

"So you'll just, what, watch?"

Ape Mom nodded in confirmation. Chicken Legs grinned. Gramma made a hole with one tentacle and shoved another tentacle in and out of it lewdly.

"Gramma," Chicken Legs said approvingly, "you're such a pervert."

"Okay, then," Eli said, making a face. "Definitely not."

Other random acquaintances entered, dozens and dozens of them. Eli was pleased to witness his own popularity, but he felt compelled to ignore anyone who wasn't a major player in his life. The importance of the task at hand began to loom before him, and he worried that he wouldn't choose the correct resolution.

Ginger entered then. The girls were with her: the older child, Blythe, who sought out Vanessa and ran to her happily, and the younger girl, Ruby, who held a stuffed rabbit tightly to her chest. The girl's eyes were wide and searching. A thin scar trailed down one side of her face into the armpit of her dress.

Compared to Gladys's scarred head, Ruby's scar, however long, was delicate and faded, like a line of pretty pink thread.

"God," Eli said. "Why would she bring the children here?"

"Why not?" said Ape Mom. "It's not like it's an open casket."

He watched Ginger as she crossed the room to his photograph. She took off her jacket. She was wearing a blue short-sleeved dress.

"She looks well," he said. "Pale, though. What is that tattoo on her arm? A fucking unicorn? What is she, thirteen?"

He peered closer and saw that she was fighting not to sob.

"She's still my little girl," he said. "My baby."

"I like the tattoo," Chicken Legs said, and it was the first kind thing Eli had heard from her.

Eli felt Ginger's emotions surge through him, and he brought his hand to his chest. "She wonders if it's her fault."

"What, the tattoo?" Chicken Legs asked.

Ape Mom hushed her.

"My death. My heart attack. My issues with Amelia. Even Ruby's scar. All of it." He rifled through Ginger's brain. "She blames herself for everything."

"That's a pretty self-important thing to do," Chicken Legs said.

"No, it's not that," Eli said. "She's hated herself for a long time." Saying this aloud broke his heart. "But she knows better. I can tell she knows better now."

"Ah," Ape Mom said. "Here's a noble task for you, then. Give her a much-needed confidence boost! One short haunting from you and she'll be strong and guilt-free in a heartbeat."

Eli considered this seriously. He groped through his daughter's thoughts one more time. "No. Like I said, she's doing better. And she has Vanessa, who is a good mom. I think she'll be okay."

Just then an old woman swept into the room, energetic and ancient. She was sharp-eyed and liver-spotted and, Eli saw, anxious to pay her respects and then leave. She darted like a minnow up to Eli's photograph, lifted it, kissed it, set it back down. Then, nostrils expanding, she retreated to a corner, where she stood for a minute or so, eyeballing the crowd nervously. Then she hurried back outside to the Gertrude Elms van.

"Agnes," Eli said darkly.

"She's practically immortal, isn't she?" Ape Mom said. "Anything you'd like to do for her? Forgive her, perhaps?"

"No," he said firmly.

It was a comfort to him that the final abandonment would be his own.

Music kicked in on the stereo, a song Eli didn't like but that he tolerated because it was one of Vanessa's favorites. Vanessa, always selfless in such matters, spoke with the deejay.

"Not that CD," she said. "The other one."

A Beethoven string quartet began. "I'm glad I get to hear this one last time," he said.

"You have a good wife," Ape Mom observed.

"Had," Chicken Legs corrected.

Eugene Ferm entered, and Eli was almost happy to see him.

"He's not a bad man," Eli said to Ape Mom. "Quite a good man, in fact."

"He liked you," Ape Mom said. "He respects your work still."

This pleased Eli. "I wish him well."

"As you should," Ape Mom said.

Eli's pleasure was disrupted, however, by the arrival of Amelia. She entered with her husband. Jim was respectfully sad, Eli noted, but Amelia was a million emotions: angry, bereft, confused, afraid, mournful, and even relieved. Eli gazed upon her emotions for a long, silent minute and then, for the first time, understood: Amelia, of the two daughters, was the more mortally affected by his life's choices. Ginger was distraught and weepy because she had lost a father who had loved her; Amelia was distraught and weepy because she had lost a father whom she had never truly known.

She really believed he loved her less than he did the others.

"Amelia," he said. "It's not that. How could you think that? I loved you. Always, I did! I just—" He stopped here, thinking. "I just never loved your mother."

He saw then how he had unwittingly let his hatred of Gladys

spoil his emotions for Amelia, too. He felt the unjustness of it keenly now.

"Oh, Amelia. I'm sorry you felt this way for so long."

He tried to go to her, to comfort her and embrace her, but it was as though his ankles were fettered. He looked down. Heavy iron chains encircled his legs.

"It's policy," Ape Mom said. "Until you make your wish, you're rooted to the spot."

"Amelia," he said, tearing up. "My poor baby. Why does she think I never wanted her?"

All three Fates watched him. Even Chicken Legs and Gramma were touched.

Ape Mom said, "You once told her—maybe more than once— that you wished you'd never met her mother. Did you mean that?"

He said that he had meant it, yes. "But just because I wanted Gladys out of my life, that doesn't mean I wanted Amelia out of it, too."

"I think," Ape Mom said, "that you've happened upon your fix. Say the word, Eli, and we'll arrange a good haunting. This will do wonders for her, believe me. It will do wonders for everyone, really: Gladys, Ginger, even Vanessa. You can tell her, plainly, how glad you are that she's your kid. Why you never thought to communicate this to her while you were alive is beyond me. Anyway, that's why we do this, I guess. That's what makes our work so satisfying. Am I right, ladies?"

Gramma took up one of Chicken Legs' hands with an oily tentacle. There was love between these monsters, Eli saw, not unlike the love he felt for his daughters. Unconditional love. It was a love that Amelia believed her parents had never truly felt for her. But they did! Both of them! They had simply failed at communicating it, maybe at recognizing it, although Eli recognized it painfully now.

Eli turned to Ape Mom, about to make his official request.

Right as he opened his mouth to speak, an enormous, crude

figure limped through the door. The man was both graceful and awkward, his long arms swinging down to his knees. He held a long cane in one hand.

"Mr. Krantz," Eli said, and tried to move forward again, but the chains held him.

Mr. Krantz's wife quivered excitedly beside her gigantic husband, all smiles and boobs. She was downright plucky in her pink coat and high heels. She chattered inanely at anyone who made eye contact with her. Eli read annoyance on Vanessa's face, sheer horror on Gladys's.

Gladys leaned in to her companion. "What sort of harlot would wear pink to a *memorial service*?"

Ginger, standing with Amelia and Jim now, took a sip of boozy punch and said, "Who are those people?"

"They were friends with Dad," Amelia said. "They were with him when he had his heart attack."

The evening came rushing back to Eli: the misfired rifle, the scuffle, Mr. Krantz's astounding power and speed, the taste of Mr. Krantz's mouth against his own.

I meant to kill him, Eli remembered, *and I failed.*

"Can I kill someone if I wish?" he asked the Fates.

Ape Mom soured. "I guess. I mean, it's up to you."

Gramma made her cutting motion again, eagerly, pleadingly. Chicken Legs, too, bobbed up and down in place, excited.

"But, you know, death is in the cards for him, anyway, so why worry about it?"

"I just . . ." He stopped here, thinking. "I want to prove who he is."

"Your life's ambition, right?" Ape Mom said.

Eli said yes.

"So, ask yourself: Do you really think he's a monster? Or—I know—a hominid, as you call him? I mean, I know he looks that way. Sorta looks like me, huh?"

Eli looked at Mr. Krantz. He could still feel that breath circulating in his lungs. And as he groped through the file cabinet of Mr. Krantz's thoughts, he happened upon this discovery: Mr. Krantz would be a father soon. A father, like himself. He could sense in Mr. Krantz an eagerness about his impending role, as well as fear, expectation. He remembered all of that so well, the mingling worry and hope, the inability to relax until the baby was with them, out in the world, in his arms.

"Let him go," Ape Mom said, and motioned at Ginger, then at Amelia. "Because there, in the flesh, are two women—your daughters—who could use the help of a good ghost."

Eli scowled. It was vain, he knew, but he wanted credit for the discovery of the Sasquatch, even now.

Eternal glory and all that, he thought.

The three women seemed to read this in him, and they exchanged a knowing look.

"Well, we could arrange that for you, too, I guess," Ape Mom said, but she sounded discouraging.

Chicken Legs said, "We could. Just choose *something.* The service is almost over. If you don't use it, you lose it."

"Where do we go after this?" Eli asked.

"Everyone's going to the forest to scatter your ashes," said Ape Mom.

"And we go with them?"

"We'll leave here when they do," Ape Mom said, "but not for the forest."

"Where, then?"

Ape Mom was silent. "We'll go wherever we want. When you're done with your haunting, or whatever you choose, you'll sit by the Gray Lake and experience pretty much nothing for all eternity. Unless they force you into the new labor pool. In which case—"

A man knocked his fork against a glass. Everyone turned toward it. *Oh, no,* Eli thought. *A toast. I specifically requested* no toasts.

Eugene Ferm cleared his throat.

"So it's been said," the round, charming man began, "that our lovely hostess, Vanessa Roebuck, requested no toasts, but I find myself too moved not to speak." He raised his glass to Vanessa. "My apologies, dear girl."

"It was my husband's request. But, please, go ahead. It's too quiet in here. I'd appreciate some kind words."

"Typical," Gladys muttered to her companion. "Typical of her not to honor him, even now. I would have honored him."

The nurse shushed her.

"We lost a fine man to a heart attack," he said, "and although I didn't agree with all of his opinions, I don't believe a finer man walked the planet, and I know for a fact that no man influenced my career and my entire belief system to such a degree. I was star-struck when I finally met him, giddy as a schoolboy. I made a fool of myself, in fact, but he was gracious and kind, and I owe him a great deal. I hope to repay him one day, although I'm not sure how. Maybe that's what I'm trying to do now, with this awkward speech." Everyone laughed kindly here, except for Eli, who was hanging on Ferm's every word. "It saddens me to think the day I met him was the day he died." Mrs. Krantz put her face in her hands. Vanessa bit her lip. Ferm continued, "I just want to raise my glass to you, Dr. Roebuck, and to your beautiful family. I want to say thank you for allowing me to believe in magic."

Everyone clinked glasses. Ferm drank deeply and then wiped at his eyes, and then he smiled and the speech was over.

Vanessa went up to Ferm and embraced him.

"Poet," Gladys said. "Harlot. Throwing herself at him as we speak."

Eli saw that Amelia stood with her mother now. She gave Gladys a strong hug.

"Mom," Amelia said, keeping hold of Gladys's shoulders. "I know how hard this must be for you, and I'm sorry."

Gladys said, shaking slightly, "Thank you, dear. I'll feel well in a moment. Thank you for taking the time, finally, to greet your lonely old mother. You don't visit me enough, Amelia. You don't care for me. No one cares for me."

"Mom, I saw you just last week."

"Only for a night! That blue-collar husband of yours keeps you from me. I know how it is. You won't even let me see my own grandchildren."

"You told Jonathan he was fat. You told Mary Ellen she had no courage. I don't want you speaking to them that way. I warned you—"

"Your father didn't love us, but here we are, all the same, honoring him. Do you remember how he never fought for you? How you would miss your scheduled weekends with him and he never noticed? It's just pathetic. You and I have no self-respect, Amelia. I feel very sorry for us."

Amelia had fallen silent. Eli could hear the thoughts lifting from her then, a vapor that seemed to rise from her shoulders like a poisoned cloud, all of it directed at him. *You cheated on her and she was unwell. You left her and you left me. You left me alone with her. You left me all alone. I was a child, a little girl. You left me and I had no one. You were never there to begin with, Eli, and then you left me.* She turned to a darker place, far away from him, where even his ghost self could not intrude. Eli watched the darkness shift and expand in her. He felt deeply afraid of it.

After a moment, Eli leaned over to Chicken Legs and whispered in her ear.

Chicken Legs, simpering, turned to Gramma and whispered Eli's request to her. Gramma chortled in response.

"What?" Ape Mom demanded. "What'd he say? What'd he choose?"

Chicken Legs said, "You'll never guess. He chose Amelia. He's going to tell her he loves her. Or he's going to try, anyway."

Eli set his jaw. Even now he was uncertain of his decision, and the monster's mocking tone worried him.

But, he thought, how difficult could it be to communicate his love to his daughter? It wouldn't take long. He would do it and then she would benefit and he would continue on with his afterlife, whatever that was.

Ape Mom was silent for a moment. Then, somberly, she said, "I was scared there for a moment. I thought you'd choose Mr. Krantz. I thought you'd want us to kill him. I don't say this usually, but I'm proud of you, Dr. Rootbutt."

"Roebuck," Eli said.

"Right. Roebuck. Anyway, it's refreshing when someone makes the right choice for a change."

Eli didn't respond at first. He had made his choice. He was stuck with it now. But he watched Mr. Krantz longingly as Ape Mom spoke. The great man was by far the most awkward person in the room, tall and jagged and silent as a large stone.

"If you willingly save a man's life," Eli said, more to himself than to anyone else, "or try to, anyway, does that automatically make you human?"

Ape Mom shrugged. "What do you think?"

Eli saw it not as a fact or a fiction now but as a choice. "I suppose," he said. He considered Mr. Krantz's baby, growing in the tummy of the new wife. "Mr. Krantz is a man."

"Can we stay for the rest of the party?" Chicken Legs asked her mother. "They're serving beers."

Ape Mom sighed, throwing up her hairy hands. "We'll stay for one beer. Just one, Gramma. Don't go ten-fisting again. Last hurrah, ladies."

Eli floated over to Vanessa's side, as close as his fetters would allow, wanting to be near her for just a little longer. She was speaking quietly with Eugene Ferm.

"I hope you don't mind what I said," Ferm was telling her apologetically.

"No, it was wonderful, thank you. I'm glad someone spoke. He was a wonderful man. We were all lucky to know him."

"I feel the same," Ferm said.

Mr. Krantz lumbered by with his perky wife, and Vanessa narrowed her eyes. Ferm followed her gaze.

"Who's that fellow?" Ferm asked her.

"Mr. Krantz," she said. "No first name, as far as I know."

Ferm's bushy eyebrows shot up. "Huge man," he said. "Bigger than I am."

"By a long shot." Vanessa waited for a moment, considering, and then confided, "You know, I feel I can tell you this, Eugene, because of your background. My husband . . . he thought Mr. Krantz was, well . . ."

She couldn't quite say it, but she'd said enough, and Ferm's eyes snapped onto Mr. Krantz's long figure as though magnetized. "You don't say," he said.

"That's why Eli went there," she said, "to Mr. Krantz's apartment. I think he meant to . . ."

Eugene Ferm's expression shifted. "Your husband," he said, "was always ahead of his time with his theories."

"I don't know, Eugene," Vanessa hurried to say. "Maybe I'm a fool for mentioning it. Monster or not, maybe he should be left alone. He tried to save Eli. He really did." She wrung her hands. "Wow, I feel pretty guilty. I don't think I should—"

"Nonsense, my dear; feel nothing of the sort. You were merely conveying your husband's astute observations, no more." Ferm's tone was hurried, dismissive. "My dear, thank you for this wonderful celebration of your husband's life." He took up her hand and kissed it, lingering for a moment. "If you'll excuse me, Mrs. Roebuck. I have a desire to introduce myself to this *Mr. Krantz.*"

And he took his leave, with Vanessa standing back on her heels to allow him room. She looked very worried.

"Oh, Eli," she said to herself. "I hope I did the right thing here."

Eli shook his head. It was too late, however, for Eli to fix that mess. He had already committed to Amelia. Mr. Krantz would have to fend for himself. And if anyone was capable of fending for himself, Eli thought, it was Mr. Krantz. He turned his attention elsewhere.

Across the room, Amelia's conversation with her mother continued, unimpeded.

"Here you are," Gladys said, "with that *blue-collar* husband of yours, giving your halfhearted respects, and we don't even *belong* here. He didn't love us. He didn't love me and he didn't love you, dear. He ruined us."

"That's a touch dramatic, Gladys," Amelia said. "You're wearing Chanel, and that *blue-collar* husband of mine is a fantastic dad and is mind-blowing in bed. So don't worry too much about our ruination. Could be worse."

But Eli, groping around in his daughter's thoughts, could see how much Gladys's comments had unnerved Amelia. The darkness in Amelia hardened and cooled. Eli could see how it walled her off from everyone—from Jim, from her own children, even from herself.

"Please," he said to Ape Mom. "When do I begin?"

Ape Mom presented him with a bright silver key. As he fitted the key into the lock around his ankles, she warned him, "Now, don't go expecting immediate results. These things take time. A day, a decade, a lifetime. Time is strange in the afterlife. Before you know it, you'll be beside the Gray Lake again, watching your toenails fall off."

"I won't miss the Gray Lake," Chicken Legs said.

Gramma gurgled in her throat, agreeing.

"So we're done here," Ape Mom said when Eli's shackles fell free. "None of this is our problem anymore."

"So long, underworld," Chicken Legs said.

"It's nice to end on a good note," Ape Mom said, and she gave Eli an affectionate look. "Take good care of Amelia, now."

"So long, you dumb mortals," shouted Chicken Legs.

Gramma threw her tentacles around at everyone in the grange, as though flipping them all off.

"Let's go, girls," Ape Mom said, and turned for the door.

Eli followed them out of the grange and watched as they began to walk through the thin snow, toward the south. A gray trail opened up before them and they followed it, moving forward swiftly, shuffling and sprinting both.

"Goodbye, now," Eli called after them.

They were gone.

He returned to his eldest daughter and stood at her side. He could not, in fact, move away from her. The shackles had returned. They now attached him to Amelia, threading their clean metal rings from his rib cage into her chest.

Amelia glanced at him, looked away, glanced back. She drew in a long, slow breath.

"Hiya, Eli," she said, more annoyed than surprised.

"Hello, Amelia," he replied.

She furrowed her brow, leaned in.

"Hello," he said again. "I'm here to tell you I love you. I love you so very much."

She shook her head, pointed to her ears. She couldn't hear him.

It dawned on him that he was mute. Amelia could not hear him, could only see him mouthing things at her, gesturing at her.

Oh, goddamn it, Eli thought. The Fates! Why did they have to make everything so difficult?

Amelia watched him impatiently, waiting for him to speak.

Bracing himself for the long haul, Eli began to wave.

ACKNOWLEDGMENTS

VARIOUS ARTICLES ABOUT GROVER KRANTZ—AN ANTHROPOLOGIST at Washington State University and an enthusiastic Sasquatch apologist—inspired a few of the (very fictitious) details in this manuscript, as well as the name of one of its characters. I also reference Spokane and Colville tribal beliefs concerning "the Tall Man of Burnt Hair," who was called S'cwene'y'ti (pronounced *Chwah-knee-tee*). Without a timely reading of Sherman Alexie's "The Sasquatch Poems," found during a random Internet search, I might never have committed to a second draft of the book. I am grateful for these inspirations and to the lives and memories of those involved in their journey.

I researched and read articles at the Spokane County Library District's Moran Prairie Library, usually on their ProQuest database. I wrote much of this novel at either that branch or at the South Hill Library of the SPL (Spokane Public Libraries). Thank you to these beautiful spaces and to public libraries everywhere for all that you do for our communities.

I had the best editorial team on my side during the *Almanac's* evolution. Thank you to Nat Sobel, who contacted me after reading one of my short stories in *Fugue,* and who gave invaluable input throughout the editing and submitting process. My agent at Sobel Weber, Julie Stevenson, worked with me to reshape two full drafts of the book, and my editor at Henry Holt, Caroline Zancan, guided me through several more. Both women are brilliant and funny and flipping generous as hell. I'm so lucky they understood the vision of the book and advocated for it so passionately. Thank you, Julie and Caroline!

Other readers improved on the book, too: J. Robert Lennon, my good buddy; John Paul Shields, my brother; and Sam Mills, my husband. I could not ask for a better group of creative geniuses to hone my work. You dudes rock: Thank you for reading earlier, deeply flawed drafts of *Almanac*. I also want to thank Kathy Lord for her detailed copyedit, and Will Staehle for the beautiful jacket design.

I'm also hugely indebted to my sister-in-law, Astrid Vidalón Shields, and to my mom, the best grandma in the world, for watching my kids with so much love and care despite their own busy schedules, and for being there for me emotionally when things got weird (my MS diagnosis). Friends and family, including the Conways, Rupperts, Tenolds, Yahnes, Sonia Gustafson, Aileen Luppert, Linda Carlson, DarAnne Dunning and Corbin Schwanke, Sorensons, Zoeanna Mayhook, Colin Manikoth and Amber Williams, Gayle and Greg, Roewes, Welckers, Greiners, J. Robert Lennon, Jason Johnson and Liz Rognes, McLains, Lisa Heyamoto and Todd Milbourn, Suzanne Mulvey, Katie Thompson, Elaine Madigan, Debby and Jesse Mills, Jon Mills, Jeremy Smith and Crissie McMullan, J.P. and Astrid, Dad and Mom (and probably scores of others I'm forgetting to mention here), all brought food, cared for my kids, played host and/or hostess, walked with me in my first MS walk, and, most importantly, gave verbal support when health issues became overwhelming. Thank you to countless others who sent kind messages and good wishes my way. Thank you to my dad for answering questions about rifles and Mount Saint Helens, and to David Renwick for fielding inquiries regarding Super 8mm film processing. I also want to give a shout-out to stellar literary organizations like Humanities Washington, Autumn House Press (and Michael Simms), Artist Trust, Washington Library Association, Pacific Northwest Booksellers Association, and Late Night Library (and Paul Martone), who all do an awesome job of getting debut authors recognized.

It's a good idea to marry your best friend or your best editor, and I managed to do both. Sam: I LOVE YOU. It's amazing to have such a fearless partner; you make me a better writer, a better mom, a better person.

And to my young children, Henry and Louise: You are the first thought in my mind, always and forever. Mommy loves you kids so much.

ABOUT THE AUTHOR

SHARMA SHIELDS holds a BA in English literature from the University of Washington and an MFA from the University of Montana. She is the author of the short story collection *Favorite Monster* and the winner of the 2011 Autumn House Fiction Prize. Her work has appeared widely in such literary journals as *The Kenyon Review* and *The Iowa Review* and has garnered numerous awards, including the Tim McGinnis Award for Humor and a grant from Artist Trust. Shields has worked in independent bookstores and public libraries throughout Washington State and now lives in Spokane with her husband and children.